THE MO

For some time they didn't speak or touch. Each knew what was being asked in this encounter in the forest, what it would mean. Finally, Ceci raised her hands and began to remove her dress. Anthony watched her. Then he drew her into his arms.

The kiss was a long one, gentle at first, tasting of the salt of both their tears. She could feel his hands on the bare flesh of her back, the pressure of his broad chest against her breasts. They parted for a moment and sank to the carpet of pine needles.

"I love you," he said.

"I want to give myself to you," she whispered, surprised by the truth of the statement. Until this moment she had not known . . .

Fawcett Gold Medal Books
by Beverly Byrne

THE OUTCAST

THE ADVENTURER

JEMMA

FAWCETT GOLD MEDAL • NEW YORK

A Fawcett Gold Medal Book
Published by Ballantine Books

 Published in the United States by Ballantine Books, a division of Random House, Inc., New York, and simultaneously in Canada by Random House of Canada Limited, Toronto.

Library of Congress Catalog Card Number: 83-90010

ISBN 0-449-12487-8

Manufactured in the United States of America

First Ballantine Books Edition: September 1983

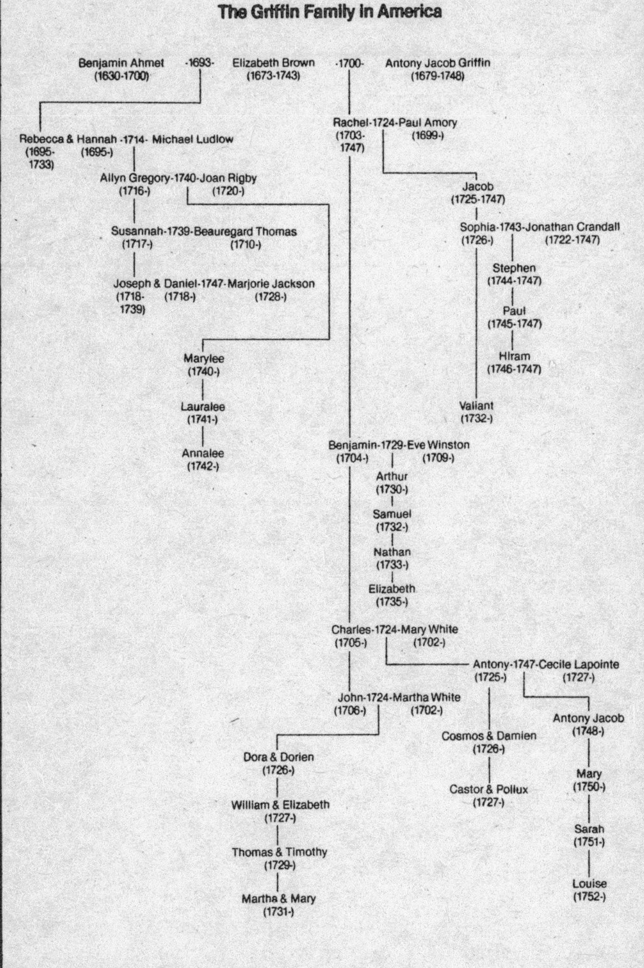

The Griffin Family in America
Benjamin Ahmet (1630-1700) -1693- Elizabeth Brown (1673-1743) -1700- Antony Jacob Griffin (1679-1748)
Rebecca & Hannah -1714- Michael Ludlow
(1695-1733) (1695-)
Allyn Gregory-1740-Joan Rigby
(1716-) (1720-)
Susannah-1739-Beauregard Thomas
(1717-) (1710-)
Joseph & Daniel-1747-Marjorie Jackson
(1718-1739) (1718-) (1728-)
Marylee
(1740-)
Lauralee
(1741-)
Annalee
(1742-)
Rachel-1724-Paul Amory
(1703-1747) (1699-)
Jacob
(1725-1747)
Sophia-1743-Jonathan Crandall
(1726-) (1722-1747)
Stephen
(1744-1747)
Paul
(1745-1747)
Hiram
(1746-1747)
Valiant
(1732-)
Benjamin-1729-Eve Winston
(1704-) (1709-)
Arthur
(1730-)
Samuel
(1732-)
Nathan
(1733-)
Elizabeth
(1735-)
Charles-1724-Mary White
(1705-) (1702-)
Antony-1747-Cecile Lapointe
(1725-) (1727-)
Antony Jacob
(1748-)
Mary
(1750-)
Sarah
(1751-)
Louise
(1752-)
Cosmos & Damien
(1726-)
Castor & Pollux
(1727-)
John-1724-Martha White
(1706-) (1702-)
Dora & Dorien
(1726-)
William & Elizabeth
(1727-)
Thomas & Timothy
(1729-)
Martha & Mary
(1731-)

FIERY SPLENDOR

BOOK I

1739 – 1745

1

THE REBELS

". . . the plantations . . . of this province cannot be well managed . . . without the labor . . . of slaves; and forasmuch as the said slaves . . . are of barbarous, wild, savage natures . . . it is absolutely necessary that . . . laws be made . . . as may restrain the disorders, rapines and inhumanity to which they are naturally prone."

—Preamble to South Carolina Slave Code of 1712

1

In the beginning, when wild Cherokee roses bespecked the June landscape and crickets made a pleasant, even sound, the rumors were confined to the banks of the James in Virginia. "They say Finchley Thomas has settled on a bride for Beau . . ." The recipient of this news would nod and remark contemptuously, "Yes, but did you hear, he's getting her from South Carolina!"

By late July the intelligence reached the Ashley. "Michael Ludlow's agreed to wed his daughter to a Virginian. Now why should a beautiful girl like Miss Susannah be banished to some tobacco farm on the James? Ludlow must be mad."

In fact, neither Michael nor Finchley had disposed of their children without first seeking the sage advice of the Jameson's agent. The representative of the London factor had conferred separately with both men for many weeks before the decision was made.

Such consultation was to be expected. Was it not the factor's money that bought their seed, his ships that carried their crops to the market in England and returned with the amenities of London? Where would the gentlemen of the south be without those books and furnishings and fashions and so much else that made their lives civilized and gracious? To be in debt to one's factor was sometimes unavoidable; to incur his displeasure by arranging a marriage of which he disapproved was unthinkable.

"Despite what you hear, Mr. Thomas," the Jameson's agent

told the man from Virginia, "not all the planters of South Carolina are spending fools. Blackwater's one of the best-run plantations in the south. And the girl's been properly reared."

"She'll have all this to see to. It's a big job." Thomas made a slight inclination of his graying head to indicate the gracious house, the charming gardens, and the extensive slave compound.

"Of course. But I'm certain she's capable. This young lady is the proper mistress for Tamasee."

"Good." The old man sighed with satisfaction. "Then we can discuss the dowry . . ."

At Blackwater they were equally cautious. Here the agent had to convince both father and mother, for Ludlow always included his wife in important discussions concerning the children. "You say," Michael asked for the third time, "this boy inherits everything? There are no other children?"

"None. Beauregard is the sole heir to Tamasee. It's a superb tobacco plantation."

"And,"—Hanna Ludlow's voice was gentler than her husband's but equally firm—"his mother is dead? Susanna will be mistress of the place from the first?"

"That's right, ma'am. Mrs. Thomas died some years back. Finchley never took another wife."

This decided Hannah. Her daughter would respond well to a challenge of that sort. At twenty-two the girl was ripe for it, just as she was for marriage and motherhood. With a signal only her husband could decipher, Hannah indicated her approval of the match and then left the men to settle the financial arrangements.

In the stifling heat of August, when most flowers had burned away in South Carolina and only a few rugged and flamboyant sorts still bloomed in Virginia, Hannah replaced rumors with certainty. In the comparative cool of dusk she sat at a desk in the small tower room she loved and wrote invitations to the wedding on the seventh of September, 1739, of Miss Susannah Ludlow to Mr. Beauregard Thomas of Virginia. Outside the mosquitoes buzzed threateningly and the even sound of the crickets became an angry reproach to the uncompromising climate. But Hannah was serene and comfortable in her tower.

A few years before, a particularly clever sewing slave had

managed to weave a loose linen cloth which let in both air and light while keeping out the mosquitoes. Hannah had seen its potential immediately. She ordered great bolts of the stuff to be made, then had it affixed to all the windows of the house. By day the ordinary curtains and shutters were closed against the sun; in the evenings they were opened so that such moving air as there was could cool the rooms.

It was an innovation which gave Michael Ludlow enormous satisfaction. For years he had refused to join his fellow plantation owners in their summer exodus to Charleston. He knew as well as they that the city was refreshed by sea breezes which died before they could find their way up the Ashley, but he wasn't willing to sacrifice his personal supervision of Blackwater's vast acreage for any slight improvement of physical comfort. "Disastrous," he commented. And put the alternative forever out of mind.

The others laughed at him. New-money miserliness they called it. "Ludlow's a stranger. Didn't come to Carolina until he was a grown man. Doesn't understand how we do things." They built their seaside houses and summered in them with an enthusiasm unmarred by Michael Ludlow's disapproval.

It was to those Charleston homes that Hannah sent her slaves to deliver the wedding invitations. And it was at Charleston parties that the unlikely match was discussed. "Always knew the man was a fool. Virginians are unprincipled idiots. Too easy on their slaves and too hard on their land. Tobacco's a killer crop: the fields are starved in a handful of years, then they have to clear new ones . . ."

But no critic could fault the management of Blackwater. It was known for its orderly productivity, and for the high quality of its rice nurtured by well-disciplined niggers. Everyone admitted that despite Ludlow being an Englishman come to Carolina just twenty-three years ago, he was a wise man where property was concerned. A good master of slaves: firm, yet understanding of the Negro's basic character deficiencies. He fed and clothed his blacks adequately, and demanded absolute obedience and unremitting labor in return. It was the essential balance that made for a good plantation.

Hannah Ludlow too had the respect of her neighbors, although they viewed her with no more affection than they did her husband. She set a bountiful and delicious table and kept the cook-house slaves under careful supervision. Her four children were attractive, well mannered, and clever. Like her gardens, her sewing rooms, and her home, they were tended by niggers managed with intelligence.

Why, since his return from Oxford last year, her eldest boy, Allyn Gregory, had even begun to find a welcome in Carolina society. Allyn had the makings of a true southern gentleman. The youngest Ludlows, the twins Daniel and Joseph, were only twenty-one, an unknown quantity whom few felt able to judge. Still, taken all together, Blackwater and the Ludlows had always been grudgingly admired. Until, of course, this mad sortie into Virginia to find a husband for Susannah.

Two days after the wedding—when the last bottles of wine were nearly empty, the fires of the cook house cooling, the chickens and suckling pigs all consumed, and the delicious crabs brought from Virginia but a memory—the last of the guests prepared to depart Blackwater. "She did make a beautiful bride," one of the ladies said in a conciliatory fashion. "Is there any truth in that story about Jewish blood, do you think?"

The woman to whom she addressed the question had no opportunity to answer. "There is indeed," Hannah Ludlow said as she joined the pair on the verandah. "My father was a Turkish Jew named Benjamin Ahmet. Of course, on my mother's side we know little of ancestry. She was an orphan left at a workhouse in Salem, Massachusetts, when she was newborn."

Hannah smiled benignly at her guests, ignoring their embarrassment. She knew they were looking at her more closely than ever before, trying to discern evidence of the bizarre lineage to which she admitted. Her high cheekbones perhaps; they were certainly foreign. Her eyes, on the other hand, were a vivid, intense blue. Nothing semitic about them. She suppressed a grin and patted a stray lock of hair into place with a deliberate motion. Brown curly hair, not a trace of gray despite her forty-four years. And no wig to disguise it; Hannah never wore a wig. "Your husbands are waiting on the levee, ladies," she said finally. "Nehemiah here will shade your way."

Hannah chuckled as she watched them walk toward the dock and the waiting sloop, little Nehemiah struggling to hold a large parasol over their powdered heads. Too bad they couldn't have met that "workhouse orphan" who was her mother. Lizzie, her second husband Antony Jacob Griffin, whom everyone called Tonyjay, and all the Boston relations had been invited to the wedding, but they'd pleaded the impossibility of making the long trip. Hannah hadn't been surprised. She knew Tonyjay's opinion of the south and slaveholders. He despised them, and doubtless her half brothers and sister and their numerous children had been poisoned with the same nonsense.

Fools, Hannah thought, as removed from the real world as those empty-headed females now settling themselves for the journey down the Ashley. Let them live in their dreamworld—it was no concern of hers. Hannah had problems closer to home.

Allyn Gregory, for instance. She hadn't seen him since a few minutes after the ceremony. He had kissed his sister, shaken the hand of Beauregard Thomas, and disappeared. She knew where he'd gone—to the cabin at the far western edge of the plantation, to Lucinda. It wasn't the thought of Allyn's bedding one of the niggers that bothered Hannah. It was a fact of life she accepted as she accepted most others. But the manner and style of this alliance disturbed her greatly.

Allyn hadn't chosen one of the house slaves whom Hannah herself had trained in cleanliness and a semblance of civility; he'd selected a field hand. As soon as she became aware of the affair, Hannah had made a point of seeing the girl. Lucinda was as black as the earth she tilled. Her eyes had a wild, insolent cast, and when Hannah inspected the girl's back it showed evidence of how often the overseer found it necessary to discipline her. To make matters worse, Allyn hadn't brought her to the house—something the other boys managed to do discreetly; instead, he'd had a cabin built beyond the slave quarters of the western fields and installed Lucinda there. Doubtless that's where he was now. Hannah shook her head. Something would have to be done about Allyn Gregory. He was not preparing himself to inherit Blackwater in a manner she found acceptable. Now, with Susannah wed and gone, she must turn her attention to the matter.

"Yore mama looked at 'em too. She made me take off my blouse and turn round so's she could see if I was a good nigger or a bad one."

"Yes, Lucinda, you've told me that story a dozen times.

And she learned what you and I both know—that you are a thoroughly bad nigger girl." Allyn laughed as he traced the scars of the lash. They were shallow, seeming to make little impression on the thick, supple skin that covered her well-muscled back. "That's why I enjoy you. You're wild and untamed."

"What's 'untamed' mean?" she demanded.

"Not broken. Not biddable like a good animal should be."

"No." She smiled. "I ain't broken. What's a gen'man like you want with a broken woman?"

"Nothing at all," he hooted. She turned over and he threw his leg across her thighs. The contrast of white and black excited him. He placed his hand on her full breasts and studied the effect further. Satisfying. Particularly in this raw and primitive setting, with the fierce sun beating down on the tarpaper roof and the drone of insects filling the air. He had no desire to bring Lucinda to his elegant bedroom in the big house. She might disgust him there. Here she delighted him.

"You want to screw me again, Mr. Allyn Gregory sir?" She addressed her question to his semi-erect member. "You think you's able?"

"Oh that's insolent, Lucinda. Sassy. You'll have to pay for such impertinence."

"How, sir, how I gonna pay for bein' a bad, sassy nigger girl?"

"In good biblical fashion. With the part of you that caused the offense."

"What's that got to do wit' de Bible?" Her curiosity was real, not part of their game. Mr. Delevant, the overseer, read the Bible to all the slaves and she'd heard nothing she could connect with this moment.

"If thy right hand offended thee, cut it off . . ." Allyn quoted.

"You wants to cut off my hand?" She was puzzled but not afraid. Lucinda knew she had nothing to fear from this white man at present.

"No, it wasn't your hand that offended. It was your mouth. That's how you must pay."

"Oh." She smiled with understanding and changed her position. "Now I knows how you wants to punish Lucinda."

He moaned aloud with pleasure as she bent her head to the

task, and for a brief moment he considered again the wisdom of building this isolated cabin. Laying a piece of black ass like Lucinda was not something a man should be forced to do in silence.

"Where's your husband and the boys?"

"I'm not sure." Hannah looked at the man with some alarm. She knew him slightly. He was Bill Myers, overseer of a nearby plantation called Tuttle's Folly. Michael had been good friends with the owner before he died. Never had she seen Myers look so white with fear and rage. "What's wrong? What's happened?"

"Sorry, ma'am, no time to explain. I've got to find Mr. Ludlow—"

"Nehemiah, come here! Hurry and find the master. Tell everyone to look for him and ask him to come immediately." Having issued the order she turned back to the caller. "Now there's nothing to be done until my husband arrives, so you might as well sit down and have a glass of lemonade." She poured a drink even as she spoke and the man accepted it gratefully, but he said nothing more. Whatever was agitating him, he didn't intend to tell her about it.

Three blacks were raking the lawns clear of the wedding debris. Two more performed the same office on the long path leading to the levee. A few minutes earlier she had inspected the cook house and found it being scrubbed from top to bottom as she had instructed. Inside, a bevy of hands were restoring order to the rooms the guests had occupied. All was right with Hannah's kingdom. She could afford to speculate on what misfortune had befallen Tuttle's Folly. "I hope your mistress isn't ill," she ventured after some minutes.

"Thank you, ma'am. Mrs. Babcock's well." He stared glumly at his glass.

Hannah might have tried again but she saw Michael coming toward them from the direction of the stables. Daniel and Joseph were with him. Hannah rose. "Here comes my husband. I shall leave you gentlemen alone."

"What's the trouble, Bill?" Michael asked. "Something we can do?"

Myers looked around him carefully. No blacks seemed to

be within earshot, but still he motioned the three Ludlow men closer. When he spoke, his voice was a harsh whisper.

"Niggers down on the Stono. Running wild. Burning and looting everything in sight."

"Sweet Christ!" Michael cursed. "When did it start? Have they weapons?"

"Started yesterday, near as I can make out. And they got guns. Broke into a store and got 'em. Powder too. Killed the storekeeper and his clerk and left their heads on the front step."

"Bloody savages! How many?"

"Don't know for sure. Some say more'n a hundred. And if the others hear about it and join . . ." He left the consequences of this terrifying possibility unspoken.

"I'll get the weapons." Daniel was gone before Myers had finished speaking.

"Where's Allyn?" Michael demanded of the remaining twin.

"In the western fields, sir," Joseph answered unhesitatingly. Both he and his father knew what Allyn was doing in the western fields. "Shall I get him?"

"No time for that now." Impossible to send a slave with a message such as this. Allyn's help would have to be forfeited. "Go explain to your mother. See you're not overheard."

Within five minutes the three Ludlows and Bill Myers were sailing a small swift sloop toward Charleston. They passed two other boats headed the same way, but no one spoke or even called a greeting. On this occasion no slaves could be used as crew, and the white men were too busy manning their crafts to exchange pleasantries. Besides, their errand was too grim. Fear for wives, daughters, infant sons filled their minds. The thought of black rebellion, of savage niggers raping and rampaging through South Carolina, silenced them all. Michael breathed a prayer of thanks that this abomination had not struck before Finchley and Beauregard Thomas were clear of the colony. Susannah at least was safe.

2

The Ibo was not happy with the manner of their progress. True the dancing and the singing and the drums had helped to attract other blacks—they numbered ninety-seven now, whereas they'd been fewer than twenty when they stole the guns—but it was attracting the whites as well. He had envisioned a furtive run from the colony, successful because the slaves were armed and had sufficient numbers to defeat pursuers. Instead the escape had become a noisy, marauding passage. "Can't you fools keep you mouths shut!" he muttered.

"What for, Luke? Why we need be quiet now?" The man turned his head and looked over his shoulder. "You hear sumpin'? You think dey's comin' after us?"

"Ain't heared nothin'—but dey's comin' after us."

"Then we'll kill 'em." The second man swung his gun as if it were a cutlass. "Kill 'em all jus' like dem others."

The Ibo shrugged his broad shoulders and kept walking. An hour later they reached the wide body of water known as the Edisto River. The elders determined to camp there for the night and cross to Spanish Florida and freedom in the morning. It was a singularly bad decision, and when he heard it the African shrugged his shoulders again.

Black men born in this terrible country were all fools. They made camp in a place they couldn't defend and from which they couldn't retreat. Once or twice he tried to tell the leaders this, but they wouldn't listen and he didn't speak their language well enough to convince them. Seven years the African had waited and plotted for this opportunity. Now it was being squandered by idiots who had forgotten the wisdom of whatever tribes had spawned them.

The Ibo toyed with the notion of crossing alone. But how would he find those other white men, the ones who had promised freedom to any slave who reached their land? He couldn't speak their language either, and he didn't understand their quarrel with this tribe. Impassively, with that discipline to which he'd been bred as a young warrior, he settled down to await the morning. But when the man to whom he had spoken earlier approached with some idle question, the African turned on him with rage. "Don' call me Luke," he spat out. "Not my name. My name Yogami." It was his personal declaration of war to the death.

At Blackwater, Hannah mounted a day and night watch on the levee. She recognized the inherent lunacy of setting black slaves to guard against black renegades but she saw no choice. Since the whispered words with which Joseph had alerted her to the terrible danger, she had done what she could. It was little enough. Allyn Gregory she'd summoned with a cryptic message that he was wanted. He had listened white faced to her tale, then gone to check the locks on the fence surrounding the compound nearest the house. It was his only constructive action. After that he sat in his father's study with a shotgun over his knees and a bottle of spirits at his elbow.

By herself Hannah sailed the short distance to Tuttle's Folly. She found there an air of calm normalcy. The slave who showed her upstairs to Illona Babcock's bedroom was the same girl who had cared for the old woman these past twenty years. Certainly nothing in her manner toward her mistress had changed.

"It's Missy Ludlow come to pay you a visit, ma'am."

"Hannah! I'm delighted to see you, such a kind and thoughtful gesture so soon after the wedding. I hear Susannah made a lovely bride. Sit down and tell me all about it."

Not until her guest had been made comfortable and served with a glass of lemonade did Illona dismiss the slave. "Thank you, Verona, that will be all for the moment. I'll ring when

Mrs. Ludlow's ready to leave." Then she gave her visitor a look that bespoke her knowledge of the threat they all faced.

"You know, Illona? You've heard?"

"I know. Bill Myers told me before he left to fetch your husband."

Hannah was glad to be spared the necessity for explanations. "Good. I've come to take you to Blackwater until things are safe again. Allyn Gregory's home. He wasn't there when the message came, and then he decided he'd best stay with me." In truth Allyn had said nothing of the possibility of going after his father and brothers, but there was no need to mention that.

"Thank you, my dear." Illona reached out an aged and wrinkled hand to grasp Hannah's. "It is kind of you to remember me and risk coming here. But I prefer to stay where I am."

"You can't, Illona! It's madness. You're old and ill. Please, you must come with me."

"That's what Bill Myers said too. I told him the same thing I'm telling you. This is my home. I have no intention of being driven from it by a band of rebellious savages. Besides, I can protect myself."

"How?" the younger woman demanded scornfully. "Be reasonable, Illona. You can't even walk."

"No. But I can shoot." She turned back the lace-trimmed sheet that covered her withered body to reveal four pistols. "In my youth I brought down more pigeons than any man or woman on the Ashley. More than my husband could dream of bagging. Niggers," she said with a grin, "are bigger than pigeons. Go home, my dear Hannah. Go to Blackwater and give your son just cause for remaining clear of the battle."

"They're in the woods a mile ahead," the advance scout reported.

"How many?"

"Couldn't tell."

"Damn it, man, are you a blithering idiot? We have to know how many." The speaker was Samuel Davis, overseer of a nearby plantation and head of the so-called militia.

"Don't get angry, Samuel." Michael Ludlow often spoke with the calm voice of reason when others lost their temper.

"It helps nothing. He'll just have to go back and develop an estimate of their strength."

"I ain't goin' back. Send someone else." The scout was a local farmer's son. Neither he nor his family owned slaves, and the blacks made him nervous when they were peaceful; at a time like this they terrified him. "I been once. That should be enough."

"But no one knows this area as well as you do," Davis protested. "You've the best chance of remaining unseen, preserving the advantage of surprise."

The boy wasn't interested in discussions of military tactics. "I ain't goin'," he repeated.

"I'll go." Joseph Ludlow checked his weapons as he spoke and adjusted the strap of one slightly uncomfortable boot. "Tell me exactly where you spotted them."

His twin wasn't there when Joseph made this decision and acted on it. He'd gone into the distant bushes to obey the call of nature. "Why did you let him do it, Papa?" Daniel demanded angrily when he learned of Joseph's errand. "I'm the one that should have gone. Joseph can't track half as well as I can, and he's not much of a shot. You know that."

"Yes," the senior Ludlow agreed. "I know." Daniel was the best woodsman in Carolina. Quite possibly he would one day be the best in all the colonies. The boy had been born with the instincts of an Indian, the wiliness of a fox, and the tenacity of a bloodhound. He was, in addition, intelligent, well spoken, and possessed of at least the potential for great charm. In short, he was the absolute best of Ludlow's three sons and on him rested all Michael's plans for the future. "I need you here," was his only further explanation.

Daniel turned away in impotent rage. He understood why Joseph had been sent and not he. His father was husbanding his resources through careful management, just as he always did.

"Daniel," Michael called after the boy. "You're not to follow him, you understand! I forbid it. Joseph will be all right. All he has to do is assess their strength."

An hour later Joseph still hadn't returned. Samuel Davis looked at the sun and the lengthening shadows and said, "We'd best take 'em now regardless. If we don't, it'll be dark and we'll have lost the chance." The others nodded their agreement and the group of some seventy men headed south toward the river.

Daniel was in the vanguard of the advance. His father could find no way of preventing that. Many of the others were familiar with the lad's considerable skills and content to follow his lead. When after ten minutes he held up his hand to halt their progress, the others stopped without question. Daniel motioned forward the two men closest behind him and pointed to the path. They looked at him blankly.

"There was some kind of a scuffle here," he explained, trying to keep the impatience from his voice. Few of his comrades in arms had made any study of the woods. They weren't even particularly good hunters. "We're getting close. We'd best fan out and attack from two sides."

"Not on your life, son." It was Samuel Davis who spoke. He fancied himself knowledgeable in military matters. "We go straight in and strike the enemy at his heart."

Daniel looked at the older man with disgust. When the group pressed forward under Davis's instructions, he placed himself a few paces back from the front. Daniel was brave, but he was not a fool. Michael fell into step beside his son, grateful for the obstinacy of Sam Davis which had removed the boy from the leader's position.

The two Ludlows were thus walking together when they came upon Joseph. His torso had been slit from pelvis to neck and his entrails torn out and scattered. Wordlessly Daniel fell to his knees beside his twin. Michael couldn't even move that far. He was frozen in his tracks by a wave of hatred and rage so great it threatened to choke him. That's how they were when the first shots rang out and the blacks' bloodcurdling cries destroyed the peace of the woods.

For nearly ten seconds both Ludlows ignored the battle now raging around them. Then, when Daniel at last turned to look at his father, he saw a renegade slave hurtling toward them with a knife in one hand and a pistol in the other. Perhaps it was the black man's unfamiliarity with firearms that defeated him, or maybe it was Daniel's formidable talent. Young Ludlow had his shotgun aimed and fired before the Negro had even tightened his finger on the trigger. The man's face was blown away, and he pitched forward with his weapons still in hand. The knife entered Michael's thigh as the black fell.

They had no time then to attend to the wound or exchange the recriminations and denials begging to be uttered. The blacks came in wave after wave, hatred and desperation supplying a kind of suicidal courage. By himself Daniel killed five of them and wounded half a dozen more. He and Michael fought back to back, Indian fashion. Some of the others did likewise. Still others lined themselves into walls of gunfire.

Against such expertise, moderate though it was, the blacks had no defense. Generations of enslavement had stripped them of the skills of their African forefathers. Only the knowledge of the fate that awaited them if they were captured and the sweet taste of a few hours of freedom kept them going. It was inevitable that in little over an hour the Stono rebellion came to an end.

The bank of the Edisto River was red with blood. The air stank of powder and death. Some sixty-five bodies were strewn over the ground, two-thirds of them black bodies, and nearly half a hundred slaves were trussed and staked to the ground to await the sentence of their captors. No one even suggested tending their wounds.

"Daniel! You all right? Where's your pa?"

"I'm all right, Sam. Papa's got a knife wound, but he's alive."

"Glad to hear it, boy. You two were . . . Oh Jesus! That's Joseph, ain't it?"

The Ludlows had fought the entire battle not two feet from Joseph's mutilated body, as if to protect it from any further abasement. "Yes," Daniel said quietly. "That's Joseph. I'll need help getting them both home, Sam. Papa can't walk."

"I'll get a couple of the boys. You want to go now or wait till mornin'?"

"Now, please."

The old overseer nodded and went to find the promised assistance. On his way, he spat on the decapitated body of one enormous Negro whose rich ebony color proclaimed his African origins. "That's the cause," Davis muttered. "Bringin' niggers in straight from Africa like Palmer does. Ibos like this one. Got to breed 'em here if we want peace."

Later, sailing up the Ashley in the moonlight, Daniel considered the future. What he most wanted, he realized, was to slip Joseph's body quietly over the side and let the silent water cover him.

All their lives the twins had loved the little river. Their affection was born of different impulses and found different modes of expression. Daniel probed the secrets of nature as it existed in this particular confluence of land and water; Joseph tried to capture its small mysteries with words or sketches. But when Michael wanted to send his younger sons to school in England, it was to the Ashley that both boys looked as they shook their heads and resisted. Yes, the river was the appropriate burial ground for Joseph.

Still, Daniel knew he couldn't dispose of his brother's body thus. Neither could he do the second thing that seemed most right to him. He wanted to jump from the skiff, swim to the shore, and set out for parts unknown. With the reeking carnage of the fight still in his nostrils, and the bitter anger at Joseph's cruel and unnecessary death churning like acid in his stomach, Daniel longed to go but didn't.

His father was ill, burning with fever and muttering in delirium: crazy sentence fragments about people sold to the Tyburn hangman . . . Daniel grimaced. Was a man haunted by the same ghost all his life? He knew the specter that pursued his father. Grandfather Ludlow had started life as an errand boy working for the Griffins in London. He'd repaid their kindness by accusing Mark Griffin of conspiring with Jesuits to murder the king. Mark was a Catholic, and he and his wife were hung, drawn and quartered at Tyburn.

Resentful of this day's work though he was, Daniel thought of his mother, and sponged his father's forehead with the cool waters of the Ashley. He whispered. "It was a long time ago, nothing to do with you." The words were wasted. Ludlow continued to mutter and groan. Death casts a long shadow, Daniel thought—violent death worst of all. He glanced at Joseph's still form and swallowed his tears.

His thoughts returned to his mother, how she'd react to all this. But she was tough, he knew that. She'd been raised as a ward of the Griffins, yet when she wanted to marry Michael Ludlow, son of the man who'd betrayed them, nothing would stop her. That's the sort she was. He sighed with the complexity of it all, tended the lanterns burning fore and aft, and adjusted the jib to make the best of the breeze.

Hannah was apprised of their coming when they were yet some distance away. She was waiting on the levee when the skiff docked.

"Joseph's dead, Papa's badly wounded, I'm fine, the rebellion's ended," Daniel reported tersely. Hannah quietly gave orders and set in motion the necessary courses of action.

Three days later, after Joseph had been buried in the field behind the magnolia trees and Michael's fever had broken, she summoned Daniel to the little room in the tower. "You need not be ashamed to weep for your brother," she said, hoping to ease the grief she knew the boy carried.

"What good would it do? Tears won't bring Joseph back."

"No. But they might do you some good." When he made no reply to this, she said, "You haven't been to see your father. He's much better today, and he's asking for you."

"I don't want to see him."

"Why, Daniel? What happened out there?"

"He knows. He can tell you if he cares to."

"I'd like to hear your version of the story."

Stubbornly Daniel shook his head. "There is something I want to tell you, though. I'm going away. As long as Papa and Allyn are here to take care of you, there's no reason for me to stay."

"No reason! Blackwater's your home, your inheritance."

"Not my inheritance, Allyn Gregory's."

"It need not be so if . . . if things don't change. We're not blind, Daniel. We mean to leave Blackwater to someone who'll care for it as it deserves."

"No, Mama, I've made up my mind. I only waited to see that you didn't need me."

"Of course I need you. You're my son. I've buried one child this week and sent another off to a distant home. Am I to lose you too?" Again he shook his head in that familiar stubborn way and Hannah knew it was pointless to argue. "Very well," she sighed. "I see I can't stop you. Here," she said, reaching for a pouch of coins she had secreted against a possible emergency. "Take these." It pleased her that he didn't refuse the money.

"Good-bye, Mama."

"Good-bye, son." She kissed him lightly and turned her back so as not to see him leave or betray her tears.

Three days later, when it was far too late to recall Daniel, Michael took a turn for the worse. The infection in his leg spread from ankle to groin. His flesh was swollen and mottled with ugly blue and black stains. Hannah tried every remedy she knew but it was no use. On Friday morning she woke Allyn Gregory and told him that his father was dead and Blackwater now belonged to him.

3

"Evening, Mrs. Amory. They've started without me from the sound of it."

"Good evening, Sam." Rachel managed a smile as she greeted the boy, but it changed to a frown when she nodded toward her husband's study. "I expect you know the way. Doubtless you're expected."

"Yes, thank you." Sam Adams started for the door then stopped. "You don't approve of us, do you?" he asked suddenly.

Rachel was startled by his directness. She paused before answering. "I would not say that exactly. All our friends are welcome to our home. The door of The Roses is always open."

Her voice betrayed her pride in the beautiful house on Boston's rural Summer Street. "But," Rachel continued in a more serious tone, "I do not always think it wise to discuss certain matters."

"Everyone says you're the most intelligent woman in Massachusetts Bay, Mrs. Amory. With which remark Adams turned and went to join Paul and the others.

A few moments later, Rachel could hear Paul's voice rising in defense of a point and three or four others trying to shout him down. She shook her head and walked away. The smell of tobacco and strong punch followed her all the way upstairs.

The worrisome thing was that talk like theirs could be misunderstood. Unification of all the colonies, a direct voice in Parliament . . . Why did Paul take such risks? Rachel had no better answer to that persistent question than she ever had. If I were a man, she told herself for the hundredth time, I'd not waste my energies on political theories—I'd do something!

And therein lay the true nub of her animosity to Paul's sympathies. She knew full well that there was a logic to his position; even her father, Antony Jacob Griffin, the most thoughtful of men, agreed that the relationship between England and the American colonies was often mismanaged. But her husband was content to play at the edges of that distant drama, and this Rachel could not forgive. It bespoke all the other failings she found in him.

Paul Amory was a gentle, considerate, and kindly man. Many women envied her his love and devotion. But oh God, he was such a . . . Rachel stood with her hands on her hips and searched for a word. A jellyfish. That was it. Paul was a jellyfish. You could squish him about this way or the other. And the freethinkers and theorizers who met here did just that. Whether Paul agreed or disagreed with them, they could come to The Roses and speak their truth. They would stay awhile, drink endless toasts, tell each other how noble were their ideas, and move on—often a bit richer with Amory money.

Rachel paced the turkey carpet in the bedroom and her anger grew. In girlhood she had been known for her quick and clever mind—like a man's, people often said. Hah! The thought of that perverse compliment rankled. Like a man indeed! She could do most things better than any man. Hadn't she taken the thousand pounds Paul brought with him from England to

America and turned that into the far-flung network of the Amory markets? Did anyone imagine Paul could have done that without her? Or without the Griffins, said a voice in her head.

What of it? Certainly she had capitalized on the advantage of her successful family. The Griffin shipping empire stretched from Boston to London and the four corners of the earth. She'd have been a fool not to trade on that. But by itself that wouldn't have been enough . . . Oh bother! What difference did it all make?

She dropped to the bed and buried her face in her arms. If it weren't for the children, she would simply ignore the whole thing. Let Paul do whatever he liked and the devil take him. Of course Val was only seven, and at thirteen Sophia was the kind of girl who considered politics purely the province of men. She cared for nothing but domestic chores and pretty dresses. No, Sophia wasn't likely to be harmed unless some terrible catastrophe befell them all. But Jacob . . . If somehow what Paul played at with these plotters and . . . yes, revolutionaries, endangered Jacob . . .

The son for whom Rachel felt such fear was at that moment being invited to join the meeting taking place downstairs. At two months short of fifteen, Jacob Amory was already taller than most grown men. His wasn't the enormous bulk of Paul; no one would ever dub Jacob with his father's sobriquet, the gentle giant. Jacob was all Griffin to look at him—long and lean with dark hair and blue eyes like his mother. But he had the Amory set of mind. "Papa said I might join you to discuss this paper I've written." His voice was soft, a bit shy. But his pride was unmistakable. This was the first time Jacob's efforts had been considered worthy of presentation to the Socratarians. Paul looked at his son and waited. Jacob cleared his throat and started to speak.

There was another member of the Griffin family who shared Rachel's dislike of Paul's political sympathies. Her brother Benjamin Griffin had a special reason for being concerned, and he pointed it out to his father with his usual scrupulous honesty.

"I admit it's not just Rachel and the children that worry me,

Papa. I don't deny that Paul's carryings on could hurt my chances of being on the governor's list. It could deny me my rightful opportunity for a title."

Tonyjay smiled and leaned back in his chair. Poor Benjamin. Somehow the older he grew, the more he looked and sounded like a pompous ass. Tonyjay knew that wasn't a fair judgment. Benjamin had many sterling qualities. Nonetheless, that was the impression he gave, even to his own father. "Tell me," Tonyjay said after some thought. "Just what does Paul actually do?"

"He . . . well he receives people at his house. People with . . . with seditious ideas."

"Seditious? That's a strong word, isn't it, Ben?"

"Not too strong, I think." The younger man pursed his lips, unaware that the gesture made him look rather like a toad. "He was a known Jacobite, you realize."

Tonyjay leaned forward. "For God's sake, Ben, that was sixteen years ago. In England. Paul's been here since he married your sister. Surely you aren't accusing him of being a Jacobite now."

"I never said that. But you must admit that for one who doesn't believe George the Second to be the true king, it's easy to be rebellious about royal authority—"

"Seditious, rebellious," his father interrupted. "You're talking rubbish, Ben. Paul and that group—what do they call themselves, the Socratarians?—all they do is study philosophy. The same concepts are being published here and in England. Time changes things, Ben. It always has and it always will. Surely you aren't ready to condemn Paul because he discusses the ideas behind those changes?"

"No, damn it! Of course not." Benjamin was beginning to perspire. Trying to wriggle around his father's relentless logic always made him nervous. "You know that's not what I mean."

"Yes, I know that. Calm yourself, Ben. I do see the problem. I just think you're making too much of it. Paul and his friends don't actually do anything but talk. Can't you just ignore the whole thing? I don't see how there can be any real danger to Rachel and the children."

"Maybe not," Benjamin agreed. "But I've already admitted my personal interest. You can call it selfish if you wish but—"

"I never said it was selfish, Ben. Just foolish."

"Foolish! To seek a baronetcy. I fail to see—"

At that moment Lizzie Griffin burst into the study without knocking. "Tonyjay, I've just had a letter from Hannah, the most terrible news— Oh Ben, I didn't know you were here."

"I just came to ask Papa something." He kissed his mother dutifully, then asked, "What's happened? Is Hannah in some sort of difficulty?"

"A pile of them. There was a revolt of the slaves and both Michael and Joseph are dead."

"The Stono rebellion. I was reading about that just before Ben arrived." Tonyjay motioned to the news gazette on his desk. "Small wonder it hasn't happened before now. Came to nothing but a lot of bloodshed apparently."

"But I just told you," Lizzie reiterated. "Both Michael and Joseph were killed." Lizzie couldn't share her husband's concern with the general evil of slavery when it affected her own family so intimately. "And Daniel's run off someplace. Either Hannah doesn't know where or she isn't saying. In any case, it's a terrible thing."

"Who does that leave to manage the plantation?" Benjamin, ever the businessman, asked.

"The oldest boy, Allyn Gregory. Hannah doesn't sound too confident of his ability."

"Pity." Ben shook his head. "Blackwater's said to be a fine holding. Let's hope he'll grow to suit the task."

Tonyjay felt a surge of anger. Ben's lack of concern with the larger issues was typical. "Yes. Well, as you can see, Ben, your mother's upset. You'd best be going. And tell the others. They must all write to Hannah."

"Yes, Papa." Benjamin knew there was no point in pressing for an answer to his questions about Paul Amory. He reclaimed his elegant three-cornered hat and let himself out. The condolence letter to his half sister he would leave to his wife; she was much better than he at that sort of thing. He'd have to stop at the Ark, though. John and Charles would need to be told. In his present frame of mind the thought of a visit to that noisy, ill-run establishment was not pleasant but Benjamin was never one to shirk his duty. Manfully he strode on.

* * *

The proclivity for producing children in pairs existed on both sides of the two families who cohabited in the house called the Ark. Like their half sister Hannah, Charles and John carried the trait through Lizzie. Then fifteen years earlier, in 1724, they'd married twin sisters, Mary and Martha White, and waited with interest to see what would happen. It might be nice to have a twin or two, the young husbands speculated. They could hardly have been prepared for the largesse their wives bestowed.

Mary began by lulling her husband into a false sense of security. The first child she presented to Charles was a single boy, whom he named Antony. Then in rapid succession Mary produced two sets of twins.

Not to be outdone by her sister's prolific childbearing, Martha went her two better. John was the father of not two but four sets of twins.

The effect of all this duplication was intensified by the fact that from the first Charles and John and their wives had lived together in the house on School Street where the White sisters were born. When the spate of procreation was ended there were nine little girls in the house as well. Naturally it wasn't big enough for seventeen people, so they added on. Not all at once and not with any plan. Just a room here and a room there as needs must and space could be found. The result was a big ugly house that was full of children, toys, and laughter. Huge cauldrons of soup or stew constantly simmered in the kitchen, innumerable loaves of bread came in eternal procession from the ovens, the clotheslines were always full of washing, and the garden was always full of weeds. Most people adored visiting the place. Even those who didn't chuckled whenever they thought of the wag who first said, "They enter two by two just like in the Bible. Darn place is a regular Noah's ark." The Ark it became, and so it was known from that day forward.

Benjamin was not one of the Ark's admirers. His own home at 26 Marlborough Street was an elegant brick townhouse. His wife, Eve, was a woman of culture who knew about music and art and poetry and how to talk to important people. The four children she gave him came one at a time and at decent intervals—no, Benjamin didn't like the Ark at all. Still, he knocked on the door as he knew he must and prepared to pass on the news of the misfortunes that had befallen the Carolina branch of the family.

The Boston Griffins might not entirely approve of their southern relations but neither did they ignore them. Family loyalty was a virtue they had early been taught to prize.

4

Sometimes, early in the morning when the most ordinary day seemed pregnant with potential, Paul would look at his sleeping wife and see the girl with whom he had fallen so passionately in love. Rachel's black hair still curled appealingly around her finely chiseled features, her lashes still made evocative shadows on her cheeks, and the determined chin was still contradicted by the full, sensual mouth. All he had once read, or thought he had read, behind the unyielding façade of Rachel's public person seemed yet to be there. But whether the woman of his dreams and longings was real or a product of his imagination Paul still didn't know.

Nearly sixteen years they had lain together in this bed. She had borne him three children, stood beside him through good times and bad. Beside him yes, but he seldom felt he really touched her. Only in the cataclysmic retreat from self that was their lovemaking could he probe the depths of her, the inner core—for the rest, nothing. That bridge which he sensed between married folk grown easy and forgiving with each other never spanned the chasm that separated him from Rachel.

Now, on this bleak November morning that promised snow

and with his breath hanging like a small cloud in the cold of the bedroom, Paul reached out and lay a tentative finger on her cheek. "Are you awake, darling?"

He could feel her stiffen beside him. "I'm awake," she said in a voice that denied intimacy.

"It looks like snow."

"Probably. It's November, after all."

He would not accept the refusal implicit in her words. Instead he let his hand wander from her cheek to her neck and thence to her breast. She didn't move. "It's very early," he whispered. "No one's up yet."

"I've much to do today."

"Yes, I know. But not yet." She always had much to do. Rachel's days were a series of self-assigned tasks which she tackled as if doing them were the key to her salvation. Paul had learned that to reach her through that screen of busy doing he must ignore it. He rolled closer so that his big frame could touch the length of her tiny one. The warmth of their bodies made an island in the ocean of cold.

"Not now, Paul. Please." Her voice was a small echo outside the island, an effort to escape the swelling tide, the last cry before drowning. He ran his hand over her taut, flat belly and stroked the softness of her thighs. With a strangled gasp she pummeled her fists on his chest. "No, no, no," she muttered even as she turned to him.

Easing her nightdress above her waist, he let his fingers flutter over her small, firm breasts, the nipples now hard and hot. She was trembling from head to foot just as she always did. When he touched her buttocks she rammed her pelvis against his hip. She never spoke during the act. The Rachel who thought and talked and moved of her own will was gone; only the feeling remained.

Many times he had tried to be tender, even playful. She rejected that with bitter ferocity. All she would permit was the act itself. Naked, unadorned. Savage. He entered her with a single movement and felt her teeth sink into his shoulder. The rhythmic thrusts of her body matched his own. When the shuddering release came, they were united as they were only at such moments.

Afterwards he fell back and waited. She said nothing. She

seldom did. For some minutes he let the pleasurable ebb of sensation hold back the tide of bitterness. Then, because he knew this time would be like all the others, he rose, pulled on his clothes, and went into the garden to see if frost had taken the last of the mums.

On that same morning young Antony Griffin did not breakfast at home. The sixteen people with whom he shared the Ark were all finding their sleep-fogged way to the warm and steamy kitchen, but Antony donned his heavy coat and knitted muffler and let himself quietly out the back door. No one would question his absence. It was Thursday, the day he always spent at Beacon Street.

The ritual had begun nearly twelve years ago when he was a lad of four and the Ark was full of squalling infants demanding attention. In those days Lizzie would come and get him and carry him off to her quiet, sweet-smelling house. By the time he was six he had learned to make the journey alone. Over the broken corner of the back fence—it had been repaired innumerable times but never stayed that way—across Treamount Street and up Beacon. He could traverse the distance to his grandparents' home in under five minutes.

This morning the Common was covered in hoar frost and the dome of the Powder House was rimed with ice. Antony paused, sniffed the air with the practiced gesture of a born and bred Bostonian, and knew it would snow before nightfall. Good. Tomorrow he would have an excuse to go to Beacon Street again. They would need him to shovel the paths. They didn't, of course. He realized that. There were men whom the better Boston families could hire to perform such tasks, but Antony had kept the walks clear at Beacon Street ever since he was old enough to wield a shovel. They always said they depended on him utterly.

His grandfather was waiting in the breakfast room. "Good morning, Antony," Tonyjay said with a wide grin. "You're two minutes late. The porridge is getting cold."

"I stopped to look at the Common. Frost as thick as my finger. It's going to snow."

"Yes, I expect it is. Ah, here's your grandmother."

"Oh boy!" The lad looked appreciatively at the platter of

crisp donuts Lizzie carried. "My favorites."

"Indeed," Lizzie said, laughing. "And just the thing for a morning like this."

Later, when his grandmother had gone to help the ancient servant with the washing up—Abbie Tucker was over eighty, but since her sister died she was the only full-time help Lizzie employed—Antony asked, "What's the plan for today, Grandpa?"

"Still want to see that new schooner?"

"The one they're building down at Gee's? Yes, I hear he's done something new with the rigging."

"Very well. We'll go over there this morning. And this afternoon you can tell me how you're getting on with that book I gave you last week."

The boy's gray eyes clouded over. "Not very well," he admitted. "I liked that chap Plato much better in English."

"Nonsense, lad! Any civilized man must read Greek. Besides, you're almost sixteen. Time to realize that only original sources are reliable."

Antony smiled. He had a puckish sort of grin that spread across his face and with his always untidy mop of curly black hair confirmed a devil-may-care impression. His next words were typical. "Doesn't matter. I'm going to be a sea captain, not a civilized man."

Tonyjay ignored the assertion and the casual reference to the boy's dreams. Charles expected his son to join the business, but Antony wanted to sail ships not manage them. There was little point in discussing that again. The older man smiled at his favorite grandson and they continued to plan their day.

"Rachel, I think I saw her again."

"Saw who?" Rachel looked up from the ledgers spread on the table to where her husband stood in the doorway of the study. His boots were stained with mud and he held a pair of pruning shears. Understanding dawned and pulled the corners of her mouth into a forbidding scowl. "Oh no, not that business with the nun again."

"Yes. I'm not sure, mind you, but I think so. Just a bit of black out of the corner of my eye."

"Paul, we've been over this so many times. How can you

see what isn't there? Do please forget about it. Come look at these accounts. Something isn't well with the warehouse in Salem. I think there may be pilfering."

"Damn the warehouse in Salem!" he exploded in a rare show of temper. "I saw her I tell you. And you're as much involved as I am. She said '. . . the pair of you—'"

". . . have a debt," she finished the sentence for him. "Yes, Paul, I know. But there is no Kirkslee priory, so how can there be a debt?"

He shrugged in defeat. "That's what I can't figure out. Your mother can't figure it out either. And she saw her too."

Rachel sighed. She couldn't divert him. They would have to go over it all again. "Look, it's sixteen years since your . . . your apparition, and well over thirty since my mother's. If this nun exists, she's been silent for a long time. Maybe she's forgotten about it. Or maybe the debt's already paid."

"How?"

"Look," said Rachel, rising and beginning to pace, "she's supposed to have told my mother that my birth would heal the 'wound of Kirkslee.' Well it did, didn't it? My father stopped mourning his first wife, the one killed there at the site of the old priory."

"Sit down; you make me nervous. And you're talking rubbish. Do you really think that's all she came for? Just to patch up a quarrel between your mother and father?"

"Oh, I don't know!" Rachel walked to a chair as if in obedience to Paul's request but she remained standing. "How can I know when frankly I doubt this vision even exists?"

"She does," Paul said stubbornly. "And the debt she told me about exists. It's something you and I must take care of. If only I knew how." There was nothing spectral about the misery in his face.

Rachel went to kneel beside him, blue eyes peering earnestly into his. "Please, darling, forget it; relax for a bit. Perhaps you're overtired. I'll have some tea brought in here and we can go over these accounts together."

Paul smiled. Trust Rachel to consider the examination of figures a restful thing. "Very well. But promise me you'll think about the idea I mentioned last week."

"Sending money to England, to Harwood Hall, you mean?

I can't see what good that would do."

"It's the only thing I can think of. That's where the priory is."

"Was. That's where the priory was, Paul. Now it's nothing but an old ruin on a piece of Harwood land. And my cousin Mark certainly doesn't need any money from us to take care of Harwood land." He looked so dejected she couldn't just leave it there. "Look, maybe you should go to Harwood for a visit. Go see the old place where the nun's supposed to have lived. Perhaps—"

"I can't go to Yorkshire. You know that. She said it plain as you please. The same day she told me to come here to America and marry you. 'Take what you prize of England with you, for you'll not return here again.'"

"And by your choice you make it a self-fulfilling prophecy. I don't understand, Paul. I will never understand."

"No," he said, looking at her with something of strangeness in his eyes. "No, I don't think you ever will. But you have to cooperate in this, Rachel. You're part of it. You must help to heal the wound of Kirkslee just as the nun told your mother before you were born. It's got to mean more than the old trouble between your parents."

"Very well, Paul. I'll think about it some more and we'll discuss it again." She sighed with the futility of attempting to exorcise a ghost with logic and went to order the tea.

Out of the kitchen window she could see Jacob. He was supposed to be picking the last of the apples; she had heard Paul assign him the task earlier. Instead, he was standing quite still, oblivious to the late autumn chill, lost in a book. Rachel couldn't see what it was, but she could guess. One of those radical tomes of which he was so fond—politics and philosophy; they were all Jacob ever thought of, thanks to his father's influence.

Oh God! She pressed her forehead against the cold glass as if it could ease the pain of her thoughts. *Poison, that's what Paul's feeding him. He doesn't realize it, of course, but it's true all the same . . .* For a moment she couldn't breathe. The sense of impending doom was so strong it was almost suffocating.

"Shall I bring the tray to the study, ma'am?"

The maid's voice brought Rachel back to the present. "Yes, Maggie. Do that, please. I'll be right along." For another few moments she watched her son. Then she turned away. When she walked back to where her husband was waiting, Rachel could feel a dull ache in her thigh muscles. Evidence of the morning's animal lust. In her disgust she didn't consider the fact that her beloved Jacob was the result of that same despised impulse.

5

In Carolina this summer of 1740 was proving to be one of the hottest in memory. The July sun was an unremitting yellow glare. Beneath its onslaught everything that wasn't shriveled or burned dry could only be silent. Even the mosquitoes were still. Hank Delevant wiped the sweat from his forehead and waited. He was nearly the color of his charges. For all twenty-six years of his life he had lived beneath the Carolina sun, and his skin was the tough leathery brown of an old man. In that sered face his eyes appeared as yellow as the sun.

"You gonna do like I say, girl," he threatened, "or your back's gonna bleed worse'n his."

Lucinda looked not at the overseer but at her brother Hiram. He was naked and tied to a post in the middle of the field. The hundred or so watching men and women stood well back, leaving a wide circle of parched earth around the prisoner. Lucinda could see the muscles of Hiram's shoulder twitch where a fly landed and bit. It was the only motion. She didn't answer the overseer.

"It's the law, nigger girl," Delevant said.

"Ain't never heared it afore," Lucinda muttered. "When yore pappy was de boss he read us all dem laws. Don' say nothin' bout makin' a girl whip her own brother."

Delevant smiled. "New law. Just passed. Needed a new law cause niggers was gettin' funny ideas. Like that bunch down-river on the Stono. Here," he said, extending the whip. "Take it, girl, and do like I say."

She stood for some seconds longer. Once her hand jerked as if she were going to obey, but it fell back to her side. Then she heard the sound of hooves and raised her head to see a familiar gray mare coming toward them. Lucinda smiled slowly and her eyes at last met the overseer's. "Here come de massa," she said.

Delevant wrenched his glance away and turned to greet his employer. A hundred blacks watched in silence. "Afternoon, Mr. Ludlow."

"Afternoon, Hank. What's the trouble here."

The young man jerked his head in the direction of the slave tied to the post. "It's Hiram, sir. Troublemaker. Always has been. Been stirrin' up discontent down here in the western compound. I heared it myself. And just so these folks know nothin' like that's allowed on Blackwater, I aim to give him twenty lashes."

Allyn Gregory nodded. "What's she got to do with it?" He pointed to Lucinda with his riding crop.

"He's her brother, sir. And accordin' to this here new slave code its right an' lawful for slaves to be made to do the punishin'. Teaches 'em best like I reckon. Lucinda here's strong as any man. She can do it an' I say she should."

"I see." Allyn looked from the overseer to Lucinda and then at the crowd of onlookers. The sun picked out highlights in his golden hair and beard, making him appear almost a god astride a mythical beast. "Can you all hear me?" he called out. They signified that they could. "Good. Now listen well. I think you should understand this new code Mr. Delevant's mentioned. The legislature has made some fine new laws. They are concerned for all of you just as we are here on Blackwater. They want to be sure you're properly cared for. No slaves should ever again feel they've cause to rebel like those on the Stono did. You all know what happened there and you've heard that it started on the plantation of a man who didn't feed his slaves enough or give them proper clothes."

Ludlow paused. He could see Lucinda watching him with her wild and knowing eyes. Casually, so it didn't appear that he meant anything by it, Allyn pressed one polished boot against his mare's side. The horse moved closer to the crowd and left the three main participants in the drama behind.

"In this new code," Ludlow continued, "it says that any owner who mistreats his slaves is to be fined twenty pounds. Now you all know that's a lot of money. Man's going to think twice before he takes that risk. But you know too that no one is mistreated on Blackwater. My father always saw to it you had all the food and clothes you need to do your jobs and raise your children. Now that I'm master here it will remain that way, just as it has this past year. But Mr. Delevant's right too. Any slave that deserves punishment will receive it, and the law says another slave can be made to perform the whipping." Deliberately he turned the horse so he once more faced the overseer and Lucinda and her brother. "That's why Lucinda must do as he says."

There was a barely audible drawing of the collective breath. The girl stared at her white lover and he stared back. "You ain't gonna make me do it, Allyn honey, I knows you ain't," she whispered pleadingly.

He knew the others had heard, that he and his relationship with this nigger woman were on trial here in the western fields. Ludlow adjusted the cuffs of his white silk shirt, flicked some imaginery dust from his twill riding breeches. "Delevant," he said at last. "This girl sassed me. See she does as she's told, then give her six lashes so she doesn't forget her place."

Hanna was pleased that he no longer went to the cabin in the western fields. In the year since Allyn Gregory had taken over management of Blackwater it was the first thing he did that pleased her. Among other mistakes, she felt he gave Hank Delevant too much authority and didn't supervise him as closely as he should.

"There's no point in letting the new overseer get carried away," she said to her son when the story of Hiram and Lucinda reached her. "Slaves respond to firmness, not to cruelty."

"There's no reason to suppose young Delevant's cruel, Mama. Any more than his father was. Why should you say that?"

She shrugged. "I hear things."

"What things?"

"Just cook-house gossip," she said placatingly. "I'm not questioning your judgment, Allyn. Just Delevant's."

"Leave him to me."

"Very well. I had a letter from Susannah today. Both she and the baby are well, and Tamasee sounds a lovely and productive place."

Allyn poured himself another brandy and refreshed his mother's glass of lemonade. The verandah was delightfully cool tonight. A rare respite from the summer heat. Fewer mosquitoes than usual too. He was in a mood to be cordial. "I'm delighted to hear that. Our Susannah deserves the best. Does she say anything about coming for a visit?"

Hannah sighed. "No, I wish she did. The house seems so empty so suddenly."

"You ought to get about more, Mama. Maybe you should go to Virginia."

"No, my place is here. At least until—"

"Until what?" He was sensitive to any criticism, even the implication that he needed watching.

"Until I feel more recovered from the flu I had this winter," she added smoothly. "And besides, we might hear from Daniel any day now."

"Yes, I suppose we might." Allyn knew there was no reason to expect word from his younger brother, and he had no desire for any. Still, he had determined to be sociable. "I was thinking of spending next week in Charleston," he said casually. "Melissa Harvey's giving a gala on the first of August."

"Oh, but the Peak fields need draining! I thought that job was scheduled for next week." She had spoken quickly, without forethought, schooled by the years when she and Michael had discussed every detail of the running of Blackwater.

"The Peak fields are my concern, not yours," her son answered sharply. "Besides, old William will see to it. He's done it with Papa a dozen times."

"Yes," she said. "With Papa."

Allyn made no reply to that. He merely got up and left her sitting alone on the verandah. Hannah remained there for some time, thinking and planning. When at last she went up to bed, she had decided what to do and resolved to start her campaign the next morning.

Hannah was up early, chivying the cook-house slaves and seeing to it that there were hot rice cakes for breakfast. The coffee she brewed herself—black and strong, the way Allyn Gregory liked it. Then, when he had eaten and seemed in the best possible humor, she launched her first salvo. "My dear, have you considered that it's time you took a wife?"

"A wife? Well, Mama," he said with a grin, and he was undeniably handsome even in Hannah's disapproving eyes. "I admit the thought's crossed my mind. But so soon after Papa and Joseph—"

"It's nearly a year now. Not too soon to start discussing the question at least."

"I know you." He was still in good spirits, even laughing. "If you've said this much it's because you've someone specific in mind. Am I to know who you fancy as my bride?"

"Well . . ." Hannah toyed with a crumb of rice cake on her plate. "There's Melissa Harvey's girl Beth Ann."

"A decoy, Mama," he hooted. "A red herring. I know damn well what you think of the Harveys. You're trying to put me off the scent. Beth Ann's not your idea of a daughter-in-law, and we both know it. Come on now. Who?"

"Sarah Lee Myers," she said firmly.

"Sarah Lee . . . ? Mama, her father's the overseer at Tuttle's Folly. I hardly think—"

"Listen to me, Allyn, and don't be a snobbish fool. The Myers girl is the pick of the crop. I've watched her grow up and she's a remarkable young woman, as pretty as any—you must admit she's pretty." Hannah didn't wait for him to agree to the obvious. "But most important, she's educated and strong and has the will to be the kind of wife a plantation owner needs. She came here to visit me on Saturday. She's been off to school in Richmond, you know. A special school for training young ladies. Illona Babcock sent her because of her gratitude for all Bill Myers has done for Tuttle's Folly since Illona's husband died. And—"

"Whoa, Mama . . . slow down. I admit Sarah Lee's pretty and she may be all the other things you say she is. But an overseer's daughter. Really, my dear, I think you've had too much sun." With which remark he kissed her dutifully and went off.

Despite Allyn Gregory's reaction to his mother's suggestion, the idea of taking a wife began to grow in appeal. At the party given by the Harveys in their charming summer house in Charleston, he found himself appraising all the young ladies with new perceptiveness.

Beth Ann, his mother's decoy, was beautiful but not to be trusted. A flirt. A man would never know where he stood with a wife like that. The Washburn sisters were too fat and the James girl too thin. Cindy Sherman was a pretty thing and she had no brothers, which made her heiress to a considerable fortune, but there was something about her . . . And so it went. Forcing himself to analyze the marriage potential of the young ladies he knew, Allyn Gregory realized that not one of them fulfilled his requirements.

It wasn't until some days later, when he was making a pretense of checking the job William and his crew had done at the Peak fields that the idea came to him. The fields themselves provided the clue. In viewing them Allyn realized that every man has a proper function. He himself really knew very little about the preparation of land for planting rice. William knew a good deal more because all his life he had done little else. Allyn's own job, no, his role, was to set the seal of approval on the work and thus inspire the slaves to go on doing what they did best.

"That's it," he murmured as he rode back to the big house after the ceremonial inspection. "I want a girl who has been bred to be the wife of a gentleman. Not just for one generation or two. For centuries." There was only one place he knew where such a woman was obtainable, and he contacted the Jameson's agent the following week.

* * *

It was three weeks short of Christmas when they went to Charleston to meet the ship. The summer homes of the planters were all closed and boarded up for the winter, and the town had the air of a sleepy little village.

"She won't think much of Charleston, I fear," Allyn Gregory said.

"It's not Charleston that will be her home," Hannah replied, thinking of her own first sight of the place. It had been half this size then. The only thing that looked the same were the rows of cleaning sheds. They were used to house Negroes from the time the slave ships docked until the blacks were sold. In that interval it was necessary that the men and women be cleansed of the filth from the journey. The low, long white buildings where that task was performed lined the wharfs as they had for decades.

Allyn wasn't interested in the cleaning sheds. He was trying to conceal his excitement at the thought of seeing in the flesh the woman whom he had only heard about. True, there was the little miniature painting he carried in his waistcoat pocket, but he wasn't sure how reliable that might prove to be.

For her part, Hannah was praying it wasn't reliable. Ever since her son had announced his intention to import a bride from England she had been mourning his foolishness and her own lack of influence. Mourning too the decision she and Michael had taken to send Allyn Gregory to be educated at Oxford. At the time it had seemed wise, but in retrospect it struck her as tragic. Well, maybe she was wrong. A weak chin in a portrait wasn't to be taken as an absolute truth. Maybe the artist thought women with dainty little chins looked more attractive.

There was no way of predicting the arrival of the English ship with certainty, so they had to stay in town for two days. Hannah kept to her room in the inn. City life held no fascination for her. Allyn, on the other hand, was out and about from morning to night. She wondered what he found to do but didn't like to ask. Now, on the afternoon of the second day, he invited her for a walk and she felt it would be rude to refuse. "Come along up here, Mama," he said. "There's something I want you to see."

They were on the Cooper River side of the town, where the most fashionable houses were. The Cooper was broader than the Ashley but Hannah didn't think it as beautiful. When she said as much to Allyn, though, he disagreed. "There's nothing but fields and farms on the Ashley side," he said. "The best people all live over here in the summer."

What did it mean, Hannah wondered, to be one of the best people? She was about to ask when he steered her toward a funny little bit of waterfront that curved out into the river. "They call this the half moon. Isn't it charming?"

"Well, yes, yes I suppose it is." A suspicion was dawning but she didn't care to examine it. "Shouldn't we go back to the wharf now, Allyn? The ship may be in."

"Just a moment more. I want to show you a piece of land."

Oh no! A piece of Charleston land for a summer house. She had guessed, but she wouldn't face it before now. Allyn would be away from Blackwater for three or four months at a time, maybe longer. It would be disastrous, just as Michael had always claimed.

"Right here," her son was saying. "This is the piece I've bought, Mama. I'm going to build a wedding present for my bride. We'll call it Half Moon House."

She didn't know what to say and she was grateful when at that moment they heard the deep resonant sound of a ship's bell. "She's in," someone called from the next road. "The *Antigone* from London!" The Ludlows joined the suddenly materialized throng hurrying toward the wharf to see what treasures the *Antigone* was bringing to South Carolina.

6

Sir George Rigby, Bt., had inherited little of value beyond the baronetcy that had been in his family for six generations. It was a minor title that granted him merely a certain social precedence on formal occasions and a large piece of indifferent land between Bury St. Edmunds and Stowmarket in Suffolk, which he didn't know how to make profitable. He had been a widower for many years, and his son and daughter were raised with much the same ineptitude Sir George brought to his other endeavors. For all of that, Rigby was an honorable name and among his ancestors were romantic cavaliers as well as solid English gentlemen of less heroic stripe.

And no man lives fifty years without making a small mark on something or someone. In the case of Sir George there was a favor he had once done for a man of far greater talent and initiative, Clive Jameson. In 1740 Jameson was old and looking toward the end of his life. He was a man who liked to leave things in a tidy fashion and it niggled him that he had never repaid Sir George. So when Ludlow's letter reached his desk it seemed a heaven-sent opportunity. The last paragraph gave him leave to follow his inclination.

"I do not seek," Allyn Gregory wrote to his factor, "a girl of substantial dowry and little else besides. Indeed I have no interest in the daughter of some city merchant who has recently made his fortune. What I want is a girl of breeding . . ."

"It's an excellent opportunity for Miss Joan," Jameson told

Sir George. "Just the sort of marriage she should make." He had no need to add that considering the limitations of the dowry Rigby could provide, it was a miraculous chance.

"He looks all right," Sir George said, fingering the small portrait that accompanied Ludlow's request for a bride. "Still, America—"

"South Carolina, sir. It's a cut above the other colonies, you know. Real ladies and gentlemen. Joan will settle in beautifully."

So it was done. Allyn Gregory would have a wife born of noble lineage, and Joan would be quit of the restrictions of genteel poverty.

In the first few weeks following the marriage, Hannah reassessed her judgment of the girl. The miniature was inaccurate—Joan did not have a weak chin. She was pretty but not beautiful. Hannah deemed that an advantage: truly beautiful women were often empty-headed. She seemed genuinely delighted with South Carolina and Blackwater and, best of all, she seemed able to read her new husband's character and adjust her actions accordingly.

"It is proper that I be called Lady Joan," she told everyone. "It's my title, and it will distinguish me from Mrs. Ludlow senior."

Hannah, who knew that the daughters of baronets had no title, was amused but pleased. Allyn Gregory beamed when he heard his wife addressed as her Ladyship. It was a good beginning.

Hannah's hopes for the success of the union, at least in her terms, received their first setback over the matter of the home in Charleston. Allyn and his bride spent hours poring over the plans. "I shall design the house itself and you must do the decorating," Allyn told Joan.

"But . . ." She looked a bit puzzled. "I didn't see many shops in Charleston. Where am I to buy the furnishings and the pictures and the fabrics?"

"From London of course. Just make your lists and give them to the Jameson's agent."

Later Hannah drew the girl aside. "Do you understand our relationship to Jameson's?" she asked.

"No. I can't say that I do."

"They are our factors. The rice we raise here on Blackwater is carried to London in Jameson's ships and sold by them. The money from that transaction is credited to our account, less the cost of transport and their commission."

"I see. That's all right then. Whatever I order from London for Half Moon House will be debited to the Ludlow account." Joan looked pleased at having it all spelled out.

"It may not be that simple," Hannah cautioned. "If we buy more from Jameson's than our accounts cover, we're in debt. Besides, there are some things we *must* order from them. Things for the plantation that can't be made here."

"Will they not wait for the next shipment of rice to make the accounts tally?"

"Hah!" Hannah said briskly. "They're only too glad to do that. Gives them a hold over us. When my husband was alive we avoided that like the plague. It can be disastrous for a planter."

Joan realized that her mother-in-law was attempting to put conditions on the openhandedness of Allyn Gregory. "But my husband told me to order the furnishings for Half Moon House from London."

"Well," said Hannah with a smile meant to include the girl in the universal female conspiracy, "you know how men are. They never really understand how we ladies do things. Why right here on Blackwater we have a fine carpentry shop and a slave who makes lovely pieces from our native woods."

"Is there any mahogany in South Carolina?" Joan asked.

"No, not mahogany. But—"

"That settles it," the girl interrupted. "Allyn Gregory wants nothing but the best for our Charleston residence."

In the matter of the management of blacks, Joan proved equally stubborn. Hannah was conscious of the difficulty a young woman faced in becoming mistress of a home her mother-in-law still managed. She was quite willing to turn the running of Blackwater over to Allyn's new wife. Indeed, it was important to her plan to do just that. She spent days taking Joan through the cook house, the sewing rooms, and the compound where the house slaves lived. Joan was polite and gracious to them all, but she never remembered the names of any of them except Delilah, the girl Allyn Gregory had given her as personal maid.

"They respond to firmness," Hannah explained. "You must remember that they are Negroes, not white servants such as you have in England. You must oversee everything."

Joan, who considered that back in Suffolk they had far too few servants and who was thrilled with the numbers of blacks available to take on all the chores of daily living, said, "I'm sure you've trained them well. They seem to know their jobs."

"With constant supervision, yes," Hannah agreed. "Just remember that they are like children. Left to themselves they're idle and shiftless, but intelligently handled they're treasures."

"But if it's so much bother, why have them? Why not get proper white servants?"

Hannah was reluctant to mention the mosquitoes and the terrible heat of summer, a phenomenon her daughter-in-law had yet to experience. She said only, "Time has proved Negroes best in the south."

She waited for Joan to begin assuming command but she waited in vain. The girl continued to presume that Blackwater would function by itself. Only in Delilah did Joan have any interest. She spent hours with the slave's taking her to the master bedroom while she tried on clothes and ordered new frocks to be made in the sewing rooms or, better yet, sent from London. Often Hannah would hear the two young women giggling together and she would shake her head and feel the terrible anger of frustration.

Then one day in March she saw the possibility of a solution to the problem. Joan came to her on a sunny humid morning with a tiny paper packet clutched in her hand. "Do you think the gardener could start these seeds for me?" she asked. "They're clove pinks from my home, and I thought it would be nice to have some growing here."

Hannah's eyes lit up. "Do you like flowers? And gardening?"

"Oh I do!" the girl answered with spirit.

"Come with me."

She brought Joan to the shed where all the tools used for the gardens surrounding the house were stored and introduced her to Zebedee, the slave in charge. Then, before Joan could question Zeb about the possibility of growing clove pinks, Hannah led her on to the stables. "This is the secret of the garden," she said. "Good rich muck. There's nothing like horse manure to make things grow."

Joan pressed a lacy handkerchief on her nose. "I expect the gardener knows that."

"Yes, after a fashion," said Hannah, refusing to be put off. "But if you leave him to himself, Zeb always spreads it fresh because it's easier. That just burns everything up. You must insist he pile the muck and age it before he puts it on the beds. And see he doesn't let it get wet while it's aging. That just leaches out the goodness. Remember, nothing is of greater benefit to a garden than the foot of the owner."

Joan was already backing out of the stable. "You'll tell him that, won't you? And do ask him about these clove pinks." She pressed the paper packet into her mother-in-law's hand and ran for the house.

Hannah wanted to weep. She had hoped to waken in the girl a love for the land, had thought perhaps it was there just waiting to be stirred. If she could get Joan interested in Blackwater's rich alluvial soil, everything could be saved. Once she learned to revere and respect the black earth that fed and clothed them, Joan would share the commitment to the plantation that had motivated Michael and Hannah in the old days. Now, knowing that it was no use, Hannah had to face defeat.

She had always loved the little room in the tower. From its height one could look down the Ashley a good two miles, or over the plantation as far as the line of palmettos that marked the eastern border between Blackwater and Tuttle's Folly. Hannah took to spending more and more time there. She wouldn't admit to anyone that she was watching for a boat carrying Daniel home. Daniel was her last hope.

"What you stayin' up here for, Missy?" old Belle demanded. "You knows what dem young nigger gals is like if you don' keep an eye on 'em."

"I've been keeping an eye on them for twenty-four years, Belle. It's Lady Joan's responsibility now."

"Hmph!" Belle had served Hannah since the first days. She

wasn't afraid to be familiar. "That lady don' know nothin' bout this here plantation. She don' care nothin' neither."

"You mustn't say that; she's the master's wife." But there was little conviction in the reproach.

"All I know is if'n you don' come downstairs and do like you allus has, we's gonna be in a terrible mess."

Hannah refused to heed the advice. Increasingly it seemed to her that keeping watch on the Ashley was the most necessary thing in life. She never said what she was looking for, but Belle and the others knew.

"She done pinin' out her poor heart for Daniel," the old slave said to anyone who would listen. "Losin' the three bes' men on this here plantation like she did, all in one week, it jus' broke Missy's spirit."

A week later Belle went to the cook house in a rage and said, "You know what she tellin' me now? Gonna sleep up there too. Right there in that itty-bitty room what's not big enough for a baby. Made me bring up a li'l ole bed and won't come downstairs for nothin'. Not to eat and not to sleep. An' that Allyn Gregory an' his Lady whats-her-name, they don' care neither."

She was right; they didn't. After a few desultory attempts to draw Hannah from her aerie they gave up the effort and went about their own affairs. On Blackwater and on the other plantations the word spread: "Hannah Ludlow's become a hermit . . . won't see or speak to anyone but old Belle." The news wafted down the Ashley, and by the time it reached Charleston they were saying that poor Hannah Ludlow had lost her mind.

7

"Tell me again what year Great Aunt Sophie died. I forget."

Lizzie cut another spray of yarrow and sat back on her heels. "That's the second family question you've asked me this week. Why the sudden interest? Besides, she was your great, great aunt, your great grandfather's sister."

Sophia Amory sighed with resignation. "I'll never get it all straight. There's so many of them."

"Griffins are notably prolific." Lizzie smiled at her granddaughter. "Like the crowd at the Ark."

"Not always like them I hope!" the girl said with horror. "It's such confusion over there."

"That it is. You didn't answer my first question. Why are you so interested?"

"Here," said Sophia, withdrawing a carefully folded square of linen from her apron pocket. "I'll show you. I'm embroidering a family tree. To give my children someday."

Lizzie examined the half-finished work. "The stitching is quite good, Sophia. I think your crosshatching particularly fine."

She noted the missing date. "Sophia Griffin died in 1688. I think you look like her. She had one blue and one brown eye too."

"Mmm. Mama says that's why she named me Sophia. But Mama can't ever have met her if she died in 1688. Neither could you. Is it true she was a nun?"

"Yes, it's true. And I saw her portrait when I was in England. Hard to believe that was so long ago. This is 1741. . . . that makes it thirty-nine years since we were there." Lizzie paused for a moment, remembering. So much had happened. Why, if they hadn't gone to England, Rachel would never have been born and she wouldn't be standing here with Rachel's daughter.

"What are you thinking about, Grandma?" the girl asked, both interest and affection warming her voice.

"Nothing important," Lizzie answered quickly. "Anyway, as I was saying, I once saw Sophia Griffin's portrait. And so did your mother. That time she visited Harwood Hall in Yorkshire, before she and your papa were married. That's how she knew about the eyes."

Momentarily satisfied, the girl returned the family tree to her pocket and picked up a trowel. Watching her, Lizzie was tempted to relate more of the story. Sophia was such a mature and perceptive child. At fifteen she almost seemed a grown woman. How would she react to the tale of her namesake's visions, the conversion to the Catholic faith of half the family, the martyrdom at Tyburn? No, she daren't. Because to tell her granddaughter all that, she must tell of the Kirkslee nun; and if Rachel found out she'd be furious. She'd call it filling the girl's head with romantic rubbish.

The thought of her daughter sobered Lizzie and she returned to gathering yarrow. Sophia worked on with deft, quick movements. A natural gardener, like her father—and in this, as in much else, unlike her mother. Maybe that's why Lizzie got on better with Rachel's daughter than she ever had with Rachel. Sophia had her father's tawny brown hair but she also had Rachel's stubborn will, Rachel's single-minded way of pursuing what she wanted. Lizzie was sure of that. Only Sophia wanted different things; that's why Lizzie understood her better than Rachel did.

"Which garden do you like best?" she asked the girl suddenly. "Mine or the one at The Roses?"

Sophia paused and considered the question. "Well, Papa's garden is more beautiful to see all at once," she said thoughtfully. "It sort of takes your breath away as soon as you step through the gate. But yours is more, well, more productive, more practical."

"You're forgetting the apples and pears and all the other

fruit your father grows. Isn't that productive?"

"Yes, the orchard is very nice and the fruit's delicious." Sophia's tone implied reservations. "But your garden . . . well, I guess I like it because it's a mystery."

Lizzie didn't understand. "How do you mean a mystery? Most of the things here—not all, mind, but most—are very common."

"Not the things you make from them, though," the girl said. "All your simples and potions and physics—they aren't common. That's the mystery. How you grow these ordinary herbs and make such extraordinary things from them. That's what I like. When I'm married," said Sophia, digging in her trowel with energetic firmness, "I shall have all three. The flowers, the fruit, and the herbs."

"That will take a very big garden," her grandmother said, laughing.

"Then that's what I shall have. A very big garden."

The idea of educating the children at home with a private tutor had originally been Rachel's. If she'd been a different sort of mother Paul might have felt an obligation to at least try and resist, insist that the boys go off to Boston Latin School or Mr. Brownell's. But as it was, he knew that his wife's purpose was not to keep her offspring at home so they could be mollycoddled. Rachel had never coddled anyone in her life. No, she had conceived the plan so that her daughter could have the same education the boys received. Paul saw no harm in agreeing to that.

All her life Rachel had been bitter about not learning Greek and Latin and declamation like boys did. Just being able to read and write struck her as grossly unfair, and when she bore a girlchild she resolved to see that imbalance redressed. Sophia had always had the same lessons the tutors gave to Jacob and Val. Not that she appreciated the fact. Sophia dawdled through her instructions with a bit of embroidery or mending on her lap. The tutors took a dim view of teaching a girl such rarefied topics in any case, so they let her be; but Rachel was first perplexed and then angry. Why could Sophia not recognize her opportunities and take advantage of them?

Paul thought Rachel was going to complain about that when

she broached the subject of education. She was always chivying him to insist the tutors demand better performance from the girl. "Maybe Sophia will like French better than Greek or Latin," he said, hoping to forestall a long argument. "I've been thinking of engaging a French tutor for the children."

"Sophia's too stubborn to give me the satisfaction of doing well," Rachel said frankly. "She has made up her mind not to learn any more, and she won't. It's Jacob and Valiant that concern me."

He looked up from his book in surprise. "Aren't they doing well? No one has said anything different to me."

"As far as I know, they're doing as well as they always have. But Paul, isn't it time we introduced a few practical lessons for the boys? Jacob particularly."

"Practical, Rachel?" He sounded genuinely puzzled. "I'm not sure I know what you mean."

"For heaven's sake! Jacob will be seventeen in a few weeks. It's time he started learning about the business he's to take over."

"But he's meant to go to Harvard next term. You know that."

"I know that our son has a head full of radical ideas and little else." She was across the room and kneeling by his chair in one quick movement. "Please, Paul, don't fight me on this. Not this time. I'm right about Jacob and about Val too. They must be shaped to the real world, the world they live in. Not some fantasy Utopia of your imagining."

He lay one big hand on her black hair. So soft, Rachel's hair. So beautiful. "I want only the best for our boys, you can't doubt that."

"I don't. I merely question your interpretation of what that is. They are Boston lads, Paul. They shall be Boston men. And the lifeblood of this city is commerce. That's what being a colonial is all about. Whether you like it or not, it's true."

"Do we have to talk about it now?" he asked softly. His wife's nearness still had the power to excite him. He could smell the scent of her, the natural, exquisitely familiar perfume of her skin.

Rachel read the message in his eyes and retreated back to her chair. "Yes, now," she insisted. "I've been telling you for years that Jacob was headed for trouble. Today he told me that he wants to visit Philadelphia. Talk to some men there whose writings have intrigued him. Philadelphia, Paul! Can you imagine anything more absurd."

He dropped his eyes. He himself had given the boy the journal published by a group of Pennsylvanians calling themselves the Heralds. The notion of a trip to Philadelphia wasn't a complete surprise to Paul. "It is the nature of men to be concerned with ideas, my dear. You're a woman, so I don't expect you to understand—"

"How dare you!" she cried. Her face went white with rage and she almost spat the words. "How dare you make such a remark to me. Where would you be, Paul Amory, if I were not concerned with the only ideas that matter, surviving and winning!"

"I didn't mean that, Rachel." He was pleading now, just as he always did when the specter of her temper and rejection threatened. "I know that Amory's markets owe all their success to you. I've never denied it. It's just that—"

"Just nothing." She stood up, and tiny as she was she seemed to tower over him. "I don't want to hear any more of it, Paul. Not of Philadelphia or of Harvard. Jacob must begin an apprenticeship in the business. If you don't arrange it, I will."

2

THE LEGACY

"The fathers have eaten sour grapes, and the children's teeth are set on edge . . ."

—Ezekiel 18:2

1

Sophia Amory's birthday came in that most cold and bleak of months, February. In 1743, on the day she turned seventeen, there was at least sunshine. Outside Sophia's bedroom window the frozen garden appeared a crystal wonderland. The branches of the fruit trees shimmered in their coating of ice, and the bright red of the few rose hips that had not become food for the birds, or jars of jelly, was intensified by a robe of frost. Even the snow-covered paths glowed with reflected sun. It was ample compensation for the lack of flowers. When Sophia went down to breakfast she was bubbling with high spirits and a sense of excitement.

"Good morning, Sophia. Happy birthday."

The girl acknowledged her mother's greeting with an uncustomary kiss. Rachel looked up from the letter she was writing and smiled. "Where are Papa and the boys?" Sophia asked while she helped herself to porridge and a liberal amount of cream.

"Gone to the Plymouth warehouse. Papa had to collect some papers and he took Jacob and Val with him."

Rachel had prevailed. Jacob was learning the business rather than wasting his time at Harvard. Val was headed in the same direction. The thought gave her a sense of real satisfaction, and she almost missed the slightly crestfallen look on her daughter's face. "They'll be back in time for your birthday dinner," she added. Then, having dismissed the matter of the day's celebration, she turned to the subject most on her mind. "I find I need some records from Lyn Street. You'll have to go and get them this morning. There's no one else."

"Very well." Sophia didn't trouble to ask what they were or why they must be fetched today. Of late her mother was involved in some engrossing scheme that required the assembly of data from all the Amory markets. So far as Sophia knew, no one else was privy to the plan and she for one didn't care. Never had she shared her mother's concern with trade. "May I stop at Beacon Street on the way home?"

"No. I want the information right away." Rachel's eyes gleamed. Whatever her intentions, she certainly found them exciting. "Anyway, Grandma and Grandpa will be at dinner this evening. You can wait till then to see them."

Sophia nodded her assent. She never opposed her mother in small things. She merely did as she wished on large issues and complied on minor ones. It kept the peace, a commodity Sophia had come to value.

The walk to Lyn Street was invigorating. The cold air put color in her cheeks and a bounce in her step. Sophia knew she was pretty despite her odd two-color eyes. She was small like her mother and grandmother, with the same full breasts and curved hips. Her hair was lighter than theirs, though. A bright chestnut brown with golden highlights. Sophia was proud of her hair. When she let it down it almost reached her waist.

Being pretty was nicer, she had decided some years past, than being ugly, but it wasn't the most important thing in life. It was how you used your assets that mattered. Sophia knew exactly what she wanted to attain with hers, but as yet she had not determined how best to go about it. This morning the question was not uppermost in her mind. She was too full of the simple joy of being young and alive to worry about anything. "Good morning, Jack." She greeted the Lyn Street manager with easy familiarity and handed him the list her mother had prepared. "Mama needs these records right away. I'm to wait for them."

The man examined the request. "Quite a bit here, Miss Sophia. It'll take a while to get it together. Do you want to come into the office and sit down?"

"No, that's all right. I'll just wander around until you're ready."

Lyn Street was the heart of the Amory operation. Here the vast assortment of manufactured goods that arrived on the docks a few steps away were sorted and stored. From Lyn Street those items destined for sale in Boston were hauled to their appointed places and those apportioned to the outlying markets and warehouses were assembled and made into consignments for transport by road or water.

Sophia gravitated to the section housing bolts of cloth. It was while she was examining a bit of blue chintz with an eye toward making new curtains for her bedroom that she saw him. He was of medium height, but beneath his heavy rough jacket he seemed to have remarkably broad shoulders. It was not his frame that attracted her, however; it was his hair. She'd never before seen a man with bright red hair. Nor heard a voice quite so softly appealing.

"Will thee not take these in payment for the seed?" He was holding out a package of something Sophia couldn't identify. She moved closer.

The clerk shook his head in answer to the young man's question. "Got all the hinges we need at the moment. You'll have to do better."

"But I've nothing else with me."

"Let me see those, please." Sophia interjected herself into the conversation without asking anyone's permission. The boy looked at her with some surprise, then showed her the four iron hinges he had offered the clerk.

"Yes," the girl said firmly. "These are exactly what I've been looking for. We'll take them."

"But Miss Sophia," the workman protested. "We've a dozen sets just like those in the back. Your mother would—"

"Not like these, Seth," Sophia corrected. "This is particularly fine workmanship. You can see that."

"Aye. He's a good smith. I ain't denyin' that, but . . ." He shook his head and continued to ignore the boy. "What do you want with hinges anyway?"

Sophia drew herself up to her full five feet of height. "That's my affair. Now, are you going to give this gentleman the seed he wants or am I going to have to speak to my father?"

The clerk muttered his disapproval of young ladies who interfered in business as he filled a burlap sack with the stranger's choice of corn.

Sophia was suddenly embarrassed at her presumption. When she saw Jack approach with the ledgers her mother had requested, she took them quickly and fled into the street.

"Hey! Will thee not wait a minute . . . ?" The redhead overtook her before she had gone ten feet up Lyn Street. "Thee forgot the hinges." Then seeing how burdened she already was, he shook his head. "Has thee a carriage waiting?"

"No, I walked. I don't live very far."

"Thee doesn't need these at all," he said with a hint of accusation.

"They are very well made."

"Aye. But thee doesn't need them."

"Oh bother! They have tons more seed than they'll ever sell in there. Why shouldn't you have some?"

"Thee doesn't understand—"

"Why do you do that? Say 'thee' instead of 'you' all the time?"

"It's the speech of Friends," he explained stiffly.

"You're a Quaker then? How interesting. I've never met any before. Not to speak to. Do you live in Boston?"

He made a face that indicated his distaste for the mere idea. "I live in Rowley. Tis a fair place and not so crowded as this."

"What's your name?"

"Jonathan Crandall. Is thee one of the Amorys?"

"I am. Sophia Amory."

"I thank thee for thy kindness, Miss Amory. When next I come to town I shall bring thee something of more use to thee than hinges."

He was gone before she could say anything more.

It was many weeks before she saw Jonathan Crandall again but Sophia didn't forget him. She made inquiries of her grandfather about the nature of Quaker beliefs and the condition of the village of Rowley. Tonyjay didn't ask why she wanted to know. He instructed her as best he could and kept his own counsel.

At the beginning of April, on a day when spring seemed at least a possibility, Sophia was working in the garden among the tender shoots of the newly emerged daffodils. Behind her a voice said, "Thy maid told me I could find thee here. I've come to pay my debt."

"Good afternoon, Jonathan Crandall." She finished the bit of weeding she was working on before turning around to face him. "You owe me nothing, but I'm happy to see you again."

"I am in thy debt for five pounds of seed corn," he insisted. "I hope thee finds this adequate payment." He held out a small wooden stool. It was round with three tapered legs and a low back that would just fit the curve of her spine.

"It's very beautiful," Sophia said gravely. "It's made of apple wood, isn't it? That's a hard wood to carve."

Crandall shrugged. "It's strong. The chair will last."

"Yes, I expect it will. So you have talents besides those of smith and farmer." She smiled as if that fact pleased her enormously. "Come into the house, Jonathan. We will have tea and you can tell me of Rowley."

Later Rachel questioned her about the strange young man. Sophia said very little beyond the fact that she had met him at the market and he had come to bring her a present. Rachel examined the small stool silently and with no pleasure.

The mysterious project on which Rachel was working so diligently involved extensive letter writing and waiting for replies. It occupied her to the point where she took little notice of Sophia's activities. When Rachel wasn't at her desk reading or writing letters she was at Marlborough Street having lengthy private discussions with her brother Benjamin. Not even Paul knew what was afoot, and he, like the rest of the family, dared not ask. Rachel would reveal all in her own good time.

The situation suited Sophia. It left her free to arrange "accidental" meetings with Jonathan Crandall. She managed two of them in April and one in May. It wasn't difficult since the clerks at the market could tell her of the young man's routine and how often he came to Boston to trade his ironwork for farm needs.

In June, however, on a day he was expected, he did not arrive at Lyn Street. And on the two successive days he was likewise absent. Sophia concealed her disappointment and waited. By the end of the month Crandall still had not come to Boston. The girl resolved to take matters into her own hands.

No one was awake in the very early morning when she readied a small trap, hitched up two horses, and set out on the Post Road.

At Beverly she asked directions and was told to continue on toward Ipswich and ask again. When lunchtime came, she pulled off by a stream and ate the bread and cheese she had brought with her while the horses drank and nibbled on the fresh summer grass. Then, refreshed and as determined as ever, Sophia continued on her way.

In half an hour she came to a sign directing her to turn right if she wished to go to Ipswich. There was no mention of Rowley. Sophia tried to remember the map her grandfather had shown her months before. Should she take the detour into Ipswich or go straight ahead? Fortunately, a farmer driving a hay wagon came into view just then. "Rowley's three miles farther on," he told her. "You'll come to a small track by a red barn. Tis just a short piece up this road. Turn there and you'll find Rowley after a bit. Who are ye seeking?"

"The smith, Jonathan Crandall."

"Ah, the Quaker lad. His place is half a mile beyond the Rowley church. You can't miss it."

It was close to three when she arrived, and the sound of an anvil led her to where Jonathan was working. He was naked to the waist and his body gleamed with sweat. His shoulders were even broader than she had realized and the sinews of his arms stood out as he swung the heavy hammer of his trade.

"Good afternoon, Jonathan," she called out, but he didn't hear her over the noise of his work. Sophia climbed down from the trap and waited for him to notice her presence. In the meantime, she studied the flat marshy landscape and the neat house and barn that were attached to the forge. The fields surrounding the establishment were green with crops and there were two cows and a horse in a nearby pasture. In the back of the barn a few ducks and some geese roamed a small enclosure, pecking at the earth and squabbling with each other.

Suddenly the air grew still. All at once Sophia could hear the drone of bees busy in the honeysuckle that climbed up the side of the forge. She turned around to find Crandall staring at her in astonishment. "What is thee doing here?" he demanded.

"You didn't come to Boston all this month. I came to see if you were all right."

"Of course I'm all right. There's been a lot of work." He shrugged to indicate the forge and the fields. "I've gone to thy father's market in Salem for what I needed."

"You could have done that before," she said.

"Aye." He stared at the ground and was silent.

"You came to Lyn Street in hopes of seeing me. After that first time, I mean." Crandall continued to stare at the ground but he didn't deny her claim. "Well, now that I'm here, will you not invite me inside for a bit of refreshment? I've been traveling since early morning."

"I live alone here. It isn't fitting," he said.

"I know you live alone, Jonathan. I found that out long ago or I wouldn't have come. As to its being fitting . . . it doesn't matter, seeing that we're going to be married."

He drove her home. He wouldn't hear of her making the journey alone, and he made better time than she had since he knew the route. He had also exchanged her horses for two fresh ones of his own. When they arrived at The Roses it was nine in the evening and even the lengthy June day had given way to dark. The house was ablaze with candles and Sophia guessed that her parents would be waiting for her in the front hall.

"You need not come in and speak with my father tonight," she told Jonathan. "It's late and you're tired and they'll be upset because they didn't know where I was. Come tomorrow or the next day." She wanted to prepare them for the event. Sophia knew that Jonathan would get on all right with her father, but she doubted he could stand up to her mother.

"I'll not start our life together with an act of cowardice," he said as he helped her down from the trap. She couldn't prevent him from walking with her to the front door.

2

There was none of the fiery rhetoric that Sophia had predicted. "They won't give in easily," she had told Jonathan on the long journey back to Boston. "You're not their choice of husband—you're mine. If you want me you'll have to fight for me."

"I want thee," he had answered softly, his brown eyes speaking love more eloquently than words. "All these years since my parents died . . . alone in that silent house . . . I've dreamed of the sort of wife I wanted but didn't believe I could find. Thee is that woman, Sophia Amory. I knew it the first time I saw thee there in the market. But I dared not hope thee would feel the same."

"I want thee, Jonathan." She emphasized the pronoun, as if in adopting his speech she was joining herself to him. "But I repeat, it won't be easy."

He said no more. In the little trap his silence had seemed a promise; the silence he maintained in the Amory drawing room was a bitter disappointment.

Paul listened to Crandall's straightforward request for Sophia's hand and then looked at his wife. Rachel shook her head slightly. Paul waited a moment more as Rachel's eyes held his. Finally he cleared his throat and spoke the words his wife expected. "I'm sorry, it's out of the question. We do not know you or your family. Sophia has been raised to expect a certain standard of living. I do not mean to be rude, but you cannot provide that standard. Besides, she's much too young to marry."

Sophia drew in her breath and waited to hear Jonathan's reply. He said, "I love thy daughter and she loves me. It is right that we should wed."

"No!" Rachel's voice was firm and without any of Paul's apologetic gentleness. "It is not right. Please go."

And Jonathan Crandall, after one long, suffering look at Sophia, had turned on his heel and left.

"How dare you," Sophia spat out when he was gone. "How dare you interfere thus in my life!"

"Sophia, you're too young. We're only doing what we know is best for you. The boy's a Quaker and no part of your world." Paul pleaded with his daughter, stretching out his hand in a gesture of conciliation.

"My world! What do you know of—"

"Enough!" Rachel placed herself between the man and the girl. "Stop arguing with her as if she was an adult and an equal, Paul. She's a stubborn, willful child with no thought in her head but how to wound me. Go to your room, Sophia."

The next morning, when Sophia didn't appear at the breakfast table, Rachel came into her bedroom without knocking and stood beside the chair on which Sophia sat staring out the window.

"Let us understand each other here and now," she told her daughter, speaking in stiff, formal sentences that lent weight to her words.

"When the time comes for you to marry, you must be old enough to appreciate what we have built for you—what I have created for you in the Amory markets. I do not say that you shall have no choice in the matter. I would not wish an unhappy marriage for you. But you will choose a man who can contribute to the business we have built, who can add to your legacy, not milk it dry. When that day arrives you will thank me for not allowing you to throw away your birthright."

Sophia knew it was useless to argue. She wanted to say that neither she nor Jonathan desired anything from the Amorys except permission to live their own lives, but she knew her mother too well to believe that she could prevail in a head-on confrontation. Besides, Sophia was still disillusioned by Jonathan's behavior. He had given in so easily. After everything she had said, when it came to the test he'd turned tail and run like a scared rabbit. She could not understand how she could have so misjudged the man.

But later, despite Jonathan's failure, she looked for a time when she could speak to her father alone. Two days after the abortive engagement she found Paul working by himself in the orchard. He was thinning the tiny fruitlets on the apple trees, and she worked beside him for some minutes before either of them spoke.

"Silly trees," Paul said at last. "Imagine their setting all this fruit when they couldn't possibly ripen it. Wouldn't you think nature would know better?"

"Perhaps nature has a different aim than you do," Sophia answered. "You want big juicy apples to eat, she only wants to produce seed and thus more apple trees."

Amory smiled. "A wise observation for one so young. And a true one. Do I detect a moral in your story, Sophia?"

She dropped the pretense of allegory. "Why, Papa? Why will you not stand up to her?"

"Stand up to your mother, I expect you mean. But really I disapprove of the match as much as she does. You are too young to wed, my dear. And the boy is not of your class."

"I know you better than that, Papa." Her voice was calm and reasonable. "Even if you believed those things, you would still discuss the matter. If it was up to you, you'd give Jonathan a chance to prove himself. It's only because she wants to sell me to the highest bidder like some piece of merchandise that you oppose the match."

"I won't have that, Sophia," he said quietly. "You can't insult your mother if this conversation is to continue. She wants the best for you and your brothers. If you don't realize that, you're a fool."

"The 'best' according to her own interpretation," Sophia retorted. "Mama must have the final word in everything. I understand that. What I don't understand is why you give in to her all the time." Then, seeing that he would not answer her, she dropped the apples she'd thinned in a heap on the grass and walked away.

News of Sophia's escapade and the trouble it caused spread throughout the family. With the Griffins it was always impossible to keep anything secret from the censorious Benjamin or the chattering crowd at the Ark. "Went all the way to Rowley she did, and brought home a strange farmboy. Said she was going to marry him. Can you imagine what Rachel's reaction must have been!"

At Beacon Street they did not say those things with pleasure or amusement. Her grandparents grieved for Sophia and for their own children. Tonyjay remembered the questions with which the girl had plied him some months back and he knew Sophia had not acted on sudden impulse when she went to Rowley. Lizzie, who had been looking more and more tired of late, showed her worry in the lines of her face and the way her hands trembled as she moved about the house.

Tonyjay became increasingly concerned for his wife as the days passed. "You do too much, my dear. Won't you let me hire someone to help you in the garden?" He had made the suggestion before and always she had refused. This time she nodded her agreement, and that frightened him.

"Yes," Lizzie said. "Get someone to do a bit of the weeding and trim the paths. That will give me more time to—"

"To what?"

"Nothing. It's just something I want to finish while I have the time."

"You have all the time in the world," he said hastily. "We've earned our retirement. You can do as you please."

She smiled because that was not what she had meant and he knew it, but she only said, "Will you talk to Rachel about Sophia?"

He shook his head. "It's years since I've had any influence over Rachel. Besides, in this instance she's probably right. Sophia is still very young. I doubt I could do anything. But Antony—"

"Yes," Lizzie said. "I think you could exert some influence there, and it is right that you should."

He had the opportunity later that same day. Charles came to him with some question about old bills of lading from transactions that had taken place years before when Tonyjay still ran the company.

"I'm trying to have all the old records in readable order, Papa. It may be useful someday." Charles was looking ahead, already convinced that Griffin's Importations had a permanent place in the business world of the future, that the history of the firm would be of interest to coming generations.

Tonyjay observed his son. Though he wasn't yet thirty-eight, Charles had run to fat and a bit of a paunch. And like his brothers he was a true Boston man. Comfortable, secure, convinced that trade was all-important. Tonyjay answered Charles' question and wondered if this was the right time to speak of other things. The younger man gave him the perfect opening.

"I suppose you've heard about our naughty Sophia," Charles said, chuckling. "Imagine the cheek of the child. I'd like to have seen Rachel's face when that farmer lad walked in the door—"

"If I were you, Charles," his father said sternly, "I'd leave those at The Roses to settle their affairs and put my own house in order."

"I don't know what you mean, Papa." Charles was puzzled and a little hurt by Tonyjay's tone. "None of my children are old enough to marry."

"I'm not speaking of marriage," Tonyjay said. "I'm speaking of young people in general. Their hopes and desires and the things their parents want of them. Do you remember that day your mother and I returned from Carolina and you and John were waiting for us with the news that you wanted to marry the White twins?"

"Of course I remember. But what's that to do with—"

"It has to do with realizing that children grow up. That they have their own notions of how to live."

"But I told you, none of mine have even whispered the word *marry*." Charles was becoming yet more astonished at this outburst.

The elder Griffin sighed. "Sometimes I can't believe how dense you can be, Charles. I'm not talking of marriage, damn it! I'm talking of your son Antony and his future."

"Ah, Antony . . . I see." The younger man put his hand over his eyes as if the thought were painful. "You mean this madness about going to sea, right?"

"Right. And it's not madness, Charles. It's an honorable profession. Do you imagine that every Griffin ever born has sat behind a desk? Or that every one must do so?"

"Of course not, but—"

"But nothing. Antony thinks he wants to be a ship's captain. You think you want him in the business. Very well, send him out. Let him ship on one of our vessels with some captain you trust and get a taste of the life. If nothing else, it will serve him well in Griffin's."

"But he's still at Harvard. I've told him that when his education is complete, if he yet insists on this plan, he can try it."

"He's eighteen, Charles. Have you no memory of how long three or four years looks to an eighteen-year-old? And do you imagine he will do well at Harvard when his heart is miles away?"

Charles shook his head. "I just can't see . . ." Then, noting his father's face, he stopped speaking. After some moments he said, "I'll think about it, Papa. I know how close you are to the boy. How much you have his best interest at heart. I'll think about it."

Later Lizzie asked him, "Were we so foolish in our day? So insistent that the children do things our way?"

He chuckled softly. "I prefer to think not, but I warrant they would have a different story."

No one was more disturbed by events at The Roses than Paul Amory. Sophia's accusations in the orchard pained him more than she could possibly realize. Not because he imagined that his children did not know how often he gave in to his wife, but because he knew that in a way she could not dream of, he was using his daughter.

Had she announced her wishes at any other moment, he might have tried a little harder to overcome Rachel's resistance to the match. As it was, he could not do so because he needed to save his strength, his ammunition as it were. Paul had plans for Jacob—plans that Rachel would find far more objectionable than Sophia's proposed marriage. He needed to bide his time and keep the peace so he'd be able to win that battle when it came. It wasn't fair to Sophia, and he felt guilty about that, but the stakes were too high to do anything else.

Then, before he was ready to tell Rachel his intentions, she announced hers with a hoot of triumph and a kind of excitement he'd not seen her display in years.

"It's come," she cried out when a bulky parcel was delivered to the door by a drayman from the wharf. "And here's the letter and all the necessary papers!"

"What's come?" Paul came into the front hall and stared at the wooden crate and the sheaf of documents his wife was waving. "What is all this?"

"This"—Rachel pointed to the crate as if it contained the Rosetta Stone or at least the crown jewels—"is the new Pennsylvania Stove. I've been corresponding with Ben Franklin for months. At last he's given Amory's exclusive distribution rights in Massachusetts Bay."

3

The friendship between Benjamin Franklin and Benjamin Griffin dated back some twenty-five years. They had gone to Mr. Brownell's school together and despite the fact that the Griffins were much the social betters of the son of a candlemaker, the two Benjamins had become close friends.

In 1723, when Franklin had difficulties with his brother James and needed to leave Boston in haste and secrecy, the Griffins had provided him transport to New York on one of their ships. Through all the intervening years the contact had been maintained, mostly through letters in which Benjamin Griffin argued with Benjamin Franklin about the future of the American colonies. "We must strengthen our ties to the mother country, preserve our heritage," Griffin said over and over.

"Britain must loosen the bonds," Franklin replied each time. "We must grow together, partners and equals—not willful parent and stubborn child."

Despite this difference of outlook the affection between them survived as such early born affection sometimes does. They had shared the experience of youth and the memory remained fresh.

So when Rachel had approached her brother with the stove scheme, he was willing to listen. "Have you seen this?" she asked, pushing a copy of *Poor Richard's Almanack* across his desk and pointing to an advertisement for the new stove.

> TO BE SOLD at the Post-Office Philadelphia, The New Improved Fire-Places; Where any Person may see some of them that are now in Use, and have the nature and advantages of them explained.

Her brother smiled. "Trust Franklin, he's always inventing things and finding a way to make them profitable."

"This could be profitable for us too, Ben. For Amory's, I mean."

He looked mildly interested. "Oh, how's that?"

"These fire-places of his, they're stoves really, and they're truly remarkable." She shoved a pamphlet across the desk. "Here's the full explanation printed by Franklin and his friend Grace." She didn't wait for him to read it but continued enthusiastically. "The important thing is that they use a quarter of the fuel to produce three times as much heat. With the way wood prices are going, Ben . . . Once these things are seen, every family in America is going to want one!"

Ben pursed his lips and nodded. "You're probably right. What do you plan to do about it?"

"Secure the exclusive distribution rights in this colony for Amory's markets."

Ben Griffin wasn't known for wit or levity, but he said, "Only this colony, Rachel? Only Massachusetts Bay?"

"For the present," she shot back, ignoring any hint of mockery. "Will you help me with Franklin? There's no profit in it for Griffin's just yet, but—"

"Of course I'll help you," her brother said quickly. He was

a trifle wounded that she imagined he would put business over family loyalty. "If someone's going to earn a bit from this invention it might as well be you and Paul."

Together they had begun the secret campaign of convincing the inventor of the stove that Amory's would serve him best in Boston and the surrounding towns. Rachel compiled endless figures to prove the efficiency and strength of their network of markets. Her brother wrote to Franklin, subtly reminding him of old loyalties and confirming the capabilities of Amory's. The fruit of all that careful planning sat in the hall of The Roses on this morning in late July.

"I see," Paul said as Rachel explained the terms of the arrangement and extolled the new stove's virtues. "Residents of our area will be informed that they need not order their stoves from Philadelphia but can purchase them from Amory's. Why should they do that?"

"Because the cost to them will be the same as ordering direct and they will get faster delivery. We're going to stock the stoves, Paul. This is only a sample. I've ordered a dozen to be made for every warehouse."

"Won't that involve a lot of money? Money we must invest before the stoves are sold?"

"Franklin has agreed to take half now and the rest after the sale. And he will accept a slightly lowered return on each stove. That gives us our profit while the customer still pays the advertised price."

"I see. But why . . . ?" He looked puzzled, and he obviously didn't see at all.

"Volume, Paul." Rachel's voice had grown shrill with excitement. "Volume! People will buy more of these when they can actually see them, not just read about them. Now, you must leave on a tour of the markets no later than tomorrow."

"A tour? But why?"

"Please stop saying that. No matter what I say you answer 'But why?' This is a great opportunity," she said, lowering her voice and struggling to be patient. "And my brother has used his friendship with Franklin just to help us. You must visit each of the warehouses. Demonstrate the stove, convince our people that it's a remarkable value for their customers. We are going to make a fortune from this little beauty, Paul." She patted the crate with affection.

"Very well," Paul sighed. "But I can't go until next week or the week after. There's some correspondence I'm waiting for. It's important."

"No." She shook her head, expecting to put an end to the discussion. "Whatever it is will have to wait. You must leave on the tour tomorrow."

"I can't, Rachel," he said with unusual stubbornness. "It's out of the question. This damned thing's waited all these months. It can wait a couple of weeks more."

His wife looked at him in amazement. "I don't think you understand one word I've said." Then, convinced that the economic aspects of the issue were lost on him, she changed her tack. "Paul, I really want you to do it." Her voice grew gentle. "I . . . I think many of the employees don't understand that you are the power behind Amory's. They think it's me because I make the most noise. I want them to respect you more, to understand. And the children too; you can take Jacob with you."

"I cannot go before my letter comes," he repeated as if he'd not heard a word.

Rachel looked at him in silence. Paul stared at the floor. After some moments her face hardened into a mask of fury and she went upstairs and began selecting the clothes she would take for her tour of the markets. When that was done she sent for Jacob and told him he would leave with her the next day to introduce the Pennsylvania Stove to all the Amory warehouses.

Sophia watched them leave from the window of the drawing room. Uncle Benjamin had lent his splendid coach for the journey. It was a comfortable vehicle and had the Griffin coat of arms emblazoned on the doors. "Azure a bend or. With two griffins rampant." She had learned the formula from her grandfather years before. And the meaning of the Latin motto written beneath the blue shield, "*Regum in via recta dirige*" (Guide straight the king), it referred to the fact that supposedly the first Griffin to arrive in England had been the navigator of the ship carrying William the Conqueror at the time of the Norman conquest.

Sophia dropped the curtain with a sigh of disgust. She didn't care a bit about her illustrious ancestry or her mother's quest for profit. And none of them even tried to understand the things she did care about. That's why she was so miserable now.

She spotted him then. There was a flash of red behind a tree in the overgrown meadow across the road, and she knew the color came from the hair of Jonathan Crandall. He was over there watching the house—too frightened to come up to the front door and carry her off, as he would have done were he the man she believed him to be. Sophia ran to the kitchen and let herself quietly out the back of the house.

She knew the field well, having played in it through all her growing-up years. It was easy for her to come up behind Jonathan before he knew she was there. "Why are you standing over here mooning like a sick calf?" she demanded without preamble.

He looked at her with love and pain and enormous regret. "I know thee thinks I failed thee. I wanted to try and make thee understand."

"Understand what?" Her voice was still harsh. "That you lied when you said you loved me. That you've not the courage of a puppy dog. I told you what she would be like. What she would say. And you let her get away with it."

"Don't, Sophia. It is not right that thee speaks of thy mother thus. She bore thee, she deserves thy respect and affection."

"My mother is a bitch out of hell."

That's when he slapped her—one swift, irretrievable gesture that left a red stain on her cheek and brought tears to Jonathan's eyes, not to hers. "Oh dear Lord . . . I beg thy forgiveness, Sophia. It is a terrible thing to strike another human being, a woman. Thee makes me forget all the teachings of my faith."

Sophia was trembling not with pain or shock but with exultation. She had not been wrong; she hadn't misjudged him. The blow had quickened all the love she felt for him. "If you are very angry," she said softly, "it's right to take action."

"No, not violent action. That is a sin against God and thyself."

He was shaking his head, but she stopped the motion by throwing her arms around his neck and kissing him full on the mouth. It was their first real kiss. They had behaved very properly when they were alone in the house in Rowley. For a brief second he was merely stunned. Then his youth and his passion for the girl gained the upper hand and Jonathan wrapped her in a tight embrace.

He could feel the softness of her breasts against his broad chest, her tiny waist like a delicate sculpture in his hands. When she drew back he looked at her as if he could not believe she was real. "Oh Sophia, I love thee so."

"And I love thee." She slipped into his speech again. "Why did thee not stand up to my parents, Jonathan? We must be married. It is ordained for us to be together."

"I thought that too. I still think it. But to aid thee in willful disobedience to the guardians under whom God has placed thee . . . I wanted to do it. Oh how I wanted to! But I could not. I still can't. It's a sin, Sophia, an offense against God."

Sophia thought for some seconds. She moved away from Jonathan's grip and sat in the shade of a big maple tree, then motioned him to sit beside her. A bright butterfly landed between them, fluttered its vibrant wings, and flew away. The drone of summer insects made a soft accompaniment to her words. "When I first met you," she began hesitantly, "I wanted to understand about your religion."

"Say 'thy,' Sophia," he said softly. "I like it when thee uses our speech."

"Very well, *thy* religion. My grandfather is a very wise and learned man. I hope someday you . . . thee . . . will meet him. He gave me books. I read a bit of the teachings of George Fox and William Penn and others."

"They were good men," Jonathan commented. "They perceived the truth and spoke it."

"And did they not risk much in speaking their truth?" she asked.

"Yes, very much. But it was right that they do as they did."

Sophia nodded. "Truth is worth fighting for, then?"

Jonathan shook his head stubbornly. "Thee will not trap me thus, Sophia. To fight with words and ideas, that is right. With violence and with sinful actions, that's something else."

"Listen to me." She turned and placed her hands on his shoulders so she could look directly into his eyes. "If my father can be made to see what we feel for each other, to give his consent to our marriage, will thee feel better about it? Easy in thy mind?"

"I would feel," he said simply, "such joy as I cannot put into words."

"Then come." She rose and took him by the hand. "We will go and speak with him now."

Sophia knew the advantage she gained by approaching Paul while Rachel was away. She knew too that Jonathan could not be expected to understand the unusual relationship between her mother and father. If they gained the permission of one parent, the father and head of the household, Jonathan would see their union as blessed by both parents. She would leave him in his ignorance and thus achieve happiness for them both.

They found Paul in his study surrounded by books and papers. He looked up, saw the pair, and said quietly, "Good afternoon, Mr. Crandall. I did not think to see you here again."

"I could not stay away, sir. I love thy daughter mightily, and she loves me. We wish to marry, and I will provide for Sophia with the last breath I draw. I've a forge and a good farm, sir. My parents were killed by Indians some years ago and it's—"

Paul held up his hand to stop the flow of words. Before he could say anything, Sophia asked, "Can we not go into the garden to talk, Papa? It's so warm in here."

They walked together into the orchard and shared the cool shade of the burgeoning trees. The fruit was bigger now than on that day when father and daughter had pruned in bitterness. The pears were as large as a man's fist, the apples the size of a woman's. Sophia knew that the orchard had a calming effect on her father. It brought out all his natural gentleness. She was not surprised to hear him say quietly, "I am not enamored of position or wealth, Crandall. It is my daughter's happiness that concerns me."

"Have I been happy these past weeks?" Sophia asked. "Without Jonathan?"

Paul shook his head. "At your age, weeks seem a long time. I'm thinking of years, of a lifetime."

"Sophia has seen my house and my fields and my forge, sir," Jonathan said. "She does not wish to marry me with any false ideas of what the future will hold." He didn't consider that mentioning the disastrous journey to Rowley might not be a wise thing.

But Paul chuckled at the memory. "Sophia is more like her mother than she cares to admit. She goes after what she wants."

"Papa . . ." Sophia stopped walking and placed herself before her father. His great bulk had never seemed so enormous to her as it did now. "Once a long time ago you told me how you came to America to marry Mama even after she had refused you."

"That's true."

"And how your own parents disowned you because they didn't approve of—what was your term?—'colonial adventures.'"

"That's true too." Watching the girl, Paul felt the conviction rise within him that her truth was stronger than his.

"I know you and Mama don't always agree," she said next. "Sometimes you argue and are unhappy. But Papa, tell me honestly, would you rather that you had listened to your family? Would it have been better if you had never come and married Mama? Never had the boys or me?"

"But I was twenty-five, Sophia. You're just seventeen . . ." Even as he spoke, he knew the argument was over. The decision had been made.

4

Sophia and Jonathan were wed three days later in King's Chapel, where Paul was a token member despite the lack of religious conviction he and most of his generation of Griffins shared. At first the rector balked when the hasty ceremony was proposed, but the promise of a generous emolument convinced him.

Only Lizzie, Tonyjay, and Paul himself were witnesses to the event. That saddened Paul, for he thought Sophia looked incredibly beautiful and that she deserved to begin her new life with a greater celebration than this. But she had wanted it thus, and looking at her serenely joyful face and that of Jonathan Crandall he was content with his decision. It would cause more trouble than Sophia could dream of, but Paul knew it was the right thing to do. The girl must not be sacrificed because of things between Rachel and himself.

Later, in Lizzie's garden where they shared a bottle of champagne and some little cakes before seeing the youngsters off to Rowley, his father-in-law confirmed Paul's judgment. "You've done the right thing," Tonyjay told him in a moment of privacy. "That young man will be a good husband for her."

Paul looked at Crandall and nodded. The lad made an incongruous picture in the bright garden. His somber Quaker garb looked out of place among the soft yellows and blues and grayed greens of the herbs. Only Jonathan's red hair belied the dour image, and the radiance of his smile when he looked at his bride. But more than the externals, it was an indefinable something else that reassured Amory. Crandall exuded a strength of purpose, a kind of moral armor that sprang from deep within him.

"They will be good together," Paul said to his father-in-law.

"Yes, I think so."

They neared Rowley with the encroaching dusk, riding in Jonathan's rough but sturdy cart. The seat across the front was hard but big enough for the two of them. The capacious rear had been scrubbed of all traces of the muck and hay and corn that were its customary cargo. Jonathan had spent all of one day preparing the wagon for this journey. He'd even given it a coat of fresh red paint, then worried all night that it wouldn't dry in time for the trip to Boston. But it had. And the refurbished vehicle made his announcement for him.

One of the villagers had come to leave some pots for mending at the forge and he asked the smith why he was working so hard on his old cart. "I'm going to Boston to be wed," Jonathan said. "I wish to bring my bride home in cleanliness." The villager nodded and left to spread the word.

Now the wagon looked bright and happy as it toiled over the narrow road through the quaking grass. The heat of August brought a sheen to the flanks of the chestnut gelding that did the pulling, and shimmered in a haze over the yellow-brown salt marsh on either side. A few venturesome gulls squawked loudly overhead, and Sophia turned to look for the sea but she couldn't find it. "Are we far inland here?" she asked.

"Not as far as it seems. Just six miles. Over there is the ocean, but the dunes hide it from view."

Sophia nodded. It was good to know that the familiar Atlantic was nearby. Behind her the boxes and trunks she had hastily packed with her grandmother's aid were tied securely in place, and on her lap was the most precious bundle of all. Every once in a while she would pat it with love and adjust its position so the contents wouldn't be disturbed by the jouncing of the trip.

When they approached the village it was sunset and the fiery red that suffused the landscape promised an even hotter day tomorrow. Sophia looked carefully at the houses of her new neighbors. They were few in number—it was a very small and isolated place—but each was neat and tidy, and looking at them gave her pleasure. Then her heart leaped and for the first time in that extraordinary day she felt the sting of tears behind her eyes. In front of each little house stood its occupants. They had heard the cart and come out to welcome the newlyweds home.

Most simply smiled and waved as Sophia and Jonathan passed. A few whispered "Good luck to you" or "God bless." One woman began a long discourse starting with, "Thee must both remember that marriage is ordained by God for thy . . ." They were beyond her before she reached the end of the sentence, but the drone of her voice followed them for some distance.

"That's Ellie Mann," Jonathan explained. "She is a Friend and she always has a message. I'll introduce thee to her on First Day at Meeting."

Sophia noted his assumption that she would go with him to his church though she said nothing. Finally they were at the forge, but Jonathan drove the wagon a few paces beyond it and stopped by the front door. "Come inside," he said. "Thee must be tired. I'll take care of the horse and the baggage after thee is settled." He put his hands around her little waist and lifted her to the ground.

"Careful of the package," she said.

"What's in it?" He had contained his curiosity as long as he could.

"A present from my grandmother. Thee will see."

In the house was another present. Jonathan had left the kitchen table scrubbed and clean, but bare. Now it contained a loaf of bread still warm from the oven and a pitcher of milk still warm from the cow. There was a crock of fresh butter and a round of cheese as well. "Do you keep a servant?" Sophia asked, forgetting to say "thee" in her surprise.

He chuckled. "No. These are presents from my neighbors. They must have put them here as soon as word came that we were home."

They ate their simple supper in shy silence. When they had finished, Jonathan left to see to the livestock and Sophia spent a long time washing the few plates in the unfamiliar kitchen. While she worked she was thinking that the place had been without a mistress for many years. The windows had no curtains and the crockery and cooking utensils were arranged without thought for efficiency or attractiveness.

"I must have another shelf here," she mused aloud. "And Jonathan must make me some hooks over here for towels. This table would be better against the window. And perhaps he can make me another for this corner. It would be convenient for working dough."

"I'll do all those things," he said, startling her, for she had not heard his return. "Tomorrow thee can make a list of what's needed and I'll begin."

"I'm not complaining," she said quickly, embarrassed to have been overheard. "Thy house is very nice." She was glad she had remembered to say "thy."

"*Our* house," Jonathan corrected. "It's thine as well as mine now."

Sophia smiled, and when he stretched out his hand she took it. "Would thee like to see all of it now?" he asked.

"Not now. Tomorrow."

It had grown dark outside the circle of light cast by the single candle on the table that was in the wrong place. They knew what the next step of their adventure was to be and they both wanted very much to take that step, but they were young and tongue-tied with love and excitement and strangeness.

"It's a hot night," Jonathan said. "Is thee too warm?"

"No. I never mind the heat . . . or the cold."

And their conversation seemed exhausted.

"Come," Jonathan said at last. "We will go to bed." And having uttered the word that was on both their minds, he seemed to gain new sureness.

He led her up a narrow winding staircase to an equally narrow hall; and in the light of the candle he carried, Sophia could see that the floor was of wide pine boards polished by time and the walls were painted a faded yellow. When he opened a door on the right, however, the room was not small as she'd expected but spacious and airy with two windows that looked out over the fields and another that faced the marshes. There were woven rugs on the pine floor and a crocheted spread on the big four-poster bed.

"This was my mother and father's room," Jomathan said. "I have never slept in it before. But I think it is right that we sleep here."

"Yes." Sophia felt like a fool. She had never in her life been at a loss for words, and she had known about the rites of marriage ever since she could remember. Why was she acting like such a child now? Hoping to shake herself into some confidence, she walked around the big chamber examining every detail of the wainscotting and the pine washstand and the little cupboard in the corner. Jonathan had brought the trunk containing her clothes up here earlier without her noticing. It stood by the cupboard waiting.

Jonathan had often thought about this moment in the days since he knew they were to be wed. His plan had been to leave her alone for some minutes so she could undress and climb into the bed in privacy. Now, faced with the reality, he impulsively changed his mind. He drew her near and loosened the top button of her wedding frock.

Jonathan undressed her slowly and solemnly and she stood very still while he completed the task. Then he moved away and carefully turned back the covers of the bed. When he had done that he returned to where she was waiting, lifted her into his arms, and lay her on the sweet-smelling sheets.

She watched him take off his clothes, and in the light of the candle she could see how dark the sun had made the skin of his back and how white his hips and buttocks seemed in contrast. The hair of his chest was as red as that on his head. It grew in the shape of a vee and came to a point above his waist. As he walked to where she lay, Sophia made herself look at the spot between his thighs and the hair was red there too. His maleness stood up with desire and for the first time she felt not just shyness but fear.

When he lay beside her the springs of the old bed creaked and she could feel the heat that emanated from his naked body. "I love thee, Sophia," he said softly. "Thee must not be afraid of me."

"I'm not afraid," she lied.

Jonathan lowered his head and kissed her for a long time. She could taste the strength of him on his lips, and she let her arms rise up and circle his neck. His hairy chest pressed against her and it tickled; she heard herself giggle softly. The laugh opened her mouth and admitted his tongue and the kiss changed in mood.

He did not hurry; he was not a hurrying man. He had blown out the candle but there was a full moon. It lit the room and shone on Sophia's white skin, the dark pink of her nipples, and the triangle of gold-brown hair below her belly.

"Thee is beautiful all over," Jonathan said softly, as he stroked her with his hard callused hand and with his soft gentle mouth.

"You don't think my two-color eyes are funny?" she demanded suddenly, and it was his turn to laugh.

"I don't." He squeezed her buttocks playfully, and all at

once she pressed against him with a new urgency. He could feel the wetness of her secret places as they touched the skin of his thigh, and he knew instinctively that the proper moment had come.

Sophia knew it too. "Make me your wife, Jonathan," she whispered. "Make me truly your wife."

"Please," he asked, for he knew this to be a most solemn moment. "Please say it again, in my speech."

"Make me thy wife," she repeated.

So he spread her legs with his hands and lay over her and sought entry to her depths. At first he was clumsy and terrified of hurting her, but Sophia wanted this consummation with a wanting she had never before experienced and she squirmed her hips and even used her own hand to help him.

When his first thrust met resistance, Sophia raised her buttocks and completed the entry. The sudden stab of pain made her gasp, but by then Jonathan couldn't hear her. His blood was pounding in his ears and his heart was beating too loud to admit any other sound. He poured himself into her with joy and his strong young body trembled from head to foot like a newborn colt shaking itself into the world.

"Is thee all right?" he asked anxiously afterwards.

"I'm wonderful," she replied.

Jonathan touched her lightly between her thighs and he could feel that she was hot and sticky. He rose and wrung out a cloth in the tepid water of the pitcher on the washstand and came back and sponged her with it.

"That feels nice," Sophia said softly. And before he had completed his task it had become something different than he'd intended, and he put the cloth away and continued stroking and rubbing her with his hand. He went on doing this for some time because she obviously enjoyed it and because touching her so intimately somehow gave him a greater sense of possession than the other had done. Soon she was trembling as he had a few minutes before, and he watched her in the moonlight until the last explosive shudder had come and gone and they slept.

5

Paul stood on the front step to welcome his wife and son home. Jacob was first out of the carriage. He called a cheerful greeting to his father while he helped his mother to the ground, then went to instruct the driver about the luggage.

"Was it a good trip?" Paul asked.

"Oh yes, marvelous!" She had left in anger, but her ire had dissipated itself in the course of the journey. That kind of thing often happened with Rachel. Her furies were so intense they burned themselves out quickly. Now she was full of the pleasure of a job well done, and Paul felt the knot in his stomach relax a little.

"Would you believe it," she said breathlessly while she pulled off her bonnet, "we took orders for over thirty stoves in just twelve days! Paul, it's going to be everything I said it would and more—" Val interrupted his mother's speech with a flying hug, and she ruffled his hair and commented that he had grown even in this short space of time. Then finally she asked, "Where's Sophia?"

"She's not here," Paul said, hating himself for the cowardice of the evasive answer. He shot Val a look and the gangly twelve-year-old removed himself from the room without a word. Val hated scenes.

Rachel might have asked when her daughter would return but Jacob came in and distracted her. "I've had them put the cases in the box room, Mama. Is that all right for now?"

"Oh yes, fine. It will all want washing anyway. You can't imagine the dust and heat of the roads, Paul."

He took it as a reproach, though she hadn't intended it as such. "You needn't have gone, Rachel. I would have done it if you'd been willing to wait a few days."

She waved her hand as if the acrimonious dispute over the trip had never taken place. "I didn't mind. I enjoyed it. Wonderful to see the countryside and learn firsthand how well all the markets are doing. They are, aren't they, Jacob?" She turned to the boy for confirmation.

"I guess so," he said with a laugh. "I can't make sense out of all those ledgers and figures as quickly as you can, Mama."

That annoyed her. "You could if you'd put your mind to it," she insisted. "You're eighteen, Jacob, and in a few years you'll be running this business. Which reminds me . . ." She sat down and addressed her remarks to her husband. "I've been thinking. Why doesn't Jacob spend six months working with the market in Plymouth. Starting this September. I'm very impressed with the Plymouth manager, and I think it would be valuable for Jacob—"

"That won't be possible," Paul interrupted. He hadn't planned to say anything this soon and certainly not in the boy's presence, but the opportunity could not be passed by. Besides, delay would probably make it worse. "I've made arrangements for Jacob."

"What arrangements?"

She was looking at him through narrowed eyes. He couldn't tell what she was thinking. "Here, read this." Paul withdrew a sheet of heavy vellum from his pocket and passed it to his wife. Jacob stood by in silence. He could feel the gathering storm and he knew he would be at the center of it, but he didn't know anything else.

Rachel looked at the unfamiliar crest on the top of the page. "My dear Mr. Amory," she read aloud but under her breath. Jacob had to strain to catch the words. "How pleased I was to receive your letter. I should be delighted to welcome your son to Philadelphia and see he has the opportunity—" Her voice broke off.

"Philadelphia," Jacob whispered. He made it sound like a prayer.

"Have you completely lost your senses, Paul?" She didn't shout or even raise her voice.

"I don't think so." He had rehearsed his explanation a number of times. Despite the fact that his shirt was soaked with perspiration and he dreaded the whole scene, he continued. "I've thought about it for many months. Jacob needs to travel. I propose he spend a year or two with this gentleman in Philadelphia, then see some more of America, travel south perhaps. He needs a sense of . . ." She was silent while he fumbled for a word: ". . . a sense of roots."

"Jacob's roots are here in Boston." Rachel still didn't raise her voice.

"I want to go, Mama. I've wanted it for ages, but I didn't think . . ." The boy prayed that he could avert the explosion, but he didn't have much hope.

"We need discuss it no further," Paul said quickly. "I've written to Mr. Markham accepting the offer. He does this sort of thing often, by the way. He's a kind of tutor. Jacob leaves—"

"Jacob is going nowhere." Rachel stood up and faced them both. Her blue eyes were smoldering but she was still outwardly calm. "Nowhere. Do you hear me? I mean what I say, Paul. I will not allow you to do this thing."

"I don't see how you can—"

She didn't let him finish. "I can," she said softly. "You know I can."

Jacob looked from one to the other in bewilderment. His father's broad shoulders were sagging. Defeat was written on his face. "Papa," the boy said pleadingly. "I want to go. It's a wonderful idea, a wonderful opportunity. I can, can't I?"

His father didn't answer and Jacob turned and ran from the room. Rachel followed him and Paul was left alone. He sank into a chair and stared into space. It was some time before he realized that his cheeks were wet with tears.

She came back in a short while. By then he had stopped crying but he remained seated in the same place, staring into space.

"You've upset Jacob terribly," she said. "Why, Paul? It was so unnecessary. You must know how foolish it would be to send him so far. His life is here, his future . . ."

"It's not right, Rachel," he said, as if he hadn't heard her. "You force me to choose between the children and you. All the time."

"I think you must be mad," she said. "What has come over you lately? And where is Sophia?"

He looked at her then. "Sophia is married. She's living in Rowley with her husband."

All the color drained from Rachel's face. "I don't believe you," she whispered hoarsely. "You're just saying that to wound me. To get back at me."

"She wed Jonathan Crandall three days after you left." He said it so simply she had to know it was the truth.

"For the love of God! What did you do? Didn't you go after her? How could she do such a thing without permission? She's only seventeen!"

"She had permission. Mine. I gave it when I saw how much they cared for each other. How well suited they were. Your mother and father were at the wedding. They agreed with me." His voice was expressionless. He was saying what he knew had to be said, but he knew too it would make no difference.

"Well suited . . . ? Sophia and a penniless farmer. An ignorant Quaker with dirt under his fingernails! My daughter—"

"She's my daughter too. And Jonathan is none of the things you say."

Rachel stared at him. There was still no color in her cheeks. "Get out," she said finally. "Get out of this house. I don't want to look at you. The sight of you makes me sick to my stomach."

He had never been a drinking man. A bit of brandy, a glass of wine—those were his usual indulgences. Paul would have been hard pressed to name more than two or three of the public houses of Boston, although he'd lived in the town nineteen years. He preferred his home, family, and garden to the boisterous company of inebriated men. When he realized that he wanted a drink, he didn't really know where to go.

He wandered the streets in the August twilight, his head pounding. There was a great pain in his chest. He wished he could sob like a woman. Rant and rave and accuse himself of being weak and stupid and afraid to risk one love for the sake of another, until in the end he lost them both. Jacob was as disgusted with him as was Rachel. And Paul despised himself more than either of them did.

When he reached Cambridge Street he looked up and realized he had wandered into a part of the city he didn't know. It was a maze of little crooked alleys and dark unsavory-looking buildings that smelled of fish and urine. He turned left and found himself in a rope walk. Great coils of hemp were everywhere and the place was deserted. Paul doubled back and walked aimlessly west. He had come almost to the bleak peninsula called Barton's Point when he finally spied the taproom. He only identified it because a small door opened and a man staggered out reeking of spirits. Behind him Paul caught a glimpse of dirty yellow light and a sawdust-covered floor. He went inside and ordered rum.

The drinkers around him were silent, serious about their imbibing. The huge, well-dressed man excited only momentary curiosity. They looked him over carefully, then turned back to their liquor. Paul was equally oblivous to them. More so in fact—his lack of interest was genuine, while the others were simply waiting for an opportunity to test the heft of his purse. Only his size delayed a frontal attack. Better to wait until the stranger had a bellyful of rum.

They would not have to wait long. He was pouring back the golden spirit as if it were water and he dying of thirst. When the second bottle was almost empty and he had to hold on to the edge of the heavy oak counter to keep himself upright, four of the others edged a bit closer. It was then that the woman came into the room.

Her skin was the color of coffee laced with cream and her hair was black and tightly curled. She wore it in an extraordinary short cut, like a man's. In that exotic, foreign-looking face the deep emerald green of her eyes was startling. Paul tried to bring her into focus, but she kept wavering and he couldn't see her as clearly as he wished.

"Get out o' here, Mattie," one of the men said softly. "This one may give a bit o' trouble."

The woman called Mattie looked at the huge stranger and shook her head. "No he won't," she said. "Cause you ain't gonna provoke him none."

"Mind yer own affairs," the man said.

"Anything what goes on in here is my affair," she answered. "I says you gonna leave him alone, and you gonna do jus' that."

The meanest of the four thugs spat on the floor and looked as if he would strike her, but the others held him back. "How often's a chance like this come along?" he whined. "You gonna let her talk you out o' easy money—"

"Shut up," the woman said. "And get out o' here. All o' you."

They left, muttering curses under their breath, and the man serving behind the bar sighed. "You're gonna bite off more'n you can chew one o' these days, Mattie."

"When I do it'll be me what chokes," she said. "Meanwhile, you help me get this big animal upstairs where he can sleep it off."

He seemed already asleep when she pulled off his boots and loosened the buttons of his breeches. "You needs to breathe, you poor thing," she said, chuckling. "You ain't used to the kind o' rum we serves here in Mount Whoredom."

He wasn't as unconscious as he appeared to be. His bulk was capable of absorbing more alcohol than even he had realized. When Paul heard her say "Mount Whoredom," he opened his eyes and asked, "Is that where I am . . . Mount Whoredom?"

"So you's awake, big man. Yes, that's where you is. In the meanest, most sinful part o' this here town o' Boston. Is you a stranger here?"

He wanted to shake his head but he hadn't the strength. When the coffee-colored woman sat down next to him he could smell the strange and tantalizing scent of her but he couldn't speak.

She ran a quizzical finger over his eyebrows and the side of his face. Her touch felt cool and welcome. "I think you got some big pain inside you. So big it fills up all o' you, giant that you is. You got grief, big man?" He still didn't answer, and she watched him in silence for a few seconds. Then she stood up and took off her dress. "You wake enuf' for lovin'?"

His tongue wouldn't respond but his hand would. He touched her breasts and they were firm and exciting. She was thin enough so that he could feel her ribs but she didn't seem in the least fragile. "Come on, big man," she said softly. "You need a woman to make you forget, and I's here."

He fell on her like a rutting bull.

He did not sleep as long as might be expected. Amory woke when it was still dark, and the airless, fetid room threatened to suffocate him. His memories of where he was and what had happened were rum soaked and confused. The terrible scene at home, Jacob's pleading eyes, Rachel's accusing ones—all that he could remember clearly. But everything after was a blur.

He threw back the rough cover and was startled to find that, while he still wore his shirt, his breeches were gone. Stumbling in the darkness, he felt around until he found them and his jacket and boots. A sick sourness was rising in his gorge and his only thought was to get outside and breathe some fresh air before he covered himself with vomit in this stinking hole.

It seemed to him that he made an awful racket while he tried to find a door to the street. He banged his shins once and his head two or three times before he managed to locate something that at least felt like an exit. There was a heavy wooden bar across it, and when he tried to lift it free his arms were leaden. At last the bar came away from the brackets in which it was set. He couldn't hold it and it banged to the floor with a tremendous crash. The door blew open on squeaking hinges. Paul waited a moment as it occurred to him he might be in some danger. But nothing moved outside or in. He stepped into the night and got as far as the dirt road before he doubled over and puked for what seemed a very long time.

There was no moon but the stars were incredibly bright. By their position and the distant sound of the ocean at his back, Amory could judge where he was. He turned left and began walking. His pain was physical as well as mental now. He'd solved nothing with his drunken spree. And he could remember so damned little.

The name Mount Whoredom flashed in his mind and quickly he felt for his purse. It was in his jacket pocket, where he'd put it before leaving home. Its weight told him he'd not been robbed. But there had been people. Men drinking, thugs, and a woman—an exotic half-caste with a man's haircut and green eyes. He stopped short and leaned against a building. He'd lain with her, lain with the mulatto woman. But had he? Or was it just a rum-induced fantasy? He couldn't remember, so he shook his head clear and walked on.

Dawn was a suggestion of pink in the sky when he reached The Roses. He'd met no one; no one had questioned him. The days when Puritan bailiffs patrolled the night streets of Boston were past, thank God. And they would all be asleep inside too. Not even the servants would be up at this hour. He fumbled for his key and let himself in.

"I've been waiting for you." Rachel stood in the hall fully dressed. She had a candle in her hand and in its light her skin seemed to glow with whiteness and her eyes looked as blue as precious sapphires. "My mother died this night. We will be expected at Beacon Street in a few hours."

"Lizzie, dead? But—"

She ignored his shock. "Go out to the garden shed and wash," she said. "You smell like a cesspool."

6

Tonyjay had been anxious about his wife for some time. Her small frame had seemed to shrink this past year, her skin to stretch taut over spare bones. Lizzie was seventy, after all, six years older than he. But she seemed so alive, lit by the inner flame of spirit that had always been hers.

When the sun set on that hot August day he had been sitting behind the house in the little summer room where they sometimes breakfasted. The windows were all open and there was even the suggestion of a breeze. He had a book on his lap and every once in a while he could look up and see his wife puttering among the fluffy stands of wormwood or the erect stalks of angelica. Over the years she'd taught him the names of the various herbs. On this evening, in the year of grace 1743 he could watch her and smile at the thought of all the wisdom she had acquired not from books but from life.

An hour later he glanced at the garden again and didn't see her. Gone into the house, or the small potting shed perhaps, in search of some tool. Tonyjay returned to his reading. Nearly twenty minutes passed before he became conscious of her continued absence and rose to see where she was.

Lizzie lay on the grass path that separated the tall tansy plants from the low-growing horehound. It was apparent from her position that she had not fallen. She had merely been overcome with tiredness and stretched out on the soft, warm earth. She was smiling and a trowel was still loosely gripped in her fingers. Next to her body was a basket of freshly gathered lavender waiting to be brought inside.

Tonyjay knelt beside his wife for a long time. They had been through much together; the peace of their later years had been purchased with fire and blood and tears. But he could not weep now. All that was in the past. He was grateful for what she had been, what she had given. Her loyalty had been a beacon shining day and night, never betraying even the suggestion of a flicker. That unfailing light had flared to sustain him at a time when he deserved it least. Remembering that, he was glad her death had been such a serene and fitting thing. His sorrow was for himself, for the loneliness he must face, the void her passing would leave in his life. And for himself he could shed no tears. All that was behind him too.

Because there were so many mourners the funeral could not be called quiet. It defied anyone to make a simple thing of the numerous Griffins and the dozens of townspeople present. Still, Tonyjay had done what he could to avoid the sort of ostentatious show Lizzie would have despised.

By his decree the burial took place within two days of Lizzie's death. He wanted just that, a burial, but Benjamin opposed him and Tonyjay gave in. In the event, it didn't seem such an important thing. What if he and Lizzie had never been believers? Benjamin had become a pillar of the Church of England in these years of his social rise. He was a respected member of the parish of King's Chapel, and at his insistence they held a service there before interring the body. The eldest Griffin listened to the words read from the Book of Common Prayer and it struck him that they were mellifluous and soothing if nothing else. So be it.

Later, leaving the burial ground next to the church, Tonyjay was glad it was such a short walk to his own house. For him the entire ceremony had little meaning. Lizzie would live in his heart, in her children, and in her garden. If she had a spirit, he would find it there. The mound of earth behind him was only that.

Many of the family seemed to feel the same way. They straggled up Beacon Street and let themselves not into the house but into the garden. There they could best mourn their loss. "I shall miss her, Grandpa," Antony said quietly. He'd not left his grandfather's side since the early morning, but these were the first words he had spoken.

"So will I, lad." Tonyjay nodded. "So will I."

He wanted to say more to the boy but he was distracted by Martha and Mary passing trays of punch and little cakes and by Rachel's direct question as soon as she could get near him.

"What will you do now, Papa? Have you thought of coming to live with us at The Roses?"

"Or at the Ark," one of the twin wives said.

Even now he could never be sure if it was Martha or Mary speaking. But it didn't matter. His answer would be the same in any case. "I have no intention of living anywhere but here," he said firmly. "Why should I?"

"Well, it would be easier for you, Papa." Rachel again. "More convenient."

"Nonsense. That O'Malley woman will look after me. She comes in every day. Has done ever since old Abbie Tucker died."

"Yes but—"

"But nothing, Rachel. The subject is closed. I'm not a fossil yet; I still arrange my own life." Then, having silenced his daughter in the way only he was ever able to do, he asked, "Where's Sophia?"

Rachel's lips pursed into a thin, hard line. "In Rowley, Papa. You should know that. I'm told you gave your blessing to the marriage."

"I did. You still withhold yours, I take it. Not even willing to notify the girl that her grandmother died?" Rachel made no reply. Tonyjay looked at her with more sadness than anger, and she walked away. Over the heads of the crowd he could see Paul standing by himself, a pained and miserable expression on his face. Tonyjay sighed and shook his head. There was nothing he could do about that situation, but the other one might still be salvageable.

He was trying to attract Charles's attention when Benjamin appeared at his elbow. "I just wanted to tell you, Papa, I wrote to Hannah this morning."

"Thank you, Ben, that was thoughtful. I'll write her myself later in the week but—"

"Is it true, Papa, what one hears . . . that Hannah's lost her mind?"

The older man shook his head. "I can't quite believe it. I remember . . ." He was remembering many things: Hannah's determination and vitality was the thread that united the reminiscences. "She's tough, Hannah, strong. Always was. It's hard to imagine her otherwise. But we've not heard from her in almost two years. The note her son sent . . . well, Lizzie wasn't satisfied. She wanted to go and see but she wasn't well enough for that . . ."

The conversation drifted into a discussion of how long Lizzie had been failing, and Hannah Ludlow wasn't mentioned again.

Eventually Tonyjay managed to get Charles into the study without anyone noticing. "What are you going to do about your son, about Antony?" he asked.

"Today, Papa?" Charles said in surprise.

"Yes, today. Doesn't it tell you anything? Death, the short span we're allotted. The tension out there between Rachel and Paul, Sophia's conspicuous absence. Is that what you want?" He was sharper than he might have been at a less emotional moment.

"I don't see . . ." Charles began in customary fashion. Then he stopped and didn't say anything for a while. Father and son watched each other.

"I'm sorry, Papa, I know you mean well and I don't want to upset you," Charles stammered at last.

"Sweet Jesus, Charles! Stop talking to me as if I were a doddering old fool. Upsetting me's got nothing to do with it. What about Antony?"

"He must finish school and come into the firm. Just as I've always intended. This talk of going to sea, it's nonsense—for a Griffin, at any rate."

Tonyjay sighed and shook his head. "You're making a mistake, Charles. You're going to regret it bitterly one of these days."

Antony Griffin moved away from the door of the study feeling a mixture of rage and shame. He'd not meant to eavesdrop. He'd only been looking for his grandfather, afraid he'd locked himself away to brood. If their voices hadn't been so loud he would never have realized his father was in there with the old man. Nor would he have heard the pronouncement.

Damn him! Antony thought. He promised I could go to sea if I finished at Harvard first. Now he's saying . . . The thought broke off as he heard a chair scrape and realized his father was about to leave the room. As he moved away from the door, Antony heard his grandfather ask that Rachel be summoned. So the old man was all right, not too depressed at any rate. Antony hurried from the house. For a moment he stood in the garden, watching the great milling crowd of relations. He saw his father come out and whisper something to Aunt Rachel. Then, because it looked as if Papa might be going to speak to him, he eased himself out of the gate and began walking. He wasn't conscious of any intention to go to the docks; it was merely a long-standing habit.

"You sent for me, Papa." Rachel was still angry. Tonyjay could see it in the stiff set of her shoulders.

"I wanted to give you this in private. The others might not understand. It's the only personal possession your mother left with specific instructions."

Rachel reached for the small paper-wrapped parcel. "What is it?"

"I have no idea. I just found it among her things. But I think she'd been working on it for some time, whatever it is. You must see that it's delivered, Rachel. It's the last thing your mother will ever ask of you."

She glanced down at the spidery writing on the brown paper. "For Sophia," it said.

7

The ship was small and of a type seldom seen in Boston. Antony recognized her as a barkentine only because he'd spent years studying the old pictures in his grandfather's library. "Hey!" he called when he recognized one of the workers from Gee's Shipyard perched high in the mizzenmast. "What's this?"

"'Tis a French lady," the man yelled back. "The *Notre* something or other. Ran into trouble off Norman's Woe." Antony stood for a while examining the rather squat and ugly lines of the vessel, then moved away.

The sky had clouded over and the smell of salt mingled with that of pitch and pine. He could see whitecaps forming on the choppy water. There was a storm brewing. It felt like autumn, not like August. That suited his mood, for he felt as bleak as the weather. He didn't hesitate when he came to the door of the tavern. The Mermaid was a favorite haunt of seamen. Few of Boston's land-based population went there to drink, certainly not Griffins, but today Antony didn't care about that. The conversation he'd overheard less than an hour earlier churned in his stomach like acid, a mockery of all the conventions with which he'd been raised. What was honor if a man lied to his own son?

"What'll it be, lad?" the barman inquired.

"Rum." He pushed a coin across the counter, then took the tankard and moved back into the shadows. When his eyes became accustomed to the dim light of the interior he could make out the dozen or so men drinking with him. Mostly local sailors. There was even a Griffin's captain, Alex Haycock, among them. To the rear were a pair who looked foreign—from the French ship no doubt. Antony moved toward them. His French wasn't bad. Maybe a conversation with these strangers would take his mind off his own misery.

Just then the door opened and a clutch of newcomers entered. They were obviously British officers. Their uniforms were unmistakable and their presence cast a strange pall over the place. Officers didn't often come to drink at the Mermaid. "Claret, landlord," one of them said. "That is if you've any that's a cut above poison."

His voice wasn't loud but it carried. So did the laughter of his companions. For a brief moment Antony thought there would be trouble. It wasn't that anyone moved or said anything; it was just a kind of vibration in the air. Then the barman produced a bottle of wine and the officers took it to a table without further comment. Antony resumed his progress toward the Frenchmen.

"Is that your ship I saw in the harbor?" he asked in English. They looked at him blankly and he tried again in French.

"Yes," the older of the two foreigners said. "My ship. I'm Captain Jacques Bonde." He was a small, wiry man with dull red-rimmed eyes and an oily-looking black goatee. His speech was slurred with drink when he introduced the fellow with him as his first mate, Mr. Marguet. Antony bowed and told them his name. Bonde motioned to a seat.

"I've not seen a barkentine before," the boy said. "What's she like?"

"She's a good ship, at least she was until yesterday." The French captain looked morose and took a large swallow of the drink at his elbow.

"Yes," Antony said. "I heard you had some bother off Norman's Woe. Cape Ann can be treacherous."

Bonde slammed his fist on the table. His goatee seemed to quiver as he spoke. "Everything in these cursed English colonies is treacherous," he said loudly. One of the British officers glanced in their direction.

"I'm interested in your rigging," Antony said quickly. "Most of it's fore-and-aft isn't it?"

The first mate recognized the boy's efforts to avert trouble and hastily entered into a discussion of various methods of setting sails. Marguet was a good deal less drunk than his captain.

For some moments there was peace. The officers called for more wine. The Frenchmen accepted Antony's offer to buy them another round. The technical discussion continued. Bonde took no part, seemingly lost in his rum and his thoughts. When he jumped to his feet he startled the pair at his own table as well as everyone else.

"It's piracy," he shouted. "Nothing but damned piracy! Anyone but the English would have better markers off that hell coast." He spoke in French but his manner was explanation enough. When he hurled his tankard to the floor most of the men around them melted into the shadows. Marguet tried desperately to quiet Bonde, as Antony stared at them both in astonishment.

Suddenly a fourth man was standing at their table. "Have you some complaint to lodge, *mon capitaine*?" The French was perfect as befit an officer and gentleman, but there was an ugly undertone to the naval man's words.

"Yes, I've a complaint. You and all your English kind—"

"Captain! Please." Marguet said, turning to the stranger. "He's had too much to drink. We were in a bad storm yesterday and—"

"But I'd like to hear." The words were soft, ostensibly placating. "If your captain has a grievance against his Majesty's navy—"

"Here is my grievance, you pig!" Bonde tore free from Marguet's restraining grip. He was shorter than the English lieutenant by almost a head but the jetty of spittle he aimed hit the other man full in the face. Within seconds the Mermaid was a mass of flailing arms and legs and splintering furniture.

Later Antony tried to figure out why he had automatically fought on the side of the Frenchmen. Because the naval officers had come to the tavern looking for a fight? Because Bonde was obviously drunk and no gentleman should have paid him any attention? Merely because he had been sitting with the foreigners and it seemed the natural thing to do? Possibly none of those reasons or all of them. As to why he had fought so fiercely, that he understood.

When the opportunity to strike out came, he reveled in it. It was his family he was pummeling. Every satisfying contact of skin and bone and sinew was a gesture of revolt. He'd even been conscious of Alex Haycock watching him, glad that this escapade would be reported to his father. Griffins didn't engage in tavern brawls. Well damn them all, here was one Griffin who did.

They backed out of the Mermaid over sprawled bodies and debris. The two Frenchmen were formidable fighters. Antony was astounded to realize that three of them had bested all the others. But as they stood in the street gasping for breath, he saw the glint of a knife in Bonde's fist. "Hey," he said quickly. "Put that away. Fighting's one thing, but . . ." He realized he was speaking in English and switched quickly. "You can't use a weapon! Do you want to end your days in a Boston jail?"

Marguet understood him even if the other man didn't. "Help me," he commanded as he started to drag the captain down the street. Between them they pulled and carried Bonde back to his ship. Halfway there he obliged them by passing out. It made things easier.

"We're casting off right now!" Marguet yelled to the handful of crewmembers on deck. "Get rid of that one." He gestured to the shipwright still working on the mast.

"Yer daft, ye blighter," the man said when he understood what they were trying to tell him with their frenzied gestures. "Job ain't done yet. She ain't fit to sail. Tell 'em, Master Antony. Tell 'em I ain't through."

Antony turned to translate that message to Marguet but the first mate was occupied with the effort to ready the ship for leaving. Griffin had to chase him up to the bowspit; and when he did succeed in making Marguet understand, the man wasn't interested. "Can't be helped," he said with a shrug. "It's dangerous to remain here. We'll trust to the sea."

"But it needn't be," Antony said. "Look, I told you my name's Griffin. My family is pretty powerful in Boston. I can see to it that nothing happens. I mean it was just a fight after all."

Marguet looked at him and there was a trace of a smile about his lips. "So you're one of those Griffins, are you? I've heard of them. But it won't be enough, my young friend. Not this time. The knife—Bonde used it in the tavern. How else do you think we got out of there?"

Antony stared at him, mouth agape. "But—"

"But nothing." The first mate turned from him and called to a passing deck hand. "Here, give this money to the shipwright and get him ashore. Throw him overboard if you have to." Then he turned back to Antony. "You too, *mon ami*. Thank you for your help, and good-bye."

Griffin drew a breath. The idea was born in one swift second and decided upon in the next. "Take me with you."

"You! Why should you come with us? You're in no danger from the law."

"I could be. Plenty saw me fighting beside you."

"But you're a Griffin. You yourself said—"

"That's not the only reason. I want to go to sea. I've always wanted to."

"Have you sailed before?" Marguet asked. Antony shook his head. The Frenchman began to understand the situation. "I see. So you want to be a sailor not a rich merchant. Is that it, *mon ami*?" He didn't wait for an answer. He shrugged and said, "Very well, the choice is yours. The captain may not like it when he wakes up tomorrow and finds you aboard but . . ."

For some seconds neither man said anything more. Then Marguet stretched out his hand and Antony shook it warmly. "Welcome aboard." After that the first mate was occupied with his job. "Prepare the foredeck halyards!" he shouted. "Hoist the foresail and the bowsprit jib!"

Antony stood stock still while all around him men rushed to obey the familiar commands. The breeze stiffened as if it too were obedient. Griffin watched the sails fill with wind and felt the deck shudder beneath his feet.

"So you decided to join us." Bonde looked little changed by his long sleep. The excesses of the day before were evident on his bruised face. Griffin guessed that the bloodshot eyes were a more or less permanent condition. He'd already heard much of the captain's fondness for strong drink.

"Yes. I hope you are not angry with Mr. Marguet. It seemed necessary to act quickly and I—"

Bonde stopped the explanation with a quick gesture of his hand. "I don't care about your reasons," he said. "I just want you to know that on the *Notre Dame* we carry no excess baggage. You work for your keep or you pay. Have you any money?"

"No." Antony shook his head. "I mean no more than the bit I had with me yesterday. I hadn't intended any of this, you see. It just happened."

"Yes, I see. It will have to be work then. What are you good for?"

Antony shrugged. "Not much as far as you're concerned, I'm afraid. I'm, that is I was, a student at Harvard College."

Bonde chuckled. Somehow it wasn't a friendly sound. "A student. Yes, I guessed as much. With a rich father. No, no, don't deny it. I know who you are. My first mate told me. So we've a high and mighty Griffin on board and he's good for nothing but swabbing decks?" The chuckle again. "Very well, Griffin; we shall see how good you are with a mop."

The *Notre Dame* had sailed from Montreal with a cargo of furs and fish to trade in New Orleans, and another shipment as well—two women to be sold as indentures when they reached Louisiana.

"From Acadia," one of the crew explained to Antony. "Debtors. All poor as church mice, the Acadians. This pair"—he jerked his head toward the mother and daughter standing over by the rail—"got no men to look after 'em. Was workin' the farm themselves. Small wonder they got in debt."

Antony could see that, and more. The older woman was very ill and the younger very beautiful. The mother was a gray wraith. The daughter had golden hair which she kept tightly plaited and eyes of sea green which sometimes watched him, just as he watched her.

"What's your name?" he asked when he managed to find the girl alone on deck.

"Cecile LaPointe," she said, then looked away as if she

were not willing to engage in further conversation.

"I'm sorry about . . . well, about your trouble." She didn't answer. Antony reached into his pocket and pulled out an orange. "Here, take this. It's for your mother. Do her good."

Cecile made no move to accept the offering. "Where did you get it?"

"From the captain's stores. He has a crate of them—he won't miss this one. Besides, your mother's ill. She needs it more than he does. Take it. I'll get you another tomorrow."

She reached out and grabbed the treasure as if it might disappear, hid it under her cloak, then darted toward the hold where she and her mother slept. "Don't forget," Antony called after her. "Tomorrow."

The girl paused as if she were going to say something but changed her mind. Antony watched her legs as she disappeared. They were exposed by the short skirt she wore, a fashion he'd heard was customary with the Canadian women as it was with the Indians. Her legs were as beautifully proportioned as the rest of her. He found himself wondering if all of Cecile LaPointe's skin was that same bronze color. She seemed to him a very different sort of girl than any he'd ever met in Boston.

8

Cecile knew Antony Griffin wasn't the only one looking at her. Her mother knew it too. "You must be careful, Ceci," the old woman whispered urgently. "Very careful. You're so young, so beautiful, these men—" Her voice broke off as another spasm of coughing began.

Ceci tried to ease her with soothing words. "Don't upset yourself, *Maman*. I understand, I'm careful. It will be all right." Even as she spoke, she knew the claim was a lie. Nothing was all right. They spent most of their time in a filthy hole behind the cargo. It was a damp, dark prison below the water line, where the pitching and rolling of the ship was most pronounced. Still, it could be worse. The girl looked at the iron rings attached to the wall and the pile of chains lying in one corner.

"Come, Ceci, bring me my beads. We will say another rosary, ask the Blessed Virgin to protect you."

The girl complied because it made her mother feel better. For herself, Ceci had given up expecting help from God or His mother. If they were going to do anything for the LaPointes, they had left it far too late. Divine providence should not have let her father die before she was born; it should have made the stony ground of the little farm near Beaubassin fertile, prevented the terrible drought of the past two years. If God had wanted to help, He could have done so before now.

"You're not praying, Ceci, we must pray."

"Yes, *Maman*, yes I'm praying. *'Je vous salut Marie . . .'*"

Griffin kept his promise. Every day that week he managed to deliver some bit of extra nourishment for Madame LaPointe. Ceci took his gifts eagerly, grateful for any small comfort she could provide her mother. Antony was more interested in the opportunity to spend time with Cecile.

She wasn't the first girl he'd found attractive. Antony'd always had an eye for the ladies, and it wasn't just women of his own class that caught his fancy. Last winter he'd lost his virginity to a lass from Paddy's Alley in South Boston. She was a winsome little creature who was quite willing to lift her skirts in the snow behind the woodshed outside the hovel where she lived. He'd paid her a shilling for the privilege and decided it was money well spent. But neither she nor any of the three or four others he'd succeeded in wooing made him feel as he felt when he looked at Cecile LaPointe.

It wasn't just her beauty, real though that was. He sensed a fire in Ceci, an inferno waiting to be set free. It seemed a primitive, wild thing, and it promised delight unparalleled to the man who released it. Griffin couldn't actually verbalize all that, not even to himself, but it was there and it drew him more powerfully than her golden hair and sea-green eyes.

"Why do you do this?" she asked him one day. "You've brought me six oranges and each one is a terrible risk for you. Do you care so for my mother?"

"Not your mother, for you." He reached out a hand to touch her hair.

She didn't move away but neither did she encourage him. It was as if she were unaware of his touch. "I have never been able to understand," she said. "Men are willing to face such danger when they wish to lie with a woman. But they can be so cruel. The men on this ship look at me with longing, but they're prepared to see my mother die a slow and painful death."

He was startled by the matter-of-fact way she referred to the feelings she roused. "Have many men wanted to . . . to lie with you?" said Griffin, stumbling over the words.

"Yes." She nodded and her eyes were solemn. "But I always refuse. I am a good girl, Antony Griffin. You will not buy me with oranges."

"I never meant that!"

"No, of course not. You meant only charity and sweetness." Her voice was scornful. The way he blushed crimson seemed a confirmation of her opinion. "I'll tell you something: when I do give myself to a man, it will gain me more than a piece of fruit!"

Griffin did not recognize the warning she was issuing. He knew only that afterwards she refused to accept his stolen bounty, and when they were ten days at sea he came to understand the import of her words.

It did not seem to Ceci that she had been considering the step since they were put on board the ship, but when she went to knock at the door of Captain Bonde's cabin she knew that she had.

"What do you want?" he asked.

His voice was gruff, but his eyes looked at her appreciatively. The lust she saw in them frightened her, but it also gave her courage. "My mother is very ill. I've come to ask you to do something."

"Oh?" Bonde was enjoying the sight of this beautiful wench coming to him for aid. "And what do you think I should do for your sick mother?"

"Move her to better quarters, see she has adequate and nourishing food." Her hands were like ice but she didn't allow her tone to falter.

"I see." Bonde stepped away from the door and motioned her to enter. "Come inside Mademoiselle, and tell me why I should do these things." He reached for the glass of spirits he'd been drinking and took a long swallow.

"You will get more money for her in New Orleans if she is well," Ceci said.

He chuckled. "Do you think it possible that an old ruined hag like your mother could bring any money? Whatever I did?"

"Then why did you accept our indentures?" she demanded although she knew the answer.

"Because you, my little pretty, will fetch a very good price. Very good indeed."

He reached for her then—just a hand on her shoulder, but it made the hair rise on the back of her neck and started her trembling. Still she wouldn't run. She had made up her mind, she would go through with it. "What do you want?" she asked. "To make things easier for my mother, what will it take?"

His voice was a hoarse whisper now. "What do you think I want, *cherie*."

"Me."

"*Eh bien*, you are direct, aren't you! I like that. Yes, I want you. But I do not have to bargain, *cherie*. I can take you without making any promises. Why do you suppose I've not done that?"

"I don't know," she answered honestly.

"Because"—he was fondling her blond plaits as he spoke—"I knew you would come here just like this and for these very reasons. I preferred to wait for that. You see, little Cecile, I enjoy seeing a woman beg. And now you must show how well you can do it. Get on your knees, *cherie*, get on your knees and tell me how willing you are to do anything I want."

There was a red haze in front of her eyes. Her breath was coming in short gasps. She'd known it would be hard, humiliating, but this . . . Yes, part of her mind said, this. She knelt before him, and the floor of the cabin swayed and pitched with the waves. Ceci thought she would topple over, be sick there at his feet. But her determination was stronger than the elements, even stronger than nature. "I beg you," she whispered. "I beg you to take me to your bed and make things a little easier for my mother. Please, *mon capitaine*, please."

"Good. Very good!" His laughter bounced from the walls of the cabin. Ceci thought it must fill the whole ship. "Tell me, how old are you?"

"Sixteen," she lied. Somehow it seemed better not to admit she was only fifteen.

"And how many men have you lain with, my sixteen-year-old Cecile?"

"None." Her voice was so low he didn't hear her, made her repeat her answer.

"None!" he said incredulously. "A virgin? I can hardly believe it. Well, I shall soon know if you're telling the truth—won't I, *cherie*?"

"Yes, but—"

"But nothing." He lunged for her, ripped her blouse from her shoulders. Ceci's full, dark-nippled breasts were exposed to his eyes.

"No," she screamed as she tore from his grasp and tried to cover herself with her hands. There was a big chair in one corner. Quickly the girl darted behind it. "You must keep your part of the bargain first," she insisted. "My mother—"

"Ah yes, your sainted mother." Bonde looked at her. He need do nothing except what it pleased him to do—on the *Notre Dame* he was God—but he knew ways to serve his needs that were beyond the imaginings of this golden-haired child.

He walked to the door of the cabin and opened it. "You," he bellowed to a crewman. "Come here." Then, when the man was standing in the door where he could plainly see the half-naked girl, Bonde said, "Move the old woman. Give her the cabin next to Mr. Marguet. And double her rations. This one," he said, nodding his head in Ceci's direction, "will stay in here and amuse me for the rest of the voyage."

For a few seconds she thought the shame would kill her. Then Bonde was on top of her, pulling off her clothes, slobbering over her with his whiskey breath and rotten teeth. Ceci realized that nothing so merciful as death could be expected

* * *

"Don't fret, lad," one old sea dog told Antony. "Most women is whores. Look like madonnas some of 'em, but whores none the less."

Griffin turned away. He'd thought his feelings well hidden. It wasn't just the notion of Ceci lying beneath a filthy animal like Bonde that bothered him; it was his own inability to win the girl. Wasn't he the handsome and wealthy son of a powerful family? No woman had ever rejected him so thoroughly, or for such an unworthy rival. It didn't please him that an illiterate old man might be thinking the same thing. "It's nothing to me who shares the captain's bed," he answered quickly.

"No, it ain't," the other man said. "See you remember that. It'll keep you out o' trouble. Besides, wait till we get to New Orleans. There's plenty of women for everybody in New Orleans."

In Boston the fact that Antony Griffin had run away was soon known to all the Griffins as well as most of the townspeople. Charles learned the facts from Alex Haycock, the captain who had been present in the Mermaid tavern when the fight occurred. Haycock, a long-time employee who cared deeply for the family, wasn't likely to spread the tale.

But the shipwright from Gee's yard also knew. He repeated the story the length and breadth of the city. It wasn't often that the high and mighty Griffins gave the lesser folk a chance to snicker. "Bad blood croppin' up in this here generation o' Griffins," the shipwright said to anyone who would listen. "Didn't that Amory lass run off and get married without her own mother even knowin'? Now Master Antony's gone and joined the French. The French, mind you!" He shook his head at the treachery of it. "But he'll be sorry, I warrant. Whole damn crew will be sorry. I hadn't got that mast secured proper like afore they sailed. She'll topple in the first good blow and it won't be my fault."

9

Not being in Boston, Sophia Amory Crandall knew nothing of her cousin Antony's behavior. And she wouldn't have cared if she did. Sophia was busy creating a miracle.

The changes being worked at the Crandalls' were not immediately visible to the other occupants of Rowley. Besides, most had nothing to do with the forge itself, the part of the establishment open to public view. Sophia was working her magic in the house.

Despite her youthful impatience she did not move precipitously. She went from room to room cleaning and rearranging the things already there before she made any major additions or subtractions. It was a good house. The rooms were well proportioned and designed for their function. The thing most wrong with them when Sophia became mistress was their bareness and a lack of softening, homey touches.

"The curtains grew old and faded," Jonathan explained, "so I just took them as rags for the barn or the forge."

Sophia nodded and opened the trunk packed with cotton and chintz that had been part of her hastily assembled dowry. She spent an entire afternoon trying bits of cloth in different rooms until she was satisfied, then set about sewing with a feverish intensity. By the time they had been wed a month, there were curtains in every room. And she had found a storeroom full of old rag rugs. When she asked Jonathan about them his explanation was rather like that about the curtains. "They always seemed to be dusty, and I'd no time for cleaning." The rugs were beaten, washed, and aired in the sun, and now they lay on the floor, lending warmth and color where none had been before.

But perhaps the greatest change was an impermanent one. Early in the morning, sometimes before cock crow, Sophia would be out gathering flowers for the house. She had only the wild and fragile blossoms of the fields from which to choose. There had been no proper garden at the forge since Jonathan's mother died. And there were none of the silver and crystal vases that had graced The Roses. But there were a few old pewter mugs and some heavy stone crocks. These she found pleasing to the eye when filled with meadow grasses or wild ox-eye daisies.

"Thee likes flowers," Jonathan said, viewing her charming arrangements. "And thee has nothing here like thy father's garden or thy grandmother's."

"Don't thee start mourning what I've left behind," Sophia said firmly. "I don't. Not a bit. Besides, I'm going to make a superb garden here. Come and see." And she led him to a secret she had kept for weeks.

In a neglected bit of dirt behind the barn, a place Jonathan never had reason to visit, she had dug a small square bed. A great quantity of tiny plants were tucked in there now. "These are the slips and cuttings my grandmother gave us the day we were married," she said. "That was the parcel I was carrying. There's a great number of different herbs here. Many are very rare and almost impossible to find anymore."

"But Sophia," he said, looking puzzled. "Thee has put them so close together. Surely it can't be right for them to grow so? I'd have dug thee a bigger plot if thee had but asked—"

"Silly!" She giggled. "They aren't going to stay here. I've only heeled them in until their permanent home is ready. At this stage they do best close together in the shade."

He looked suitably impressed with her skill. "Thee has learned a lot about plants from thy family," he said with pride. "I shall enjoy helping thee make a garden. Where will we put it?"

"I'm not sure yet. I'm still trying to make up my mind."

She thought about the question while she worked at other things. When her hands were buried deep in bread dough, and when she pulled the fresh hot loaves from the oven beside the fireplace, she considered and vetoed a dozen different sites. While she skimmed the cream from the milk Jonathan brought into the cool stone dairy room, or churned butter with slow rhythmic motions, Sophia thought of and rejected a dozen more. Then one afternoon in September, Jonathan found her standing beneath a small maple tree a dozen paces from the far corner of the barn. "This is the spot," she said.

"For what?" He'd forgotten about the garden, having too many practical concerns on his mind.

"The spot for our garden. Look," she said, gesturing to the area around them. "This bit of land is removed from the rest of the fields, isn't it? So it's really not too good for crops."

"No," he agreed. "I've not planted here for years. It's out of the way."

"Yes. But the windows of the sitting room look out on it, and the barn's close enough to provide a windbreak but far enough not to intrude. That other field up there . . ." She pointed to the side of a gentle hill that adjoined the land she had been discussing. "What are your plans for it, Jonathan?"

"I can't really say. It's bothered me to have that lie fallow, for tis good, rich soil. But the slope makes ploughing a long hard job. Longer than is warranted by the amount of crops there's space for."

"Yes," she said, smiling broadly. "I thought of that too, but I wanted to hear thee say it. Now, Jonathan, this will be the garden of herbs and flowers." She began pacing out a substantial site.

"From the maple tree to this corner we'll make a stone path. And someday when thee has time, thee can fashion a fence and a gate to mark it off. Then, over here, there'll be another little path." Sophia looked at the proposed garden area ruefully. "We've no lack of stones, that's for sure. As for the hill, thee won't believe what a marvelous idea I've had!"

It was a mark of how she'd settled into being this man's wife that Sophia now remembered to say "thee" even when she was excited. "We'll make an orchard, Jonathan: apples and pears and plums. The finest orchard in Rowley—on the whole of the north shore. And what we can't use ourselves, we'll sell. I've drawn a plan of the whole thing. Come inside and I'll show thee."

They went inside but it was some time before Jonathan saw her sketch of the garden and orchard to be. He was full of the joy of her, the wonder of her vision and sense of purpose. The happiness she gave him demanded expression in something more real and intimate than mere words.

Paul Amory thought frequently of his daughter in the ripening days of late summer. Sadness hung from him like a clumsy shroud, tripping him when he walked, blinding him when he would see—the way Sophia was cut out of their lives by Rachel's implacable opposition to her marriage was yet another fold in the shroud. Not that Rachel was content to let the matter rest there. She would not speak to her husband, wouldn't even dine at the same table with him. She had moved his things from the bedroom, and now Paul slept alone in a room once reserved for guests.

Jacob was not like his mother. Disappointed though he was, Jacob tried to make peace. But Paul was convinced that he could read disgust and pity in the boy's eyes, and not even Jacob could ease him.

Behind The Roses the garden rejoiced in abundance. The fruit trees were heavy laden, the roses rich with fragrant blossom. In one curved bed that traced a line beneath the drawing-room windows dark orange lilies bloomed. They stood nearly waist-high, and their arched petals sailed above a sea of purple and blue asters. Paul took joy from none of it.

And it was in this frame of mind that he found his thoughts harking back to the coffee-colored woman in the miserable tavern. For a time he thought he might have dreamed the woman as well as the episode in which he'd bedded her. But he made discreet inquiries on the waterfront where men know such things and found out she was real.

"Name's Mattie Sills," an obliging sailor told him. "Mulatto. Nigger mother and white father. Came to Boston ten, maybe twelve years past—from Virginia, I think. Owns a place called the Bucket o' Grease over in Mount Whoredom." The sailor waited to be told why a man like Paul Amory was interested in such a woman, but Amory simply thanked him and walked away.

Must be the kid, the seaman thought. His boy's what . . . ? Eighteen, nineteen maybe. Must be that young Master Jacob's sowin' his wild oats over on Cambridge Street and the old man wants to know who with. He chuckled and went back to his mates with the bit of gossip.

That same night, while Paul lay awake and thought about his life and about Mattie Sills, Rachel came to him. The clock downstairs had struck three when the door to his bedroom of exile opened and his wife entered. Paul's heart gave a leap of joy. "Rachel, oh my love . . ." He held out his arms and she came into them, but she didn't say a word. When he tried to speak she pressed her hand over his mouth.

"Don't talk. I don't want to hear your voice. I want to pretend that I'm not here and neither are you."

He was confused. None of it made any sense. For the first time in years she had yielded, come to him after the most bitter argument of their marriage, but she wouldn't let him explain, apologize, heal the wounds. She would accept only the physical from him, and when it was over, when they were both spent and trembling with the aftermath of an act that was almost violent in its ferocity, she rose and left the room.

It had been no part of peace Rachel came to offer. She had given in to her own need, her body's need, and now she would loathe herself as well as him. Paul cursed the stupidity and the waste of it, but he knew no way to change things.

Two nights later he returned to Mount Whoredom. He found the Bucket o' Grease easily. He'd not been drunk when first he went there, only when he left. This time he was dressed in simple clothes and he carried very little money. Those precautions turned out to be unnecessary. The woman saw him as soon as he entered, and she approached him with a smile.

"Evening, big man. I was wonderin' if'n you was ever comin' back. How come you left in such a hurry?"

"I don't know, I thought . . . I'd had a lot of rum. When I woke I was a bit confused."

She chuckled, a soft sound, and her green eyes crinkled up at the corners and danced with merriment. "I'll jus' bet you was. Well, you recovered enough now to have a hair o' the dog what bit you? I mean rum, not me," she added. "I's still sore from the last time."

Paul looked at her in astonishment. "Yes, some rum please," he said quickly to cover his embarrassment. If he had understood her correctly, it hadn't been a dream. He had lain with this remarkable creature. She seemed to read his thoughts.

"You don' remember what's real and what's not bout that night, do you, big man?" She was laughing again, and some of the other drinkers were looking at them curiously. Paul shook his head and felt his cheeks redden.

"You's blushin'. I don' know how long it is since I seen a man honest enuf to blush. Come on, lover man, we's gonna go someplace private and talk. 'Sides, if you remember so li'l bout me, I's gonna have to refresh your mind."

She led him upstairs to the same dirty, airless room he had been in previously, but he shook his head and said, "Is there someplace else? Someplace more . . ."

Mattie looked at the boxlike chamber with its peeling walls and narrow ugly bed, and she seemed to see it through his eyes. "Yeah, there's someplace else. Come." She held out her hand—it was the first time she'd touched him this night—and led him along the corridor and down another set of stairs. Soon they were in a kind of alley between two buildings and then in a wide, open space overlooking the copper works and pounding surf beyond.

"This here's my cabin." Mattie opened the door to a shack hidden by the blackness of the night. Paul had to duck to avoid hitting his head, but once inside he could stand upright. "Wait a bit," she said. "I's got some candles and a lantern right here." She slid the words together so it sounded like a different language than that spoken by anybody in Boston. Gentler, with more music in it.

When the candle flared he looked around. The shack was built of wood, not matched timbers but bits and pieces of what looked like driftwood. There were rushes on the floor and brightly colored fabrics hanging from the walls to keep out drafts. The furnishings were a pile of mattresses in one corner and a table with two chairs in the other. It was as primitive and exotic as Mattie herself, and it was spotlessly clean. "You like it?" she asked with a trace of defiance. "It ain't fancy, but I built it myself with my own hands and not much else."

"I like it very much," he said. "It's warm and welcoming, like you."

"Oh my . . . warm and welcoming. Well there's some as

would agree and some as wouldn't. I welcome who I likes, big man. But I ain't for sale. You understand?"

"I understand, Mattie."

"How come you knows my name?"

"I asked. After the last time, I mean."

"I don' know yours."

"It's Paul, Paul Amory." He had not intended to say that. It seemed an indiscretion. All the while he'd walked toward Mount Whoredome he had promised himself he wouldn't reveal his true identity. He'd even tried a few aliases to see how they felt in his mouth. None of that mattered now. It would be unthinkable to tell Mattie Sills anything but his real name.

"So, Mr. Paul Amory, now we's introduced, you sit yourself down over here and I'll give you some proper rum. Not that poison I sell back there." She chuckled while she uncorked a big jug and poured a portion into a pewter mug. "That stuff in the tavern can kill a man. But I s'pose you knows that now."

He grinned. "I almost died but not quite. Felt like it for a while, though."

"Yeah, I bet you did."

For some time after that they seemed to have nothing more to say. It wasn't a harsh silence, though. It was quiet and companionable, and it was shot with the sound of the sea and the calling of the gulls.

10

In all the time they'd been married, this was the first day she did not know Paul's whereabouts. The thought created an icy place deep inside Rachel. Not because she cared, but because she didn't. Something was dying and she was saddened by the fact, but not mournful, and that frightened her. It portended empty years and a battle lost.

All that morning she found herself watching Jacob and Val with new intensity. Jacob was so perfect he took her breath away. From the tangled skein of their lives, she and Paul had produced this fine thing. Or had they? Were young men like Jacob a result of heritage and upbringing, or did they just happen at the whim of a beneficent creator? She didn't know.

And what of Valiant? Such a misnamed child. Had Paul made the younger boy the whining, timid creature he was with that silly, romantic name? Or was the younger child a kind of joke on the part of the same creator? There was a strain of sweetness in Val; he could be loving and gentle. But he was weak—an inherent, fundamental weakness Rachel realized she could never change. Just as she'd never change Paul. She sighed at the thought and went slowly upstairs to her bedroom.

The package marked for Sophia lay on her dressing table. It had been there since the funeral four weeks earlier. Half a dozen times Rachel had started to give it to one of the servants with instructions that it be taken to Rowley, but each time something had held her back. What was behind that impulse she couldn't say. Not spite or meanness. The parcel belonged to Sophia and the girl would have it, whatever it was. Rachel ran her fingers over the package. She wouldn't open it; that sort of dishonesty was no part of her makeup. She despised liars and cheats. But she despised weaklings even more. Rachel made up her mind and went to arrange for the delivery of Sophia's legacy.

They told her it would take at least five hours to get to Rowley, even using the best carriage and a team of four. Rachel had no desire to spend the night on the road, so she didn't leave until the following morning. They were on the way by sunup. Paul had still not returned, and Rachel considered leaving him a message but decided against it.

It was a reasonably cool day for September. And it had rained during the night, so the road wasn't dusty as it might have been. She sat in the swaying coach and tried not to think of much. Few of her thoughts would be pleasant. Having made up her mind to take this step, she preferred not to dwell on it.

By noon they were in the small village square, asking directions to the Crandall house. "Aye, the forge. Just down there bout half a mile." The man pointed with a sturdy arm bronzed by a summer working the fields.

Rachel motioned the driver forward and pondered this new element. She'd not known the boy was a smith. Did that bode well or ill? Well, she decided; craftsmen were often intelligent. If Jonathan Crandall was bright enough to recognize an opportunity, her task would be easier.

He was standing by the anvil when she arrived. Not hammering yet, but with his arm raised as if he meant to start. He looked up when he saw the carriage and left his work to approach the vehicle. "Good afternoon," he said politely. "Can I help thee?"

He was squinting into the shaded interior, and Rachel knew he didn't recognize her. "I'm Sophia's mother," she said. "I've come to see my daughter."

Jonathan smiled. "I'm glad thee is here, Mrs. Amory. Thee is welcome. Sophia will be pleased."

Rachel grimaced. He didn't seem to know Sophia as well as she did. Nonetheless, she let him help her out of the coach and lead her to the front door. "Sophia," he called from the front hall, "thee has a visitor."

She came in, wiping her hands on her apron. There was a smudge of flour on her nose. When she saw Rachel she stood stock-still for a second or two then said, "Hello Mother. We didn't expect thee—I mean you." It struck Sophia that using the Friends' speech would heap coals on the flame of the dispute. All her instincts told her that would displease Jonathan. The thought flitted through her mind quickly, in the seconds it took her to speak her cool greeting. She saw her mother raise her eyebrows at the obvious correction and waited for her reaction.

But Rachel only said, "No, I know you didn't expect me."

The two women looked at each other and Jonathan sought a way to bridge the awkwardness. "Please come into the sitting room, Mrs. Amory. Thee must be tired from the journey. Sophia, get some refreshments for thy mother."

Rachel waited until the pitcher of cider was produced. "The first of the season," Jonathan said, trying to make conversation. He offered to take her bonnet, but she said she would keep it.

The awkward silence descended again. Finally, Rachel took a deep breath and began speaking: "I have not much time and it is foolish to mince words. You both know I disapprove of this match. I think, Sophia, you were cruelly disobedient to deceive me as you did." The girl started to say something but Rachel held up her hand. "Let me finish, please. I haven't come to berate you, however much I think you deserve it. What's done is done. I've come to say that despite everything, you are still my daughter. And you"—she turned to Crandall—"are now my son-in-law."

She rose then, needing motion to help her marshall her thoughts. Rachel always paced when she was making an argument. Now she walked up and down in front of the windows of the small sitting room. Outside she could see stakes tied with bits of white cloth and newly turned earth. An incipient garden. It passed back and forth before her eyes as she spoke.

"I presume, Mr. Crandall, that you are aware of the nature and extent of the Amory markets. You may not know that I—that is, my husband and I . . ." A lie, she'd done it alone, but it suited her purposes. "We built those markets from nothing. We worked and planned and struggled to create a legacy for our children—Sophia as much as her brothers. It is not my intention to see Sophia cheated of that legacy, despite her disobedience."

"Mother, I think you should—"

"Be quiet, Sophia." Jonathan's voice was gentle but firm. "Thy mother has more to say. Let her finish."

"Thank you, Mr. Crandall." Rachel nodded at the boy in appreciation and continued: "I'm nearly done, anyway. I simply came to tell you that, despite everything, I will permit—" She bit her lip. It was a time for absolute honesty, not pride. "I want you to take your rightful place. Both of you. You may come into the business, Mr. Crandall. We will train you and in future years you will share an equal inheritance with my two sons." She sat down and waited.

Sophia was struck dumb. She knew how uncharacteristic of her mother was this swift and frank reversal. Jonathan was deeply moved. He swallowed hard a couple of times before he spoke. "Thy generosity is a great kindness, Mrs. Amory. I shall never forget it."

"Good, that's settled then." Rachel sighed and took a long drink of cider.

"I don't think you understand, Mother." Sophia remained in her chair as she spoke, her hands folded in her lap. "Jonathan means that he is grateful for the offer. So am I. But we cannot accept."

"Nonsense!" Rachel said quickly. "Sophia, I've swallowed my pride and come here. Can't you swallow yours?"

"It's not pride, Mama. I do so want you to understand that. You mustn't think I'm spiting you or anything—"

"What Sophia means," Jonathan interjected, "is that I've no interest in being a man of business. We have discussed all this before, Mrs. Amory. Thee must not imagine it is a hasty decision. I told Sophia my feelings before we married, so she should not wed me with any false ideas."

"Jonathan loves this place, Mama, this land. Surely thee can understand that." The girl's voice was strained with anguish. Tension made her forget herself and use the Friends' speech. "He's a farmer, and I want nothing but to be a farmer's wife—Jonathan's wife." Sophia knew that any chance of peace between her mother and herself was being systematically destroyed, but she couldn't do anything about it.

Rachel seemed to note only her daughter's use of "thee," not the import of her words. "Have you become a Quaker, Sophia?" she asked quietly.

The girl was startled by the digression. "I can't say for sure," she answered honestly. "I go to Meeting with Jonathan and I use his speech, but I don't think I'm a Quaker. At least not yet."

"God speaks to our hearts in His own time, Mrs. Amory. I pray He will speak to Sophia's, but that is between her and God. I make no demands."

Rachel smiled but there was no warmth in it. "I see. And you make no demands of life either. Is that it? You're content to grub a living out of this . . . this marshland and let an opportunity like Amory's markets pass you by." She rose and started for the door. "There is nothing more for us to discuss. I came to offer, not to plead. I'll leave you both to your chores. I'm told they are numerous in a place like this."

The young people watched her but they said nothing. Then,

just before she left, Rachel turned to her daughter. "Your grandmother died a month ago. She left this for you." She removed the brown paper package from the satchel she carried and set it on the table. "Good-bye, Sophia, Mr. Crandall."

It was late in the evening before Sophia opened the parcel. She held it in her hands for some time before undoing the string. Jonathan sat nearby at the kitchen table, but he didn't speak. He had said little since the events of the afternoon. He'd heard Sophia weeping in the privacy of the barn. He knew his wife was grieving for her grandmother, and for the little death she had endured today. It did not occur to him to intrude at such a time.

Now her eyes were swollen and red-rimmed, but her small, beautiful face was composed. "It's a book," Sophia said after examining the gift. "Written by my grandmother." She passed it to him.

The cover was of heavy linen cloth. On its front was embroidered the Griffin coat of arms: "Azure a bend or. With two griffins rampant." The stitching was extraordinarily fine—even Jonathan could tell that. When he opened the book, methodically, starting with the first page as was his wont, he saw the inscription, "A Herbal for Sophia: Her Legacy." Inside were lists of plants with an inked sketch and a description of the properties and propagation of each.

"There are receipts in the back," Sophia said. "Her methods of making simples and such."

"It seems a fine thing," Jonathan said. "Thee has been given a treasure, Sophia."

She nodded solemnly.

11

Rachel wasn't there when Paul returned to The Roses. Just as well. He would prefer to see Jacob alone first. Many decisions had been made while he lay beside Mattie in the little cabin. Jacob was central to all of them.

"You got some kind o' grief, big man?" she asked him that first night. "I think you needs Mattie cause you is a sad man."

"You make me happy, Mattie," he had said.

It was true. The warmth of her, the giving. It was balm for his soul. Mattie made no demands, didn't try to push him into a mold for which he'd never been cast. More important, she made no demands on herself. That was the worst thing between him and Rachel. The way his wife would not allow herself just to be and feel. With the mulatto woman there was nothing like that.

Her lovemaking was easy, even playful. She kissed him and allowed herself to be kissed. She explored his body with interest and affection and offered her own in like manner. Mattie enjoyed sex; she seemed to enjoy him. "I like you, big man," she said, smiling broadly. "I likes every part of you. It's all big, inside and out." And she stroked his member with familiarity while she spoke. "This part's nice, but what's in here"—she tapped his chest—"that's nice too. Now love me again. Slow and gentle."

He stroked her full breasts and rounded buttocks and luxuriated in the warmth of her pale brown skin. "That's nice," she said. "That feels good. That first time, upstairs over the taproom, you was like an animal but I knowed it wasn't your natural way o' bein'. That's why I hoped you was comin' back. Now I'm glad you did."

They enjoyed each other thus many times in the forty-eight hours he spent in the cabin. Toward the end, when he was tired and not quite as active as he'd been at first, she chuckled and said, "When you gets worn out with fuckin', I likes you best. Then you's kind o' like a li'l boy and I likes li'l boys."

There was obscenity in neither her words nor her actions, no matter how unbridled. Paul listened to her laughter and knew he would return many times to Mattie's cabin. That's when he decided about Jacob.

He had mourned his inability to choose between what he believed best for his son and his dread of finally losing Rachel. Her love had always been such a tenuous thing. He had fought so hard and long for it. Now he was ready to let go. What he felt for this colored woman had nothing to do with Rachel, but it gave him a foothold and from that position he was ready to stand and defend Jacob, whatever the cost.

On his way home, Paul stopped at the Griffin office on Ship Street and spoke with Charles. "Yes," his brother-in-law told him, "it can be arranged." Charles didn't ask any questions and Paul gave no lengthy explanations.

At The Roses he asked first for his wife, thinking that discussion would have to be dispensed with before anything else could be done. When he learned she was out he sent for Jacob.

"Pack your things," he told the boy. "You're leaving for Philadelphia tomorrow morning on the *Elizabeth G*. You'll be there in two weeks. I will give you a letter of introduction to Mr. Markham."

Jacob didn't dare let himself believe. "But Mama said—"

"I'll deal with your mother. When is she expected home?"

Jacob had never seen his father so calm and so certain. "I don't know exactly. She left early this morning. For Rowley."

Paul raised his eyebrows. "Is something wrong with your sister?" It was hard for him to imagine anything but a crisis of magnitude taking Rachel to Rowley.

"I don't think so. I think Mama just decided to go."

"Very well. Hurry off now, lad, you've a lot to do and a short time to do it in."

"Papa, you're sure . . . ?" Jacob looked at his father searchingly. He couldn't bear another scene and another disappointment.

Paul smiled. He knew the boy's thoughts. And who could blame him? Experience had shown Jacob that in a contest of wills Rachel always won. How was he to know that everything had changed because a mulatto woman laughed when she made love. "I'm sure, Jacob," Paul answered firmly. "You needn't worry."

Jacob's trunks were stacked in the front hall when Rachel arrived in the evening. For a moment the thought struck her that Paul was moving out, making the rupture between them permanent. She had no time to examine her reactions to that idea. Paul called her into the study and told her the truth before she could say a word.

"Jacob is leaving for Philadelphia tomorrow morning. The *Elizabeth G.* sails on the early tide and he will be aboard."

She stared at him for long seconds. She could see the change that had come over him, hear the determination in his voice. "I will not permit it, Paul," she said. But even as she spoke, she suspected she had lost.

"You have no choice," her husband answered. "I am Jacob's father. His training is my responsibility and my decision alone."

"Paul," she said. Her tone was low, without feeling, but she spoke each word with awful clarity. "If you do this thing, if you send Jacob away . . . you know what the cost must be?"

"I know." He reached out a tentative hand as if to prevent them both from tumbling into the abyss that was opening between them. "It need not be like that, Rachel. You don't have to make it so."

She recoiled from the suggestion of his touch. "It's not I who have done this, Paul. It's you. First Sophia and now Jacob. Do you expect me to forgive you for tearing my children away?"

"Not away, Rachel. Just free. Free to live their own lives, follow their own dreams. You saw Sophia today, I'm told. Was she not happy?"

Rachel laughed, and it was a bitter sound. "Happy. I often

wonder at the definition of that word. Sophia is slaving day and night over a scrubby piece of land, a vile little house, and a clod of a husband. At this moment she thinks she's happy because she has defied me. In a few years' time she will have to live with her regrets. I wanted to spare her that. But you wouldn't let me."

Paul sighed. Rachel could never see anyone else's truth because she was so intent on her own. "I think time will prove you wrong," he said. "Can we not wait out that time in peace?" He made his final plea. "I've loved you from the first day I saw you, Rachel. You were Maeve, Queen of the Fairies at the masquerade ball. Do you remember?"

"I remember."

"Has it never occurred to you that if you'd not made that visit to England, we would never have met? Does it seem to you it would be better if we hadn't?"

She shrugged. "You're speaking of the past. I'm looking to the future. We can't change what has happened, Paul. But the future is yours to decide. Jacob need be on that ship tomorrow only if you insist on it."

"He's going, Rachel."

"So be it. It's on your head, all of it." She turned and left the room.

3

THE TESTING

"I cannot praise a fugitive and cloistered virtue, unexercised and unbreathed. . . . Assuredly we bring not innocence into the world, we bring impurity much rather: that which purifies us is trial, and trial is by what is contrary."

—Milton

1

The sailor working beside Antony cursed him again. They were splicing frayed lines and Griffin was incredibly clumsy at the job. His fingers were raw from the effort, but the joins he made still looked lumpy and insecure. Nonetheless the stream of abuse from the seaman named Rickles was a worse trial than his bloodied hands or even the still and sultry weather.

"Look," Griffin said finally. "I'm doing the best I can. Keep your mouth shut, will you!"

Rickles looked up from the coil of hemp and Antony braced himself for an explosion of foul language. It didn't come. "Getting to ye, is it lad? Small wonder. Ten days we been becalmed—ten bloody days."

"I can take that," Antony grumbled. "It's your swearing at me morning till night that drives me mad." He dropped his end of the rope and strode to the railing. Below him the sea was a muddy green. Barely a ripple showed on the surface. "Looks like damned swamp water," he muttered.

"Aye, it does." The seaman was English, but he'd been on the *Notre Dame* for years. Despite his impatience with the boy's ineptitude he seemed to feel the kinship of their common language. When other people were near, they spoke in French. Alone, they reverted to their native tongue. Now Rickles glanced quickly right and left. There was no one else on deck. When he spoke his voice was pitched low and bore a trace of something like fear.

"Tain't natural, lad." he said. "Doldrums like this so far north. We's only about level wi' Carolina. Should be a good breeze still."

"What does it mean then?" Antony sensed the old man's distress but didn't understand it. "Is there a storm coming?"

"Yes. A big one, I reckon. Mind ye, we's been in storms afore this." He glanced at the mizzenmast that had been repaired in Boston. "But I don't fancy ridin' out a real blow with that thing only half fixed."

"Will it give, do you think?" Griffin stared up at the tall wooden spire. Its sheets hung limp and bedraggled, waiting for the wind. "Shouldn't we do something about it now, while there's time?"

The sailor spat into the water and waited to see the distance he'd achieved before answering. "Takes a prudent cap'n to do that sort o' thing."

"And Bonde's not?"

"I knows yer inexperienced, laddie. I didn't take ye for an idiot. Course he's not! That old Frog bastard cares for three things: hisself an' his drink an' his women. Ain't you figgered that out? Like that poor little girl. You know any Englishman would o' took advantage o' her that way?"

Antony grimaced. "She didn't have to—" He broke off. Discussing Cecile LaPointe raised a knot of anger in his throat. He didn't want Rickles to know it. "What about you?" he countered quickly. "If you think so little of Bonde, why do you sail with him?"

"Some o' us is free to make choices," the man replied softly. "Some o' us ain't. Rich folk, don't never understand that." For a few seconds he stared at Griffin as if he were going to say something else. Then he turned and walked away.

Ceci had not come near him in almost five weeks, not since she'd begun sharing the captain's bed. Antony told himself he was glad of it. Why should he waste his time talking to Bonde's whore? Still, he was intensely conscious of her presence on board. Somehow he always knew when she was near. It was as if he'd developed a kind of unwelcome communication with Cecile LaPointe. That night, standing on the foredeck in fog and silence, he knew she had come up behind him.

"Can you not sleep either?" she asked. Her words were edged with a tentative friendliness.

"The weather makes sleeping difficult," he answered stiffly.

"Not for the rest of them. We're the only ones awake."

"Oh, and is the captain asleep then? Comfortable in his drunken, sated stupor? You must be good to him, Mademoiselle LaPointe."

She recoiled from him as if he'd struck her. There was a lantern nearby, and in its dull glow he could see the gleam of her golden hair as she whirled around to stare into the fog. No plaits tonight. The glorious hair hung free to her shoulders. He had to clench his fists to keep from stroking it.

"You despise me, don't you?" she said. "Think I'm just a—what is your English word?—a whore."

"I never said that; you did."

"But it is what you think."

"Why should you care what I think, Mademoiselle? You owe me nothing."

"No." She whirled to face him now, and her green eyes flashed sparks. He could see them despite the dim light, see too the way her wide mouth curved and the appealing tilt of her small upturned nose. "No, I owe you nothing. So why should I take the risk of telling you—"

"Telling me what?" he asked. He took a step forward, knowing he was going to kiss her.

"Nothing. I will tell you nothing. I don't care what happens to you—" He stopped her words with his mouth.

The kiss lasted a very long time. When at last they broke apart, Cecile stood quite still. She had not fought him. Antony's heart was hammering in his chest. He reached for her again, and again she didn't resist. This time he was more demanding. His hands moved across her back; he pressed her to him and felt the softness of her breasts and thighs. His lips moved from her mouth to her ear. "I want you," he whispered. "Now, here... No one need know, not even Bonde—"

She broke from him with a gasp. "Damn you!" She didn't raise her voice, didn't take the risk of disturbing the captain or one of the crew. Still, her whispered curse was as cutting as a scream. "I'd lay with Satan before I'd lay with you. I hope you rot in hell, Antony Griffin. What's more, I have reason to know you will."

The tension was gathering with every passing hour. Everyone on the *Notre Dame* knew the storm was coming. There was not yet even the suggestion of a breeze, but they knew.

"Gonna be a hell of a blow," Rickles told Antony. "Ain't never been in a storm afore, have ye?"

"Only on land."

Rickles chuckled. "Tis a bit different at sea, a bit different." Suddenly his mood changed. "Listen, lad," he said quietly. "You watch yer chances. Could be as this bit o' bother might be a help to ye."

"I don't understand . . ." It crossed Griffin's mind that the old man was somehow referring to the girl, that somehow Rickles knew of Antony's feverish longing for her. "I don't need any help," he muttered. Damn the meddlesome old bastard. What business was it of his?

Rickles pursed his lips and sucked air between his toothless gums. "Don't get high and mighty with me, laddie. Ye got no call for it. I'm tryin' to do ye a good turn. Make o' it what ye will."

They had no time to say more. The wind rose with swift and sudden energy. There was no prelude, no tremulous announcing breeze. One moment they were becalmed as they had been for two weeks, the next the sails were luffing madly and the small barkentine was fighting to steady herself and move.

Antony had no part in the burst of activity that broke over the deck. He knew nothing of setting and trimming those huge sails that had suddenly spread themselves like the wings of a caged bird longing for freedom. All his life he'd dreamed of moments like this, pictured himself in command of a fully rigged vessel sailing before a fierce gale. Now he saw with awful clarity the difference between theory and action. He had read everything written on the subject of sailing, but when the real crisis occurred his book learning was useless. And that's what he was, Griffin realized—useless. No one even bothered to shout commands at him. His worthlessness was as apparent to them as to himself.

Bonde staggered on deck and began giving orders. The weather was sobering him, and within minutes the Frenchman was a changed personality. No longer a drunken sot, he was the captain of a ship in danger. "You," he shouted to Antony just as the rain started, "get below. You're no use up here. Besides, I want to keep you safe." Bonde laughed, an ugly and chilling sound. "I don't want anything to happen to you, *mon ami*. Not to a Griffin."

An hour later they were facing real danger. The wind was coming from the east, forcing the ship ever closer to the shore. And the wounded mast was straining; the sound of its struggle to remain upright was audible even over the howl of the storm.

They had taken in the sails of the mizzen some time earlier—they'd had no choice—but the loss of her spread of canvas made the *Notre Dame* more difficult to control. When Antony went above, driven by the need to at least see what was happening, he was astounded at the degree of list they'd developed.

"We've got to deal with that mast," he heard Marguet shout at the captain. "If we don't, she'll crash and take the others with her."

Bonde yelled back. "Get some lines and a saw. We'll cut her off at the deck level. But we'll have to wait for the lull to do it."

Men were rushing in all directions; the deck was awash. It was impossible to tell if it was the sea or the rain that poured over them. Griffin looked around and knew his first moment of actual fear. A cold hand clutched at his viscera and icy water dripped down his neck, plastering his shirt to his chest. It took all his strength to remain upright.

"I told you before!" a voice shouted in his ear. "Get below. If you come up here again I'll have you shackled!"

Bonde's face was distorted by the curtain of rain. His red-rimmed eyes stared at Griffin. The boy saw hatred and rage in them for a brief moment before the Frenchman moved away. The world was coming apart within Antony. Terrified and disoriented, he staggered backwards toward the protection of the hold. He'd bumped into Cecile before he realized she was there.

"Quick! Come in here," the girl whispered urgently as she drew him into the small cabin assigned to her mother.

Antony's eyes darted across the tiny room. He could just make out a slight figure huddled beneath a mound of blankets. Madame LaPointe. He'd not seen her since the change in her quarters. "Is she all right?" he asked.

Cecile shot a glance in the woman's direction. "She is dying."

"Oh God! I'm sorry, Cecile. Really . . ." Cecile's calm acceptance of her mother's condition startled him. "Is there nothing to be done?" he asked.

"Nothing. I will be with her until the end. That is all that matters."

Her face was so close to his, he could smell the lemony scent of her skin. "Listen," he said. "You stay here. I'll make my way to the stores, get some brandy—"

"No. We're fine. You are the one in danger."

"We're all in danger."

"I don't mean the storm," she said. "We'll ride that out. I know, Jacques told me."

"Jacques" was Captain Bonde. So she was on first-name terms with him. Griffin had no time to react to that, because she was still speaking. "I wasn't going to tell you but . . . Oh, there's no time to explain. The captain's planning to sell you to pirates operating off the coast of New Orleans."

Antony stared at her incredulously. "You're mad!"

"I'm not, it's true!" Her small fists were pummeling his chest in her anxiety to be believed. "You're valuable, aren't you? Son of a rich and powerful family? Don't you see? The pirates will hold you for ransom."

"Are you sure?" He knew she was, even before she nodded.

"Antony, this storm . . . Rickles came in here a few minutes ago. He said the wind is pushing us close to the shore of South Carolina. You could get away. Now, while everyone's too busy to notice."

There was no time to argue or protest. Griffin instantly knew the truth of her words and the wisdom of the advice. He had only to remember Rickles' earlier hints and the way Bonde had looked at him to confirm the story. "Come with me," he said quickly.

"I can't. I can't leave my mother."

"We can take her too." The absurdity of the idea was obvious to both of them. There was no way they could move the old woman. They might just as well kill her outright.

"I'll be all right," Cecile said firmly. "I can manage. I've learned to handle him."

"But to go off and just leave you . . ."

"Why should you care? You think I'm a whore, remember." The acid in her words recalled the bitterness of their last meeting.

"No, I don't. I never meant that. I'm sorry, Cecile—"

"Don't waste time with apologies." She moved away, as if

afraid he would kiss her again. "Or with anything else. There'll be a lull soon. There's always a lull in storms like this."

"Yes, I know that. I'm not so stupid as you and everyone else seem to think I am."

"Good. Then you'll be wise enough to get yourself to some spot where you can slip overboard when the time comes." Then, as a new thought struck her, "Can you swim?"

"Yes. And we're pretty close inland. You can see the shore every time there's a flash of lightning. But I can't chance that; I'll have to try and take the tender."

"Then go, for God's sake! Hurry."

He waited one more moment. "Cecile, why did you tell me? I mean, after the other night . . . You must have hated me."

She shrugged and then smiled. "I am not remembering the other night," she said softly. "I'm remembering the oranges."

"Listen, I'll come to New Orleans, find you, buy your freedom."

She didn't look at him when she said, "Yes, well, it's a nice dream. But as I told you, I can manage."

2

Antony ran his eye over the bay. Perhaps the *Notre Dame* had called in at Charleston for repairs. But there was nothing resembling the French barkentine to be seen. He hadn't really expected it. Still, since arriving here ten days earlier he'd kept hoping. It was October now, two weeks since the storm. Either the *Notre Dame* was at the bottom of the Atlantic or she was in New Orleans. Sighing, Griffin turned away and started toward Tradd Street.

Funny name for a street. They'd told him it was in memory of the first white child born in the province. That was damned funny too. Griffin had seen a few Negroes back in Boston, but he had never experienced anything like the two-color society into which he'd been plunged lately. Darkies were everywhere, fetching and carrying and waiting and running. Most of the things a man expected to do for himself in Boston, as well as the ordinary tasks of servants, were done by black slaves here. All the same, they didn't seem to object to their status. Behind him he could hear their voices raised in song as they worked among the boats at Elliott's Wharf. What would Grandfather say if he was here, the boy mused. Nothing he thinks less of than slavery. But this time maybe he's got the wrong idea...

The thought of family brought him back to the present. When he'd sailed out of Boston two months earlier, Antony certainly hadn't expected to be so quickly retangled in the web of his relations. Now he was confronted yet again with the difficulties, and the privileges, of being Charles Griffin's son.

"Mornin', Mr. Antony. Fine mornin', ain't it." The black woman nodded a greeting. The road was thronged with people, and dutifully she stood aside for Griffin and the other white folk to pass.

The woman didn't seem to count that an indignity. Her grin was broad and even the basket over her arm bobbed with the enthusiasm of her gestures. "I's going to market to get the biggest, juiciest chicken you ever seen, an' the finest oysters. Jus' you wait, Mr. Antony, you gonna have a lunch like you never dreamed of."

"I'm looking forward to it, Lilac." He answered her smile with one of his own.

"Lady Joan, she told me you was needin' decent food after all you been through, and that's what you's gettin' today. Decent food." Lilac laughed as she moved off through the crowd.

Antony walked on, thinking about the solicitous attention these southern relatives had bestowed on him, and clenching his teeth at the thought of the reasons that kept him here.

Allyn Gregory's wife was waiting for him when he arrived at Half Moon House. "Oh, there you are! I was getting a bit worried. You must rest, Cousin Antony, regain your strength." Lady Joan beckoned him to sit beside her on the verandah.

They weren't alone. Half a dozen guests sat with them, invited that they might be regaled with the tale Joan delighted in telling.

"Would you believe it! Antony escaped from pirates and some Cherokees found him on the beach ten miles above Charleston—"

"Not pirates, Lady Joan," Antony corrected softly. "From a French merchant ship. The captain planned to sell me to pirates."

"Well, it comes to the same thing," she said, her gray eyes dancing with the excitement of it all. The others murmured that such dealings were what one could expect from the French. Joan went on with her story, her pleasure increasing as each remarkable detail was revealed.

"Can you think how it would have all come out if the Indians weren't on their way to Charleston to trade? Or if they didn't bring Antony with them? He was unconscious, you see. Couldn't speak at all for three days. Then someone realized he was a Griffin, so naturally—"

"It was Reverend Wills and his wife that took me in," Antony interrupted again. If the story were to be told, at least the kindness of the family Wills should be part of it. "I'd have been a lot worse off if Mrs. Wills was not such a fine nurse. The vicar learned my name and knew I was related to the Ludlows of Blackwater."

"Yes." Joan nodded solemnly. Her face was rather long and narrow, and this morning that trait was accentuated by the high puffy crown of the lace cap she wore. Antony found himself studying her. When he realized that he was comparing this woman's ordinary prettiness to Cecile's beauty he forced his eyes away. He didn't want to dwell on Cecile LaPointe.

"So of course," Joan was saying, "when Allyn Gregory heard that his very own cousin was here in Charleston, a cast-away as it were, he rushed right to the vicarage and brought Antony straight home." She smiled with satisfaction at the rapt attention of her audience.

Antony knew Joan enjoyed telling the story. It gave her a decidedly novel bit of social success. Still, he cringed when he found himself displayed for public consumption like this. His cheeks were red beneath the black beard he'd grown at sea, and he was unprepared for the question one of the ladies asked.

"But Mr. Griffin, I still don't understand. How did you come to be on that French ship in the first place? And how did you escape?"

Joan jumped in before he could answer. Relating the tale was her prerogative and she wasn't prepared to relinquish it. "Now Maryanne, you mustn't ask the first question. It's indiscreet. Antony's still quite young, not twenty yet, and he had a small disagreement with his papa."

She reached over to refill her guest's glass with wine punch and her eyes met the other woman's in conspiratorial fashion. "You know how boys are. Allyn Gregory and I have told Cousin Antony we won't press him about that side of it. When he's ready to make up his quarrel we'll send word to Boston. But the other part! Do you know, my dear, he actually jumped overboard in that storm we had two weeks past and made his way to shore!"

"I had a boat, Lady Joan," Antony interrupted again. "And there was an English crew member who befriended me. He helped me launch the ship's tender during a lull in the storm. Everyone else was busy with a broken mast. I rowed to the coast."

"And did he come with you, this Englishman?" The man who spoke had heard the first bit of news that truly interested him. "Should have thought he'd have been as anxious to get away from those foreign villains as you were."

"No, sir, he didn't," Griffin answered. "Chap's name is Rickles, and he's sailed on the *Notre Dame* for years. My guess is that he's wanted by the British for some crime or other, but he was a true friend to me nonetheless. I didn't expect his aid, but if I hadn't received it at the last minute I'd never have gotten away."

"Damnedest story I've ever heard. Excuse me, ladies, but it is. Proves we English can best anyone if we put our minds to it."

"Careful, Roland. Cousin Antony doesn't approve of saying 'we English.'" Allyn Gregory had joined them just in time to hear the last comment. "He tells me we're Americans, and that's a different thing."

Ludlow's grin was friendly enough but Antony felt compelled to interject a small disclaimer. "I just mean that we colonials have an identity in addition to being English. Grandfather says that—"

"Hmph," Roland said. "Maybe in Boston. In South Carolina, sir, we're English gentlemen and proud of it."

That discussion occupied them all during lunch. Antony did more listening than talking. This was a new world, as different in its way as life aboard the *Notre Dame*. He was wise enough to realize he had much to learn.

"Thirty-eight, thirty-nine, forty!" The man dropped his arm, muscles aquiver with exertion, and let the whip trail on the deck. Rickles's back was a thing less than human. Flesh hung from it in shreds, blood oozed down his naked buttocks and thighs to form a pool below his dangling feet. The man groaned once, a strange high-pitched sound like the scream of a tortured cat. Ceci drew in her breath. She had been sustained throughout the last terrible minutes by the thought that Rickles had lost consciousness. Now that small mercy seemed to be ended.

"Throw a bucket of water over that lump of *merde*," Bonde ordered. "I want him awake."

"Jacques, please . . ." She turned to him, her green eyes pleading.

"Shut your mouth," he answered. His tone was flat. There was little of passion in his anger, only calculated evil. That was the impetus behind his insistence that everyone watch this spectacle, even his mistress and her mother. "Keep saying your beads, old woman," the captain said, turning to Madame LaPointe. "This one isn't dead yet, and he'll need your prayers before he is."

"Let him live, Jacques!" Ceci had to try again, despite the small chance of success. The agony before her eyes demanded it. "You've punished him. And he's a good sailor, I heard you say so."

When he turned to her, the expression on his face was a warning. "You know," he said softly, "I begin to wonder why you're so concerned. Do you feel responsible, perhaps? I saw the way you used to look at the boy." He didn't wait for an answer but left the veiled threat between them. Ceci dropped her eyes and stared at the deck. A rivulet of blood trickled toward the toe of her shoe. She wanted to move away but couldn't. She was still frozen with horror when she heard Bonde's next command.

"Hang him from the yardarm!" he shouted. "And see he doesn't die too quickly."

For two days and nights Rickles's body was suspended from the rigging. They had tied him under the arms, not by the neck. When death came, it was the result of exposure and loss of blood, not hanging. As the ship swayed, his maimed form swung out over the sea, rolling and rocking with the swell of the waves and the lumbering movement of the damaged vessel. His sounds of agony, more squeals than groans, ceased after a few hours. Ceci prayed that he was gone, but she never knew for sure how long he suffered.

Only when they were nearing New Orleans did Bonde order Rickles to be cut down and dropped into the water. Madame LaPointe might have said prayers for his burial if she had been there, but she wasn't. She had died in her sleep that same morning.

"My mother is dead," Ceci announced to Bonde in a voice without any trace of feeling.

The Frenchman shrugged. "You expected that, didn't you? I'll have her body disposed of."

She wanted to scream, to protest, to beg that the body be taken to New Orleans and given a decent burial. But she wouldn't. Not now. In the end he wouldn't comply and he would have had the satisfaction of seeing her beg once more. Left alone in the cabin, Ceci stared at her reflection. What had she bought with her submission to the lust and cruelty of an animal like Jacques Bonde? Some small comforts for her mother's last days, yes. But what of herself?

The eyes that looked out from the cracked glass seemed harder than she remembered. And there was some change in the set of her mouth. I'm learning fast, she thought. So this is what the world is really like. Not the dreams and hopes of Acadia, not the promises of love and justice preached by the *curé* in his little wooden church with the sun coming through the windows lighting the statues of the saints. Life is about dying alone in an ugly little cabin on a ship carrying you to be sold into slavery. Or being flogged and hung from the yardarm to die because you helped a boy escape kidnapping.

It was perhaps the measure of her own death, the death of

hope and innocence, that she could not weep. Not for her mother, or for Rickles, or even for herself. Ceci could only stare dry-eyed at the sea that had swallowed them both and concentrate on her future survival. She had not forgotten Antony's words about coming to find her in New Orleans, but she had little faith in them. Life was rapidly teaching her to believe in no one but herself.

As for the other, deeper mystery, the small unfamiliar emotion that stirred when she thought of Antony, she would ignore it. Romance was as false as peace. Neither could exist for her. She turned from the ocean. Perhaps he had reached safety, perhaps he hadn't. Boys like him, born with all the privileges of wealth and position, maybe they weren't strong enough to weather storms. For her part. Ceci was determined to do so.

3

Ceci found it hard to believe that it was the end of October and the year was 1743. For one thing, every October of her life until now had meant the onset of the frozen Acadian winter. Here in New Orleans the air was soft and warm; and judging by the streets around the harbor, winter would never come. Even from the deck of the *Notre Dame* she was conscious of this perennial summer. In the distance, at the foot of the road leading from the wharf, was a low, spreading tree with reddish-brown bark and broad, glossy green leaves. It bore great saucer-shaped blooms, and on some afternoons their heady scent carried across the water.

"They call them magnolias," Jacques said. "Damn things grow everywhere like weeds. Smell terrible, make me sick."

She looked at him and said nothing. Bonde's inability to see beauty was not a surprise. It was confirmation of all she had come to know about him. The fact that she understood the extent of his evil and was not shocked by it was one of the reasons Ceci found it difficult to accept that the year was still 1743. That meant she was two months short of her sixteenth birthday. Last year, when she'd turned fifteen, she had been a child in Acadia. In nine months she had become a woman who knew that men were vile and life was a cheat.

Ceci sighed and turned from her watching place at the ship's rail. Rain was beginning, a faint warm mist that might continue for hours. Still occupied with her thoughts, the girl walked slowly to the protection of the cabin. She must make a decision, she knew that. No matter how hard it was to predict the outcome, she had to act. The last nine months had changed her life; the seven to come promised far more drastic upheaval.

For days she had been analyzing the dilemma. Should she tell Bonde she was carrying his child or should she not? For the moment he was content to keep her on board while he went about his business in town and the *Notre Dame* was repaired. What he planned to do with her when he was ready to leave New Orleans she didn't know. He could sell her into six years of indenture as previously planned, or he could keep her with him when he sailed back to Quebec. She couldn't decide which way the fact of her pregnancy might tip him.

Quebec . . . Ceci drew the letters of the town into the dust of the table, then wiped them away with a vicious sweep of her hand. What was the point of longing for home, of praying that Bonde would take her back to Canada? Had any of her other prayers been answered? And why should she want to have Jacques Bonde's child?

"Because," she whispered aloud, "because it's my child too. And because maybe this time my prayers will be answered."

He rolled off her, grunting his satisfaction. In the darkness Ceci could hear the sound he made as he drank from the tankard of wine always by his side, and the way his breathing deepened as he prepared to sleep.

"Jacques, wait a moment. Don't fall asleep just yet. I need to talk to you."

"Wait until morning."

"No, you'll be gone in the morning as you always are. It's important." There was no reply. She took a long gulp of air and clenched her fists by her sides. "I'm pregnant," she said finally. "I'm going to have your child."

"*Merde*!" Bonde cursed loudly as he sat bolt upright in the bed. He fumbled for a candle and managed to get it lit, then held it above her face and stared at her. "When?" he asked.

"In May."

"Stand up." She looked at him incredulously and he repeated the command. "Stand up and take off that nightdress." He shoved her roughly from the bed. "Do as you're told and don't waste time."

Then, after studying her carefully in the light of the candle, he said, "Well it could be worse. You don't show yet. It won't cut your price. But I'll have to take care of it right away. Tomorrow, in fact. Too bad, *cherie*. I thought to enjoy you another week or two."

When he led her from the ship in the morning her hands were shackled behind her back. That had been Bonde's response to her attempted escape the night before.

"You're lucky," he told her after he woke to find her creeping from the room. "If it wasn't that I don't want you marred for tomorrow I'd give you a beating you'd never forget." Any idea that he might have been moved by the knowledge of the child died then. And any hope for the future. The only consolation Ceci could find was the revenge she was planning.

"Keep your mouth shut," he had warned. "If you say one word before the deal is finished, I warn you, I'll kill you." Well let him kill her. If he did, it would be in public, with witnesses. This time Jacques Bonde was going to pay.

That thought sustained her as she walked along the wharf and felt the eyes of strangers staring at her with disdain, or worse, with pity. Until now she had been fascinated by the colorful New Orleans population. She'd never seen a black person before, and the Indians of Louisiana looked very different from those she'd known in Acadia. Today she ignored them all. Her head was high and her eyes stared straight ahead. You'll be sorry, Jacques Bonde, she kept thinking, you'll regret this morning's work.

"*Eh bien*, she's a nice bit, I admit that Bonde, but a thousand livres. Ridiculous."

"Nice!" Bonde sat back and smirked at the man. "She's a beauty, Paton. What's more, you know it. Do you think to outwit me with this nonsense about 'nice'?" He chuckled and blew a ring of smoke into the air. "Oh no, *mon ami*. You will pay me. If you don't she will be working in Lafette's house, and you can't afford that. This one is special." He jerked his head in Ceci's direction. A trickle of tobacco-stained spittle dribbled down his goatee. "In a month's time she'll be the most popular whore in New Orleans. I don't think you want her working for Lafette."

The one called Paton got up and walked over to where she stood. Before Ceci knew what he intended, he had ripped her dress down the front and pushed the frayed bits aside. The soft hand with which he touched her had nothing of lust about it. It was the hand of a businessman or a stock farmer evaluating merchandise.

She would not drop her eyes. She stared at him throughout his examination. Even if she had wanted to she could not have covered her nakedness, her hands remained chained behind her back.

"You know . . ." Paton addressed his remarks to Bonde, but he continued to gaze at the girl. "I think she may be difficult. I suspect she has given you some trouble, *mon capitaine*. I don't like to whip my girls. Customers don't like bruised women."

"You don't see any blemishes on her, do you?" Bonde countered. "If she was trouble, wouldn't I have beaten her?"

Paton was silent for some moments. Ceci continued to stare at him. He was much taller than Bonde, and in his own way handsome, even aristocratic. Gray hair but a young face. The eyes were old, however—pale blue eyes with dark pupils that looked as if they'd seen everything there was to see. "Very well," he said finally. "A thousand livres. But she stays here now."

"I get my money now and she can stay."

Paton walked to the desk and opened a drawer. He was starting to count out the agreed-upon sum when Ceci spoke. "Do not pay him, *Monsieur*. He is cheating you."

"You bitch!" Bonde lunged for her but the other man was too quick for him. In a flash Paton had placed himself between the captain and the girl. A knife glittered in his hand. Bonde's breath came in heavy, uneven gasps and his fists clenched menacingly, but he didn't move.

"Speak your piece, Mademoiselle," Paton said softly. "I can't turn around, but I'm listening."

"I'm two months pregnant with his child," she said tonelessly. "In a short time your customers would be totally uninterested in me."

No one spoke for some seconds. Then Paton broke the silence. "Sit down, Bonde. I intend to pay you your money, but I do not intend that you should damage my purchase more than you already have."

Ceci's gasp was audible. Bonde said nothing. He backed to a chair but remained standing. Counting softly, Paton doled out a thousand livres. After that the only sound was the slam of the door as it closed behind the captain of the *Notre Dame*.

"Now," said Paton, turning to her, "come over here and I will cut off those shackles.

Wordlessly she complied. When her hands were free, she accepted the blanket he gave her to cover her nakedness and the brandy he insisted she drink. "Sit down," he said when all that was done. "I want to talk to you."

She couldn't wait any longer to ask, "Why did you do it? Why did you pay him when I told you the truth?"

"You don't like that, do you? It makes you angry that I spoiled your little plan for vengeance. No, don't answer. Listen to me. I paid him because in spite of the fact that what you did was foolish, it was also brave. I admire bravery. I do not admire foolhardiness but in your case the one balances out the other. Do you not realize that if I had done as you expected and canceled the arrangement, you would be dead by now? You would have had to leave with Bonde, and once he got you out of here he'd have killed you."

"I thought of that."

"And it didn't matter? How young you are, *ma petite*. Only children think that cheating someone out of a little money is sufficient cause to die."

"You don't know, you can't—"

"You refer to the things he has done to you, the humiliations? I know. I know all there is to know about men like Jacques Bonde. But I know about women too." He leaned forward and his strange blue eyes gazed deeply into her green ones. "You are very beautiful, Cecile, and I suspect intelligent. Life has dealt you a bad hand of cards but you need not play them. If you wish to, you may exchange them for a new set."

"How?"

"By becoming not a reluctant prostitute whom I must watch every moment as with most of the others, but an ally whom I can trust. I will make you a rich woman, Cecile LaPointe, and a powerful one. Or you will be just another whore for the trappers. It's up to you."

"Why should you offer me such a choice?" she asked after a moment's consideration.

"I have my reasons, my . . . shall we say appetites. Besides, I have never seen a more beautiful woman in my entire life. With my tutelage you will be a vision no man can ever forget."

"You seem to forget the fact of the child," she said. "Can you wait seven months for this alliance you propose?"

"No, Cecile, I cannot. But there are ways to take care of that. The old Indian women know all about such things. Here in New Orleans it is not difficult to rid oneself of an unwanted child."

She caught her breath and he saw the look in her eyes. "So the idea displeases you. You wish to bear the son of a pig like Bonde?"

"It's my child too."

Paton shrugged. It was an elegant gesture. The hand with which he drummed lightly on the desktop was elegant too. Thin and white and long-fingered. "I will remove the burden of that choice from you, *ma petite*. Whether or not you agree to my proposal you will not carry the infant. You're my property and I cannot wait so long for a return on my investment. Now, what do you say?"

She could hear the muffled noise of the New Orleans street through the window. The rich French of the bayou mingled with the guttural speech of the Indians and blacks and the sound of horses and carriages. The window was draped in heavy red velvet, but a thin gap where the curtains met allowed a shaft of sunlight to enter and pick out the colors of the turkey carpet. Ceci stared at it. Never before in her life had she seen such a carpet. It felt soft and warm beneath her bare feet and she thought of the heavy, muddied shoes she had been required to remove before entering this office.

"Very well," she said at last. "I accept. Tell me what I have to do."

4

Hannah knew things. The others didn't suspect that. They thought she was completely isolated in her tower, that she was oblivious to the world outside. They thought she was mad.

She chuckled at the thought and turned from the window that overlooked the broad path to the levee. Allyn Gregory—now he really was insane. He was oblivious to the fact that he had systematically destroyed a plantation once worth a king's ransom, that he was living on the credit of his factor, that in a short time the debt would be called and he'd be a pauper. To ignore such a truth, to allow it to happen . . . Was anything more mad than that?

The skiff she had been watching moved to the levee, and Hannah saw her son and his wife step ashore. In the melee of slaves that surrounded them, hoisting baggage and raising parasols against the November sun, she could just make out the forms of her three grandchildren. Lady Joan produced only daughters—pale, insipid-looking children who disgusted Hannah. No blood in them, no drive. For a while she had thought perhaps it would be different when they were born. Maybe the offspring of that beknighted union would exhibit some of the vigor and drive of their ancestors. But she had known from the first it wasn't so. Her granddaughters were shadows, wraiths. They would burn away in the fire of Blackwater, be drugged by its chimerical somnolence and ease. The reality of the plantation, its demands, needs, and rewards, those truths were not for Allyn Gregory's girls. Hannah realized it though the eldest was but three. Today she spared only one quick glance for the children.

"Dear God!" The exclamation was torn from her and the tower room suddenly crackled with the vibrations of her excitement. "Daniel," she whispered. "Daniel!"

Then, just as the beginnings of joy flooded her being, Hannah realized her mistake. The young man with Joan wasn't Daniel, although he bore a superficial resemblance to him. He was as tall as Hannah's youngest son, as dark, but his walk was more deliberate, not as graceful. The proud way this stranger carried his head and squared his broad shoulders was his own, not Daniel's catlike grace. Her boy was a panther, this one a mountain lion.

She turned from the window and settled into the rocking chair where she spent her days, moving back and forth with a steady rhythm, keeping her eyes glued to the Ashley, waiting as she had waited for nearly three years.

"Sorry, old man, do hope you understand." Allyn's bluff good humor was an attempt to cover the embarrassment of the moment for both of them. "I expect it's rather different in Boston, in a business like your father's. Here in the south . . . Well, we plantation men have many things, but ready money isn't one of them."

"Thanks anyway," Antony said. "Didn't mean to make things awkward, it's just that—"

"No, no, don't apologize. Of course you were right to ask. We're blood kin, after all. That means something here, you know." Ludlow poured them both more wine before he asked, "Mind telling me why you're so anxious to get to New Orleans?

I should think you'd had your fill of the French."

"I have," Antony admitted. "It's just that . . . well, there was a girl on board. She helped me—saved my life, in fact. I promised to find her in New Orleans." He knew he need not further explain to his cousin the seriousness of such a debt of honor.

"Ah, a lady. A damsel in distress." Allyn's smile was broader than it had been. "Now I'm really sorry not to be able to help. But you could write to your family at home, you know."

Griffin shrugged. "It would take months to get a letter through. You know how poor communication is between the southern colonies and New England. Besides, my father isn't likely to be happy to hear from me. I'll have to think of something else."

"Well, while you're thinking, be our guest. Feel free, Antony, Blackwater is yours." Ludlow gestured expansively and included the entire estate in his words. "Stay as long as you like. There's just one thing more: Joan explained about my mother, I trust?"

"She told me Aunt Hannah is ill."

"Not physically, you understand," Allyn said quickly. "It's her mind. Went to pieces after my father died. Having him killed by rebellious niggers like that, after he'd always been so good to the slaves here, was just too much for poor Mama."

"We heard about it in Boston," Antony answered. "Before she died Grandma wanted to come see Aunt Hannah, but she was too old for the trip by then."

His cousin nodded. "Yes, we understood, of course. No need to discuss it further. And Mama is harmless. She just stays up in the tower and doesn't bother anyone. I only mentioned it so you wouldn't be startled if you should see her in the window or something like that."

He rose and led Antony toward the dining room where the lavish evening meal waited. Before they joined the others, Antony asked, "Would Aunt Hannah care to meet me, do you think? I could visit her if—"

"No!" Ludlow's response was sharper than seemed warranted. "No point in that. She won't see anyone. Not even my sister Susannah." He didn't mention that he was the one who'd told Susannah that a visit to her mother would be unwelcome.

"Just forget about it, Antony," he said airily. "She's perfectly content up there."

The days stretched into two weeks as Antony continued to puzzle over the problem of getting to New Orleans. He'd gone into Charleston to see if he could get work on a ship headed in that direction but was unsuccessful. For one thing, trade between South Carolina and Louisiana was practically non-existent due to Anglo-French animosity. For another, he could offer no skills to interest any captain. Griffin's sense of frustration and impotence grew.

Despite his ready acceptance of Allyn's explanation for not lending him the money to make the journey, Antony was puzzled by it. Certainly there was no evidence of poverty in the life lived at Half Moon House or at Blackwater. He'd never seen such lavish entertaining or such luxurious surroundings. The exquisite furnishings and the elegent table of his southern cousins was like nothing Antony had known. Not even Uncle Benjamin, who prided himself on being at the pinnacle of Boston society, served such food and wine or decked his house so splendidly.

Of course, Griffin mused, the darkies have a lot to do with it. The wealth of servants inside and out shaped the style of the plantation. Allyn Gregory, for instance, did nothing but what amused or interested him. He rode to hounds most mornings, spent his afternoons reading or sleeping, and his evenings with guests. If there was work to be done on Blackwater it was the slaves who did it. Ludlow and his wife never even seemed to give orders.

Walking in the garden on a December afternoon alight with sunshine and the scent of magnolia blossoms, Antony thought about these things, then pushed the thought away. Blackwater wasn't his concern, and he had decisions of his own to make. It was obvious now that the only way he would get to New Orleans was by foot—on his own. The idea was terrifying, but no matter how he tried he could think of no other solution. Getting there, that's what mattered. Keeping his promise to Ceci—

"I do not threaten sir, I inform."

The voice was too loud to be ignored, and Antony looked around him to see who was speaking.

"But it's absurd. You know next season's crop will settle everything."

Griffin recognized the second speaker as Allyn Gregory. Realizing he was standing beneath the windows of his cousin's study, he started with guilty embarrassment. Lately he was becoming a habitual eavesdropper. Still, though he didn't intend it, he heard the reply of whoever was speaking to Ludlow.

"Next season's crop will be the worst Blackwater has ever produced. You can't grow rice in neglected fields with unsupervised help, Ludlow. You know . . ."

Antony reddened and stepped back into the trees. He felt an utter cad. His cousin had shown him kindness and hospitality. Griffin had no desire to pry into his personal affairs.

"So you've come at last," another voice said. "I've been waiting."

She was standing in the heavy shade of the oleanders, wreathed by their grayed leaves and half hidden by the thicket of branches.

"Who the hell!" Not till he realized the creature was a woman did Antony relax his balled fists. "You startled me," he said quickly. "Do you usually come up on people like that?" He hadn't a clue as to who she might be, and in his anger he didn't care. He couldn't see her clearly in any case.

"I don't appear at all," the enigmatic voice said. "But I told you, I've been waiting."

"Look, if you want to talk to me, come out of there." He turned to walk toward a bench on the far side of the garden but a viselike grip descended on his shoulder and pulled him back.

"Not there. Here, on the other side."

She was pulling him through the shrubbery to a clearing beyond. It was completely hidden from the house and Antony hadn't known of its existence until now.

The sunlight after the shade of the thicket was blinding. When his eyes adjusted, he thought he must be dreaming. The creature before him was so thin as to be almost transparent. Her hair was entirely white and hung about her face and shoulders in wild disarray. The face itself was like a skeleton's, a structure of bones uncovered by flesh. Only the eyes looked alive, burning eyes which were a startling shade of blue. Those eyes told him the woman's identity.

"You must be Aunt Hannah," he said softly. "Your eyes are the same color as Grandma's were."

"Yes. My mother is dead, isn't she?"

Griffin nodded, still too stunned to say any more.

"I knew," Hannah said. "I know everything that happens. Like I know what the Jameson's man is telling Allyn Gregory now. Blackwater is going to be foreclosed on. Do you know that, Antony Griffin? Do you know things the way I do?" She was staring at him, examining him with those incredible eyes.

"I know you shouldn't be down here, Aunt Hannah," he managed to say at last. "You're ill, you should be in bed. Let me help you—"

She struck away his hand with a strength that belied her emaciated appearance. "Don't be a fool. There's nothing wrong with me. That's just what they say so they won't feel guilty. And I'm not mad. Do you imagine I'm mad, Antony? Do you think I've locked myself away and gone insane with grief because my husband is dead?"

"No, of course not. I just want to take you—"

Her chuckle interrupted his placating noises. "I have decided you are clever and a worthy ally, like all the Griffins. That's why I'm speaking to you. Don't make me change my mind."

Her laughter was unnerving. It didn't sound quite human. And he was becoming aware of the smell of her ragged clothes. They probably hadn't been washed in years. "I really must get someone to help you, Aunt Hannah," he said with as much diplomacy as he could muster. "You just wait here and I'll call Lady Joan."

"Stay where you are. I'm not finished with you." The command was spoken in tones that brooked no disobedience. Griffin stood his ground and waited.

"I am not a prisoner in my tower," Hannah continued, "whatever those fools think. I come and go as I please and I know everything that happens on this plantation. Just as I know that you need money to take you to New Orleans."

"But how can you . . . ?" He was startled into speech but her glance silenced him.

"I have the money you need right here." She removed a sack from the pocket of her rusty black dress. It could contain cash as easily as not. There was no way to tell. "I see doubt in your eyes," Hannah continued. "Here, take it."

She waited until he opened the little pouch and saw that it was indeed money. A considerable amount. "I have always managed to have a bit of money of my own. Even when Michael was alive . . ." Her voice trailed off and was replaced by that unearthly laughter. "Allyn never realized that. The other children did, but not Allyn. Otherwise he'd have tried to get it by now. But I haven't enough to save Blackwater. No amount of money can save Blackwater while Allyn Gregory remains master."

"Aunt Hannah, why are you giving me this?" He looked at her in puzzled awe. There was something magnificent about the woman despite her bizarre appearance. Some flow of power that reached out and touched him.

"Because you are a Griffin. Because that makes me believe I can trust you. At their best, they are very good stock, the Griffins. You are one of the best."

"But you don't even know me. How can you say that? And why do you need to trust me?"

"I have been watching you," she said. "Every day while you've been here. At first I thought you were Daniel come home to claim his birthright. Then I realized who you are and I decided that might do as well. It could never be a stranger, you see. No stranger can save Blackwater. But blood kin . . ." She stared at him for some seconds before continuing. "While you slept, I watched you. Standing by your bed. And today I was sure."

He shuddered at the thought of this strange person coming unbidden to his room while he lay asleep. "I offered to visit you, Aunt Hannah. As soon as I came. But Allyn Gregory said you wouldn't want to see me."

"No," she said. "Allyn is afraid of what would happen if I learned what he's done to Blackwater. He thinks I know nothing and—" She broke off with an impatient shrug. "We're wasting time. You have the money—now go to New Orleans and do whatever you have to do. Be quick about it. There is little time left."

"I don't understand." He shook his head in confusion and tried to give her back the pouch of money.

Hannah grabbed his wrist as he extended his hand. Her grip

was iron. "I must have your promise first. You must give me your solemn word to return by the middle of February. Your word as a Griffin."

"But I don't know how long my business in New Orleans will take. Besides, I can't just come and go here without an invitation. What will Allyn and Joan think?"

"They are unimportant," she said quietly. "They are dead. Aren't you able to smell the death on them? They have lost Blackwater. It has rejected them. It belongs to me. No, don't speak, just listen. In Charleston you will find a man named Willy Blood. He's a half-breed Choctaw. There's no one knows the country better than Willy. You give him the ring you'll find in that pouch. He'll know I sent you, and he'll take you to New Orleans and bring you back. There's more than enough money there to pay for the trip. When you return, I'll be waiting."

5

Old Zebedee, the slave who tended the gardens around the house, told Griffin who Willy Blood was and why Hannah trusted him. Not that Antony asked. For one thing, he never spoke to any of the niggers; for another, he viewed his strange meeting with Aunt Hannah as a matter of the utmost secrecy.

"You's goin' on a journey, Mr. Antony?" Zeb stood up and leaned on his hoe, a fuzz of white hair the only thing about him not black as pitch. "Goin' to Charleston?"

"Yes, I am. Mr. Ludlow said Nehemiah would have the

skiff ready." Antony shifted his small valise and peered toward the dock.

"That Nehemiah! He so slow it's a crime." Zeb shook his head with disgust. "Wasn't growed up like the rest o' us under Missy Hannah's rules." He wiped the sweat from his face with a red bandanna before he continued. "Long as he's late, Mr. Antony, I thought I'd make bold to tell you—I mean, you bein' a stranger to South Carolina an' all—when you gets to Charleston, if you needs a guide, Willy Blood's the one to see."

"Yes." Antony tried to keep the surprise from his voice. "So I've been told."

"Half white, half Choctaw, that's Willy. But he do anythin' for Missy Hannah's kin. You see, when he was born, the tribe throwed his mama right out. Said she disgraced 'em by bearin' a white man's son. Back then, there was an old Indian squaw here at Blackwater. Name o' Tiki. Comed all the way from Boston with Missy Hannah and Master Michael. Knowed Missy Hannah since she was born. Well, Tiki brung Willy and his mama to Blackwater and Missy Hannah let 'em stay. Gave 'em a cabin o' their own an' everythin' they needed. After Tiki an' his mama died, Willy left. Four, five years ago it was. Lives in town now, but there ain't nothin' he won't do for Missy Hannah. Or for her blood."

The Negro seemed exhausted by his long speech. He resumed his hoeing. Antony mumbled a thank you and started toward the levee. He could see Nehemiah, finally readying the boat to take him to Charleston, and he could feel the eyes of Zebedee following him as he walked away.

"Mr. Antony!" Griffin turned to see Zeb waving farewell. "Safe journey, suh! Hope you comes back real soon."

Whatever Allyn Gregory supposed, Hannah Ludlow was obviously not a silent prisoner in her tower. Antony wondered how the underground relationships between Hannah and those slaves whom she trusted could escape her son. The more he thought about it, the more he realized that a man like Ludlow would ignore any truth that didn't please him.

"You stay here," the half-breed said. "I'll go into town and ask about the woman."

Antony nodded. In the three weeks he had traveled with Willy Blood he'd learned to do exactly as the Choctaw told him. All the time. If he hadn't, they would both probably be dead. Blood had chosen the inland route to New Orleans. At first Antony had protested. He knew it to be a long and perilous journey.

"You got a boat big enough to go by sea?" Willy demanded. "And a crew to sail her?"

"No but—"

"We go by land."

In fact they traveled only part of the distance on foot. The worst parts. Blood led Griffin through swamps and forests in the dead of night when one wrong step would mean certain death. Antony learned to keep his hand on Willy's shoulder and follow his path exactly. When he asked why they must make such dangerous treks without the benefit of daylight, Blood snorted in derision.

"Indians," he explained. "Cherokees. This their land. You ain't no Frenchman, so you's an enemy. If they get you . . ." His tone said it all and Antony was grateful for his caution.

But some days Blood apparently felt they were safe. Then they would travel by water in a canoe Blood seemed able to produce at will. On those trips, Griffin came to appreciate the strength of the French in this territory. Their forts were remarkable, a string of armed outposts that Blood told him stretched from Canada to the Gulf. "Ain't nobody gonna get the French out o' here," he said. "Someday the English will be driven into the sea."

Blood seemed to view that prospect with pleasure, and Griffin knew better than to argue with him. The lesson was well learned. Antony made no protest when the Choctaw left him alone at their campsite at the edge of New Orleans and went to search for Ceci.

"Come on, Cecile! You promised it would be me tonight."

She patted the old trapper on his balding head. "I never did, Raoul. You just dreamed it. Besides," she added laughing, "I saw the pelts you brought in this afternoon. You can't afford me. Better be content with one of the others."

The crowd of men at the bar greeted this with raucous enthusiasm. A few of them tried to fondle or kiss her, but Ceci avoided them with deft movements. "Nothing for free, boys," she said lightly. "Nothing at all."

Eventually she made her way through the throng to the office in the rear where Paton was waiting for her. "Business is good tonight," he said. "It helps when they see you. Even though they can only look, not touch."

"Yes. Well that's how you want it, isn't it?" She stood in the middle of the room watching him, hands on her hips, the green velvet gown she wore feeling soft and luxurious to her touch. Three months since she'd become the belle of Chez Paton, yet inside herself she still harbored a sense of disbelief at all that meant.

Emile Paton wasn't just her master, the man who owned her indenture. For some reason she couldn't understand, he'd become her protector. Cecile wasn't for sale, no matter how much the lusty clients of the house offered to pay. She was an ornament, a spur to their willingness to spend money in the place, nothing more. They all thought she was Paton's woman. Even the other girls thought so. Only Ceci and Emile knew it wasn't true. He'd never touched her. Moreover, he'd assured her he never would.

"I don't care for women that way. Do you understand?" he'd said the first night she spent in the lovely bedroom adjoining his. "It is not for that I brought you here, Cecile."

"But I thought—"

"You thought I was like that pig Bonde, or like one of them." He'd jerked his head in the direction of the noisy trappers and traders enjoying themselves at the bar and in the bedrooms of Chez Paton. "The very thought of it disgusts me! Never forget that, *ma petite*. If you do, everything will be changed."

Ceci did as he asked. She blotted out the terrible weeks aboard the *Notre Dame* and the awful day when she had the operation that destroyed Jacques Bonde's child. She banished the face of the ugly little sea captain and that of the wizened old woman who tore at her insides with her strange instruments and made her feel such pain she wanted to die. They were erased by a conscious act of will.

The only thing Cecile allowed herself to remember was that Emile Paton had saved her from sharing the fate of the dozen girls who lived in his house, or the many others she saw on the streets of New Orleans. Not for her the humiliation of a man's pawing hands and slobbering mouth. No brute could lie over her and force himself deep into her body, none could make her do the awful things Bonde had made her do. All because of Emile.

He dressed her in the finest gowns, paraded her up and down the streets of this young and vital settlement, and when night came she could sleep warm and safe and alone. And all she had to do was remain aloof from the rugged, lusty men of New Orleans. She was Paton's goddess, his good-luck piece. He enjoyed dressing her like a queen, fiddling with her golden hair. Sometimes he even gave her a bath. But the way he enjoyed her naked body, and Ceci knew he did, was more like a father than a lover.

It was strange, perhaps even perverted, but for the first time in her life Ceci had nothing to fear. It was a heady sensation. She knew she could retain it as long as Emile had no cause to suspect her of infidelity to his rules.

"Massa." The Negro known as Pepe stuck his head through the door. "There's a fellow outside askin' fo' Miss Cecile. An Indian, I think. He say he gots a 'portant message fo' her."

Paton raised his eyebrows. "I didn't think you knew any Indians, Ceci?"

"I don't. Are you sure it's me he wants, Pepe?"

"Tha's what he say. Cecile LaPointe. Tha's you, ain't it, Miss Ceci?"

She looked startled. No one in New Orleans knew her by anything but her first name. "Yes, that's me." She turned to Paton. "Perhaps I'd best see what he wants. Maybe he's someone from home, from Acadia."

"How could anyone from Acadia know to find you here?"

"I don't know." The girl shrugged. "But it must be that. Please Emile . . ."

He nodded. "Very well. But don't be long. I want you to go out and sing for them pretty soon. Your little songs please the customers, *ma petite*, and they please me." She could feel Paton's eyes on her back as she left the room.

"Didn't you know I'd come. I told you I would."

"Yes, I know you did. But . . ."

"But you didn't believe me." Antony looked at her. It was hard to believe she was the same girl he'd last seen aboard the

Notre Dame. The golden hair was dressed in the latest fashion and adorned with jeweled clips. Her gown was white cotton embroidered with sprigs of rosebuds and spread over a wide hoop. It made her waist look even tinier than he remembered it being.

"I must say I never believed I'd find you looking like this. What's happened, Ceci? How have you managed?"

She looked about her, afraid that, despite the remoteness of this rendezvous arranged through the Choctaw, she might be seen by someone who could report back to Emile. But there was no one about. The half-breed had assured her that this deserted cabin would be safe. It appeared he was telling the truth.

Griffin saw the fear of discovery in her face. "I wish you'd explain," he said. "First you made me wait nearly a week to see you, and now you act as if we're in some kind of danger. But to look at you . . . Well, it doesn't make sense, Ceci. If someone is persecuting you, it's an odd sort of persecution."

"I never said that," she exclaimed. "I never said Emile—I mean anyone was persecuting me."

"But Bonde sold your indenture, didn't he? Who is Emile?"

Cecile moved away from him. "Tell me about yourself first. What happened after you left the ship?"

He told her the story in a few words, then waited for her to speak. He expected her story in return but all she said was, "I'm glad it worked out so well. Finding your cousins and the plantation and all. I'm really glad."

"Ceci." His voice was pleading. The sight of her reminded him of all the feelings he had tried to suppress these last months. "Ceci, won't you tell me what you're doing here? I have money. I can buy your indenture, take you away—"

"No!" Her voice cut across the space between them like a knife. "I can't start wandering again. I can't. I'm safe here."

"How can you be safe when someone owns you? What kind of safe is it when you're little better than a nigger slave!"

"You don't understand." She was twisting a lacy handkerchief in her hands, but apart from that she seemed calm, even removed.

"I know I don't, but I'm trying." Griffin moved toward her and put his hands on her shoulders. Her skin felt like cool silk to his touch. He hoped she wouldn't guess that he was trembling. "Don't be afraid to tell me, Ceci. I will understand, I promise."

The look she gave him was unreadable. It seemed both sad and scornful. "Do you know what happened to Rickles after you left?" she asked, moving away from him.

Griffin shook his head, unable to fathom what Rickles could have to do with the two of them and this meeting in New Orleans.

"He died. Horribly. Bonde had him whipped and hung from the yardarm. He suffered the tortures of the damned."

"Oh sweet Jesus!"

She took no notice of the shock and pain in his face. "My mother died too. The morning before we reached New Orleans. She was thrown overboard like a sack of refuse. Not even a canvas shroud for her burial. Bonde took her rosary beads because he said they might fetch something in trade with the Indians."

"Look," said Antony. He was recovering his equilibrium now, trying to comprehend the sufferings she had witnessed and endured. "I know it's all been terrible for you. But I've come now. We can go away. If you'll just tell me—"

"Go away," she repeated softly. "To where, Antony? To your cousins and their fancy plantation? Or to your rich and mighty family in Boston? Won't they just adore seeing you bring home a stray from Acadia!"

"It's not like that. We needn't do any of those things."

"No, we can struggle and starve instead." When she turned away from him now, it was with determination and a terrible kind of finality. "Thank you for coming, for keeping your promise," she said tonelessly. "But I am staying where I am. Where I'm safe."

Antony ran after her as she made her way down the track leading back to town. He would have caught her if Willy Blood hadn't stepped into his path. "No follow her," Blood said. "Dangerous."

"But why?" Griffin demanded. "You said you found her in the home of some rich businessman. I thought she must be a servant, but the way she's dressed . . . None of it makes any sense."

"Not servant. Whore."

Griffin stared at him. He wanted to punch the Choctaw but his hands were leaden at his sides. As if they knew before his brain did that the half-breed wasn't insulting Ceci, was merely telling the truth. "How do you know that?" he whispered.

"Everybody in town know. She most important whore in New Orleans. Live with man called Paton, like I tell you. Paton run house where trappers go when they want women. Some say she Paton's woman."

"Why didn't you tell me this before?"

Blood shrugged. "You no ask."

"And that's what she calls being safe." Bile was rising in his throat. Griffin knew he was going to be sick. He strode off into the bushes to vomit, and when he rejoined Blood he was calm and very cool. "Let's get out of here," he said. "I'm due back at Blackwater in less than a month."

For the second time, she had rejected him. The thought tore at Griffin's guts during the journey back to Charleston and it was a worse torture than the swamps or the heat or the danger. Golden-haired Cecile LaPointe apparently preferred almost any man to him, be it a degenerate sea captain or a vicious whore-master. Anguish turned to anger and in a few days he came to terms with the lesson of New Orleans. What was it that poor bastard Rickles had once told him? All women are whores. It was true, and Griffin knew he wouldn't forget it again.

6

The skiff moved noiselessly up the Ashley, her silent passage barely disturbing the black waters and the muffled night life of the banks. "Listen," Antony said suddenly. "What's that?"

"Talking drums," the Choctaw answered. "Quiet. Willy listen."

The dull thud continued, its beat first rhythmic and even, then staccato, distinct, frenzied almost. The sounds bounced off the contorted trunks of the overhanging palmettos, eddied in the drifting Spanish moss, flowed across the river, and enveloped the little boat. It was eerie, unnerving. Antony sat rigid and finally could bear it no longer. "What the hell do you mean, 'talking drums'? What are they saying?"

"Niggers," Blood said softly, "talk with the drums, like Indians use smoke. Young ones don't know how, but old ones, they remember." He listened for a moment more, then said, "Masters, they whip slaves that use drums. Scared of trouble. Big risk." As he spoke, he was turning the skiff toward the shore.

"What are you doing?" Antony asked. "This isn't Blackwater."

"Drums say we turn here. Meet someone."

"You mean the drums were speaking to us? From Blackwater?"

Blood nodded and occupied himself with maneuvering the craft. They neared the northern bank and the moon broke from behind a cloud. Griffin could see the half-breed's small, tough body strain against the pull of the current and win. A black man emerged from the dense growth and approached them.

Antony was excluded from their whispered conversation. He had the distinct feeling that if he tried to intrude, one or the other of these savages would make short work of him. Sitting there like that, a pawn in some mysterious drama shaped by two primitives, Griffin realized how far he had come. The strangeness of this life became truly apparent. Boston, all New England, even all the northern colonies, were something very different from this place they called "the south." He could smell the difference, feel it, see it. For the first time, the excitement of it called to him.

Maybe it was the bitter disappointment he'd left behind in New Orleans, or the delayed shock of finding that he neither enjoyed nor excelled at seamanship. Maybe it was simply the accumulated legacy of being the son of a rich merchant and expected to act accordingly. Whether it was all those things or none of them, the result was the same. Griffin moved up the skiff to where the two natives talked, no longer mindful of the threat their barbarism posed.

"What's the message?" he asked. His tone was quiet, but it rang with authority. He was a white man, a natural master. When he stood, he towered over both the others.

"You no come to Blackwater tonight," the Negro answered. "Missy Hannah, she say you wait here. Come day after tomorrow. Two o'clock. No later."

"You're sure these are Missy Hannah's instructions?" Antony demanded. "If you've made a mistake, you'll be whipped—I'll see to it."

"No mistake, massa, I's sure. Missy Hannah, she tell us to start the drums last week. Every night since then I wait here, watch for you. Now I go home and send word to Missy. You come in two days jus' like she say."

The staircase leading from the upper floors to the entrance of the house was Blackwater's proudest boast. It had been built by an itinerant joiner from England who happened to be a genius. He produced a long sweeping curve that descended with such grace and flow of motion it took one's breath away. Lady Joan often stood in the front hall and examined that staircase; she would picture herself gliding down its length at the next party, greeting her waiting guests in an elaborate gown. Her "entrances" had become famous.

She was standing there on the afternoon of the sixteenth of February, 1744, planning a costume for the ball they were giving in a fortnight's time. It was a date and a day she was never to forget. When she looked up, a woman was coming toward her. At first Joan had no idea who she was.

"Good afternoon, my dear," Hannah said. "Will you please summon Allyn Gregory? I wish to speak with you both."

"Mother Ludlow!" the girl gasped. "I had no idea . . . I can't believe . . ."

The woman facing her was painfully thin, but nothing else about her appearance was remarkable. Her frock was of dark brown, high-necked and long-sleeved and covered with an apron of starched white linen. Her hair was as white as the apron, drawn back into a severe bun so the intense robin's-egg blue of her eyes shone forth—the only touch of color in the vision. When she withdrew a watch from her pocket and examined it there was nothing hysterical or remotely mad in her controlled gestures. "Please do as I ask immediately. We've very little time."

Joan fled to seek her husband. Hannah walked across the hall and threw open the door of his study. It was empty as she knew it would be; no detail of this day had escaped her careful planning. She was conscious too of the unseen eyes watching from every corner. All the slaves knew what was happening. Hannah had arranged that as she'd arranged all else.

"Mama, dearest Mama! I can hardly speak for joy." By the time Allyn entered the room he'd had time to adjust to the extraordinary message his wife brought. "I've prayed that you'd recover, come back to us." He moved forward to kiss her and she allowed the gesture, presenting one creased cheek for his greeting.

"Thank you, Allyn Gregory. I have had many hours to consider the extent of your devotion to me and to your legacy. I'm pleased to hear that you welcome my return to . . . shall we say, return to life."

Something in her voice disturbed him, but he couldn't identify it. Was she mocking, or was it merely his imagination? "I shall send for a bottle of wine," he said quickly. "Something to celebrate—"

"We've no time for that," Hannah interrupted. "And little to celebrate. Joan," she said, turning to her daughter-in-law, "are you aware that Jameson's is foreclosing on Blackwater?"

"Foreclosing! No, you must be mistaken, Mother Ludlow. Allyn, tell her she's mistaken."

"Of course she is, my dear. It's nothing, Mama. I don't know what you've imagined up there all these years. But foreclosure, nonsense!" He waited for her to speak, needed the time that would give him to marshal his thoughts. Hannah was silent. "I admit," Ludlow stuttered finally, "we've had a couple of bad crops. There are debts of course . . . but next season—"

"Will be the worst ever," said his mother, finishing the sentence. "No, Allyn, it is time you stopped deceiving yourself and your wife. You have made a shambles of everything your father and I created for you. For a long time I didn't see what I could do to stop it. I hoped Daniel would return; then it would be possible. Daniel hasn't come but another opportunity has presented itself. I have made use of it."

"Mama, I don't think you know what you're saying. Come sit down."

"Yes, Mother Ludlow, sit down. I'll get you a drop of brandy."

At that moment a man appeared in the open doorway. "Clark!" Allyn turned to the Jameson's agent. "I wasn't expecting you today."

"I realize that, sir. I had word from your mother asking me to come at"—he glanced at the clock on the wall—"precisely one forty-five. I trust I'm punctual, Mrs. Ludlow." He bowed graciously to Hannah.

"Look," Ludlow said in a voice grown strident with the events of the past half hour. "You certainly know my mother's been ill. I don't know what she's told you, but surely—"

"I've told Mr. Clark nothing as yet, Allyn," Hannah said. "I merely invited him to come. Thank you for doing as I asked, sir."

"My pleasure, ma'am. I always valued your judgment as much as your husband's. I'm honored to be summoned now that you've . . . er . . . returned to society."

Hannah smiled at his polite choice of words. "Good." She ignored her son's attempts to regain control of the conversation and the muttered platitudes his wife was contributing to the meeting. "I trust you can see that I'm not mad, Mr. Clark. I never have been. Merely helpless, as a woman so often is without the proper man to act as her partner. But I've found the proper man now and he should be here any minute."

At which moment one of the house slaves appeared at the door and announced in a tone of solemnity befitting what he recognized as a great occasion, "Mr. Antony Griffin of Boston." The others turned and stared. Only Hannah smiled a greeting.

"I suppose you're here because my mother sent for you, too," Ludlow said finally. "How two grown men can give credence to the fancies of a crazy old woman—"

"Be quiet, Allyn Gregory," his mother said softly. "You are wasting the time of these gentlemen. Theirs is valuable, despite the fact that you choose to fritter away your own. Now, Mr. Clark, I shall come straight to the point."

She had been standing all this time, just as they all were. Now she moved to a large chair by the window and motioned the others to do likewise. Only Ludlow and his wife chose not to sit. "Antony is my nephew, Mr. Clark. From Boston, as you've heard. My half nephew, to be precise. His father is my half brother. But he is blood kin, and he's a Griffin. I don't think I need tell a man in the shipping business who the Griffins are."

The Jameson's agent smiled slightly. "You're Charles Griffin's boy, aren't you?" Then, after seeing Antony's nod of confirmation, he said, "Naturally I'm familiar with your illustrious family, Mrs. Ludlow. Please continue. I don't believe you've asked me here simply to meet your nephew."

"Of course not. I've asked you here to save us both a tragedy. Antony," she said, turning to the young man, "I haven't time to explain the entire relationship between a factor and a planter—"

"I understand it, Aunt Hannah," he interposed. "I was raised in the business. It's not an area Griffin's is in, but I know about it."

"Good. That will spare us a lengthy discussion. Mr. Clark is the Jameson's agent. Jameson's is our factor and they are about to foreclose on this plantation."

"Look here!" Allyn shouted.

"Shut your mouth," his mother said quickly. "If you interrupt again, I'll have the slaves remove you from this room."

He stared at her incredulously; but he knew she meant it and, what's more, could do it. In a haze of disbelief and shock, he listened silently to the rest of her speech.

"There is no advantage to any factor in foreclosing." Hannah continued to address her words to Antony. "It leaves them with a holding that is worthless unless they can sell it—which they cannot do profitably if the place has been poorly run—or find someone to manage it. I'm sure Mr. Clark will bear me out when I say neither he nor his company takes any joy from the notion of assuming possession of Blackwater."

The agent signified his agreement and Hannah went on. "I propose that you assume management of Blackwater, Antony. I think I can assure Jameson's that you'll make the place a paying operation again."

"Me! But I know nothing of running a plantation. I've no experience remotely connected—"

"Surely you don't think I'm ignorant of that fact?" she asked.

"He has a point, ma'am," Clark said. "Why should a lad with no experience do better than Allyn Gregory, who was raised here?"

"Because," Hannah answered, "he will care. Antony will make a solemn promise to work ceaselessly until this land is restored to what it was when my husband died. More than a promise, a vow. Do you know any better guarantee than a vow spoken by a Griffin?"

"Aunt Hannah, I—"

"Have you a better prospect, Antony? You've come back from New Orleans alone. I thought you might bring a wife, and that would have been all to the good. But I know you haven't. Your experience at sea was a disaster. Do you wish to return to your family with your tail between your legs and admit you were wrong?"

"I'm not saying I wouldn't be willing," Griffin answered. "Just that I don't know how."

"I will teach you how. You will be my arms and legs, and I will run Blackwater. Do you agree, Mr. Clark? Will you give us three years to pay off our debts? Promise that I will be sole owner of the plantation at the end of that time?" Seeing the flicker of doubt in his eyes, she knew he was still not convinced her plan would work.

"Let me tell you something else before you reply." Hannah rose to stand before the window. The sunlight made a white halo of her hair. Her incredible eyes flashed fire. "I could not have arranged all this without the help of my niggers. Every slave on this plantation wants to see it saved. They've no desire to be sold to some hell-hole of a sugar plantation in Jamaica, or to trust some strange new master here. They will work until they drop to see this place prosper again. I give you my word on that. They know if they don't, they'll be on the first ship headed for the Caribbean. Now, Mr. Clark, I am waiting for your answer."

"I'll have to communicate with London, of course," the man said. "But I shall make a strong case for agreeing with your proposal, ma'am. I think you can count on Jameson's approval."

"I've had enough!" Ludlow was at last shaken from his astonished silence. "This place belongs to me! Have you all forgotten that?"

It was Clark who responded. His tone was mild in the extreme, the voice of an adult explaining facts to a willful child. "As of today, sir, Blackwater belongs to Jameson's. We filed the act of foreclosure this morning—both in Charleston and in London. You do recall that I gave you this date as the deadline for paying what you owe, don't you? It appears your mother knew that even if you didn't."

"You scoundrel!" Ludlow lunged for the man, and Antony shot to his feet to restrain him.

"Take it easy, Allyn," Griffin said firmly. "Nothing's to be gained by a brawl." He was stronger than his cousin, so holding him was easy. Still, he was grateful when Joan moved to her husband's side.

"He's right, Allyn. You must not demean yourself by fighting with these . . . these plotters."

For the first time, Joan was displaying the strength Hannah had always believed she possessed. It was too late and too little and aimed at the wrong goal, but the older woman felt a moment's satisfaction that her long-ago judgment was finally being proved correct.

"I take it, sir," Joan said to Clark, "that Half Moon House still belongs to us?"

"It does, Lady Joan, as well as some half dozen slaves. They and the house were a gift to you from your husband. They aren't part of the estate."

"Thank you. Come, Allyn," she said softly. "We must pack." Then, turning to Hannah and Antony, she said, "We shall be out of here by morning. I only pray it won't be necessary for us to see either of you again after that." Ludlow let her lead him away. He was sobbing and gasping like a little boy after a temper tantrum.

Antony Griffin was still stunned by it all. He sat in the garden at twilight and tried to sort out the day's events, but they wouldn't fall into place.

"You won't be sorry," Hannah said, coming up beside him. "We're going to do great things together, you and I."

He looked at her for some seconds before answering. How different she appeared from the disheveled ghost who'd accosted him in this same garden two months earlier. Only the eyes were the same. They were the eyes of a seer or a prophetess and they frightened him. "He's your own son," Antony said at last. "Your eldest child. Yet you could humiliate him like that, destroy him."

"Allyn Gregory destroyed himself. I tried to stop it years ago, and I was unsuccessful. All I could do now was prevent his taking Blackwater down with him."

"Blackwater's the most important thing in the world to you, isn't it, Aunt Hannah?"

"Yes, and it will become so to you. I know it. I told you that first time, I know things. There's only one danger you must avoid. Do not be seduced by the plantation, Antony. Use it, take from it what you wish, but remain the master. Like pleasuring yourself with a nigger slave. Never, not even at the moment you are enjoying her most, forget who she is and who you are. If you view Blackwater that way, it will give you joy beyond your wildest imaginings."

He stared at her, saying nothing.

"It is important," Hannah continued, "that you understand the legalities. Until the debt is paid this place technically belongs to Jameson's." He could see the pain in her face when she said that. "Afterwards it will be mine. Someday . . ." Hannah let the unspoken promise echo between herself and Antony.

"I always thought," he said quietly, "that women were gentle creatures. I'm just beginning to discover that's an illusion. You're alike, all of you, willing to do anything to protect yourselves and what you see as yours."

"The best of us are," Hannah admitted. She knew he was speaking not just of her but of the girl he'd gone to seek in New Orleans. Willy Blood had told her all about that. Hannah preferred not to mention it at this moment. Instead, she said, "I remember my mother writing that you were very close to Tonyjay while you were growing up."

"Yes. I've been thinking about Grandpa. He'd disapprove of all this. He hates the slave system."

"I know, but only because he doesn't understand it. You must write to him, Antony. Whatever your quarrel with your father, you must not leave Tonyjay to worry and wonder about you."

"You like him, too. I can hear it in your voice."

"I didn't always. While I was growing up I hated him. But he did me a good turn—more than that, he saved me from a life of misery. When Michael Ludlow and I wished to marry, the entire family was against it because... Never mind, it's a long story. Let us just say I admire Tonyjay and I'm grateful to him. Will you write to him? Tomorrow?"

"Yes."

"Good. After that we can begin."

BOOK II

1746 – 1755

1

THE HEIRESS

"In the beginning there was no fire, and the world was cold, until the Thunders sent their lightning and put fire into the bottom of a hollow sycamore tree which grew on an island. The animals knew it was there . . . but they could not get to it on account of the water, so they held a council to decide what to do. This was a long time ago . . ."

—The First Fire,
a Cherokee myth

1

Herbert Markham was judged by his Philadelphia neighbors a virtuous, upstanding man. The opinion was based on the fact that he attended church regularly and no taint of sexual scandal had ever sullied his bachelorhood. The young men whom he frequently received were from the best families; they gathered in Markham's modest house on Chestnut Street to discuss philosophy and other such rarefied intellectual topics, and none were ever rowdy or troublesome. Markham's permanent boarders, two or three equally respectable and inoffensive gentlemen, were known to be paying guests. It was all quite unremarkable.

In fact, Markham had two vices: the one was a lust for food so great it could only be called gluttony; the other, a delight in making mischief. Everyone knew he was fat but they attributed it to nature. None suspected that at midnight, in the privacy of his bedchamber, Markham devoured inordinate quantities of cold joints, stale biscuits, leftover pies, and the like. His cook was accustomed to the disappearance of such items from her larder. She never spoke of it. As to his second weakness, Markham's particular delight was creating trouble without anyone suspecting that he was its author. He had no difficulty whatever in keeping his taste for destructive intrigue a secret.

It occurred to Markham on an August evening in 1746 that he was about to be given an opportunity for gratification in an area that had so far proved sterile. Jacob Amory was treading on dangerous ground after three years of being the most exemplary boarder ever to stay at the Chestnut Street house.

"I tell you," Amory said as he moved up and down the room with the long, graceful strides that were his hallmark, "the enemy's not in London; he's right here within our gates. It's not the stupidity of Parliament or the wrongheadedness of the king that threatens American growth. It's the French."

Will Randall cleared his throat. "We *are* at war with them, Jacob. What else do you suggest?"

Amory made a disparaging gesture. "England's at war—that's not the same thing. I'm speaking of conditions here, not three thousand miles distant in Europe."

Markham's fat fingers caressed the stem of his glass. He seemed to be studying the dark amber color of the sack, but what he was in fact examining was the young man from Boston. Amory was beautiful. There was no other word to describe the exquisitely modeled head, the chiseled features, and the tall, elegant frame. His hair was black and combed straight back from his forehead to end in soft ringlets at his collar. His eyes were blue and sparkled with intelligence and good humor. The mouth from which such persuasive argument issued was turned up at the corners. Men and women alike were charmed by this twenty-one-year-old Adonis, and astounded when he displayed complete unconsciousness of his appearance.

What interested Jacob was ideas; only about principles of government did he become passionate. Markham had tried to find some weakness in the lad, some exploitable folly, but until now there had been nothing. No indiscretions with ladies young or old, no unnatural taste for men or boys—nothing but moderation, clarity, and brilliance. Now there was a hint of a crack in the armor. Amory was so fired by his belief in the duplicity of the French colonists that he actually trembled when he spoke of it. And he lusted for glory, for a hand in shaping America's future. Markham watched and was delighted.

"But what is there to do?" The fellow who asked the question was Stuart Reed, a newcomer to this group. Most of the discussion had been over his head and Jacob's impassioned speech was the first thing he'd understood.

"Do! We've got to rid ourselves of them." Jacob sat down and stared morosely at the floor. He knew as well as any of them what an impossible task it would be to drive the French from North America.

"Can't be done," Randall said. "They're building forts from Canada to the Gulf. We've nothing like the arms or the men it would take to defeat them."

"I know." Amory tossed back a tumbler of ale with unusual speed. "Nonetheless, it is ridiculous to speak of growth in these colonies while we're hemmed in by the French. The entire virtue of this continent is its size and wealth of raw materials. The colonists must be able to expand."

Markham cleared his throat, and the others were reminded of his presence. "Jacob," he began hesitantly, "I'm not one to pretend a cleverness beyond my abilities, but it does seem to me you're all overlooking something."

"What's that?" Amory barely looked at his landlord. He had little respect for Markham's intelligence.

"It isn't necessary to go to war with the Canadians. Not open war, I mean. The greatest part of their strength lies in their alliances with the Indians. If that could be broken, if the savages could be persuaded that the English settlers were their natural neighbors in this land, why the French would be no threat at all. The Cherokees, for instance, they've seesawed for years. At the moment they favor the French. Could be someone might change that." Markham sat back and waited.

Robert Grace looked unhappily around the table. The faces of his five young guests told him his arguments were wasted. "Will you not talk to Franklin before making a decision?" he asked again.

"It's pointless, Robert. You know as well as we do that he doesn't approve. Believe me, I mean no disrespect when I say we would be arguing with a deaf man." The speaker was Jacob Amory. Like the others in Grace's study Amory was a member of the Junto, but this was not an official meeting of the philosophical club Ben Franklin had founded. Amory and his companions had come this night to engage Grace's support for a scheme the Junto had already heard and rejected.

Grace stood up and the visitors sensed their welcome ending. Quickly they finished the last of the Madeira and sack and ale that had lubricated the discussion. The older man shook his head. "You're wrong. I can't dissuade you, I see that. But you're wrong. Oh, not in principle—I grant you that. But the notion of a mission to the Cherokees such as you propose is a lunatic idea. I won't conspire to assist the five of you in throwing away your lives."

There was nothing more to say. The visitors knew their way out. The Junto met weekly in this house, and Amory and the others had been coming here for nearly three years. Grace sat in his armchair for some minutes after they'd gone. He could hear the wind howling around the chimney and he took satisfaction in the warmth generated by his Pennsylvania stove. "Damn fine thing," he muttered aloud. "Damn fine thing, Franklin's stove, practical, realistic." Grace sucked in his cheeks, as was his habit, and toyed with the glass of Madeira he'd poured but not drunk. Suddenly he sprang to his feet and started for the door. Outside, the November wind was more ferocious than he'd imagined. He wrapped his heavy cloak tighter and ignored the icy blast that pursued him all the way to the High Street.

"Robert! Come in, man, you look frozen. Here, sit by the fire."

"Sorry, Benjamin, to arrive so late. I hope I didn't wake you." The look of Franklin's small study indicated he hadn't. The fire roared behind its cast-iron plates and a fresh candle burned on the desk. "You were working?"

"Mmm, doing a bit on that electrical experiment I mentioned to you." Benjamin wore a dressing gown and slippers but his wig was in place and well groomed as always.

Grace found himself examining his old friend with a touch of envy. Franklin was forty but looked younger. Grace didn't think the same could be said of himself. Women, that was the difference between them. Ben might have a roving eye but he managed to preserve domestic tranquillity with his Debbie. Grace wondered if he should ask Franklin how it was done. He pushed the thought away; he'd not come here at this hour to discuss marriage. "It's Amory," he said finally. "He and that crowd of hotheads came to my place tonight."

Franklin nodded, waiting for Grace to continue. He was a good listener; he never hurried a man or made him feel a fool.

Robert didn't seem to want to say more, however. After some seconds, Ben prodded him gently. "This business about a treaty with the Cherokees? Is that it?"

"Yes." Grace sprang to his feet, his agitation showing in the way he pounded his balled fists together to punctuate his remarks. "They're bent on doing it, Ben. Going into the Cherokee country like some damned knights of old on a crusade. Young fools! They wanted me to help them, speak for them at the State House, get official approval. It's suicide. They can't expect me to cooperate in suicide."

"Here." Ben poured a mug of ale and handed it to the other man. "Calm yourself. It's not your responsibility. Or mine either, if it comes to that. We've told them what we think."

"Yes, but—"

"But nothing, Robert. If a man is determined to do himself ill, there's little point in his friends suggesting good in its place."

It was the appropriate response, and Franklin succeeded in quieting Grace's guilt and misgivings before sending him home. Still the news bothered him. Jacob Amory was an extraordinarily fine youngster. For three years Franklin had watched him develop into not just a bright boy but a brilliant young man. Not yet twenty-two, Amory had a clarity of thought that delighted Franklin. So he'd helped the lad, seen he met the right people, tried to shape his thinking. Now Jacob had fallen prey to a dream of glory and it was hard to sit back and do nothing. Besides, there was Amory's family to consider. His mother's people, the Griffins, were friends of long standing; his father, Paul Amory, had been a regular correspondent since the boy first came to Philadelphia.

It was long past his regular bedtime when Franklin took pen in hand and began a letter to the senior Amory. Jacob would not be dissuaded by any arguments from his friends. His father was the only one likely to stop him from pursuing this ill-conceived adventure.

It was cold that night in Boston too—bitterly cold and only autumn. This coming winter of 1747 promised to be a harsh one. Rachel Amory pulled her shawl tighter and moved her chair a little closer to the fire. The empty silence of The Roses seemed a tangible thing, a threat lurking just beyond the door of her bedroom and its circle of warm yellow light. Time was when she'd disapproved of having more than one candle lit in a room, considered it extravagant. These days she had half a dozen and they were all lit the moment dusk approached. She needed their glow to keep her demons at bay.

She held Jacob's most recent letter, not so much reading as remembering its contents. She wasn't staring at the page but at her hands. How thin they had become, how unsteady. Blue veins stood out in a pulsing tracery against white skin. Her nails looked blue too, flat and somehow uncared-for despite the regular attention she paid them. Useless and defiant hands, they refused to do her bidding, like everything else in her life. She couldn't still their shaking no matter how strongly she willed it.

A clock chimed softly on the mantelpiece. One in the morning. Where was Valiant? Did she want to know? A picture sprang unbidden before her eyes. Val and his friend as she'd seen them the month before. She'd turned a corner in the North End, intent on her business, and found herself looking into the window of a coffee house. Her youngest son was sitting with another lad. They were laughing together, heads pressed close, eyes locked. Beneath their table, hidden from the other customers' view but exposed to the street, they were holding hands. Their fingers were entwined like those of lovers. Rachel had stared for a moment then walked on. She'd betrayed none of her feelings at the time, but the vision of that moment still haunted her.

Valiant had always been a difficult child, whining, frightened, weak. The realization of what he'd become had not surfaced in Rachel's mind until she'd seen it behind the glass—framed, protected, held up to her view but removed from her, like so much else. It wasn't just Val who was absent. Paul was not at The Roses either. He almost never was. He was on Mount Whoredom with his half-caste mistress. They had a cabin there, a miserable little hovel hardly big enough for Paul to stand up in. She'd gone to see it one day last year. Drove herself there in the trap and studied the shack for ten minutes before returning home. It had never been her intention to go inside, to confront her husband in his infidelity. She just wanted to know what it looked like, and now she did. Like the memory of Val and his friend, it had become a picture to haunt her dreams.

The hands holding Jacob's letter still trembled. Rachel ignored them and concentrated on the last lines he had written: "...I know it's time I returned home. Three years is long enough to be away. I do promise I'll plan to be back in Boston by next summer. I'm working on a project, something that will bring glory to the name Amory. I know you'll be pleased." Next summer. Could she wait that long? She must. Everything must be held in readiness for Jacob. The house, the markets, everything. Jacob was the future.

Rachel reached for her lapboard and took out a piece of stationery. The nib of her pen was worn, and she changed it before beginning her reply. For some seconds she hesitated. He'd asked for news of Sophia. Should she break her rule of never discussing the girl? Yes. She was his sister, one more link to home. "I'm told," she began, "that Sophia has a new baby. A third son. I'm sure you won't be surprised when I say I don't know his name. Perhaps when you return you can visit her in Rowley..."

She looked up when a particularly vicious gust of wind caused a branch of the elm tree outside her window to scrape noisily against the glass. What was it like, she wondered, in the cabin on Cambridge Street? Did the wind howl through the cracks of that flimsy structure? Did Paul feel the cold and move closer to his mulatto woman for warmth?

2

Jonathan Crandall made a hood for his forge in the terrible winter of 1747. During those days of bitter cold and desiccating winds, when the absence of snow cover made the fields a network of frozen ruts and the dryness caused the water in the well to sink so low he had to lengthen the rope on the bucket, he designed and fashioned a huge wrought-iron canopy. When it was finished and installed above the raised brick furnace, it was a handsome thing. Clever too. Now only a few blasts from the bellows caused the fire to roar into life in the morning. "Twill draw," he had told Sophia. "Just like a fireplace chimney." And so it did.

His satisfaction in the success of his work was nothing compared to that he felt looking at his wife and young family. On this icy March morning he could observe Sophia and the children from his place at the anvil. She was carrying the baby born last September. Hiram they'd named him, after Jonathan's grandfather. The other two were named for Jonathan's father and Sophia's: Stephen aged three; and Paul, two. This morning they toddled after their mother as she inspected the newly planted orchard.

Jonathan could see them clearly, could see also the worried look on Sophia's face. The trees must be the cause. Cold dry weather like this, months of it, was disastrous for young fruit trees. When he looked again an hour later, Sophia was back in the orchard. She was alone this time and she was busy, doing something that involved a knife and a basket. Jonathan watched her for a pleasurable moment. His wife moved with an economy of motion that delighted him. Then he returned to his own work.

After lunch he asked her about the orchard. "I'm taking cuttings," she explained. "It's the wrong time of year for it, but I have to do something. We can't lose all that stock without a trace."

"It's bad then?"

"Very bad. Die back at almost every branch. I've taken slips wherever there seemed to be a bit of sap flowing."

He finished wiping the dishes and watched her while she wrapped the last of the loaves baked that morning. The little boys were all napping, and not a sound disturbed the peace. "Thee is beautiful Sophia," he said suddenly.

She blushed a deep crimson and pushed a lock of tawny hair from her face. "Thee mustn't say things like that," she chided.

"Why not? Thee's my wife. Besides"—he was grinning as he put his arm around her waist and drew her close—"I say it often enough. I have to, it's true."

"But not here like this—in the kitchen!" He did compliment her frequently, usually while they lay together in the big bed upstairs. Hearing the familiar words down here in the middle of the day flustered Sophia. His kiss was even more unnerving. "Jonathan Crandall, stop it! It's not seemly."

"Thee talks too much," he answered. "And anything is seemly between man and wife." She couldn't reply because he covered her lips with his own.

Sophia felt herself give way. Her spine relaxed and she melted against Jonathan's broad chest. The muscles of his arms felt wonderful beneath her fingertips. She moved her hands across his shoulders and tangled them in his red hair. "Oh," she breathed softly when the kiss ended, "thee makes me feel like a girl, not a married woman of twenty-one."

He had just lifted her into his arms and started for the bedroom when they heard the sound of a horse outside. "A customer," she said quietly. "At the forge."

"Yes, I'm afraid so." Jonathan could see the man's shadow from behind the calico curtains of the kitchen window. Reluctantly he set her down. "I'll have to see what he wants."

Sophia kissed his cheek. "Don't be disappointed. I'll still be here later."

"Thee had better be!"

But in the evening Crandall's mood had changed. They sat by the fire in the sitting room and Sophia could see the look of deep concentration on his craggy face. "What's wrong, Jonathan?" she asked.

"Nothing's exactly wrong. I . . . I'm wondering if I've a right to ask thee something."

"A right! Thee can ask me anything in the world, Jonathan. Surely thee knows that." She pushed the sewing basket from her lap and crossed the room to kneel beside him.

Tentatively, almost as if he was afraid, Jonathan lay his hand on her head. She had loosed her bun after supper, and now her hair hung down her back in a shining cascade of brown-gold silk. "Thy hair is the color of autumn leaves," he said softly. "I've never seen such a color before."

"Please, Jonathan, tell me what thee is really thinking."

"About thee, me, our sons . . ."

"We do not make thee happy?"

"Happy." He repeated the word as if it were some strange, foreign tongue. "Sometimes I'm so happy it scares me. The farm, the fact that we're so late in planting, the things that need doing in the forge, nothing is difficult or worrisome when I think of thee and the children, Sophia. I wonder how a man can possibly have such blessings."

"And that's what is making thee look so unhappy? I can't believe it." She took one of his big hands in both of hers and pressed it to her cheek. "Tell me," she said.

"The man who called today. The one who interrupted us. Twas Jeremy Jackson from Hollow Lane. Thee knows him."

"Yes, of course. Not well, but I see him at Meeting every First Day. What did he say, Jonathan? How did he worry thee?"

"He asked about thee. Not just for himself—some of the others deputized him."

Sophia sat back on her heels. "About me! But why?"

"Thee never speaks, Sophia. Never." His voice was heavy with urgency, and he was searching her face as he spoke. "It's almost four years now since thee joined us, but thee never opens thy mouth at Meeting. The others are worried about thee. So am I."

"I see." She rose and went to stand by the fire. Suddenly she felt chilled, as if the March wind had found a way into her snug and cheerful house. "Is it some sort of crime to be silent? A sin?"

"Of course not! Thee knows that, Sophia. It's just that if thee hears the voice of God, then sometimes thee feels the call to share thy truth with the others. It's our way."

"I feel no such call," she said stiffly.

Jonathan stood up and crossed to her side. He took her small delicate chin in his hand and forced her to look at him as he spoke. "But does thee hear His voice, Sophia? That's the only important question."

She was silent for some seconds. When she spoke her voice was low, tremulous. "I can't answer that, Jonathan. As the Lord is my judge, I don't know the answer."

He pressed her to him with a half-strangled cry of pain. "I know," he whispered hoarsely, "I've always known. It's why I'm so frightened. It's nothing to do with Jeremy Jackson or the others. Thee must believe that. Thy heart and thy conscience, they're no affair of theirs. I told Jackson that this afternoon."

"Then why—"

"Us, Sophia! Our joy in each other and our children and our life. It's so perfect. I wake in the night and sometimes I weep for the perfection of it." His words were muffled because he'd buried his face in her hair, but Sophia heard everything. "If the blessing of faith is withheld from thee," he said, "if God gives us all these other things but does not reveal Himself to thee . . . What does it mean?"

She said nothing, but each whispered fear entered Sophia's heart and lodged there, never to be forgotten.

In Boston, Mattie Sills often counted her blessings. They were all summed up in the shadowy figure of the enormous man lying over her in the early spring darkness. She could feel Paul's swollen maleness deep inside her belly, and the flickering lantern they hadn't extinguished etched the contortions of pleasure on his face. "Oh God," he muttered. "Sweet Jesus, it's good." Then, when he was lost in ecstasy and his cock was shuddering wildly within the confines of her hard, narrow loins, he cried, "Mattie, Mattie, Mattie . . ." Just her name over and over as if it were a prayer.

"I don't know why I loves you so much, big man," she whispered when he rolled away and lay with his head cradled on her breasts. "You's got the same equipment as every man I ever knowed. But when you takes me, I feel . . ." She stopped, overcome with sudden shyness.

"What?" He propped his head on his elbow and gazed into her green eyes. "What do you feel? Tell me." His finger traced the full curve of her lips. They were a dark plum color that stood out against her coffee-toned skin.

"I feel reborn," she said softly. "I thought I'd been everywhere and done everything and knowed all there was for a half-nigger girl to know. But I never knowed about love until you came down here, Mr. Paul Amory. Nothin' about it."

Paul brushed her cheek with his mouth and he could taste the salty wetness of tears. He wanted to say something, tell her what she longed to hear, but he couldn't. In the four years he'd been coming to the cabin on Cambridge Street, he had never said "I love you." It was unlikely he ever would.

"It's all right, honey," she whispered. "Don' you feel guilty. I knows and I unnerstan's. Now, is you thirsty? I got some hot rum jus' waitin' by the fire."

Amory lay with his arms folded behind his head and watched her as she got the drinks. God, she was graceful! Tall and slim and knit together like a picture of a jungle cat he'd once seen. When she brought him the mug of rum, he took hold of her wrist and held it. "You know what you mean to me, Mattie dearest," he said. "Don't ever forget that."

"I know." She smiled and her teeth were white and even and exciting against the plum-colored lips. "I know sumpin' else too. That wife o' yours must be the biggest damn fool female ever born on this here earth."

She'd meant it as a joke, but Paul didn't laugh. "Whatever else you can call Rachel, she's not a fool."

"Not about book learnin', I realize that," Mattie said as she climbed back into the jumble of pillows and quilts that served as their bed. "And not about business. Everybody in Boston says what a right smart business lady Missus Amory is. But I say she's a fool cause her husband loves her and he always will and she's lost him anyway. You call that smart?"

He chuckled then, and nibbled playfully on her fingertips between sips of sweet, steaming liquor. "I don't really know, Mattie. But it doesn't change anything. What's all this talk about Rachel anyway?"

"I guess I was thinkin' o' her cause I heared today she wasn't home."

"Oh?" He sat up and the covers fell away from shoulders almost too broad to be real. "Where did you hear that?"

Mattie shrugged. "In the town. I hear lots o' things. Today someone said Missus Amory was gone on a trip to visit all them markets you folks own. Been away more'n a month from the sound o' it. And I was thinkin' I better tell you cause you ain't been home in all that time. And jus' maybe this would be a good time for you to go and check on things."

"You are absolutely correct," he said, slapping her buttocks to punctuate his words. "And you deserve a spanking for being so devious."

"Devious? How I bein' devious?"

"You know I have to visit The Roses every once in a while and you want to be sure I do it while nothing so inconvenient as a wife is in evidence. Right?"

"Sure you's right! *I* ain't no fool, Paul Amory. Not like that fancy white lady you happens to be married to."

The house never showed any evidence of his neglect. Rachel would allow nothing to happen to The Roses, nothing to detract from its status as one of the most beautiful homes in Boston. Paul looked at the garden for a minute or two before going inside. These days two hired men took care of the place that had once been his private paradise. The roses were carefully tied to their supports, the herbaceous perennials neatly cut back and mulched with fallen leaves. Even from a distance he could see that the orchard had been meticulously pruned and the bark of the trees washed with lime water during the winter. Everything done according to the best principles of husbandry. It must be his imagination that made the place look less loved than once it had.

By the steps to the back door a clump of daffodils pushed through the dry, crusted earth. They belied the cold of the April morning with the tender, pale green of their new growth. Amory bent and touched them with one gentle finger. "Reborn," he whispered, "even after a winter like this." The word made him think of Mattie and her statement the night before, and when he let himself into the house he had forgotten the garden.

Maggie, the servant who had worked for them since before Jacob was born, showed no surprise at his arrival. She never did. Her manner of dealing with the strange relationship between her master and mistress was to ignore it. She just went on polishing a bit of brass as if he wasn't there.

"Mrs. Amory is away, I hear," he said.

"Yes, sir," Maggie nodded. "Went on a tour of the markets. She left five weeks ago and is due home in the next few days."

"I see. Is everything all right here?"

"Course it is, sir, why shouldn't it be?"

He ignored the implication of the remark. Neither Maggie nor anyone else believed his presence necessary to keep The Roses or the Amory markets functioning up to standard. They were right; he felt no need to deny the fact. "Is Mr. Valiant home by any chance?" he asked.

"No, sir. Mr. Valiant's not been here for most of the winter. Staying with a friend in the North End, I think Mrs. Amory said."

Paul winced and turned away so she wouldn't see the pain in his face. He knew about Val, had known for over a year. Mattie had told him, and then held his head while he wept for his youngest child. "Some men," she'd told him, "they's born like that. Don' fool yourself you kin change it, cause you can't. Jus' let the boy be." It was good advice and he'd followed it, even to continuing the lad's allowance. But he didn't like to think about Val. He was glad when Maggie changed the subject.

"There's some letters come for you, sir. I put them on your desk."

"Thank you." Amory moved quickly toward the study. It was unusual for him to go this long before collecting his post. If nothing else, he was always anxious to have news from Jacob. But this winter had been so harsh that few ships from Philadelphia had called at Boston. Word on the docks was that ice floes had broken loose from up north and were floating along the coast. He'd thought it unlikely that any mail would have arrived.

The room was cold and unwelcoming. No fires were lit in here now. The pretense of his being in residence at The Roses had been dropped two years earlier. It wasn't dusty though. Rachel wouldn't stand for dust anywhere in her house. Not even in his deserted study. Paul saw the little stack of envelopes sitting in the middle of his bare but polished desk and grabbed them eagerly. The one on top was definitely from Jacob. He'd recognize that hand anywhere. Careful, controlled, and elegant, like everything about his son. There was another he didn't recognize and a third that looked familiar albeit he couldn't immediately place the writing. A moment later it came to him. That was Franklin's scrawl. So, a letter from Jacob and one from Ben Franklin. He'd have much news of how things were going in Philadelphia. Paul settled into his chair, and ignoring the cold of the room, was warmed by pleasant anticipation.

3

"When did this Franklin feller write that there letter?" Mattie asked.

Amory looked up from the personal belongings he was quickly gathering. "Last November. That's just the problem. This damn freeze we've had slowed the ship down. For all I know, Jacob's already gone."

"You gots to go, Paul honey, I see that." Mattie moved to

his side and lay her hand on his arm. "But you mustn't feel bad if you's too late. Why your boy jus' may fool everyone and get his treaty with them Indians."

Paul smiled. "Yes, love, he just might." He hadn't yet had time to sort out his feelings. He had nothing more profound to share with Mattie and little time to do the sharing. "I have to leave," he said, buckling the strap of his valise with a final decisive tug.

"You got everything you need?" she asked.

"I think so. This lot"—he gestured toward the leather bag—"and a few things I packed at The Roses before I left. How's the tide?"

Mattie walked to the door and gazed across the scrub and brushwood that made a rugged ribbon of shore between the cabin and the sea. "Full in, from the looks o' it."

"Good. It's time then. John said the *Lorelei* would leave with the ebb tide."

"Lucky they had a place for you on such short notice."

Amory grimaced. "I'm to have the owner's cabin. That's what comes of being married to a Griffin."

Mattie's green eyes searched his face. "Does she know?"

"Rachel? I don't see how she can. She's not here. Off on some tour of inspection just as you reported."

"Did you . . ." She hesitated, thought a moment, then went on. "Did you leave any word?"

"No." He hoisted the baggage and stepped to the door where she stood. "Why should I?"

"I don't know, jus' seems right. He's her boy too, ain't he?"

Staring out at the cabin's ugly surroundings Amory made no reply at first. The barren, deserted shoreline was stark contrast to the peace he'd found in this odd little hovel. "It seems pointless," he said finally. "There's nothing she can do but worry. I said as much to her brothers, asked them to be discreet."

"They know? Where you's goin' an' why?"

"John and Charles know. Someone had to."

There was nothing more to say. The moment of leavetaking had arrived but it was devoid of drama—too sudden and unceremonious for real emotion. "Good-bye, Mattie dearest. Take care of yourself."

"Good-bye, big man. Come home soon."

"I will. I promise I will." He kissed her briefly and was gone.

Not until Paul was preparing to board the sloop that would carry him down the coast to Philadelphia did he remember Sophia. His custom was to visit her in Rowley every three or four months. He was due such a visit now. Sophia would worry. "You there," he shouted to a boy standing on the dock. "Come here."

The boy did as he was bid and Paul kept him waiting while he searched for a piece of paper. Then he realized how foolish was the notion. Mattie could neither read nor write. If he wanted her to do something he had to tell her, not send a note. "I want you to deliver a message," he told the lad. "To the Bucket o' Grease tavern on Cambridge Street. Go now while it's light and you'll come to no harm."

"Ain't nothin' I'm feared of on Mount Whoredom, sir," the boy said with a grin. "Been there plenty of times."

"Very well. Go to the tavern and ask for Miss Mattie Sills—she's the owner."

"I know," the youngster said, leering. "I know all about Mattie."

Paul winced. "Mind your manners. It's Miss Sills to you."

"Yes, sir." The smirk was barely hidden but he did make an effort to obey. He had to if he wanted to earn a few pennies from this gentleman. Lads like this one knew well how the game was played. "What you want me to tell Miss Sills?"

"Say that I told you to ask her to get word to Sophia that I won't be calling for a while. Until the autumn at least. Can you remember that?"

"Mr. Amory," a voice from the deck of the *Lorelei* interrupted. "Kindly come aboard, sir. We're ready to cast off."

There was nothing more he could do. He turned and climbed the gangplank without even watching to see if the boy set out for Cambridge Street. "Sorry to keep you," he murmured as the first mate ushered him aboard. "Important."

The sailor nodded and turned to issue the order to cast off.

The guides were white but they had the look of Indians—at least to Jacob and his four companions with their unkempt hair, long and tangled, and skins burned brown by the outdoor life they led. Taciturn too—they hardly spoke to their employers, and if they had conversations among themselves the young men from Philadelphia were unaware of it. "They look more savage than the redskins," Stuart Reed commented on the third night when they beached their canoes and made camp. "Don't exactly inspire confidence, do they?"

Jacob merely shrugged. The oldest member of their party of five, a chap named Joseph Deering, nearly twenty-six, said, "I suggest we keep a close eye on our things. It wouldn't do to lose the gifts we've brought for the Cherokee chief."

"No need to worry," Jacob said at last. "The guides can be trusted."

"Forgive me, Amory, I don't see how you can know that. I realize you hired them and you feel responsible, but—"

"They're all right," Jacob repeated with that quiet authority which made him leader. "Save your worries for our mission. We've nothing to fear from these men."

Neither Timothy Hanson nor Will Randall said anything. Still, like Deering and Reed, they eyed the guides with suspicion. There were only three of them, but the Philadelphia party could take little solace in superiority of numbers. The trio of strangers were formidably tough, alike not only in their buckskin leggings and jackets but in their hard-muscled agility and proficiency with firearms and knives. Woodsmen like these would have no difficulty in overpowering five educated gentlemen in breeches and jackets and silk cravats.

Their clothes had been a source of argument when they reached the real beginning of their adventure, at Jamestown in Virginia. They'd traveled by ship that far and it had occurred to none of them to dress any differently than they did in Philadelphia. Then, sensing the encroaching wilderness and with the smell of adventure and glory in their nostrils, they decided to buy buckskins. Two days later Jacob came to the inn where they were lodged after an absence of many hours. "I've hired guides," he announced. "And I'm told we're not to change our clothes. It's important that we approach the Cherokees looking like white men of stature, as unlike them as possible."

The others were prepared to take advice on the matter of clothing but they didn't trust the guides as implicitly as Jacob seemed ready to do.

"What makes you so sure they won't betray us to the French?"

Timothy asked. "I thought we were only to say we wanted to explore, not that we wanted to meet the Indians. We're supposed to be mapmakers, Jacob. We all agreed—"

"I know," Jacob answered. "Something came up. I'm sorry, I can't explain any further. But these men can be trusted."

They'd taken his word because they had no other choice and because he had the kind of natural charisma that usually manages to convince, but they didn't like it. And now they slept uneasily in their rough camp, with the stars like ice chips overhead and the lisping sound of the Roanoke lapping its banks a few yards away.

Jacob wasn't worried but he didn't sleep much either. The extraordinary piece of luck that had come his way in Jamestown seemed to bode remarkable things for the future of this mission. Excitement was a heady stimulant. What none of the others knew, because he'd been asked to keep it secret, was that the tall, wiry leader of the three guides was Daniel Ludlow, his cousin. Amory hadn't discovered their kinship until after he hired Daniel, but it altered the character of the arrangements.

"You know," Amory had said when the fellow whom he knew only as Dan pocketed the money that sealed the agreement to guide them inland, "you do look rather familiar. You're sure we've never met?"

The older man—he was twenty-nine or thirty, Jacob guessed—merely smiled. "I'm sure. I've never been in Philadelphia or in Boston."

Amory looked startled. "How did you know I'm from Boston? I didn't say."

The guide realized his slip. "Well, your accent, for one thing. And you did say your name was Amory. I've heard of the Amorys of Boston."

It was a weak explanation. Jacob sat back, eyes narrowed, and spoke slowly and softly: "I think, sir, you know something I do not. Since my companions and I are about to put our lives in your hands that makes me rather uneasy. Perhaps you'd best return that money."

Dan chuckled softly. "Relax," he said with good humor. "I know who you are, I admit that. Every reason I should. We're cousins, Jacob. I knew who you were the minute you spoke your name."

A barmaid came by then and Amory signaled her to bring

more ale. Not until the tankards were deposited on the scarred oak table, with its countless rings as souvenirs of past drinkers, did he say, "I'm afraid I don't believe you. You don't look like any cousin of mine."

"Don't I? Have you seen a glass lately?" The older man laughed, then tilted his mug of ale and drained it. "It's not most definitive evidence, Jacob, but look at my eyes."

Amory was annoyed with the man. He seemed to be taking this all as some huge joke. And it was outrageous of him to use his would-be employer's Christian name. Despite that, he did look at the stranger's eyes. They were the intense robin's-egg blue of Jacob's mother, his grandmother, and himself. "Griffin blue" the family called it, though it hadn't come from Tonyjay but from Lizzie. "You're a Griffin," he said incredulously.

"Not exactly. Name's Ludlow. Daniel Ludlow."

"Hannah's son? The Ludlows of Blackwater?"

"That's right." Daniel tilted back his chair and fixed the young man with a long stare. "I don't advertise it much. In the circles where I make my way, being the son of landed folk from South Carolina is no asset. But you've made me curious. Coming in here like this with that ridiculous tale about map-making and hiring a perfect stranger to guide you into Cherokee territory. What are you up to, Jacob Amory?—besides suicide, that is?"

Amory flushed with anger. He'd heard that word too often in recent months. "Our mission is secret, sir. But it is neither impetuous nor unremarked by men in high places. Now, do we or do we not have a contract?"

His oblique reference to official backing was based on a vague conversation Joseph Deering and he had had with a small group of men from the Philadelphia Assembly. It had resulted in the promise that if the Cherokees were interested, the government of the province would be interested too. That had meant a great deal to the group proposing to go to the Cherokees but it meant little to Daniel Ludlow. "We have a contract because guiding is my business," he answered. "And because you may as well have a guide you can trust as a French spy. But I don't mind saying, lad, I think you're insane."

They had parted soon after that. Daniel had told Jacob about the clothes and one or two other practical things. His last words had been personal, however. "I'd appreciate one thing, Jacob. I don't use the name Ludlow, as I've explained. I'd rather it wasn't bandied about."

"Of course," Amory agreed. So he'd said nothing, but the coincidence buoyed him up for days. His confidence could even survive the dark cold of the April night on the banks of the Roanoke and the strange sounds of the forest that surrounded them. A few feet away he could make out the shape of a guard sitting by the dying fire. As yet they'd seen only animals, but the guides assured them that the Indians knew they were there, that they were watching. The sight of the sentinel was reassuring, and Jacob rolled over and slept.

4

The carriage Mattie hired was from Frank's Livery Stable on Newbury Street. Its plain black interior was spartan and it struck her as odd that a coach meant to transport the gentry was so bare of comfort. She was content, however, knew she looked fine in her gown of crimson satin and lace. She looked finer than these dowdy Boston women at any rate. All of them so high and mighty, and so all-fired plain. Let them look down on her, she couldn't care less.

Neither did Mattie deceive herself. Of course the driver knew who she was, but he was pleasant nonetheless. More important, he was big and sure of himself and seemed able to make the four horses behave. That was vital. She was afraid of no human being walking on earth, but animals were quite something else.

"First time you been this way, Miss?" the cabbie inquired when they stopped to water the horses at a coaching house near Lynn.

"Yes, first time. I don' travel much." In fact it was the first time she'd journeyed out of Boston since arriving there from Virginia some twenty years past.

"Mmm, I guessed it. I mean, you seemed real interested in the sights and all."

"I is interested," Mattie admitted. "Never realized there was so much . . . so much space out here in the open. But I gots to get to Rowley so we'd best be on our way." She climbed back into the carriage and waited while the driver hoisted himself into his high seat and called softly to his beasts. Once they were under way she allowed herself to watch the countryside rolling past and ignore the man and the horses. For her part, she was glad to think she earned her daily bread in a building that sat immovable on the ground. The touch of spring waking the fields and woods and streams that ribboned by out the window was appealing, but—city-dweller that she was—it made her uneasy.

Three hours later the cabbie drew up to a rambling yellow house on the outskirts of a village. "This is it," he told his passenger. He opened the door and waited politely for her to climb down.

"You sure?" Mattie looked around. The place seemed deserted. Not a sound from anywhere, no faces peering from behind the crisp curtains, not even a puff of smoke from the forge. "Don' look like no one's home," she said in dismay. It hadn't occurred to her when she made the impulsive decision to carry Paul's message in person that Sophia and her family might be away.

"I asked a ways back, ma'am. This is the Crandall house. That's the forge right there. Crandall's the local smith."

"I knows that," Mattie said scornfully. "I ain't blind. But there's no one workin' it, is there?"

The driver shrugged. His job was to bring the woman where she wanted to go. What she found at journey's end wasn't his concern.

Just as Mattie was preparing to knock at the door a very small boy dashed out from behind the house. He was pursued by a young woman. "Stephen Crandall, bring that right back!" She caught up with the child and snatched a trowel from his chubby hand. "Thee is a naughty boy to tease me, now I—Oh! I'm sorry, I didn't realize we had callers." She held the youngster's hand as she walked closer to the dusty carriage. "Thee must want my husband. He's out back. I'll call him."

"You's Sophia Crandall, ain't you?" Mattie took a step toward the girl. "I'm Mattie. Mattie Sills. Your papa's friend."

"Why yes, of course. I see that now." Sophia's cheeks stained crimson. "I mean—"

Mattie chuckled. "Don' be embarrassed, honey. I knows I's hard to mistake for any other woman in this here Massachusetts Bay. Is that your oldest boy? Stephen?"

Sophia nodded. "Yes, he's three. Stephen, say hello to our guest." She prodded the child and he bobbed his head obediently.

"He's beautiful, just like your papa said." Stephen had his father's red hair. It framed his round baby face in straight, soft folds and barely skimmed his eyes—one brown and one blue, like his mother's.

Sophia looked around. "I don't understand. Is Papa with thee?"

"No. I's come to bring a message from him."

They were still standing by the carriage. Sophia suddenly realized she'd been remiss. "I'm sorry, keeping thee out here like this. What must thee think of me! Thee can water thy horses out back," she said to the coachman. "Stephen, run and tell Papa we've a visitor. Please come inside, Miss Sills. My husband is planting but I'm sure he'll join us soon."

Mattie nodded and turned to the driver. "You jus' wait for me, you hear? I won't be long, so don' you go off and leave." Then she followed Sophia to the door.

Inside there was the bustle of settling in the front room and waiting while Sophia stirred up the banked fire to cover the awkwardness. Then the girl excused herself to go to the kitchen and bring refreshments. "I'm sure Jonathan will be right along. Would thee mind waiting a moment? I'll get us something hot to drink."

Left alone, Mattie inspected the room and the view from the windows. It was simple, but wonderfully bright and cheerful. Everything gleamed, from the rag rug on the floor to the polished pine of the tables and chairs. There was even a pewter mug filled with barely budded branches despite the earliness of the season. Outside, she could see the tender green of plants that formed precise patterns against the dark brown earth. "That must be your garden," she said when she heard a step behind her. "Your papa told me all about it."

"It's my wife's herb garden," a deep voice replied. "Sophia can make anything grow. And she knows more about simpling than anyone in Rowley."

Mattie turned to see a man of medium height with well-muscled arms and shoulders bulging beneath his homespun shirt. His red hair and beard told her who he was. "You is Jonathan."

"Jonathan Crandall, ma'am." He stuck out his hand. His grip was powerful and certain. "Thee is Mattie Sills, Sophia tells me. Welcome to our home."

"Thank you." She looked at him, then dropped her eyes. "I was wonderin' all mornin' if I did wrong comin' here. I mean—"

"We are delighted to meet thee, ma'am," Crandall said easily. "Please sit down."

Then Sophia came in with a pot of steaming brew she described as tansy tea and she repeated Jonathan's words. "Please don't apologize, Miss Sills. We're glad thee's come. But the message thee mentioned . . . Nothing's wrong with Papa, is it?"

"Oh no! Ain't I stupid to let you worry bout that. Your papa's fine. But he had to go to Philadelphia real sudden like and he wanted you to know so's you wouldn't think it strange. Him not callin' for a bit, I mean."

"Philadelphia? Is there trouble with Jacob?" Sophia stopped pouring and looked at her guest.

"Nothin' really wrong, honey. It's jus' that your brother is tryin' to do something with them Indians what's sidin' with the French and your papa thinks he better go and talk to him bout it." It was the vague explanation she'd decided on during the journey and she watched anxiously to see if it sufficed.

It did. Sophia sighed and handed the cups around while she spoke. "That's all right then. Papa and Jacob always get excited about politics." A strand of her gold-brown hair had come loose and it fell over her shoulder as she leaned forward. She tried to restore it to her bun with one hand while offering a cup to Mattie with the other. "I wish we'd known thee was coming. I'd have made some preparations, Miss Sills." Her eyes dropped to her frock. She had covered the gray dress with a starched white apron while she was in the kitchen; but compared to the brilliant red satin worn by the mulatto woman, Sophia thought herself a very plain thing indeed.

"Call me Mattie, honey. Everyone does. And don' think you's not a lovely sight, cause you is. Jus' like your papa says."

Sophia blushed again. Jonathan looked from one woman to the other. Certainly the flamboyant creature opposite was unlike any visitor to the forge he could remember. "Will thee stay and take supper with us, ma'am?" he asked to bridge the strangeness that had descended on the group.

"Can't do that, Jonathan, but thank you for your kindness. I's spected back by this evenin'. Business like mine don't rightly get itself started till nine or ten, so—" Mattie bit back the words. Reminding this wholesome pair of the tavern was a mistake. She knew what Quakers thought of women like herself. "I mean—"

Sophia reached out and lay her hand over Mattie's. The contrast was less marked than it might have been. Sophia's skin, tanned by long hours in the garden, was almost the same color as Mattie's. "Please," she said softly, "don't feel awkward. Jonathan and I, we feel we know thee, that thee's a neighbor almost. Papa speaks of thee often."

Mattie's green eyes suddenly filled with tears. When she looked at the girl, Sophia's face seemed blurred. "I almost didn't come," she admitted in a voice barely audible. "I could o' sent someone with a message. That's what Paul meant for me to do. But I wanted to meet you, he's talked bout you both so much, and your babies—"

"Thee must meet the other two," Sophia said firmly. "Come with me. I'll show thee the house and the garden too."

Jonathan watched the women leave the room, then sat deep

in thought for some minutes. His wife was easily satisfied about the nature of her father's errand in Philadelphia. For his part, Jonathan didn't think Paul Amory's trip quite as innocent as it was being painted. Still, he told himself as he rose and headed back toward the field and the potatoes he was so late in planting, it's best if Sophia doesn't worry. Time enough for trouble to come if it must. He couldn't help but notice that the mulatto woman had barely touched her tansy tea. Crandall smiled. Not quite what she was used to drinking no doubt.

"But how do you know what to do with all this stuff?" Mattie asked in wonder. "It all looks the same to me." They were in Sophia's small still-room, a lean-to structure Jonathan had built between the house and the barn. Bunches of dried herbs hung from the rafters and crocks of strange mixtures covered every shelf. Everything was neatly labeled but none of the names would have meant anything to Mattie even if she could read.

"That's fumitory, good for skin ailments," Sophia said. "And that's rue, or 'herb of grace.' It's very helpful for ladies after childbirth. This is loosestrife; it's an excellent physic—" She broke off and adjusted the position of the baby she was carrying. Hiram was contentedly sleeping on her shoulder but at eight months he'd become a heavy weight. "I shouldn't be boring thee with all this," she said, embarrassed. "I do go on about it all."

"I think you's marvelous, honey. And your papa thinks so, too. He always tells me bout all the good you do here in Rowley with your cures and things. How'd you learn so much, a little thing like you?"

"My grandmother started teaching me when I was a tiny girl. Here, if thee will hold Hiram, I'll show thee." She handed the baby to Mattie and opened a cupboard. When she turned back to the older woman pride lit her face. "This is the book my grandmother made for me just before she died. That's the Griffin coat of arms on the cover. My mother's a Griffin—" Sophia broke off, and the words hung between them in the sudden silence.

"I'd best be goin'," Mattie said quickly. "I's kept that driver waitin' more'n an hour already."

Sophia put down the book of herbal recipes and held out

her arms for Hiram. He didn't even murmur as he changed hands. The two women left the still-room and walked toward the waiting carriage in silence. Then, just before they were within the driver's hearing, Sophia stopped and turned toward Mattie. "I understand," she blurted out. The words tumbled over themselves in her anxiety to speak them. "More than thee can realize. At first I didn't. Jonathan heard about Papa and thee when he went to market in Boston, and when he told me I was very angry. Then I saw Papa, the way he looked. After all the years of being so . . . so beaten by her, so miserable. He looked happy—for the first time I could remember. I can't be sorry about that, Miss Sills."

"Mattie," the other woman said softly. "You's supposed to call me Mattie. And I thank you, child. From the bottom o' my heart. For such a little slip of a youngster you gots a lot o' wisdom in that pretty head."

Sophia swallowed awkwardly. She wanted to say something more but didn't know what. Mattie Sills was almost back in the carriage before the girl called out, "Wait! Just one more minute please, driver!" Then she turned and ran toward the still-room.

When she returned she was no longer carrying the baby but she had a small crockery pot clutched in both hands. "Here," she said, thrusting it toward her visitor. "It's potpourri. It doesn't do anything, just smells sweet. I made it last autumn. An old family recipe from England." She was suddenly shy of the simple offering. "It's not very special; I guess thee has many rarer scents."

Mattie was silent while she lifted the cover and inhaled the perfume of the dark powder. "I never smelled nothin' nicer in my whole life," she said solemnly.

Sophia smiled. The pale May sun shone on the tawny highlights of her hair and sparked shafts of color from Mattie's bright red gown. "Safe journey home," the girl said. "I thank thee for coming."

Mattie didn't watch the scenery on the long ride back to Boston. She kept the precious little crock of herbs and flowers on her lap, and every once in a while she would lift it to her nose and savor the indescribable sweetness and sharpness of Sophia's gift.

5

In the four weeks of their passage through the wilderness much changed. April became May and as they inched southwards the air turned first warm, then hot and sultry. Jacob and his party minded the heat. They took to stripping off their jackets and shirts and traveling bare-chested, but that habit was not to last long.

Early on the morning of the hottest day Daniel went ahead to scout the trail. When he returned it was afternoon and the Philadelphians were half undressed. "Put your clothes on, you fools!" he shouted even before dropping his gun. "What the hell's the matter with you, Bill?" he demanded of the guide he'd left in charge. "You want to get them killed!"

The one called Bill, a grizzled, gray-haired man the size and shape of a tree trunk and just as silent, only shrugged. It made little difference to him what happened to the young men. Daniel turned away from Bill with a snort of disgust and signaled Jacob to join him a few feet from the campsite.

Amory was struggling into his jacket as he moved toward Ludlow. They had all learned to do as they were told, but sometimes, as now, they resented it bitterly. "I wish to hell you'd make some sense," Jacob said to his cousin. "What earthly difference can it make? We were sweating like horses."

"Would you prefer to die? Slowly." Ludlow raised a jug, tilted back his head, and swallowed a huge quantity of water before continuing. When he turned again to Amory droplets of moisture dripped from his brown beard and his blue eyes were clouded. "Jesus, you're such innocents. Why the hell I ever agreed to this crazy trip—"

"All right, Daniel," Jacob said. "We'll do as you say. Just explain to me so I can tell the others."

Ludlow tipped the remainder of the jug of water over his head, then wiped his face with the sleeve of his buckskin jacket. The effort seemed to cool his brain as well as his skin. When he spoke again he was calm. "To the Indians, particularly the Cherokees, there are rules, ways of doing things. It's very important. If a man breaks the rules, he's not a man but an animal. He can be neither friend nor worthy enemy. Do you understand?"

"I'm not sure. Taking off our shirts was an infringement of one of their laws?"

"No, not exactly. An infringement of what they see as your law. You are a tribe who wears things like this all the time in public." He fingered the lapel of Amory's velvet coat. "They see you dressed this way in your cities and settlements. If you remove your clothes here in their land, it's a mark of disrespect."

"I see. That's why you told us not to wear buckskins in the first place?"

"Something like that. It's more a question of honesty. The Cherokees value honesty. They know that white men like Bill and Hank and me wear these things. It's our 'badge of office,' as it were." He motioned toward the other two guides a few yards away. "The Indians understand about scouts and woodsmen. They'd never believe you and your friends were like us. It would mean you were meeting them under false pretenses. They would despise you."

"Thank you," Jacob said quietly. "We're all in your debt. It won't happen again. I'll see to it." Ludlow had turned to go when Amory summoned him back. "Daniel," he said, "I wondered . . . I've been meaning to say something . . ."

"Yes?" The blue eyes watched him, waited. "Say something about what?"

"Your mother, the plantation. I wondered if you'd heard the latest news. About her being better, I mean—and Cousin Antony Griffin managing the place?"

Daniel grinned. "I heard. My sister Susannah lives in Virginia on a plantation called Tamasee. I see her sometimes. That's what I was doing in Jamestown when you met me. Susannah writes to Mama and she told me everything. She never was mad, you know—not Hannah Ludlow. I always knew that."

For no particular reason, Jacob stuck out his hand and shook Ludlow's with feeling. "I'm glad. Really. We owe you so much. I'm truly glad about your mother." He felt a little foolish after that. This was neither the time nor the place for such family affairs. Ludlow must think him an ass. "I thought to tell you, in case you didn't know. As a sort of repayment. It sounds ridiculous, I suppose."

"No, I understand. Thanks anyway. How did you know, by the way? I thought you said you'd been in Philadelphia over three years."

"Yes, but my father wrote. They had the news in Boston because Antony wrote to Tonyjay. Our grandfather."

"I know who he is. You're both named for him, aren't you? You and Antony. Antony Jacob, isn't that Tonyjay's real name?" Amory nodded, and Daniel looked at the ground before asking, "What's he like—young Antony Griffin, I mean?"

"Antony? Oh he's a nice enough chap. We're the same age but we never saw much of each other. My father and mother and his . . . well, they're different sorts. Never visited a great deal unless it was weddings, funerals—you know the kind of thing."

"Yes, I know." Memories of an earlier life flitted across Ludlow's mind. Dances, formal dinner tables with candlelight, ladies in pretty dresses. "Sometimes I forget I wasn't born in these woods, but I do know." He looked up then and his expression changed. "Get back to the camp," he said so softly his lips barely moved. "Don't run, but don't waste any time either."

Amory did as he was told. He didn't know what Ludlow had seen, but nervous excitement sent fluttering vibrations up his spine and he could hear his own heart beating. "Something's happening," he whispered to his companions as he joined them. "Just stay still and let Daniel handle everything. Do whatever he says." He noted with satisfaction that all four of them had donned their shirts and coats.

Daniel followed Jacob to the campsite. "Indians," he said quietly. "Over there in the trees. Coming for a close look at last."

The Philadelphians felt a collective thrill of fear and anticipation. They thought to get their first sight of a Cherokee, but it wasn't to work that way. "They's waitin' fer you out there, Daniel," the guide named Hank said softly. "Is you goin'?"

"Soon," Daniel answered. "Not just yet, but soon." He went to the fire and scooped a bit of squirrel stew into a hollow gourd, eating it slowly with his fingers and making exaggerated sounds of enjoyment. Then he filled another bigger gourd with more stew and moved toward the copse of trees on the hill. His gun was left behind, lying casually and in plain sight on the ground.

Amory could stand it no longer. He sidled toward Hank and squatted beside the guide. "Where's he going? What's happening?"

"Cherokees," the man answered. "Up there on the hill. They wouldn't o' come so close if they didn't want to talk."

"Maybe they want to attack," Jacob said. He hoped his voice didn't sound fearful.

Hank chuckled softly. "If they wanted to attack they'd o' done it afore this. That bunch's been followin' us fer fifteen days and nights. They's White Cherokees."

"White? I don't understand." Amory had never heard of a white Indian.

"It's their way," Hank explained. "Cherokees is of two kinds. White and Red. Not their skin, their ways. Red ones is warriors and live in Red villages. White ones is peaceful and live in White villages. Here in these foothills mostly all the villages is White. That's why we come this way."

Gratified, Amory returned to his friends to pass on the explanation. Almost before he'd finished speaking, Daniel returned. The gourd was empty of squirrel stew and Ludlow sported a wide grin.

They slept that night at the same campsite. "We move on tomorrow," Ludlow explained. "We'll have company."

"I take it you mean Indians," Joseph Deering said. "I should like to know what you've told them."

"I've told them nothing. Neither will you if you've any

sense. These aren't the men you want to talk to. They're guides and sentries. And you better decide among yourselves who's to be your spokesman. The Cherokees will expect one of you to be the leader. It will seem a mark of disrespect if you don't have one."

Deering traced a line in the dust with the toe of his boot. The others looked away uncomfortably. "I'll leave you to settle it," Ludlow said. "It's no business of mine. When you've made up your minds, send whoever's to be leader to me. I can tell him a few things worth knowing."

Deering was the only one of the five in any doubt as to who the leader would be. He cleared his throat and waited. When no one said anything, he began the discussion. "I don't like to remind you," he said, "but I put up the money for this expedition."

"With the understanding that you had one vote, like all the rest of us," Stuart Reed answered. "You weren't even in on the idea at the first. Personally, Deering, I never quite understood why you joined us, let alone gave the funds."

"Now look here." Deering's anger was obvious. "That's hardly fair. True I wasn't at the original meeting at Markham's, but ever since you told me of the plan I've been an enthusiastic supporter and I think—"

"Your remark was uncalled for, Stuart," Jacob interposed. "None of us doubt your loyalty or interest, Joseph. Stuart's just nerved up by the circumstances, as we all are. But I submit, gentlemen, that we have no time to waste in squabbles. Everything we've dreamed about is near at hand. Let's decide on a spokesman and have done with it. There's work waiting."

Timothy Hanson was the quietest member of the group. He spoke seldom, but when he did it was always worth listening. He had a keen, analytical mind, and they all valued his judgment. "We need not spend much time deciding on a spokesman to represent us to the Cherokees," he said now. "For one thing, he's not to be an elected leader in the true sense. Among ourselves we're all equal partners in this venture. That was agreed from the first. For another, there's only one among us with the proper qualifications for doing the actual talking to the Indians. Amory's the logical choice."

"I don't see—" Deering began.

"Shut up." Hanson waved the other man to silence. "You do go on about the obvious, Joseph. The job wants eloquence and sensitivity, antennae for sensing the other chap's point of view. I've a better brain than Amory, you're taller and stronger-looking, Stuart here is probably better with the ladies, and Will"—he turned to the fifth member of the party—"speaks better French. None of it means a damn in this instance. Go talk to that guide, Jacob. Whatever he can tell you will be useful."

"First," Ludlow said, "get any notion of 'savages' out of your head. The Cherokees are as civilized as any white man in America. They just interpret civilization as a different thing. They live in villages with a head-man, a *mico* they call him. He's sort of a mayor. There's a council to advise the *mico*—old heads, wise men—and they're all subject to the White chief. He moves from village to village, but you won't be meeting him so that's not important. Whatever you've come here to get, you'll have to get it from the *mico* and his council."

"Do they speak English?" It was the question Jacob most wanted to ask. He thought he knew the answer but he was leading up to another idea.

"Some do, a bit. In this village we're going to there's an old man who speaks English. He'll be the interpreter."

"You know this particular village?"

"Yes. I brought you here with this village in mind. The *mico*'s name is Dayunisi—it means 'water beetle.' He's a good man."

"You speak their language, Daniel, don't you?"

"Enough to get by."

"I thought so. I want to make you a proposition. When we get to the village, stay with us. Interpret for us. If we succeed in what we intend, Daniel, we'll be heroes. What's more, we'll have done these colonies an inestimable service."

Ludlow chuckled, then picked up a handful of river sand and let it trickle through his fingers. "Honor and glory's not my line of country, Cousin. You can have it all for yourself."

"It's not just the glory, damn it! Think, Daniel. You've been up and down this country. Don't you see what a threat the French are?"

"So that's it. I rather thought it must be. You want to woo the Cherokees from an alliance with the French to one with the English." Then, after a pause of some seconds, "How old are you Jacob?"

"I'll be twenty-two my next birthday."

Ludlow lay back and folded his arms beneath his head. The stars hung so close they seemed touchable. "I was your age when I first struck out on my own. That's eight years ago now—"

Jacob cut short Daniel's reminiscences. "What do you say? Will you be our interpreter? You know the Indians—neither I nor my friends do. You could be invaluable."

"Sorry, lad." Ludlow rolled over and faced his cousin. "I've other plans. One more thing. Dayunisi isn't one to do anything in a hurry. You may have to stay in this village for weeks before he'll even agree to take your proposal to the White chief. Then the White will have to confer with the Red chief. All that time you'll be expected to wait with Dayunisi and his people. Some things a man can propose then go away and come back later for an answer. Trades of land or women—that sort of business—but a matter like a tribal alliance requires sitting on the spot and waiting. It's too important for anything else."

"Very well, we'll wait. But I wish you'd reconsider."

"Forget it. I'll speak for you, though. Tell Dayunisi you're my kin and an honorable man. He knows me. As long as you and that lot with you"—he jerked his head back toward Amory's four companions—"do nothing to contradict that assessment, you'll be all right."

6

The Cherokees, Jacob decided, looked rather like Daniel. They were tall, powerful men with bronzed skin, far-seeing eyes, and an ease with their physical selves that he found enviable. The six who waited for them on the far side of the stream seemed barely to look at Ludlow, whom they apparently knew, but they examined the young men from Philadelphia with care.

"What are they looking at?" Deering asked while the open examination continued.

"You," Ludlow said easily. "Just relax and act natural. There's nothing to be afraid of."

"I hope not," Stuart chimed in. "Since you let the other two guides go, we're outnumbered."

"Not exactly," Ludlow said, grinning. "There's six of them and six of us. Don't you think you can measure up man for man against an Indian?" He didn't wait for an answer but turned to Amory. "We'll be climbing the rest of the way, on foot. No horses. It's the Cherokee way of seeing what you're made of. They know you're not used to it and they'll slow the pace; but, whatever it takes, make sure you keep up. It's not far. Should be in the village by midday with any luck."

"We'll keep up," Amory promised. Then, in a low voice, he asked, "Daniel, why did you send the other two guides away this morning?"

"That was our agreement. They were to come as far as these

foothills. That's what they were paid for, and they did it."

"You didn't want them to accompany us to the Indian village?"

"No need," Daniel said brusquely. "You ready?" The Philadelphians nodded, Ludlow muttered something to one of the Cherokees, and the group moved out.

It was a steady, gentle climb, perhaps more difficult for that reason. There were no steep inclines that one could conquer in a few minutes of strenuous effort, only an ever-rising path through a dense forest of pines. The humidity abated and that made it easier, but Amory and his friends were dripping perspiration and breathing with difficulty after the first hour.

The Indians didn't seem to notice until finally one of them held up his hand and called a halt. He said something to Ludlow, who turned to the others. "Rest stop. The one leading there, his name's Achechi, says to tell you to drink only a little and breathe deep."

The break lasted fifteen minutes and then Achechi moved them on. "Buck up, boys," Ludlow said, laughing, "we'll be there in under two hours." He said nothing more, not even to Amory, but he seemed to find the sight of the struggling gentlemen amusing. Every once in a while he'd chuckle softly to himself.

"I'm glad we offer you a diversion," Jacob said at last. "Hate to think all this huffing and puffing was wasted."

"I'm not laughing at you," Daniel said. "I'm thinking about my own business with Dayunisi. He certainly never expected me to return with the five of you in tow."

The village was perched in a hollowed-out cup near the base of a hill. All around were the blue-topped peaks of the mountains; behind lay the dark green blanket of the river valley from whence they'd begun their ascent. "Lord," Jacob breathed softly, "it's beautiful!"

"Yes," his cousin agreed. "I suspect it's not what you expected."

It wasn't. There were some forty structures in the settlement—long, low buildings made of logs with bark-covered roofs. They were arranged in a kind of rectangle with an open space in the center. Behind the houses were small gardens, all carefully planted, most dotted with bent figures working among the crops. At the far end of the village was one log house bigger than its neighbors. From a hole in its roof a spiral of dense smoke curled upwards in the thin, clear air.

"That's the sacred fire," Ludlow explained. "It's never allowed to go out. The square in the middle's where they hold their council meetings and settle community business. Each field belongs to a separate clan, one field that everybody works together. The crops from that one are shared out among strangers or saved against time of trouble."

"It's remarkable," Jacob said. "And you're right. Much different than I expected."

"Yeah, well the Cherokees call themselves the *Ani-Yunwiya*, the 'Real People.' Appropriate, don't you think?" He didn't wait for an answer but strode off into the village with the Indian guides ahead of him and the five tired and disheveled gentlemen from Philadelphia behind.

They weren't in the square for thirty seconds before a crowd gathered. Women and children stared at the newcomers and reached out curious hands to touch the unfamiliar stuff of their clothes while a few old men watched from the rear. Suddenly the assembly fell back and a small, sinewy man with protruding black eyes and arms and legs too long for his short torso approached them.

"You have returned early, Santroyawi, and brought guests in advance of the feast. Why have you done this?"

Daniel bowed low to the old man and said, "It was necessary, Dayunisi. This man"—he pointed to Amory, who had sense enough to stand very still and attempt to look dignified—"is of my blood. Kin of my mother's people. He desires to speak with you on a matter of urgency. I trusted in the kindness of Dayunisi's heart and the wisdom of his head and I brought him."

The Indian gazed from Ludlow to Amory. "You have the look of the same clan, but removed by many generations. How do you share blood?"

"We have the same grandmother, Dayunisi. Her eyes are in both our heads."

The *mico* stepped forward and examined Amory, looking from him to Ludlow and back again. No one moved or spoke until finally the Indian said, "Good. It is good that you bring one of your clan. We will make our feast soon and then we will talk of the matter this one wishes to discuss."

He turned and walked back to his cabin in silence. Only after he had disappeared behind the log walls did the other Indians begin talking and laughing and touching the newcomers with curious friendliness.

Later, when the white men had eaten and drunk and were being entertained by the strange, haunting chants of the Cherokees, Ludlow explained some of what had transpired. "Good thing we're related on our mothers' sides and not through our fathers," he concluded. "The Cherokees recognize kinship as coming through women."

"I see. What I still don't understand is what your business here is all about. You said you wouldn't stay with us, but now you say you're remaining until after this feast they're going to have. Can't we talk to Dayunisi through you before then? You can explain our mission."

"Not a chance, Jacob," Ludlow said with feeling. "If I tried that—or if you did, for that matter—we'd all end up as meat for the wolves. This next week is a sacred time, not a time for talking treaties. Tomorrow I'll be taken to a cabin outside the village to wait and purify myself."

"Purify yourself! What the hell for?"

"For marriage, Cousin. I'm going to be married at this feast."

"Married! To an Indian squaw?" Amory stared at the other man in disbelief.

Ludlow seemed to enjoy the shock on Jacob's face. "Doesn't sound the sort of wife usually approved by our family, does it? Her name's Passayoro. At least that's her name here; it was Marjorie before she was captured."

"Marjorie... You mean she's a white woman? Captured by the Indians?"

"Right. She doesn't remember much except Cherokee life, though. She was only seven when she was taken. That was twelve years ago. I met her five years past but she was married then."

"I don't understand."

"She's a widow. Her Indian husband died last year and I

asked Dayunisi to give her to me. He agreed. That's when they gave me my Cherokee name, Santroyawi. It means 'Gun that sees like an eagle.' Simple enough, isn't it, once you know the details."

"I suppose so." Jacob stared for some moments at Daniel. In the glow of the fire, with his brown hair pulled back and tied Cherokee fashion and his sweat-stained buckskins that looked so much like theirs, he could be one of them. But the blue eyes weren't Cherokee—they were white man's eyes, Griffin eyes. "Will it work, Daniel? You're at home here in these woods, I see that. But will it always be thus? What if you want to return to civilization? How will this poor woman manage that after the life she's led?"

Ludlow looked for a moment as if he might say something genuinely personal, confide something of his plans and feelings to his young cousin. But the moment passed. "Don't worry about Passayoro. She'll manage fine. Any woman who can be a wife to a Cherokee can handle me and anything I have in mind."

Paul Amory was having a very different sort of discussion some five hundred miles to the east in Philadelphia. "I'm to presume then there's nothing further we can do, no other way to trace their movements?"

"I'm afraid that's the long and short of it, sir. According to this information they left Jamestown nearly two months ago with three woodsmen as guides. After that we know nothing." Franklin dropped the letter on his desk and removed his glasses, polishing them slowly while he spoke. "If only my first letter had reached you sooner . . ."

"Yes, that's the pity of it." Paul stood up and his great bulk dwarfed the other man. "Damn!" he exploded, suddenly crashing his fist on Franklin's desk and making the smaller man jump. "Damn, damn, damn! Just ten weeks. If I'd gotten here ten weeks earlier, it could all be so different." He turned away and his shoulders heaved, betraying tears of anger and frustration. "It's all my fault. If I hadn't sent Jacob to Philadelphia, none of this would have happened."

Benjamin rose and moved toward him, stretched out a tentative hand of sympathy, then pulled it back. "Please," he said softly. "You mustn't blame yourself. You did what you thought best for the boy. What *was* best. I wish you could have seen how he blossomed here, Mr. Amory. How he developed. His was often the most stimulating argument at the Junto. No young man was better thought of in all Philadelphia."

It occurred to Paul that Franklin was speaking of Jacob in the past tense, as if he was dead. "That's small comfort under the circumstances," he said. His lapse of control had ended, and when he turned to face his host he was dry-eyed but the pain in his face spoke eloquently. "His mother never approved, you know. She'll never forgive me when she learns . . ."

Franklin poured a glass of sack for both of them. "I remember Rachel well," he said. "Not just our recent dealings, the stoves and that sort of thing. I remember what she was like as a girl. I was in the house frequently, you know. Ben Griffin and I were school chums."

"Yes. I know all that." Then, perhaps because the finality of the news they'd received after weeks of waiting was so fresh and so discouraging, he asked, "What was Rachel like then?"

Franklin smiled. "Not all that different from what she seems to be now. A loyal supporter and a bitter enemy." Franklin sipped his wine and watched Amory over the rim of the glass. "It occurs to me, Mr. Amory, that young Jacob is probably a bit like his mother. We shouldn't be too quick to despair. Perhaps the outcome of this adventure will be very different than we imagine."

Amory left the house little cheered by those words. It was hard to erase the picture of Jacob that had haunted Paul since his arrival in Philadelphia over a month ago. In that vision Jacob's body was lying somewhere in the wilderness and half-crazed savages were celebrating his death. "Oh Jesus," he prayed half aloud. "If there's really a God somewhere, protect Jacob. Bring my son home safe."

Franklin's thoughts after the meeting were less mystical. "This country must have a decent postal system," he told his wife. "We're nothing but a primitive outpost until we do."

7

There it was, the Green Dragon tavern on Union Street. Holding up her skirts with one hand and clutching her breast with the other, Rachel almost ran the rest of the way through the semidarkness. Let him be there, she prayed. Let him know something.

The door gave easily when she shoved, and a cloud of tobacco smoke assailed her. "No ladies, ma'am. Tain't allowed."

"Please, I don't want to drink. I'm looking for Sam Adams. I went to his house, and they told me he might be here."

"It's Mrs. Amory, isn't it?" A second man stepped forward, more socially adept than the dock worker who had spoken first. "Wait here, ma'am. I'll check out back and see if Adams is there."

She leaned against the wall, still breathing in short gasps, knowing her hair was a sight and her gown stippled with mud, not caring. "Can I get ye somethin', Mrs. Amory? A brandy perhaps." The dock worker had decided that a woman of Rachel Griffin Amory's position deserved a modicum of civility.

"No, nothing, thank you." She craned her neck to see above the crowd of drinkers but it didn't help much. All she could discern was a confusion of men's heads, some wigged and some not. The smell of liquor was stronger even than that of tobacco, though the latter not only scented the air but colored it. Blue-gray smoke and the overwhelming reek of flip and rum and ale—it was a daunting combination. Rachel thought she was going to faint and she wondered if her body would fall in this crush or just be suspended amid the crowd.

"Adams is delivering a speech to the Caucus Club, ma'am. He asks that you kindly wait but a moment until he's finished." The second man had returned. Peering at Rachel, he added, "Perhaps you'd like to wait outside, Mrs. Amory. I'll stay with you until Sam comes."

He didn't wait for an answer but took Rachel's arm and led her through the door. In the twilight the air was heavy with late May's promise of summer, soft and warm with a hint of salt carried from the docks a short distance north.

"Thank you," Rachel said. "You are most kind. You needn't wait with me. I'm all right now."

"No trouble, ma'am," he murmured and held his ground. He didn't look at her but stared into space, as if averting his eyes from an indelicate scene. Normally she might have been amused by his stiff, proper manner but now she hardly noticed.

They remained in silence until the door swung open and Sam Adams stepped into the road. "Thank you for waiting, Mrs. Amory. Sorry I couldn't come right away. Now, how can I help you?"

She looked from the young man to the stranger and hesitated. "That's all right, Jack," Adams said quickly. "I'll look after Mrs. Amory now." The other man nodded and went inside, bowing to Rachel as he passed. "He's an old friend of your husband's, ma'am," Sam said. "You don't know him?"

"No, I . . ." She hadn't come for polite chatter. "Sam, I've got to find my husband. Now, tonight, it's urgent. I've been everywhere, without success. Then I thought of you and went to Purchase Street, and they told me you were probably here. Do you know where Paul is?"

Adams stared at the toe of his boot and cleared his throat noisily. "Well, he might be . . . I mean . . ."

"He's not in Mattie Sills's cabin on Cambridge Street, if that's what you're thinking," she said quickly. "It was the first place I tried."

Adams looked both relieved and troubled. He wasn't dealing with a wronged wife about to have hysterics—that was a good thing—but apart from Mattie's cabin, he hadn't a notion where

Paul Amory might be. "I'm sorry. I don't know anywhere else to suggest."

"You men and your political clubs," she said breathlessly. "That's the kind of information I need. Where are some of the meeting places other than this? I can try them."

"Well, there's Dawes's garret or the Bunch of Grapes in King Street. And there's the Salutation Tavern in the alley. But Paul isn't likely to be at any of those." He looked at her closely for the first time and saw how truly distraught she was. "He hasn't been active in any of our groups for some time now. I thought you knew."

"Some time," she repeated softly. "Since he took up with that woman. Yes, I knew. I just thought—" She bit her lip, leaving little red tooth marks on the soft flesh that were deep enough to be seen in the dull glow from the tavern door. "Thank you, Sam. I'll let you go back to your meeting. It was a chance, that's all."

"Mrs. Amory, what's wrong? Can I help? I'd like to, you know."

"Help? No, young Mr. Adams, you've already done enough. You and my husband and all the rabble-rousers and malcontents you court have done more than enough." As she turned and hurried away, Adams could only stare after her.

Five minutes later she was standing in silent darkness on the edge of the Common. If she turned right, she'd come to Benjamin's house; straight ahead would lead to the Ark. Rachel hesitated only a moment before turning right. The maid who opened the door recognized her instantly. "Mrs. Amory, come in, ma'am. The master and the mistress have guests. I'll announce you."

"No," she said quickly. "Don't do that. I'll wait in here." Rachel moved across the hall and let herself into her brother's study. "Get word to Mr. Griffin without disturbing the others," she instructed. "Just tell him I'm here and that it's urgent."

When Griffin came into the room he was frowning, screwing up his eyes as he did under stress. "For heaven's sake, Rachel, what is it? I've the governor and his wife in the drawing room. Eve will be furious at my leaving like that, without any explanation."

"Damn Eve. And damn the governor and his wife too," she

said heatedly. "This is vital, Ben. You should realize that. I'd never have come otherwise. It's Jacob. His life is in danger." The words, spoken aloud thus, made nausea rise in her throat and a red haze float before her eyes. She was visibly trembling.

"For God's sake, Rachel, don't faint! Here, sit down. Drink some brandy." This time she didn't refuse. Only after she'd taken a hefty swallow did her brother say, "What do you mean, Jacob's life in danger? Jacob's in Philadelphia."

"No, not at the moment. Here, read this. You'll recognize the hand." She pulled a crumpled sheet of stationery from her bosom and passed it to him.

"This is Franklin's writing," Ben said after a moment. "And it's addressed to Paul. Really, my dear, reading another man's correspondence is hardly—"

"Just forget your damned propriety for once and read it," she commanded.

He stared at her for a moment, realized the state she was in, then dropped his eyes to the page. "Oh, dear God," he whispered finally. "When did you get this? When did it come? Where's Paul?"

She ignored his questions. "You see what he says there, Ben, what Franklin says: '. . . a brave and noble gesture but certain suicide.' That's my son he's talking about. My Jacob!"

"I know. Don't go to pieces, Rachel. It will solve nothing. You haven't answered me. When did this come, and where's Paul?"

"I don't know where Paul is." Her voice had gone flat, toneless. "I've been looking for him since this afternoon. The letter came some time ago. Over two months now as far as I can figure out from what Maggie said. Paul came to the house, read it, and then left. That was around the third of April, a day or two before I returned home from the Plymouth market. I just found this thing today. I was dusting Paul's desk and it fell out from behind some books. He'd hidden it, Ben, hidden it so I wouldn't see, wouldn't know what a terrible thing he'd done. Oh God . . ." Her wail made her brother jump. Her tears unnerved him completely.

"Don't, Rachel, you mustn't. Please, I'll get Eve, make some excuse to our guests."

"No! I don't want Eve. I just want you to help me find Paul.

He has to stop this thing. Jacob will listen to him."

Benjamin glanced from his sister to the letter. It was dated last November and this was the end of May. Surely it was too late to stop anything. But if Rachel was going to be hysterical, she was her husband's responsibility, not his. "You just wait here," he said as soothingly as he could manage. "I think I know where Paul may be."

Rachel looked at him with a mixture of scorn and pity. "Don't bother, Ben. I've already looked on Cambridge Street. He's not there. The woman says she doesn't know anything."

"You spoke to her?" The audacity of it astounded him.

"Of course I spoke to her." Rachel jumped to her feet and grabbed his lapels in a gesture so unexpected it nearly knocked him down. "Don't you understand? Jacob is going to die! He's everything worth living for, the only thing! And he's going to die because his father's poisoned his mind with lies and political intrigues. I've got to do something, Ben, I've got to!"

He managed to calm her again, get her seated with another tot of brandy. "Wait here," he ordered. "Don't you dare move from this room. I'll return as soon as I can."

Half an hour later he was back. "Paul's gone to Philadelphia," he told her quickly. "I went to the Ark and John told me. John and Charles both knew but they were sworn to secrecy. Paul didn't want you to worry. He left as soon as he received Franklin's letter. So you see it will be all right."

"Gone to Philadelphia," she repeated softly. "And told me nothing."

"I told you, Rachel, he didn't want you to worry. Now you can rest easy because everything's going to be fine. And Martha's waiting outside. She's going to bring you to the Ark for tonight."

Rachel rose and smoothed her skirt with nervous little gestures. "I'm not going to the Ark. I'm going home. Thank you, Benjamin. I'm sorry I disturbed your evening." The toneless quality had returned to her voice.

They couldn't dissuade her. Not even John's wife Martha, whom she always got on with better than Mary and certainly better than Eve, could induce her to spend the night at the Ark. In the end, Benjamin drove her to The Roses himself in the elegant carriage with the Griffin coat of arms emblazoned on the doors. "Azure, a bend or. With two Griffins rampant." Rachel whispered the words to the night air as she hung out her bedroom window and watched the horses trot briskly down Summer Street.

Maggie found her wandering the halls at sunup, still wearing the mud-stained gown, her black curls hanging free, framing a face so white it seemed ghostly. "Come sit down, ma'am. Let me get you something to eat and I'll draw your bath while you're breakfasting."

"No, Maggie, nothing. I'm not hungry."

"A bath then. It'll make you feel ever so much better, ma'am."

"No, I can't." She wandered off into the garden. The men weren't working yet. It was a bit too early for that. The green wonderland was deserted, kissed with dew, its spring colors muted in the mist of morning. Such a beautiful garden, such a beautiful house. And the markets were showing more profit than ever before. It was the best year since she'd founded the business.

When she reached the orchard she could just see the sliver of pink that creased the green of the tightly furled buds. It was a promise of the glory to come. In a few short weeks the orchard would be a cloud of pink and white and silver, alive with the hum of bees. That tree over there—she remembered when Paul had planted it. It was the day Valiant was born, and she recalled watching Paul wield the spade with such energy it seemed he could dig up the whole garden without even breathing hard. "A tree for little Valiant," he'd said. Today that pear tree was straight and tall and full of bud. Only Valiant wasn't like that at all. He was crooked and bent and would bear no fruit ever.

And Sophia's tree, the quince planted at her birth because Paul said it had the most beautiful blossom of them all, was magnificent. It stood at the end of a grass path, and its spreading branches almost touched the ground. From its bounty came endless jars of pale rose jelly; they made it every autumn and always there seemed to be more than they could possibly use. But Sophia didn't taste the jelly from her tree. Not any more. This summer it would be four years since Sophia had set foot in The Roses. Four years since she had spoken to her mother.

Rachel turned, knowing the sight would be painful but unable to resist. Jacob's tree was a special variety of apple Paul had ordered from England as soon as he knew she was pregnant; he'd planted it the day of Jacob's birth. It had been the first tree of the orchard, the beginning of the fruit garden. Just as Jacob was the beginning of their family, of the generations of Amorys they would create. But she couldn't locate the tree now. In the place where she remembered Jacob's apple standing, there was only a patch of bare earth and a withered stump.

While she was staring, trying to decide if she'd mistaken the location, one of the gardeners walked to her side. "Mornin', ma'am. Tis a fine one, that's for sure."

"Where is it?" she whispered. "Where's Jacob's tree?"

"You mean the old apple what always stood right here, ma'am? The one they say Mr. Amory imported from England? No longer with us, I'm afraid. Thought you knew. That big storm last November split the trunk right down the middle. Killed that tree dead."

Her screams rent the silent morning. It took both gardeners and Maggie to drag her to the house.

8

It was lunchtime. Rachel could hear the clatter of plates in the kitchen. Maggie, the gardeners, and the stable boy were eating, their voices a steady hum of noise in the noonday quiet of Summer Street. When Maggie had come to the master bedroom a few minutes earlier, Rachel had just lay still and feigned sleep. She stayed that way until she heard the door close softly behind the serving woman.

Now she crept along the hall on silent, stockinged feet, her shoes in her hand. Mustn't be discovered. They would try to stop her; they didn't understand. This morning, the hysteria, it made them think she was ill, demented. If they found her leaving the house they would force her to remain, send for Benjamin most likely, or Charles or John. Well, she couldn't wait for that or take the time to explain. It was too complicated, too important. She'd thought it all out during the morning while she lay abed. She knew what must be done.

The door to the stable opened silently; it was well oiled and in good repair like everything at The Roses. It took a brief five minutes to hitch the two chestnut mares to the trap. They were docile, familiar beasts, as accustomed to her as she was to them. She was driving down Summer Street toward the Beverly Road before the servants had started on their hasty pudding.

Rachel didn't need to ask directions this time. She remembered the road to Rowley and the Crandall homestead clearly; she'd forgotten nothing of what dreadful day four years earlier.

When she reached the single street of the village a few people stared but she ignored them. The picture must be an odd one, she thought. The chestnuts were dripping sweat and heaving with exhaustion, for she'd not stopped once. The black gown she had hastily donned before leaving home was overlaid with the gray dust of the parched roads. She could feel her hair blowing wild and free in the hot wind of her passage through town.

The forge was quiet. No one was about. Supper time. Sophia must be feeding her young family, her three sons. The thought of them suddenly filled Rachel with wild exultation. Ever since this morning, when she'd faced the realities of Jacob's death, Val's perversion, and Paul's desertion, the thought of those little boys had sustained her. She didn't even know their names, but that wasn't important. They were flesh of her flesh, blood of her blood. They carried the Griffin-Amory legacy and they were proof that all she had built would go on.

Sophia took one look at the creature who burst into her kitchen and began to tremble with alarm. "Mama! For God's sake, what's happened!"

Rachel's blue eyes smoldered with passion, her drawn face was pasty white, but her voice was strong when she spoke. "They're all gone or dead, Sophia. I was beside myself with grief until I remembered you and them." She spread her hands to indicate the three little boys sitting at the table. "Then I knew it didn't matter."

"Mama, I don't understand. But here, sit down. Thee must rest. Stephen, run and get Papa. Jonathan's planting still—it's been such a dry, late season. But he'll come right away and then thee can tell us what we can—"

Rachel interrupted her daughter's nervous stream of talk. "Stay here," she told her eldest grandson as he rose to do his mother's bidding. "So your name is Stephen. It's a fine name." She reached out a hand to stroke his red hair and the child pulled back in fear. "Don't be afraid of me," Rachel said softly. "I'm your grandmother. Flesh of your flesh, blood of your blood."

Stephen looked in confused anguish from the stranger to his mother. Which of them was he to obey? And what was this funny speech?

"It's all right, Stephen," Sophia said. "Sit down and finish thy supper. We'll just wait for Papa to come in when he's done." It seemed best to humor her mother.

"Tell me the names of the other two," Rachel said.

"This is Hiram, the baby. He'll be a year old in September." Sophia leaned over to wipe a dribble of milk from the boy's chubby face, and he rewarded her with a smile displaying four minute teeth. "And this is Paul." She lay her hand on the black curly head of the child sitting next to her. "He's two. We think he looks like the Griffins."

Rachel stared at each of the lads in turn, studying them, assessing them, deciding. "Yes," she said finally. "This one's a Griffin. But you should never have named him Paul. It's a bad name, a curse." She looked away, and Paul's blue eyes turned to his mother in puzzlement.

"Thee mustn't say things to upset the children, Mama," Sophia said quietly. "I'm going to put them to bed now. Thee can wait here. When I'm done we can talk."

Rachel didn't wait. She followed her daughter up the stairs to the end of the long, narrow corridor with the faded yellow walls and the polished pine floor. The boys slept in a square room with a single window and one great bed big enough for the three of them. Here the walls were of soft hyacinth blue—painted recently, Rachel guessed—and the floor was covered with a shabby rag rug whose color had long been bleached away by the sun.

Silently she observed as Sophia sponged each little face and each set of chubby, dimpled hands. The pitcher and bowl of the washstand were fashioned of plain white crockery and both were chipped. Rachel stared at the utensils, disturbed by the severity and lack of comeliness. "None of this is good enough for them," she said. "They're heirs to a great fortune."

"Ssh, be quiet, Mama." Sophia recognized a shrill quality to Rachel's voice, as if hysteria was just below the surface. "We'll talk later. Thee can tell me whatever thee thinks after the children are asleep." She went on with her task calmly, knowing the familiar routine would soothe the little boys, disarm any fears wakened by the extraordinary events of the past half hour.

At last all three were dressed in flannel nightshirts and tucked into the big bed with its half-railings designed by Jonathan to keep them safe. Against the gleaming whiteness of the pillows their rosy faces stood out like a series of pictures on a blank canvas. Three pairs of eyes, one set blue, one brown, and one two-color like her own, looked to Sophia. Her hand touched each head in turn. "May the Lord keep thee as the apple of His eye," she whispered. "May Jesus guard thee this night and wake thee in blessedness to see the dawn He has made."

"You mustn't fill their heads too full of religious sentiment, Sophia," Rachel said. Her daughter didn't reply but led her firmly from the room.

Then, just as she closed the door behind her, Sophia glanced at her mother. Rachel's blue eyes looked wild and there was an erratic tic pulsing in her cheek. The girl felt a moment's panic. She had been so intent on keeping any sense of alarm from reaching the boys that she hadn't assimilated the remarkable character of this sudden, unprecedented visit until now. Hastily Sophia urged Rachel forward, and at the same time she reached behind her back and turned the key in the lock of the massive old door to the children's bedroom. When she'd slipped that key into the pocket of her apron, the young woman felt a bit safer.

Jonathan was washing at the kitchen sink. He was bare from the waist up and his back and chest were streaked with perspiration and grime. He didn't realize at first that Sophia was not alone. "I'm sorry to be late for supper," he said without looking around. "I had to come in here to wash. The pump by the barn is as dry as dust. Thee has only a trickle in here too. God willing we may have some rain tomorrow, there's a bit of cloud over the marsh—"

"Jonathan, we have a guest."

He turned to see his mother-in-law and his wife standing in the doorway. They made a strange picture—the younger woman so neat and composed, the older so obviously distraught. "Hello, Mrs. Amory," he said quietly. "Thee is welcome."

Rachel ignored him. "Sophia, I must talk with you. It's urgent."

"I have to give Jonathan his supper, Mama. He's been working hard all day. Thee can just sit over there and tell us what thee's come to say while I'm serving."

"No." Jonathan shook his head, and his red beard sprayed droplets of water on the oak handle of the pump and the floor below. "It's not necessary, Sophia. I'm not hungry. Thy mother appears to be in some sort of difficulty. We'd best all go into the sitting room and talk."

Sophia protested, but he overruled her and led both women to the front of the house. "Now, Mrs. Amory," he said when they were seated by the big window overlooking the garden. "What is the trouble? How can we help?"

Rachel didn't address herself to him but to her daughter. "Your brother Jacob is dead. He went to try and make a treaty with some Indians and they killed him. I know because the tree died. I wasn't sure before that. Then, when I learned about the apple tree, the one your father planted the day Jacob was born, I knew."

"Indians, I don't understand, Mama. Oh yes, yes I do!" Sophia's eyes widened in horror. "Last month Mattie Sills came here and said Papa had gone to Philadelphia to talk to Jacob about a treaty with Indians." In her shock she didn't consider the effect the mulatto woman's name might have on her mother.

"She's part of it, you know," Rachel said, jumping to her feet. "That half-caste. Paul lives with her; he doesn't care about the house or the markets. And Valiant too. Valiant is a pervert, Sophia." She was pacing, wringing her hands and then letting them flutter in the air. "Val has a man friend as his lover. They live together in the North End. He is diseased and cannot be the heir." Neither Jonathan nor Sophia said a word. They could only watch Rachel and try to understand her quick, half-whispered phrases.

"I didn't care before," Rachel continued. "It didn't matter because of Jacob. Everything was ready for him. He wrote me last autumn that he'd be home this summer. I was waiting, you see. I kept everything ready and waited."

"Mrs. Amory." Jonathan had found his tongue at last. "Thee can't know for certain that thy son is dead. Perhaps thee will have word he is well and all thy worries have been for nothing."

"The tree's dead!" she shouted. "I told you that, didn't I? It's a sign. It happened so I would know and be able to plan. I mustn't let them find out, though. If they realize there's no heir, it will be disastrous."

"Who, Mama?" Sophia whispered. "If who finds out?"

"Them! All of the vultures waiting to take what I've created, what I've built. But they won't get it, Sophia. They've forgotten about you, about your sons." She flung herself to her knees before the girl and grabbed both of Sophia's hands with her own. "I forgot too for a little while. I was so grief-stricken I wanted to die. But this morning I remembered and then everything was all right, so I came straight here."

Sophia tried to disengage her hands from her mother's grip. Rachel's fingers were still black with road dirt, and they were incredibly strong. No one would think such a tiny woman could have so much strength.

"You will come home with me," Rachel continued. "Tomorrow morning, as soon as the children are awake. I thought of tonight but they need their sleep—I realize that. Tomorrow will be time enough. Wait till you see The Roses, Sophia. After all these years. It's so beautiful. There's not a house in all of Boston more beautiful than The Roses. Your children will live there, and their children and their children's children. They're the heirs, you see, and you're the heiress. It doesn't matter about you and I, our quarrel. All that's in the past now. The boys can each have a room of their own, and as soon as they're a little bigger we'll bring them around and show them the markets. They're all doing so well."

"Mama, I . . . thee mustn't—"

"Not now, Sophia," Jonathan interrupted quickly. "Thee mustn't keep thy mother talking more now when she's so tired." Sophia looked at him in consternation and he shook his head firmly. "Thee and thy mother can talk more after she's had some rest. Go get her a hot drink, Sophia. Thee can see how she needs to sleep."

Rachel sat back on her heels and released her grip on the girl's hands. "Yes," she said softly. "I am very tired. It would be good to rest. I can sleep now that I know everything's going to be all right. I couldn't be sure until I saw the boys, but it is going to be all right."

"Let me help thee, Mrs. Amory." Jonathan took his mother-in-law's elbow and lifted her gently from the floor. "There's a spare bedroom just next to the kitchen. Thee won't have to climb any stairs. Hurry, Sophia, get that drink."

9

Sophia's eyes were red-rimmed with weariness. She sat at the kitchen table leaning on her elbows and staring into the darkness of night outside the window. "It's so unbelievable to see her like this," she said again. She had said something of that sort at least half a dozen times in the two hours she and

Jonathan had spent trying to find a solution to the dilemma. "I feel terrible having to expose her to anyone else in this condition."

"Not to strangers, Sophia," Jonathan said. "In the morning I'll send word to Boston, to thy uncles. They can come and get her and she can remain at her home with a nurse until the shock has worn off. I'm sure that's all it really is," he added, taking his wife's hand. "The shock of believing thy brother dead, on top of everything else."

"Everything she's built, everything she worked so hard for . . . I've always hated her for it, Jonathan, for being so single-minded in pursuit of her own goals, treating all of us children as pawns. But now I just feel terribly sad."

"Thee never hated her, dearest," he answered softly. "Not in thy deepest heart. Thee couldn't be the good woman thee is and hate. But perhaps the Lord will make that the good which comes out of this bad thing. Perhaps thee and thy mother will make peace. She can visit us as thy father does. The boys should have a grandmother."

Sophia smiled at him. Jonathan Crandall was the finest man in the whole world; he could see evil in nothing and no one. "Perhaps," she said.

"Shall we go to bed now?" he asked, kissing her cheek. "Thee has had a very hard evening. Surely thy mother will sleep until morning."

"She should. I put a calming potion in her tea. But I'd like just to sit here a bit longer if thee doesn't mind. Perhaps we can have a bit of tea ourselves." She rose to move the kettle over the fire and her foot touched the shirt Jonathan had discarded when he came in from the fields. In all the excitement it had been forgotten. "Is thee cold?" she asked, picking up the soiled garment.

"No, tis a warm night for May. Wind's coming up, maybe twill bring rain."

"Maybe," Sophia said, moving around the familiar kitchen with sure steps. The homeliness of ordinary tasks was comforting at a time like this.

Rachel could hear the drone of their talk when she woke. It must still be night. Outside her window the moon shone on the unfamiliar fields and marshlands. She was groggy, heavy-headed. What had Sophia put in the tea? Still, she knew where she was, why she was here. And she knew too that things were going to improve. They wouldn't get The Roses or the markets away from her. She had been right to come. Of course Sophia saw the wisdom of the plan. Sophia had always been a wise and practical girl. She'd do well. They would raise the boys together and see them grow to manhood and inherit all that was theirs.

The sounds from the kitchen intruded on her reverie. What were they talking about, Sophia and the farmer? Was he arguing with her, trying to prevent her going to Boston to claim her legacy? It struck Rachel that she'd not given enough thought to him. What was his name? Oh yes, Jonathan. Jonathan Crandall. The boys would have to use the name Amory of course. She'd demand that, make it part of their bequest. But she mustn't ignore this man Jonathan. He was Sophia's legal husband, after all—she should have thought of that. She must explain that he could come to The Roses too. As long as he didn't interfere with her plans he'd be welcome.

She was still wearing the dusty black frock; Sophia hadn't insisted she take it off after she protested. Rachel fumbled by the bedside for her shoes but couldn't find them. No matter, the pine floors were warm. She felt her way to the door of the room and started toward the kitchen and the sound of voices.

"Does thee think she really believes it?" Sophia was saying. Her speech was soft and tired, but in the silent hall Rachel could clearly hear her daughter. "Can Mama really believe I'll bring the boys to Boston? Leave the farm, leave thee? Oh Jonathan, if she believes that she really has lost her mind! That's what I find so hard to bear. The thought of Mama insane."

"She needs to believe it, Sophia, at least for the present. Later, when she has had time to accept reality, she'll understand. She'll get better, Sophia. I'm sure she will. Thy mother has always been such a strong woman. Thee can help her with thy herbs. There are physics to cure a fevered brain, aren't there?"

Rachel didn't hear the girl reply. She thrust herself back into the darkness, clutching at her chest to stop the frenzied beating of her heart. It couldn't be! Sophia couldn't have deceived her like that, humored her as if she were a demented old fool. It was monstrous, the final betrayal. Sophia too. After all the others had betrayed her, Sophia meant to deliver the killing blow. She was in league with them! She must be.

Well, she would pay! No one would beat Rachel Griffin Amory in the final reckoning. No one ever had and no one ever would, not even Sophia. Rachel turned and groped her way toward the stairs that led to the boys' bedroom. She would take the children someplace where they'd never be found. They would inherit everything. She'd made up her mind and nothing was going to stop her.

There was a door at the end of the hall. Was this the way upstairs? It gave easily when she shoved, but it led to the outside, not to the second floor. Where was she? Oh yes, the forge. She could see the dull red glow of the banked fire in the raised furnace. For a long moment Rachel stood very still, her eyes fastened on those sleeping embers. A fevered brain, that's what he'd said. The one called Jonathan thought she was mad, thought she had a fevered brain. And he'd twisted her daughter's mind until Sophia no longer knew truth from falsehood.

"They're his sons," she whispered into the darkness. "He's poisoned them with his blood. They can't grow up to inherit the legacy. It's too late, everything's ended." The sadness of it was overwhelming, the pain unbearable. Rachel stood trembling beneath the onslaught of her total despair, and when she moved toward the furnace it was with the stiff, jerking motions of a zombie. "Burn it all," she whispered as she located the bellows with her shoeless foot. "Burn it all so nothing is left. Burn out the poison."

The hood Jonathan had built was very effective. In seconds the fire in the brick pit roared to life. Rachel felt nothing when she reached into that blaze and pulled out the glowing coals with her bare hands. She walked to the door leading back into the hall, flung them on the floor, and still she felt no pain in her singed flesh. She didn't even smell the stench of burning skin. "More!" she screamed aloud into the night. "More fire to burn out the poison!" Again and again she grabbed bits of flame from the furnace and hurled them into the house.

Jonathan heard Rachel's voice before he smelled the smoke. "She's in the forge," he shouted, running for the door. Sophia followed him. They couldn't get through the back hall, however. It was already a wall of fire.

"Get out the front door, Sophia! Hurry! I'll get the boys!"

"No," she screamed. "Thee can't carry them alone. I'm coming with thee!"

"Thy mother's in the forge! Thee has to go and get her out, stop her! Don't argue, Sophia, for God's sake don't argue!"

She hesitated only a second, saw him bound up the stairs with tiny flames licking at his heels. Then she turned and flung herself out the front door. He'd have to throw them out the window. That was the only way to save the babies. He wouldn't be able to carry them down the burning stairs. She had to be there on the ground beneath the window to catch them. They would be so frightened, they would need her so much. She didn't even look at the forge as she ran by.

Rachel saw her as she streaked around the corner of the building. The blaze was illuminating everything now and she could see clearly. "I had to do it, Sophia!" she screamed after the girl. "I had to! Everything's poisoned, it must be burned clean, purified." Her daughter didn't hear her, didn't look back. Rachel raced after her. She had to tell Sophia the truth, make her understand. She mustn't be sorry about them, about that man and his sons; she must be made to see they carried bad blood.

She could see the girl as soon as she rounded the house. Sophia was screaming and flinging herself at the wall.

"I forgot, Jonathan! I forgot! I locked the boys in to protect them from her. I've still got the key!" There was a vine growing against the wooden clapboards beneath the children's bedroom. Sophia kept trying to clamber up it, only to crash to the earth as it gave way. Again and again the girl hurled herself at the side of the house. She was yelling the children's names now: "Stephen! Paul! Hiram! Jump out the window. Jump! I'll catch thee. Jump!"

As Rachel approached, the first tongue of flame nosed out between the clapboards. In seconds the whole rear of the house was a sheet of fire. The girl ignored it, continued to try and climb. "No, Sophia! No!" Rachel cried. She saw her daughter stagger to her feet once more and she followed her gaze as it traveled up to the second story. With Sophia, Rachel saw the flash of a small red head framed in the glass, saw the tiny mouth open wide in a silent scream of terror.

"Stephen! Mama's right here! Open the window, Stephen. Thee is a big boy, thee can do it. Open the window and jump!"

The face at the window disappeared. Howling with pain and rage, Sophia tried again to climb. The fire was all around her, she was enveloped in flames. Rachel stood immobile. Then, in the time of one single heartbeat, she saw everything. It was as if a great curtain had been drawn and truth revealed. "Oh my dear God, what have I done! Sophia! Sophia!"

She thrust herself forward and tore the girl away from the inferno. They were thrown to the ground together and Rachel kept hold of her daughter, rolling her over and over in the dry, brown grass, using her own body to beat out the flames licking at Sophia's clothes.

"There's two women back here," a voice shouted. Then hands were lifting them beyond the reach of the blaze and stifling the smoldering remains of their clothing with heavy blankets.

"Where's Jonathan and the boys!" someone yelled. "Do you see them?"

"Sweet Jesus Christ!" another voice answered. "They must be in there. We've got to get them out."

At that moment the roof crashed in. With a deafening roar the pitiless holocaust leapt toward the moon and the stars and the sky.

They carried the two women, Sophia and the stranger none of them recognized, to a nearby cottage. "Mabel Hawke's gone for ointment; she'll return straight away. I can manage, go back and help the others." The goodwife waited until the men had deposited her patients on the bed before she asked, "How did it start? The forge?"

"Must be, but I can't see how. Jonathan was always so careful."

"Aye. Is he . . . ?" Her voice faltered.

"Yes, him and the three little boys it seems." The speaker was choked with tears but he didn't pause to weep. "Got to go. We're tryin' to stop it spreadin' over to Marbelle's farm."

Later the same clouds Jonathan had mentioned seeing a few short hours earlier brought rain to put out the fire. There was nothing left of the Crandall homestead but blackened, smoking ruins and charred fields. Still later, close to dawn, someone remembered that Sophia was an Amory and they dispatched a lad from the village to carry the terrible news to Boston.

The women of Rowley took turns nursing the two victims yet alive. They cut the remains of clothing from their bodies inch by gruesome inch and they emptied cupboards and still-rooms of salves and ointments and powders to treat the fearful wounds.

The stranger was the worst. There were blackened stumps where her hands had been and one side of her face was burned away. Sophia's face was untouched. She had no hair on her head and no eyebrows but her wounds were not as deep or as extensive as those of the older woman.

"Sophia may pull through," old Ellie Mann said. "But the other one, bless her soul, the Lord's calling her for sure."

"If I were Sophia," one of the younger wives said solemnly, "I'd pray to die."

"No," said Ellie, shaking her head, "thee wouldn't. Sophia is one of us, a Friend. She'll accept the Lord's will."

Three days later Rachel was dead. She'd never regained consciousness. By then John and Martha Griffin were in Rowley to represent the family. They decreed it best to bury Rachel in the tiny cemetery behind the Quaker Meeting House. "That will be fine," the Friends told them. "She wasn't one of us, but now we know she's Sophia's mother, Jonathan's mother-in-law . . . Well, it's fitting." The Griffins looked at each other and said nothing. They didn't know how fitting it might be, but it would certainly save a lot of difficulty. When the villagers asked about Sophia's father, the dead woman's husband, John explained that Paul Amory was away on a business trip to Philadelphia.

"Poor man," someone muttered. "Tis a sad homecoming he'll have."

"His daughter's alive," another answered. "That's something at least."

Sophia regained consciousness the day of the funeral. It was clear from her eyes that she remembered everything that had happened. "God help thee bear thy cross, Sophia," Ellie Mann said softly. "We buried thy mother this day. And we've erected memorial stones for thy husband and children." Sophia turned her face to the wall and didn't reply. She didn't even groan aloud, though it was obvious she was in excruciating pain and she took the numbing draughts they gave her with grateful eagerness.

"Something's happened to her voice," John Griffin said after a day or two. "She's mute."

"I wonder if it's her voice or her mind that's mute," his wife said quietly. "We must take her away from here, John. Home to Boston. She must not remain in Rowley where everything will remind her."

Her husband agreed, and when they told the plan to Sophia she signaled acquiesence with her eyes and a faint motion of one hand. Three weeks went by before the girl was pronounced fit to travel. By then John had returned to town and only Martha remained to accompany Sophia to Boston in a handsome Griffin coach.

The morning they were to leave, Martha felt suddenly frightened. She'd not seen the girl out of bed until now, not seen what physical damage the burns had left. What if she's deformed, she thought. How will she bear that too? She needn't have worried. True, Sophia's arms and shoulders were scarred and all her hair was gone, but when they dressed her in a gray cloak and tied a bonnet on her bald head she looked little different than she ever had.

"Come, my dear," Martha said softly as she joined her niece in the cottage where she'd spent the weeks since the fire. "It's time we went home."

They were in the carriage and ready to drive off when Ellie Mann ran toward them down the road. "I found this," she said, thrusting a paper-wrapped parcel through the window of the coach. "I thought thee would like to have it, Sophia."

The girl took the offering in her bandaged hands and turned away. Ellie understood that good-byes were too painful to be borne. She withdrew into the shade of the doorway and watched while the splendid coach from Boston carried Sophia out of Rowley. She could remember the day the girl had arrived, sitting beside Jonathan Crandall in the front of the freshly painted red wagon, looking happy enough to burst. Perhaps that was what Sophia was remembering too.

In the carriage there was only silence. Since the girl couldn't or wouldn't speak, Martha didn't know her thoughts and she was secretly grateful. What did one say to a young woman who had sustained such an appalling loss?

They were nearly in Boston when Sophia indicated by clumsy motions of her swathed hands that she wished to open the parcel on her lap. Martha took it from her and undid the string. "It's a book, Sophia. It must be yours. How did it survive, I wonder?"

The cloth-covered volume was charred around the edges but its spine was intact as was the embroidered crest on its cover. "It's the Griffin coat of arms," Martha said in surprise. "And that's your grandmother's handwriting on the front page: 'For Sophia, her legacy.'" When she looked up, tears were streaming down Sophia's face. It was the first time the girl had wept since the night of the fire.

2

THE CRUCIBLE

"Dulce et decorum est pro patria mori."

—Horace

1

It was easy to see why the Cherokees had adopted this woman and why Daniel Ludlow wanted her. The squaw they called Passayoro had hair of pale silver and eyes of violet. She was tall and slim and moved with the willowy grace of the Indians, plus some trick of motion that was her own.

Jacob watched her come forward to join Daniel near the sacred fire and caught his breath. Had he seen her on the streets of Boston or Philadelphia he would have thought her a beautiful woman; but now, in the elaborately beaded and fringed buckskins of a bride, she was an exotic creature who seemed to have dropped from the heavens. His distaste for the marriage evaporated.

The chanting and dancing and ritual of the ceremony was endless. "Are they married yet?" Joseph Deering asked at one point.

"I honestly don't know," Jacob said. "Must be, though. Look, they're leaving."

The bride and groom were indeed quitting the feast. They were part of a procession led by the *mico,* Dayunisi. The group escorted the newlyweds as far as a clump of trees marking the path to the isolated cabin where Daniel had spent the last week. Then they intoned another chant and watched the couple walk off into the night. The five young men from Philadelphia were not the only ones to look at Ludlow with envy.

"That's some wife he's taken," Stuart said, voicing the thoughts of them all.

"Yes, but where are they going to live? Here with the Indians or in civilization with the whites?" Deering bit into a great slab of roasted venison and gestured with the bone that remained in his hand. "Either way seems like a bad bargain."

"Maybe," Jacob said quietly. "But maybe not."

The Philadelphians' negotiations with Dayunisi began the following day. They sat on the floor of the old man's house and spoke through an interpreter, another old man who had lived with the English some time in the distant past. Amory had worried about committing an error of protocol that would prejudice the *mico* against him, but Ludlow had insisted it was an unnecessary concern. "Just talk straight to him. He understands a bargain as well as any man alive."

"Dayunisi," said Amory, opening the discussion, "I have come to ask you to consider an alliance with my tribe."

"Your tribe are our enemies," the *mico* answered through the interpreter. "They are the enemies of the tribe of white men with whom we have now sworn to fight. You are welcome here because you are of the clan of Santroyawi who is our brother, but your tribe are our enemies."

"You have been deceived, Dayunisi. I say that with all the respect due the great Cherokee nation, but still it is the truth."

"The Red chief, who made the pact with the other white tribe, he is a brave men, a fearless warrior."

Amory remembered the advice given him by Ludlow. There was rivalry between the Red and the White Cherokees. "But is he wise, Dayunisi? As wise as the White chief?"

"Maybe, maybe not. Continue, my ears are open."

"This tribe of whites, the ones called the French, they are treacherous, they cannot be trusted. They wish to take all the land for themselves and chase the Indians from their homes."

"You say that, but we have seen differently. Your tribe drive us from our ancient places; the other ones trade and send their medicine men and live in peace."

Amory took a deep breath and settled more comfortably on his heels. It was going to take a long time and much talk to undo the harm done by Englishmen acting like bloody fools.

"Listen well, wise Dayunisi, I will tell you the things the other tribe, the French, believe and do. Then you can tell me if they are men to be trusted."

"Why has the man of your clan come to the village?" Passayoro asked Daniel on their third day in the isolated cabin.

"Jacob? Why do you care about him?" Her question was strange. Squaws didn't concern themselves with men's business, least of all when they lay naked in a man's arms beside a waterfall.

"I fear for the Real People," she answered, turning to fix him with her violet eyes. "I fear that they will be deceived by white men, cheated."

"It isn't always like that. You're white and so am I."

"It is not the same thing. We are part of the Real People; Dayunisi made it so."

Daniel sat up and held her at arm's length. Beneath his hands the slope of her shoulders was like carved marble, cool and silken and perfect. "Listen to me. How much do you remember of the time before you came to this village?"

She shook her head. "Nothing. I have no wish to remember."

"You must," he said in English. "It's in your blood; you must remember."

"I do not speak the white tongue," she answered stiffly in Cherokee.

"Yes, you do." He shook her gently and made her raise her eyes to his. "You were seven years old when the Cherokees took you. I know because I went to the settlement where you were born and heard the story. You're a girl from Providence in Virginia and your name is Marjorie Jackson."

At the mention of that long-forgotten name her eyes widened. "Marjorie Jackson," she repeated. Then, in Cherokee, "I know those words."

"Damned right you do," Ludlow said fiercely. "And that's not all you know." He spoke in Cherokee once more. "You are my woman, my squaw. You belong to my clan now. It is right that you speak my tongue and have a name in my language."

"It is right," she agreed. "Is my name to be Marjorie Jackson in your tongue?"

He grinned. "Not exactly. Marjorie Ludlow—Mrs. Daniel Ludlow. Say it. Say 'Mrs. Daniel Ludlow.'" She did. "Good, now say 'Marjorie Ludlow.'" When she complied he released his grip on her shoulders. "You'll remember. In no time at all you'll be chattering like any white woman in the colonies."

"Some things are the same in any language," she said, drawing his head to her breast and giggling when be began to suckle. "Is that a white man's way to pretend he is a baby?"

He didn't answer. His mouth was full of her breast, the nipple hard and smooth against his tongue. She moaned and he let his hands wander along the curve of her hips and the softness of her thighs. "You do not do as a Cherokee does," she whispered. "You are not so quick."

Daniel lifted his head. "Among our people a woman is to be pleasured when she mates. I'll show you."

"Like kissing with our mouths? The way you showed me the first night?"

"Not just that." He let his lips trail along her midriff and drew his tongue along her flat, hard belly. He could feel her tense with surprise. "Don't," he whispered. "Don't fight me. Relax." He said it again in Cherokee to be sure she understood. "Nothing is wrong between a brave and his squaw who have stood before the sacred fire. Everything is pleasing to the Great Spirit who will make them fruitful."

He went slowly, waited until she was moaning softly before burying his head between her thighs. "No!" she cried out, trying to push him away.

"Yes. It is right." He grabbed both her slim wrists in one hand and forced her legs apart with the other. The more she writhed and squirmed, the more she unwittingly cooperated. The secret places of her womanhood rose to meet his searching lips and tongue, spread themselves in moist invitation. When he found the tiny fold of flesh that seemed most sensitive he increased the tempo of his sucking and biting and soon her moans had turned to little gasping screams.

She was trembling from head to foot when he mounted her. She screamed again when he plunged his turgid member deep into the place he had prepared to receive it. For a few seconds he thought he'd misjudged, that she wasn't as ready as he'd hoped. But she was. The third time he thrust against her gyrating hips he knew he could hold back no longer, but he didn't need to. She shuddered and screamed and her whole body stiffened. Her nails dug into the tough flesh of his back and her teeth sank into his shoulder. With a mighty final effort Daniel let himself explode. "See," he said afterwards. "You are a white woman. You feel things as a white woman does."

Her cheeks were wet with tears when she said, "I think it must make strong braves, this kind of mating."

"Yes." He drew his blunt fingers along her belly. "It will make good sons. You will not mourn the two you leave behind with the Cherokees."

She nodded. It had been understood from the first that the children born of her union with the dead brave would remain in the village when she and Ludlow left. That was the Cherokee way in such cases. "Where are we going?" she asked.

"South," was his only reply.

Then, shyly but with a need too deep to deny, "Do I please you, Santroyawi? Are you glad you stood with me before the sacred fire?"

"You please me. And you suit my plans, Marjorie Jackson Ludlow. You suit them just fine."

They returned to the village at the end of eight days. This was the formal leave-taking and it would be conducted with solemnity and care. Passayoro went to the cabin of her former mother-in-law to collect her things and say good-bye to the other women and to her two sons. Daniel took the opportunity for a few words with Jacob.

"Making any progress?"

"Hard to say. I have hopes, you understand, but it won't be fast."

"I warned you about that."

"Yes, I know." Jacob looked at the other members of his party. They moved easily among the Indians now, but he wondered how long it would be before they became impatient. Talks with Dayunisi lasted less than an hour a day; the rest of the time they were at loose ends.

Ludlow followed his glance and understood his concern. "Keep them in line if you value your lives," he said softly. "You're safe as long as you obey the rules. If you don't you'll have no one but yourselves to blame. And for God's sake, don't touch any of the women."

The thought that they might be tempted by the squaws startled Amory. "Don't worry," he said. But when he added, "I can handle them," it was spoken with more confidence than he actually felt. Jacob's feelings were more accurately reflected in his next words. "Daniel, will you come back to guide us out? We could set a time. These talks can't go on forever."

"Not me, Cousin," Ludlow said with a smile. "I've got plans of my own. I'll set it up for you, though." He strode off toward the *mico* without waiting for an answer.

"Passayoro and I have a far journey to make, Dayunisi. When you have heard all that my kinsman wishes to say, will you guide him and his friends safely back to the land of their tribe?"

"We will," the old man promised.

Then it was time for the farewell ceremony, and the Indians gathered around Ludlow and his woman. There were chants and dances and marks were made with bright-colored dyes on the hands and faces of both the journeyers. "You will always be of us," Dayunisi told the girl. "You leave your flesh behind and we will remember." He gestured to the two small boys that were her sons and then to the pine forest beyond the clearing. "Go where the Great Buzzard leads. With his wings he made this land for the Real People and it is a good land in a good place. Go. The Great Buzzard will lead you to a land of your own."

2

Blackwater luxuriated beneath the blazing August sun. The rice crop stood waist-high, rich yellow-green, swelling with seed. Amid the undulating fields, which to Antony always appeared to be in motion like the sea, the blacks toiled in their slow, rhythmic way. They sang softly, ignoring the sweat that poured from their stripped bodies, proving the truth of the dictum that said niggers were the best workers in Carolina. Antony Griffin turned his horse toward the house and marveled again that in this, his fourth summer on the plantation, he too had learned to bear the heat.

"Go with it," Hannah told him. "Don't fight it, and don't dream of being cool. Just let it carry you." He had heeded the advice and it proved wise. Now he didn't gallop toward the slave waiting to help him dismount. Instead, Griffin walked the horse slowly into the shade of the stable yard and waited patiently while the Negro took the reins.

"Missy Hannah is inside," the black boy said. "She's got company."

Her guest was Sara Lee Myers. Antony recognized the girl as soon as he entered the drawing room. He smiled, swallowing a chuckle. Aunt Hannah was matchmaking. She didn't give a damn how obvious her efforts were, but she would disapprove of his laughing out loud. "Good afternoon, ladies," Griffin said as he bowed and accepted a glass of lemonade.

They asked him about the fields he'd gone to inspect and listened with interest to his replies, but they were not thinking of rice at the moment. At least not directly. Antony was telling himself that Sarah Lee was indeed pretty and intelligent. Perhaps he ought to drop his resistance to the idea of marrying her. The girl was confirming her prior assessment—here was the man who'd proved capable of bringing Blackwater out of its decline, a gentleman by birth but not tainted with the Carolina prejudice that made her, an overseer's daughter, unacceptable as a wife. Hannah was watching them both and deciding that if they did indeed wed, the future of the plantation would be secure.

Later, after Sarah Lee had sailed back to Tuttle's Folly, Hannah found an opportunity to speak to her nephew. They were sitting on the terrace in the moonlight and it was a time when talking came easy. "She is a good choice, Antony." Hannah was always direct.

"Perhaps you're right," he agreed. "I'm just not sure, Aunt Hannah. It's a serious business, getting married."

"All life is a serious business." She leaned forward and her blue eyes were intent. "You've made a good beginning, perhaps even a brilliant one. By the end of this season we'll have shown a profit. And we've paid off the entire debt due Jameson's. Blackwater belongs to me again. Eventually . . ." She let the sentence hang in midair. They both knew Antony expected to inherit. It was the unspoken clause in their mutual agreement.

"I'll think about it, Aunt Hannah, I promise."

"Very well. But don't be put off by the girl's age. I know she's older than you—you're twenty-two, Sarah Lee's twenty-six. It doesn't matter. She's young enough to be a fine wife and bear you fine children."

"I don't doubt that. How come she hasn't married already?"

"Because she knows her own worth and the men around here are all idiotic snobs. Sarah Lee's a workman's child. To some that means she isn't marriage material. If Allyn Gregory—" Hannah bit her lip and was silent.

Griffin stood up and started for the house. "I've got to be up early tomorrow; there's lots to do. Good night, Aunt Hannah."

"Good night, Antony."

In his bedroom Antony thought of Allyn Gregory Ludlow and his extraordinary mother. Hannah's eldest son now lived in Charleston with his Lady Joan. They barely survived on the sale of bits and pieces of her jewelry. Half Moon House was nothing it once had been, yet Ludlow managed to find enough cash to keep himself in liquor. It was common knowledge that Allyn Gregory drank while his wife and children lived on poverty's edge, but none of that affected Hannah. She'd rejected them as heirs to her kingdom and they could die in the streets of Charleston without attracting her attention.

The attitude made Griffin uncomfortable for all he knew he profited by it. It was so bloody unnatural. Not that Hannah didn't regret the way things had turned out. Tonight, when she referred to her eldest son, Antony saw the look on her face. If Allyn Gregory had married Sarah Lee Myers he might still be at Blackwater. That's what she had started to say before thinking better of it. And it was obvious that Hannah would have preferred one of her sons to her half nephew.

Antony blew out the candle and tried to sleep. No point in examining all the complexities over and over. Things were what they were. Besides, he had nothing to complain about. The last four years had been the best of his life. It wasn't just that he'd learned to love the plantation and the lifestyle of the south; it was discovering that he was so damned good at what he'd been asked to do. He was a natural manager. He knew that now. Putting all the elements together, making them work—he had a genius for it. Guess I'm more of a Griffin than I ever admitted, he told himself. Papa would be astounded.

His dreams tonight were not of Boston and the family, however, nor of Blackwater. They were of a girl with golden hair and green eyes, just as they were most nights. By day Antony didn't allow himself to think of Ceci LaPointe but at night he had no choice. When dawn came he was angry with himself, just as he always was. Waking up with a stiff cock and a hunger in his loins for a woman he'd not seen in over three years, a woman who whored with every French trapper that could pay her price . . . It wasn't something he was proud of.

Griffin glanced at the elegant clock by his bedside. It was five in the morning. Too early to start working. Too early for breakfast even. The heaviness below his waist wouldn't subside. He tossed restlessly for a moment or two, then swore aloud. When he pulled the bell cord by his head the gesture was almost savage.

He didn't have to wait long. The girl let herself into the room and stood by the foot of the bed. "You rang, massa."

"Yes, I rang." She wasn't beautiful. Even without the bandanna she usually wore around her head, or the voluminous apron, Josie looked like what she was—a maid servant, a black slave. "I'm full of aches and pains, Josie," he said quietly. "Rode a far distance yesterday. I need one of your rubdowns in order to sleep."

She nodded and came to sit on the bed beside him. Antony rolled over onto his belly and let his tight shoulders relax under her prodding fingers. Her hands were strong. Once or twice he even yelped when she touched some tender nerve. She moved systematically down his torso, rolling back the sheet as she went. As the soft flesh of his buttocks responded to her treatment, he could feel tremors of pleasure all down his thighs and legs.

After fifteen minutes there was a pause in the massage. He was drowsy, half asleep, but he heard the soft swishing sound her nightdress made when it dropped to the carpet and he was conscious of the way the mattress sagged as she stretched out beside him. When he turned to take her, it was a lazy, relaxed motion without urgency. Griffin rolled over the black woman, grunting with the small effort required. "I'm tired, Josie," he said softly. "You'll have to do all the work." She guided his half-stiff cock between her legs, inserted it, and moved her hips. The copulation lasted less than a minute. Seconds after he'd spilled himself inside her he was asleep. Josie went silently from the room.

Antony rode to the cooperage after breakfast. "We're going to need at least a third more kegs than I estimated," he told the black overseer of the vital shop. The crop's heavier than last year by half."

"Tha's good news, suh," the black they called Barrel Ralph said with a grin. "Don' you worry none. We's gonna have as many barrels as we can fill."

Behind him were enormous stacks of pine staves and oak hoops. Griffin ran his eye along the stores, judged the number of kegs they represented, and nodded. "Good, Ralph, that's very good. If you and your boys do your job there'll be an extra chicken for each of you come Christmas."

"We'll do it, massa. I kin taste that chicken now!"

One of the worst stories told about the period of Allyn Gregory's mismanagement had to do with the cooperage. Barrel Ralph was a handsome buck of a black man, big and tall and strong as a cooper needed to be. His wife was pretty—too pretty. Ludlow's overseer, Hank Delevant, raped her and when her husband found out he went wild. The upshot was that Delevant had Barrel Ralph flogged to within an inch of his life, and the black man wasn't able to work for weeks. If the nigger hadn't been such a skilled craftsman Delevant would have killed him. That season the crop was good but the cooperage hadn't produced enough kegs to transport it to Jameson's ships. Thousands of bushels of rice had sat in the fields and rotted.

Nothing like that was going to happen under his rule, Antony had promised himself. Now, checking the wooden sleds that would haul the kegs from the threshing house to the levee, he was reassured. Everything was in readiness for the harvest, nothing left to chance. "I may not be a Ludlow," he said aloud as he swung the horse's head toward the fields that were next on his day's agenda, "but damn it all, I'm sure the next best thing." His laughter rose over the still, hot land and lost itself in the motionless fronds of the palmettos.

3

"I believe," Emile Paton told the clerk, "you have a room for us."

"Oh." The innkeeper's assistant eyed the man and the beautiful young woman standing a bit behind him. "Are you sure, sir? I rather think—"

"I think you had best check with your employer before you cause any unpleasantness for yourself." Paton's voice was low, thick with his French accent, but very sure.

The boy hurried off to do as the stranger suggested. "There's a Frenchman outside, with his daughter I think, who says we've got a room for him. I thought we didn't let rooms to Frenchies."

The innkeeper was an old man who'd owned the Lord Griffin since his father died. "Not most Frenchmen. This one's different. I've business with him. Give him the rose room."

"All right. Where should I put his daughter?"

"In the same room with Paton, you idiot! She's not his daughter. That's the notorious Mademoiselle Cecile. She's his woman."

The boy's eyes bulged with surprise. "That's her? Cecile herself? Well I'll be damned! Wait till Charleston folk realize who's come to visit!"

"Johnny," the old man called after him as the boy turned to go. "You keep your mouth shut, you hear! Feelings can get out of hand in a place like this on a Saturday night. Specially where the French is concerned. Paton and the woman will be gone by Monday. I don't want any trouble. If we keep our lips buttoned, could be they'll have left town 'fore anyone knows they's been."

Johnny intended to do as he was bid but he couldn't keep himself from gaping when he returned to the front hall where the couple waited. "Sorry Mr. . . . er . . . sorry, sir. I didn't realize you was expected. Obadiah!" He beckoned to a Negro nearby. "Take these folks and their bags up to the rose room. Look sharp now, none of your dallying."

When they were finally alone in the chamber, Ceci looked about her with interest. It was a nice room, high ceilinged and spacious and hung with faded rose damask. There was even a small balcony.

"It's not bad, is it?" Paton ran a critical eye over the room and glanced with distaste at the single big bed. "You can sleep there. I'll use the sofa. I couldn't ask for two chambers. You understand."

She did. This fiction that she was "his woman" was important to Emile, just as it was important that she not be anyone else's. Ceci nodded her agreement with the arrangements. She was used to the whole pretense by now. Next month, October of 1747, would be the fourth anniversary of her arrival in New Orleans. Soon after that she would mark her twentieth birthday. There was little in life with which she wasn't familiar, less to which she wasn't resigned. "As you wish," she answered, and turned to look at the town outside the window.

Charleston had a settled sureness about it that was different from New Orleans. This English city was neat and tidy and controlled, even elegant. New Orleans was more alive, more vivid, but this place seemed somehow more secure. It was just as hot, however. Ceci stepped onto the balcony and glanced up and down the length of Church Street. It was broad and handsome and very white. Despite the waves of humid air that assailed her she was glad to be even this tiny distance outside the room. She'd thought to enjoy this trip but it was proving dull and oppressive.

"It's not bad is it, *cherie*?" Paton commented, stepping onto the balcony. "For an English city, that is."

Emile hated the English. When a force from New England captured Louisbourg two years ago he'd wept like a child. Ceci was less disturbed despite her Canadian origins. "Forget politics, Emile," she commented now. "It's just a nice town." She walked back into the bedroom and sat down hard on the side of the bed, staring at her yellow satin slippers, betraying her boredom and discontent in the pouting look of her full mouth.

"What's wrong, *cherie*? Why aren't you happy? Are you not enjoying this opportunity to travel, to see things?"

"What things?" she demanded. "All I ever see is the inside of the carriage or a room in some inn. We even take our meals alone."

"But you know how it is, Ceci, you must know. We're French. It would be dangerous to go abroad among these savages."

"Then why did we come?"

Paton sighed with exaggerated patience. "I told you before we left, I have told you every day in the six weeks we've been traveling. There is going to be peace, Cecile. Peace between the French and the English. This war in Europe will end and the consequences will spread to the colonies. It is inevitable. I'm a prudent man. I wish to take advantage of changing times. For myself, for you. There are arrangements that can be made now if one is foresighted. Business agreements, investments. It's necessary. That's all you have to know."

"Very well." She studied her hands where they lay atop the skirt of her white lace gown. Emile had bought her a ruby ring last year. It sparkled with dark fire against the whiteness of her skin. "Very well, I accept what you say. I don't care about your business anyway. I only want a little fun. Just a little, Emile, please . . ." She crossed the room to stand beside him, looking up into his pale blue eyes with a pleading expression. "We could go out for our dinner tonight at least. Just that."

For some seconds Paton stared at the girl in silence. Finally he lifted his hand and traced the curve of her heart-shaped face with one finger. "*Eh bien*, my beautiful Cecile. I have put you in a gilded cage and you wish to flap your wings in the great world. Do you not realize that there are vultures waiting to pounce on a fledgling with sea-green eyes and golden curls? Hasn't life taught you that, *ma petite*?"

"How can they get me, Emile, as long as I'm with you?" It was emotional blackmail of the basest sort and Ceci was smart enough to know it. His role as her "protector" was important to Paton, vital.

"So," he said, smiling gently. "I'm hoist on my own petard, as these English say. I am your protector, am I not? Your guardian? Very well, Cecile, we will eat at that place around the corner this night. The one we passed with the fancy sign and the ridiculous name."

"The Pig and Whistle." She giggled. "It *is* a ridiculous name. But I'm so glad, Emile, so happy!" She took his hand and kissed it, the only physical display he ever permitted, then ran to her trunk to select a frock for the evening.

The green one, she decided. It matched her eyes and she had an emerald pendant that complemented it beautifully. She'd put her hair up with silver clips and wear silver buckles on her shoes. And she could carry the lace fan with rosebuds embroidered on its folds. Just for a moment a fleeting voice in the back of her mind made itself heard. What are you dressing up for, Cecile LaPointe? Do you think the clients of The Pig and Whistle likely to break the wall that surrounds the "chaste goddess"?

It was her mocking name for herself, a secret she shared with no one. Sometimes she would think on her life with wonderment and, bemused by its ironies, try to analyze her feelings. She cared deeply for Emile, owed him everything. And she hated the thought of being pawed and mauled at the hands of men like Captain Bonde. Emile had rescued her from all that. She was grateful, wasn't she? Why then did she sometimes feel this longing for something else, something more? Why did she resent her role as the chaste goddess of Paton's fancies?

Ceci shook her head and forced the thoughts away. She was safe and she was happy and tonight there would be music and people and laughter. It was all she needed. Later she could sleep in peace and alone behind the rose damask curtains of the big bed. It was something to be thankful for, not to question. As for her other notion, the tiny hope that perhaps Antony Griffin was still in Charleston with his cousins, that was worse than silly—it was evil. She had made her choice and she would live with it. Paton deserved at least that. She lay out the green gown and stepped back to admire it.

"You say this chap's got a model of the mill in town? Now?" Griffin eyed his informant speculatively.

"Now indeed, Antony, this very day. And tomorrow he is going to demonstrate it for us if we're wise enough to see the future and take due advantage."

The speaker was a man named Claude Rilke, who owned a plantation a bit north of Blackwater and had arrived that afternoon with an intriguing suggestion. Griffin had been surprised to see Rilke so close to harvest time. It was September, not visiting season among the planters. When he heard the man's story, however, he understood. Rilke was repeating himself now but Antony didn't mind having it all spelled out again.

"Look, you take the best nigger you've got, the strongest and steadiest worker—how much rice can he clean from sunup to sunset? Using the mortar and pestle, I mean. Six, maybe seven pecks a day?"

"Five on average," Griffin commented.

"Exactly! And given that your average nigger is lazy and

shiftless and won't work unless he's beaten . . ." Rilke shrugged expressively. "Well, you just figure it out, Antony. You're no fool; you can count."

"Yes, I can. And I see what you're getting at. If the husking process were done by machine there'd be fewer niggers to buy, house, clothe, and feed. But this 'wind-driven fan' you're talking about . . . I don't know, Claude, it sounds like dreaming to me."

"It sounded like that to me too," the other man agreed. "Then I saw it. That's all I'm asking, Antony: just come to Charleston tomorrow and see it. If you don't agree it's the greatest invention ever dreamed up by mortal man you'll have lost nothing but a few hours of time. If you do, you'll have made your fortune, my friend. Nothing less."

Griffin's eyes narrowed. "One thing isn't clear to me, Claude. If this wind fan is so bloody marvelous, how come you're offering me a chance to buy in? Am I to believe you're the benefactor of mankind?"

Rilke laughed. "I sure as hell am not. I'm overdrawn with my factor, Antony; it's as simple as that. The mill is for sale and I haven't the money to buy it. Word is that there's cash available on Blackwater these days."

"There is," Griffin said softly. "If the offer is worth investment, good for the plantation."

"This is a fair proposal I'm making, lad, don't doubt it. You get an opportunity to secure the plans for a marvelous new machine you'd never even have heard of if I hadn't told you about it, and I get a loan from you so I can build one too—in time for this season's harvest. Do we have a deal?"

"Possibly," Griffin said, nodding. "If, of course, the wind fan impresses me as it's done you."

"Of course," Rilke agreed. "I'd hardly expect a man to buy something as revolutionary as this without seeing it first."

"There's one other thing," Antony added. "I can't go to Charleston tomorrow. There's too much to be done here right now; it's out of the question. If we're to see this marvel of the human brain we must see it tonight. We can be in town by sundown if we sail now."

"Now! But—"

"No buts. Now or never."

Rilke sighed but he agreed. Everyone knew that once Griffin said something he stuck to it. "As you will, my young northern friend," he said, grinning. "Have your nigger hoist the sails and we're away."

4

The Pig and Whistle was the most popular punch house in Charleston. It was comfortable and familiar and fairly spacious so that a man could drink in peace or be sociable if he wished. Antony didn't need to spend any time looking around when he slid into a seat and ordered an ale. Rilke had gone in search of his friend with the wind fan. Griffin's mind was full of the coming harvest and what it could mean if this new idea really worked.

Rilke returned in ten minutes with a big man dressed entirely in black and sporting an enormous set of whiskers to match. "My colleague, Antony Griffin of Blackwater," Rilke said. "Antony, may I present—"

The bearded man held up his hand. "No names please, sir. Not here." He had small ferret's eyes that darted about with hostile suspicion. "Just call me the Inventor."

"Very well," Antony said. "Will you have a drink, Inventor?"

"No spirits, sir. Dulls the brain. A lemonade, if you please."

Griffin placed the order and got straight to business. "Mr. Rilke tells me you've created a machine to—"

"Please, sir! I warned you: discretion, discretion. I know

what my machine does and so do you. There's no need to inform the whole world, not yet."

"I know what your machine is supposed to do," Antony said. "That's not quite the same thing. I want to see a demonstration."

"Of course." The black beard bobbed up and down in agreement. "But first we must settle on a price. Only to be paid after you're convinced, naturally."

"Wait a minute," Rilke interposed. "You said two hundred dollars cash for a working model and a set of plans. Are you going back on your word, sir?"

The Inventor shrugged. "That's not how I'd put it. I'm a businessman, Mr. Rilke. And I've recently learned of a man willing to pay three times the amount you and I discussed for the rights to manufacture and distribute my revolutionary machine."

"Six hundred," Antony said with a small smile. "For that amount it should be miraculous, not just revolutionary." Smelling a charlatan's game, he tossed back the last of his ale and stood up. "I'm afraid you're playing for higher stakes than I'm willing to gamble, Mr. Inventor. Good evening to you both."

"Wait please, Mr. Griffin." The stranger's voice was intended to be soothing. "You think me a scoundrel and a rogue and probably a liar. I'm not. Seated right behind you, sir, just there in the back of the room, is the very man who has already offered the price I mentioned. Through an intermediary, of course. He's a stranger here, a Frenchman. But his offer is genuine. Look for yourself and you'll see a man of wealth able to make good his promise."

Slowly, not wishing to appear obvious, Griffin swung around and followed the direction of the Inventor's glance. He remained frozen in that position for many seconds.

As soon as they entered the place Ceci realized it was somehow the wrong choice. She was the only woman in the room. Either the ladies of Charleston didn't dine out, or they didn't do it at The Pig and Whistle. No matter which, she felt uncomfortable and wanted to leave but she didn't dare say so to Emile after all the fuss she'd made about coming here.

If Paton noticed that Ceci was the object of everyone's

attention he didn't admit it. He ordered their supper and kept his eyes glued to the table, morose and withdrawn but determined to go through with the "treat" he'd promised her. She was glad of that withdrawal a few minutes later.

Ceci recognized Antony as soon as he walked through the door. He'd shaved off the beard he had when he pursued her to New Orleans, and the passing years had brought maturity to his face and physique, but he was in every way the lad she'd first seen on the *Notre Dame*. Even across the room she could identify the smoky color of his gray eyes. Very dark hair, almost but not quite black. And when he spoke to the barmaid his grin had that boyish, whimsical quality she'd never forgotten. Ceci's throat closed up with some emotion she couldn't name. Though she had fantasized about this possibility, the actual event left her immobile with shock and terrified that Emile would notice.

"You're not eating, *cherie*," was all he said. "Is something wrong with the food? It seems as good as anything these English can produce."

"It's fine, Emile," she murmured, toying with the chicken on her plate. "I'm not as hungry as I thought, that's all."

He grunted and returned to his silence. She kept flicking glances toward Antony, praying he would notice her, praying he wouldn't. When he finally turned around and stared directly at their table her eyes met his for a space of heartbeats outside of time.

Griffin was the first to turn away. "You know the man, Antony?" Rilke had noticed something in his companion's face.

"Not exactly. I know—that is, I once knew—the lady with him. I was surprised to see her. That's all."

The Inventor leaned forward. "Gentlemen, my time is precious. I do not wish to discuss ladies, not even one so beautiful as that golden-haired girl. The man is as wealthy as I said he was. What remains to be discussed is whether or not you will better his offer after you've seen the machine."

Griffin started to say something, but he didn't have time to get the words out of his mouth. At that instant a voice rose above the low hum of the crowd.

"This is a punch house for gentlemen. Take your woman and get out."

It was Allyn Gregory Ludlow, drunk and surrounded by a handful of the social misfits with whom he fraternized these days. He was standing just inside the door and everything in his posture said that he'd come looking for trouble. The other customers turned to look in the direction indicated by Ludlow's unsteady, accusatory finger.

"He's French. I'm sure you all agree we don't drink with Frenchmen," Ludlow said. Then, when no one contradicted him, he shouted. "Get out of here and out of this town, you thieving, miserable bastard. If you don't we'll run you out."

"Mr. Ludlow! Please, sir," the landlord begged. "There's a lady present."

"That's no lady," one of Ludlow's confederates shouted. "That's his whore, Mademoiselle Cecile!"

A murmur of shock swept over the room and a few men not of Ludlow's party got to their feet. A voice from the back said loudly but without the liquor-sodden hostility of Allyn Gregory, "Perhaps it's best you leave, sir. We have our wives and daughters to consider, the ladies of Charleston."

Griffin had tensed when the first intimation of trouble came. He was watching not the crowd but Cecile, could see the dead white of her face, her green eyes wide with terror. He was poised on the balls of his feet, ready to spring, but he didn't know at whom or for what reason. He was aware that he stood alone. Rilke and the Inventor had melted into the shadows.

There was a moment of silence as even Ludlow just waited and watched. Finally Paton carefully folded his napkin and laid it by his plate of half-eaten food. "Come, my dear," he said to Ceci in French. "We will go. These barbarians are not fit to be in the same room with you."

She stood up and adjusted a silk shawl around her bare shoulders. The emerald pendant she wore sparkled in the dimness. The quick way it rose and fell on her breast was the only indication of her feelings. Ceci's head was high and she looked neither to the right nor left as they began to move across the long expanse of room that lay between their table and the exit.

Griffin stood somewhere near the midway point of that difficult journey. He watched her every step, and as she came near to him she raised her eyes and met his. The look they exchanged was so fleeting it was doubtful that anyone else noticed it. In the few seconds before Cecile and the man drew level with him Antony wondered if she would turn her head to renew the contact. He had no opportunity to find out. There was a sudden, swift whistling sound by his ear, and from the corner of his eye he perceived some sort of projectile hurtling through the air. By the time he registered the fact that it was a knife it was too late. The blade was lodged in the Frenchman's throat. Paton stopped in mid-step, an expression of startled surprise on his face. Then he crumpled slowly to the floor.

"That's for all them women and children your kind incite the savages to murder!" someone shouted.

"Serves him right," another voice echoed.

Griffin tore his eyes from the girl and the dying man and darted a quick look toward Ludlow and his friends. They were doing most of the shouting and they'd dispersed themselves among the other men present. A very ugly mood was swiftly replacing the shock of the murder. When someone called out, "Get the girl!" Griffin wasn't surprised.

"Yeah," another agreed. "Get her! We'll shave that blond hair off her head and send her back to them French bastards naked as the day she was born!"

Cecile paid no attention. She was on her knees by Emile's body, cradling his head in her lap and staring in disbelief at his open, unseeing eyes. She didn't realize it was Antony Griffin who dragged her to her feet. "No, don't! I must stay with him. It's my fault; he didn't want to come. It's all my fault."

"Keep quiet and do exactly what I say or you'll be as dead as he is," Griffin whispered in French. Then, to the men who were coming forward to take her from him, he said, "Leave her be. She's coming with me."

"Never figured you for no French spy," someone called out.

"Yeah, he must be! Why else's he talkin' Frog to her. Give her here, Griffin. We know how to treat Frog whores."

"You know all about whores of any kind, Jack," Griffin said softly. "Everybody knows that."

Someone guffawed and there were a few murmurs of assent. The one called Jack was son of a local farmer and he'd been in trouble of one sort or another since the day he was born. It was Allyn Gregory who said, "Jack's morals aren't in question, dear Cousin Antony. Yours are. There are some here who think you may be a French spy. Isn't that so, boys?" His friends agreed with loud comments.

Antony still had hold of Cecile and he hadn't moved away from the forgotten body of the murdered man. There was a circle of space around them but it was growing smaller. The thought of what they could do to the woman gave courage to some of those standing close by. Griffin ran his eyes over the crowd and let his glance come to rest on Allyn Gregory. "What everyone here does know," he said in a loud voice, "is what your real grudge is, Cousin. You want revenge for losing Blackwater. But you're not man enough to get it for yourself. You have to choose a woman as scapegoat and get a lot of misfits and toughs to do your fighting for you."

Silence greeted that speech but Griffin sensed a slight shift in the mood of the crowd. "All right," he said. "You've had your excitement and killed your Frenchman. Now get out of my way. I'm going home and I'm taking this girl with me. Anybody doesn't like it can come to Blackwater and we'll settle it there. One man to one man, not a lot of bullies and a defenseless woman."

They fell back then, even Allyn Gregory, despite the hatred and disappointment on his face. Griffin led Ceci to the door and didn't look back as they stepped into the street. "Keep walking," he whispered. "Don't falter no matter what. My sloop's tied up at the dock. Once we get there, you're safe." The irony of his choice of words didn't occur to him. Safe, that's what she had claimed to be when she'd rejected him four years earlier.

They were moving up the Ashley before she spoke. "I suppose I should thank you," she said in English.

Griffin looked at her in surprise. "You've learned a lot since last we met, haven't you? As for thanking me, yes, I suppose you should."

"I had time," she explained. "Emile spoke English. He taught me." Then, when the mention of the man's name reminded her, she said, "Why did they murder him like that?" She spoke more to herself than to Antony, the delayed shock of the evening apparent in the tremulous quality of her voice. "Emile did them no harm. He wasn't a spy, just a businessman."

"Whoremasters live dangerous lives," Griffin said. His anger wasn't reasonable but it was real. Everything she said made him aware of the life she'd lived, the life she'd chosen. "You should know that. Someone's always looking for men like your Emile."

She didn't answer, just stared at him, then dropped her eyes. Her silk shawl had been lost back in town and the skirt of her green gown was stained with rivulets of Paton's blood. They had dried in an ugly black tracery now highlighted by the full moon. When she sketched the pattern of the disfigurement with one shaking finger, Griffin noticed the ruby ring she wore.

"You're doing well, I see," he said. "Whoring must be profitable to buy jewels like that." He reached out and touched the emerald pendant.

She didn't reply, didn't even look at him. He couldn't stop looking at her though. Her hair had come loose and it hung over her shoulders in golden waves. Her skin tones had changed during her time in New Orleans. When he first met her, fresh from the farm in Acadia, she'd been bronzed by the sun; now she was milky white. There was a lantern hanging where they sat in the stern of the sloop. It moved with the breeze and flicked shadows of light and darkness across her shoulders and high, full breasts.

The Ashley was silent, the occasional hoot of an owl the only sound other than the rhythmic slapping of the water against the sides of the boat. The black who manned the rudder and the sails never looked at them, just kept his back turned and watched the river and the progress of his craft. "Ceci," Antony whispered as he reached out and touched her arm, "I'm sorry. I didn't mean to sound so harsh. I probably don't understand—"

She pushed his hand away. "Don't touch me. You're no different from any of them. Animals, all of you."

He grabbed her shoulders, forcing her to look at him. "Is that all you can say? After everything? Every goddamn time I try to help you I get a slap in the face. It's not my fault your *patron* is dead. I didn't murder the bastard."

"Don't you dare speak of him! Don't soil him with your lips!"

"Soil . . ." He was speechless with rage. When he kissed her it was because he knew if he didn't he'd hit her instead. He'd never struck a woman in his life, not even a black woman.

"Let me go," she gasped as she struggled to pull away. "That's all you ever think of. All you men. Even at a time like this."

"Yes, you know all about men, don't you, Cecile LaPointe? You've had a liberal education in New Orleans, that's obvious. Very well, I'll claim my share now. You might as well give me a little of what you spread around so freely. In payment, as it were."

He was pushing her down as he spoke. The sharp angle of the tapered stern created a kind of wedge that locked them together. There was no way for her to squirm free. She felt his fingers fumbling with the tie of her pantaloons, felt it give way, and felt the soft silk of her undergarment tear beneath his impatient fingers. She looked into his gray eyes and she could read nothing in them. Nothing but anger. "Antony, please, I beg you," she whispered urgently. "Not here, not like this, not in front of him."

He didn't answer, didn't even acknowledge the presence of the slave in the bow. He just lowered his head and stopped her protests with his hungry, searching mouth. When he tried to stretch himself atop her, there wasn't room to extend his long legs. He had to kneel and raise her hips with his hands.

She didn't speak again, didn't protest. Her eyes never left his. She was staring at him, forcing him to stare back even when he plunged his cock into her. It was a quick, hard movement with nothing of love or softness, marked more by rage and frustration than by passion. In two or three thrusts it was ended. He didn't even feel a sense of physical release. He only hated himself for a cad and her for a whore.

Antony carried her up the avenue from the levee. He wouldn't let the slaves relieve him of the burden. "Run ahead and get Emma," he told Nehemiah before they reached the house. "The lady's been in some difficulty in town. She's fainted."

By the time he got to the front door the big black woman who was in charge of the house slaves was waiting for him. "Give that there pore chile to me, Mr. Antony. I gots the blue room all ready and we's gettin' a bath and a hot drink fo' her now."

"That's fine, Emma. Thank you. Give her something to make her sleep. She'll need that."

"I surely will, Mr. Antony. Don't you worry none. Emma knows jus' what's needed. Missy Hannah's waitin' fo' you in there." She nodded toward the study as she carried the girl off.

"There's been trouble," he told his aunt as soon as he let himself into the room. "Man was killed. A Frenchman, so nothing will probably come of it. Allyn Gregory was involved but I don't think he did the actual killing."

"I see. Will it end there, do you think?" Hannah asked in the calm way that she addressed any crisis.

"Probably. Buy I'll post some guards just in case."

"Good. Who will you choose?" He named six of the blacks and she nodded her approval. "Yes, those are all niggers you can trust. It'll do no harm to give them guns for the night. Put Barrel Ralph in charge; he'll keep the others in line."

"Yes, I thought of that." There was just the vaguest hint of irritation in his voice. He didn't need to be told anything about the Blackwater niggers. Not after four years. Still, that was her way—it always would be. His tone was friendlier when he said, "I brought a lady home. She's French too, Acadian actually, and she was with the fellow they killed. It could have become ugly."

"I'm sure," Hannah said, pursing her lips. "I'll go and see she's all right."

"You needn't bother. Emma's taken charge."

As he turned and left the room, Hannah watched him with a speculative expression.

5

In the four months since they'd been married, Marjorie Jackson Ludlow had remembered how to speak English as well as other more subtle truths about being white. When they rode into South Carolina astride the horse Daniel had purchased a week earlier, she no longer looked like an Indian squaw despite her buckskins. Still, the garments bothered her; they were so unlike the clothes of the white women she saw as they journeyed south.

"What will your people think when they see me dressed like this?"

"Not people," Daniel corrected. "Just my mother and one cousin. That's all the family at Blackwater now."

"Still, I will look strange to your mother. Like an Indian."

"You don't know Hannah," he answered with a smile. And he continued to refuse to buy her a white woman's dress. Moreover, he didn't approve when she wrapped her long silver plaits around her head and pinned them in place. Indian women allowed their plaits to hang free. "You're prettier with them down," he said. But he didn't insist when he realized the small change was important to her. She still looked like what she was, what he wanted his mother to see. That was the only thing that mattered.

When they reached Charleston he left her alone on the banks of the Ashley and went into town to trade the horse for a small canoe. He didn't worry about her. She still had a knife tucked in the thongs of her buckskin leggings and like any squaw she knew how to use it.

"I'll be back by the time the sun's reached that tree," he told her. It occurred to him that the heat of this low southern land might trouble her after the mountainous hills of the Real People, but that didn't seem to be the case. "You're sure you're all right?" he asked before leaving. She nodded and he went on his way.

Ludlow concluded his business quickly, grateful that if anyone recognized him they said nothing about it. Soon he'd deal with those who had peopled his boyhood world—soon, but not yet. Two hours later he rejoined his wife. The sun had just reached the tree he'd indicated and she was waiting by the river, never doubting he'd return precisely as promised. Daniel set the little boat into the water and motioned for her to join him.

It was close to four when they drew up alongside the familiar levee. The sun was low behind the trees, and looking along the broad avenue to the house Daniel saw that the terrace was in shadow. His mother always liked the terrace best at this time of day. She was probably sitting there now.

"Who is you?" a voice demanded and a black carrying a musket stepped close to the small canoe.

Ludlow was startled. Armed niggers were the worst sight he knew. He dropped his hand to the gun lying beside him and asked quietly, "What are you doing with that weapon, boy? Does Missy Hannah know you've got it?"

"Mr. Antony gave me dis here gun," the black said nervously. "I's s'posed to stop anybody what's comin' here to make trouble." He was too young to remember a Ludlow who'd left the plantation eight years before. He peered closer at the couple. They were strangers but they didn't look like enemies, just a man and a woman.

"I'm Mr. Daniel," Ludlow said. "Missy Hannah's my mother. Help the lady out of the canoe and tie it up right here." He stepped ashore without waiting for the nigger to drop his weapon. Whatever was going on, it wasn't armed rebellion.

Daniel walked alone toward the house. The sounds and sights and smells of Blackwater rushed to meet him. There was the low distant music of the field hands singing to maintain the rhythm of their work, and the call of a mockingbird sitting on a nearby tree. The scent of honeysuckle filled the afternoon and mingled with the smell of the heat. The last was indescribable, unique. It was the odor of skin and sweat and effort called forth by the relentless sun, the peculiar odor the very buildings exuded as they stood in the sultry air. It was something he had smelled nowhere else in America. It was home and the things he had suddenly come to yearn for after his long absence.

Hannah saw him coming—not from the window of the tower room as she'd dreamed it for so many years, but from the terrace. She stopped the motion of the rocking chair on which she sat and looked carefully, shading her eyes with her hand, not letting herself feel anything until she was sure. Then she knew—how could she not know?—and she stood up and waited.

"Hello, Mama," he said when at last he reached the house.

"Hello, Daniel."

Marjorie came up behind him and he took her hand and pulled her forward. "This is Marjorie, my wife."

Hannah looked at the girl and saw what she was meant to see: strength, courage, the will to survive. All were writ large in the mixture of white and Indian the girl epitomized. If Hannah found the sight extraordinary, it showed in neither her face nor her voice. "I'm pleased to meet you," she said. "Come inside. You must be tired and thirsty."

Daniel jerked his head back toward the levee. "How come that nigger has a gun?"

"There was trouble in town last night. Your cousin, Antony Griffin, is here now. He thought it best we post some guards. It's all right. He chose the ones we can trust."

"Is there trouble? Here on the plantation?"

"No. It seems to have been a false alarm." She made no reference to the French girl still asleep upstairs.

"Send someone to take the weapons and put the guards back to work then," he said quietly. "Armed niggers make me nervous."

Hannah nodded and waited for her son and daughter-in-law to precede her into the house.

"I suppose Allyn Gregory was part of the trouble," Daniel said to his mother a few minutes later when they were alone in the drawing room. Marjorie had been sent with a slave to have a bath and change her clothes. Hannah had commented that buckskin leggings were too hot for Blackwater and Daniel had agreed. It no longer mattered. He knew from the look on his mother's face that she'd seen what Marjorie was.

Now, when he asked about his brother, Hannah glanced at him and for the first time her blue eyes were questioning. "Yes," she said, nodding. "Allyn Gregory was part of the trouble. He usually is. How much do you know, Daniel? Of what's happened here, I mean?"

"Everything," he answered and saw her eyebrows raise.

"Everything? How does that happen to be true? I've had no word from you for eight years."

"I've been to see Susannah a number of times. At her place on the James. She's kept me informed."

He walked to the sideboard and poured himself a brandy. In the slanting light that came through the long windows Hannah thought his dark brown hair, tied back Indian fashion, looked strangely alien. But the way he moved, even the way he spoke, was just as it had always been. She crossed to his side and asked, "If you knew everything as you say, why didn't you come sooner?"

"I couldn't," he answered. "There were things I had to do for myself first. Things I had to prove. Besides, I knew you weren't mad. When Susannah told me that I just laughed."

"I wasn't mad, Daniel, but I wasn't laughing. I was weeping for everything your father and I had built. Weeping to see it destroyed by a son unworthy of the name. I needed a man to help me put things right. I needed you."

He shook his head with the stubbornness she remembered so well. "You managed anyway. Just as I expected you to. The place looks wonderful. People say it's the most profitable plantation in Carolina again."

"Yes, it is. When Antony came, I found a way, and now everything's as it once was." She touched her snow-white hair with her hand and turned away, then added, "Almost everything. But you should have come, Daniel. You owed me that."

"I'm here now, Mama."

"Yes," she said softly. "You're here now. Go up and change, Daniel. All your old clothes are still in your room. Antony's due back from the western fields in an hour. We'll dine as soon as he returns."

Later, needing to see him again, not able to wait until dinner time, she went and knocked on the door of his bedroom. Marjorie let her in. The girl looked lovely in a blue gown the slaves had found for her, and Hannah smiled. "Do you like this dress better than buckskins?" she asked.

"It is the right dress for this place," Marjorie said. Her English was still slightly stilted. It made everything she said sound solemn and rather formal. "When I was with the Real People it was right to wear buckskins."

"Yes, I see that." Hannah nodded. "Where is Daniel?" she asked, looking around the empty room. "I came to ask him if you both have everything you need."

"We need nothing. Daniel has gone to find the black man who cuts hair."

"Oh!" Hannah smiled more broadly at the news. "I'm glad. He's better-looking with his hair a bit shorter." Marjorie made no reply, and the older woman put up a hand to touch the girl's braids. "Would you like your hair fixed the way women here wear theirs?"

When Marjorie nodded, Hannah led her to the dressing table and sat her down in front of the glass. Her fingers were deft as she undid the plaits and combed out the long silvery tresses. "Your hair is a remarkable color," she said. "I've never seen anything like it." Then, when the job was done, she stepped back and asked, "Do you like it this way?"

"It looks as the hair of Daniel's wife should look," Marjorie answered. She turned to her mother-in-law and some unspoken communication passed between them in a long moment of mutual assessment. The younger woman was the first to break the silence. "Soon this gown will not fit me." She pressed her hands across her belly. "I have Daniel's son growing here."

Hannah caught her breath. "Good. Oh, Marjorie, that's very good."

"Yes. Daniel's son will be born on Daniel's land. That is good."

Antony let himself into the house and asked first after Ceci. "She still sleeping, Mr. Antony," Emma told him. "Pore thing ain't opened her eyes but once today. All tuckered out."

Griffin started for the stairs. "I'm going to wash and change; then I'll go to see her." There were things he wanted to say to

Ceci, things that had been haunting him all during this long day while he rode and worked and thought, and realized how unspeakable his behavior of the night before had been. "Tell the kitchen to hold dinner for half an hour, Emma."

"I dunno, Mr. Antony," the black woman said slowly. "I don' think I'd best do that. Missy Hannah's boy comed back this afternoon. Mr. Daniel whats been gone these eight years. Brought his wife an' everything. I don' think I's s'posed to hold dinner late tonight." Her eyes were full of worry and confusion. What was going to happen here now that Mr. Daniel had suddenly returned?

Antony read the consternation in her face. "Very well, Emma, we'll dine at the usual time and I'll see Miss Cecile afterwards," he said quietly. "Oh Emma, just one more thing. Who ordered the guards disarmed?"

"Mr. Daniel, sir. He done it soon as he come."

Antony didn't say anything but as he climbed the stairs to his room he was asking himself the same questions he'd seen in the slave's face. Later, when he entered the candlelit dining room and heard Hannah's gleeful announcement—"Antony, I've a wonderful surprise; I want you to meet my son Daniel"—he didn't have to wonder. He knew.

6

Griffin didn't go with the Ludlows to the drawing room after dinner. "Please excuse me," he murmured, bowing to the ladies. "It's been a very long day and I've a guest to see to."

"Oh yes," Daniel said. "The young Frenchwoman. The niggers told me about her." His eyes seemed to be saying something about harboring such guests but Antony ignored the message.

"Yes. The young Frenchwoman, Cecile LaPointe." He threw the name into the space between himself and his cousin and waited. Daniel just smiled. Griffin realized that while Ludlow probably knew the girl's reputation, he wasn't prepared to make an issue of it. Fine, that's what he'd meant to discover by mentioning it. "Good night ladies. Daniel." Bowing again, he left the room.

Ceci was still sleeping. Her face was white and still against the pillow, her hair spread out like some kind of golden mantle. Antony stood by the bed and watched her for many minutes, then left the room.

He didn't even try to sleep that night, just sat by the window and stared into the blackness. Griffin didn't need to see the plantation to know every inch of its rich, fertile ground. In four years Blackwater had graven itself on his heart, etched its contours into his blood and bones. He would smell it, taste it, feel it, to the end of his days. But he would not be here. He knew that now.

Incredible. This morning he'd ridden out to do a day's work believing the land beneath him would one day be his, that he was earning it with every sweaty hour of effort. In half an hour at dinner he'd realized the dream was an illusion. Daniel Ludlow had come home, brought a wife of whom Hannah approved, and announced over champagne that the woman was carrying his child. Daniel had snuffed out his dream, made a mockery of everything Antony had worked so hard for.

"The bitch!" he cursed aloud. "How dare she. She used me, made do while I was available. Now she's going to give it all to him." The rage lasted for less than an hour. What Hannah was going to do, had in effect already done, was so in keeping with everything he knew of her that it was ridiculous to be angry. She was being herself and she'd never claimed to be otherwise. Hannah was a painfully honest woman, and by her own lights a fair one. The mistake, the stupidity, had all been his.

Why hadn't he realized Ludlow would return? How could any man know Blackwater, grow up beneath its spell, and not crave it? Even that ass Allyn Gregory craved it. The difference between the brothers was only that Allyn Gregory was a fool. The younger man was not. Allyn had been unable to hold on to Blackwater when he had it but Daniel would not make the same mistake.

Take the way he'd come here today, for instance. Without warning, bringing his extraordinary wife in her buckskin leggings—the slaves had been quick to tell Griffin about that—announcing she was pregnant. It had the elements of a Greek drama. All carefully staged, designed to elicit from Hannah the very response she instinctively wanted to make. It was bloody brilliant, which is just what Antony had not been. Brilliance, even ordinary common sense, should have made him get something in writing from Hannah years ago. But he hadn't even considered it, and now he would pay the price.

Staring into the night, Antony tried to puzzle out that strange oversight on his part. He wasn't really stupid, never had been. Why had he done it then? Taken everything on trust like a babe in arms, set himself up for just the fall that had come? Because, he told himself, God help me, I'm a Griffin. Where the family is concerned you don't expect to need a written contract. You expect honor, and in the end—whatever infighting takes place—you get it.

The Ludlows were cut from different cloth apparently. They were Lizzie's stock, not Tonyjay's. The thought of his grandfather made Antony grimace. The old man had written him a twenty-page opus on the evils of slavery in '44 when he first learned of Antony's involvement with Blackwater. Since then not a word. What would Tonyjay make of this development if he ever found out? And how would Hannah handle it? Promise him a lifetime job as overseer most likely. With a handsome salary and a house of his own on Blackwater land. Yes, something like that. As if he'd ever accept second best in Camelot, ever agree to be court jester rather than prince royal in the enchanted kingdom.

There was a light but urgent tap on his door. Griffin looked out at the pale flush of dawn on the horizon. Hannah? So soon with her explanations and her cheap offers? Maybe, but not likely. She'd choose her time and place more carefully. "Come in," he called softly and waited to see who opened the door.

It was Emma. Despite the warmth of the night, she was wrapped in a flannel nightdress that looked rather like a tent.

Her grizzled gray hair hung in one fat plait over her enormous bosom. "Is you awake, Mr. Antony? I gots to tell you sumpin'."

"Yes, Emma, I'm awake. What is it?"

He saw her eyes take in his fully clothed condition and her lips were pursed when she said, "It's that girl what you brought home, that Miss Cecile. She's gone."

"Gone! What are you talking about? I just saw her a few hours ago. She was sound asleep."

"Well, she ain't asleep now. She's gone, like I said. I went to her room bout half an hour ago, just to check on her like, see she was all right. There weren't no sign o' that chile nowhere."

"Did you look in the house? Outside? Maybe she went for a walk, needed some air—"

"Course I looked! Had Nehemiah look too. Everywhere we could think of, inside and out. She ain't here, I'm tellin' you, Mr. Antony. And that's the truth. Canoe ain't here neither."

"Canoe? What canoe?"

"The one Mr. Daniel rowed home in. He left it at the levee and Josh tied it up like he was told. Now Nehemiah says it ain't there."

"It must have broken free. We can look for it tomorrow. That's not important, Emma. What matters is to find Miss Cecile."

"Mr. Antony, ain't you listenin' to what I'm tellin' you! The canoe is gone cause Miss Cecile is gone. She took it. I knows she did. Took it and run straight from here to that 'Cadia place she kept mutterin' bout while she was sleepin'."

"Oh sweet Jesus!" He knew she was right. He was exhausted, preoccupied with his own crisis, that's why he hadn't seen it at first. "What did she take with her, Emma? Can you tell?"

"Near as I can make out jus' that green dress she was wearin' when you brung her home. And them jewels o' hers. They ain't gonna help her none, Mr. Antony. Jewels won't help if she's all alone out there on the Ashley at night and the spooks come to the river." Her eyes widened with horror at the thought.

"It's not spooks I'm worried about," Griffin said grimly as he grabbed for his jacket. "She probably can row; considering where she's from, it figures she can. But the currents on that river are treacherous if you don't know them. And if she does get to Charleston she won't find much in the way of welcome. Damn fool, what the hell's she thinking of—" He broke off. No time for that now. "Get Nehemiah," he said. "Tell him to ready a sloop. I'll take it downriver myself; he needn't go."

She hurried off to do as he said, and not until she returned with word that the sloop was waiting did Griffin step into the hall. He'd made use of the ten minutes that had passed. He had a gun and a knife—if there was trouble in town he'd be ready for it. And for some reason he couldn't explain he'd also taken as much cash as he could lay his hands on. A pouch of coins was secure beneath his shirt.

Thus armed, Griffin bounded to the top of the elegant curved staircase, then turned with a last instruction. "When the family wakes up tell them I've gone off on private business. There's a lot to be done today—the harvest is starting. Tell Mr. Daniel I said I was sure he could handle it." His grin was ironic but the black woman didn't answer his smile.

"I'll tell 'em, Mr. Antony," she said softly. There was a wealth of knowledge and sadness in her eyes when she said, "Good-bye Mr. Antony. You take care o' yourself, you hear. An' find that chile afore she come to any harm."

"I'll do that, Emma. I promise. Good-bye."

He traveled as quickly as the breeze and the current would allow, always hoping he'd see her paddling the canoe just around the next bend, always disappointed. She must have reached town before him. It was impossible to know how much of a head start she'd had, and how adept was she at handling the small boat? Only questions, no answers.

By midmorning Griffin was tied up at Elliot's wharf and scanning the harbor for any sight of the canoe. Nothing. And there was no one around who looked remotely like Ceci. He hurried up to Tradd Street and turned in at The Pig and Whistle. "The woman that was with the Frenchman the other night," he asked the barmaid, "have you seen her?"

"Not since you carried her off, Mr. Antony," the girl said, sighing over the romance of it all. "Wasn't she beautiful! And you were so gallant, coming to her rescue like that." She looked at him with an obvious invitation. Antony managed a grin before leaving the punch house.

Neither the clerk at the hotel nor the proprietor of the Exchange Coffee House could tell him anything. They were willing enough to discuss the dramatic events of two days past, even the details of how they'd dumped the Frenchman's body into the water with curses instead of prayers, but they knew nothing about the infamous Mademoiselle Cecile. They'd all thought she must still be at Blackwater. At Dillon's on the Corner someone asked him if it was true that Daniel Ludlow had returned home; but while they knew all about that, they knew nothing of Ceci. No joy at Shepherds Tavern or the Sign of the Two Brewers either. Antony had exhausted his possibilities.

It wasn't that he thought Ceci would go to a punch house as soon as she got to town. It was just that wherever she went, it would be at the punch houses that her arrival would be discussed. If there was nothing to be learned at the taverns, there was nothing to be learned.

Griffin walked through the streets once more. He felt aimless, frustrated, frightened for her, and horribly guilty because he knew better than anyone why she'd felt compelled to leave the refuge at Blackwater. But in a way he was less worried than he had been. The worst danger he could conceive for Ceci was the angry mob that might materialize in Charleston. Obviously nothing like that had taken place this morning. He'd know by now if it had. So where was she? In his mind's eye he went back over the familiar course of the Ashley as it made its way from the levee at Blackwater to its mouth near the town.

So many coves and inlets. She could have pulled in at any of them. But would she? He'd assumed she would come to town and seek transportation to wherever she wanted to go, maybe even try and raise cash on her jewels. Apparently she hadn't done that.

Griffin walked back to the dock and stood staring at his sloop, debating the wisdom of setting out up the river to try again. He was still considering the wisdom of that plan when he saw Willy Blood. "Willy," he called as an idea struck him. "Come over here. I've a job for you if you're interested."

The half-breed listened impassively to Antony's story. Griffin didn't say that the woman he was looking for was the same woman Blood had taken him to find in New Orleans four years earlier, but he guessed Willy would know. The Choctaw always knew everything that happened in town. He'd have heard the story of the rescue of Mademoiselle Cecile and put it into a perspective none of the others knew.

"You no see canoe on river?" was all he asked when Antony had finished speaking.

"No, I didn't. And I was looking. That's why I want you to sail back up with me, Willy. You're much better at seeing that sort of thing than I am. Better than any white man. Maybe you can spot where she went ashore. If she did."

The Choctaw shrugged. "If she no come to town and she no go ashore, she drown. If you want, we look."

They sailed off together minutes later. Griffin kept his eyes glued to the northeast bank. Blood watched the southeast side but he didn't wholly trust Antony; he kept glancing over to the shore the white man was supposed to be patrolling. And he was right. It was to the northeast that he pointed when he said softly, "There—bring the sloop in there."

Griffin did as he was told. He'd not forgotten how pointless it was to argue with Willy Blood, nor how unwise. This time too the half-breed was correct. When he pointed out the signs, Antony could see them. "She come ashore here," Blood said. "Here she grab hold of the trees to pull herself in."

Antony inspected the torn palm fronds and nodded. "You think she landed deliberately then? She didn't run aground?"

"No run aground here. Water deep. Lady bring boat in and go on foot."

"But where, damn it? Where the hell did she think to go in this bloody wilderness?"

The Indian didn't answer as he strode a few yards inland with his eyes intent on the black earth and the swampy undergrowth. "Here's canoe," he said finally as he pulled back a curtain of trailing moss.

Griffin whistled through his teeth. The little boat had been well hidden, its oars tucked carefully inside the small frame. "Did she plan to come back, do you think? Is that why she left it like this?"

"No come back," Willy said. "Not right away. Head north, six maybe seven hours ago."

"North to Acadia," Antony said softly. "Oh Ceci, you little

fool!" He looked again at the well-secreted canoe. Force of habit, legacy of her girlhood in the wilds of Canada. Ceci wanted to go home in every sense of the word. And because of him she'd chosen a dangerous, even a suicidal, way to do it. If he'd not pushed her over the edge she might have waited, planned more carefully, more sensibly.

"I've got to go after her, Willy," he told the other man. "Will you come? Track her for me? I'll pay you well, you know that."

"I come," Blood answered. It occurred to Antony that it wasn't the promise of money that engendered that ready agreement. Maybe it was the memory of the beautiful golden-haired girl.

"Do we need to stop for supplies?" he asked Blood. "Should I go back to town and get some things?"

"No time," the Choctaw answered. "Go now. Live on what we find. You have gun, Mr. Antony? Knife?"

"Both," Antony told him. "And I've learned a lot since last we traveled together. I can handle them."

"Good. Willy lead."

He moved off into the swampy land and Griffin followed. There was some element of urgency in the half-breed's behavior that wasn't in keeping with his character, but Antony knew there was no point in asking about it. Willy would explain, if he could, in his own time. Until then, Griffin must only do as he was told and keep praying that Ceci would be alive and well when they found her.

7

By Thursday evening Griffin was miserably frustrated. "Three days and nights, Willy! How the hell can she stay ahead of us all this time? She's just a slip of a girl and she only had a few hours head start. It doesn't make sense."

"Danger," Willy answered. "We go slow, no travel by night."

"Yes, so I've noticed. Why Willy? Why are we going so slow and why is it dangerous?" The Choctaw looked away and made no reply.

Then, Friday afternoon, without warning, while Griffin was slogging along through a streambed behind the guide, they came to a stop. "Girl up there," Willy said, pointing to a tree-covered rise some two hundred yards distant.

"How the hell do you know that?"

"Come, I show you."

He should have known better than to doubt. They pushed aside a thicket of branches and saw her sitting in the clearing. She jumped to her feet in terror but it was only the space of one deep-drawn breath before she recognized them. "I don't believe it. How did you get here?"

"The same way you did," Griffin said drily. "On foot, tramping through those swamps. You led us a pretty chase, lady. Are you all right?"

"I didn't ask you to come," she retorted. "And I'm fine. I don't need you."

Antony couldn't repress a smile when he looked at her. She'd ripped the bottom half of her skirt away and somehow made the remainder into leggings of a sort. It was really just an arrangement of bits of green satin cloth tied with vines, but it was damned clever. So were her shoes. God alone knew what had happened to the silver slippers. What she wore now were mocassin-style coverings of bark, wrapped with more of the green satin. Her hair was tied back and her face was flushed with sunshine and toil. She looked incredibly like the Ceci he'd first seen, fresh from Acadia. "You've certainly been inventive," he commented.

"I was raised to make do," she answered with just a hint of scorn. "I've told you many times before, I can manage. I can always manage."

Blood hadn't spoken until now, but like Antony he'd observed all the survival tactics the girl had employed. "You hungry," he said finally. "Here." He handed the girl a piece of the rabbit he and Griffin had caught and cooked the night before and she took it eagerly.

"No knife," she said to him by way of thanks.

"I know," Blood answered.

"How Willy, how did you know she was hungry and how did you know she was here?"

"Yesterday we climb out of the berry places. No more fruit, no more berries. Missy make no fire so have no knife. Kill nothing."

"And you knew she had no fire because you've seen her campsites." Antony spoke more to himself than to Blood or the girl. Ceci wasn't listening in any case; she was too busy eating. Willy wasn't standing in rapt attention either. He was busy checking the perimeters of the little clearing, making small adjustments in the way of the leaves lay, scuffing the earth. He'd repeated that performance time after time in the past days. Now Antony realized that he'd been destroying the evidence of Ceci's passage as well as their own.

It wasn't quite the same as that last trip, the one to New Orleans. This time Antony didn't feel outclassed by the half-breed's skills as a woodsman. He'd proved his own worth in the world where men fight and scratch and struggle to make a living, so he could admit that he wasn't good at everything and admire what someone else could do better than he could. That change in attitude was important. It allowed him to evaluate with a cool head and he needed to do that. He was rapidly becoming convinced of something he'd suspected since the journey began.

"Willy," Griffin said, crossing to where the other man was examining a bit of earth and squatting beside him. "I want to know what's going on. What do you know? What are you afraid of?" They were out of Ceci's hearing but Griffin pitched his voice as low as possible.

"Later we talk," Blood said. "Now you stay with Missy. Willy go get something to eat. Good chance now." He was gone before Antony could protest.

"I meant it," Ceci said when she realized they were alone. "You didn't have to come after me. It was my choice to go. I didn't expect you to follow me."

"Don't like being rescued, do you?" He tried to keep a bantering tone. There were funny prickles of fear running up his spine when he thought of how Willy hadn't denied that something was wrong.

"Maybe I don't like the price you charge," she answered quietly.

He felt as if she'd punched him in the gut. "I deserve that, I know I do," he said when he could speak. "If you want the truth, it's one of the main reasons I came after you. All the next day, after I . . . after that night on the river, I kept thinking about what I'd say, how I'd apologize. Then, before I had a chance, you ran away."

"I'm going home," she said. "North. Home to Acadia."

"Very well. I'm not trying to stop you. I'll help you if you'll let me. That's got nothing to do with saying I'm sorry." She didn't answer and he repeated it. "I am, you know. Sorrier than I can tell you. It was a rotten thing to do. Despicable. I don't know what came over me. I guess if I'm honest I have to say you pushed me away once too often. Every time, Ceci, every time I come after you, reach out for you, you push me away."

When she answered he had to strain to hear her. "I don't mean to," she whispered. "I never mean to. It's just that I know I have to protect myself. I've always had to."

"Not from me." He hadn't known he was going to say it until the statement was out of his mouth, hadn't even admitted it to himself. "I love you, Ceci. I think I've loved you from the first day I saw you."

She raised her green eyes to his and was silent for some seconds. Then she opened her mouth to speak but it wasn't possible. Willy had crawled into the clearing, come up behind her, and at just that moment clamped his hand over her lips. Griffin read the meaning of his actions instantly, even before terror had time to form in Ceci's eyes.

He bent forward and placed his lips against her ear, speaking so softly it almost wasn't speaking at all. "It's just Willy. Don't make a sound." The Choctaw released her and they crawled after him into the shelter of the band of trees surrounding the clearing.

Blood had scouted this spot as soon as they came to the clearing. The place he chose to hide them was the best one possible. They were amidst a mass of fir trees with dense, low branches. No one could possibly see them without a deliberate search. They could barely see out. Griffin had to strain his eyes to detect cracks of light in the tent of needle growth surrounding him.

A minute passed, two, three. At first he held his breath. When that became impossible he allowed himself a few shallow, silent, intakes of air. On either side he could sense his companions doing the same thing. He could smell the heady scent of the firs, and something else. He could smell fear.

Four years ago, in the weeks when they'd traveled to New Orleans, Willy had reminded him often that they were passing through hostile country, that they had to be careful. What Blood exuded now—what Griffin could actually feel, it was so palpable—was nothing like the respectful caution the half-breed had displayed back then. Blood was terrified. The realization of that truth turned Antony's mouth dry. He was going to puke. He knew he was. Whatever or whoever was stalking them would have an easy job. All that would be necessary would be to follow the sound of his retching.

He didn't of course. He'd have choked on his own vomit before doing anything so stupid or cowardly. For a time he thought that might happen. Then he saw what it was they were hiding from and the nausea of terror abated. In a queer kind of way, seeing was a relief.

Just beyond the canopy of branches that shielded them a

pair of moccasined feet passed by, then another and yet another. Griffin counted sixteen in single file before he dared raise his eyes and look at the bodies of the Indians. They were taller than any red men he'd ever seen in Charleston or Boston. Their torsos were bare from the waist up and their broad chests were covered with markings in various colors. Twenty-two had passed before Antony managed to get a brief glimpse of the head of the last, the twenty-third. His hair was confined to a single band running front to back along his skull. A scalplock, Griffin thought to himself in a moment of strange academic removal from the reality of fear. He noted too the feather that decorated the hairstyle. Then, as silently as they had come, the Indians were gone.

Blood kept them in their hiding place for twenty minutes more. Finally he signaled that they could move back into the clearing.

"Jesus!" Griffin murmured. "Is that why we've been moving so carefully?"

"Yes. Renegades. Far from their home country. Come from north. Last month, month before, I hear of them. When I see Missy went into forest afraid. We follow slowly. Very careful."

Antony turned to Ceci. She was ashen and he could actually see her trembling. He reached out a hand and tried to put his arms around her in comfort, but she turned to Blood instead. "I know them," she whispered. "Dear Mother of God, they're Iroquois, aren't they?"

"Yes, Iroquois."

Cecile swung around, doubled over, and did what Antony had been afraid he'd do—retched violently. It wasn't merely the brief time of terror just passed that brought on the reaction. It was the knowledge that all these days she'd been alone in the forest and the renegades had been there too.

"It's all right, Ceci," Griffin said, wiping her face and pressing her close. "They're gone now. It's all right."

For once she didn't push him away. "You don't understand," she said, looking up. "I know about them. At home we used to hear stories. They're Iroquois!"

"It is done," Dayunisi said finally. "It is good."

"Yes," Jacob Amory agreed with feeling. "It is very good."

The messenger from the White chief, the one they'd awaited

for almost five months, stood up. "I go and tell that the white men will carry our words to their chiefs. Then chiefs come and the Real People will see these new friends."

"Tell the great White chief of the Cherokees that I am honored to carry his promise of peace and alliance," Amory said. The translator interpreted and the messenger nodded.

Dayunisi spoke again. "Tonight we make a feast to celebrate this good thing. Tomorrow Achechi who brought you here with Santroyawi will select four of our best young men to guide you and your friends back to the land of your tribe."

The *mico* raised his eyes to sycamore trees grown red with the early cool of the September nights in this high country. "Before the last leaves have fallen to the ground you will be with your own people. When the new leaves come you will return with your chiefs and we will make our alliance with you, and not with the people who do the abominable things of which you've told me. It is good," he repeated and motioned to the women to prepare the feast.

Later Joseph Deering asked Jacob, "What do you think really did it? The point that actually tipped the scales in our favor I mean."

Deering's voice was husky with the sweetness of success. Amory felt it necessary to add a word of caution. "Don't be too elated, Joseph. Remember, it's not a real treaty yet. Just the promise that they'll talk to us of one."

"Doesn't matter." Stuart was as happy as Joseph and he couldn't be deflated by Jacob's caution. "It's more than anyone has ever achieved. Wait till we tell them back in Philadelphia. Nobody thought the Cherokees could be wooed from the French, but you've done it, Jacob. You've really done it." He slapped Amory on the back and laughed aloud from sheer high spirits.

"Yes, you have," Deering agreed. "I still want to know what you think was the *coup de grace* as it were."

"Well, your idea really. What you suggested I tell Dayunisi about the French being Catholics. That they worship a devil man who lives in a far city and tells them all what they must do, even here in a place he's never seen. And that they claim to eat their God and drink his blood. I don't know how much Dayunisi really understood, but he certainly was astounded. Said that among his people the eating of live flesh was an abomination, that the Cherokees couldn't be allies to any who admitted to such atrocities. That's when he agreed to send a message to the White chief. Anyway," he said, stretching out and looking up at the stars, "I told you about that at the time. Why are we going over it all now?"

"I don't know," Deering said. "I guess it's just so unbelievable I enjoy talking about it."

"Yes, me too," Amory admitted. He closed his eyes and allowed himself to dream of a hero's return to Philadelphia and thence to Boston. Wouldn't Mama be proud when she finally heard the story.

8

Using the point of his knife, Griffin drew a rough map in the dirt. "Look, Willy—here's Blackwater, here's the Ashley, and here's about where I think we started north a week ago. Now, where do you think we are?"

"We here." The Choctaw plunged the point of the knife into the ground with certitude.

"You're sure?"Griffin looked at the still quivering blade. "If you're right we've traveled over a hundred miles. It doesn't seem possible."

"We here," Blood repeated.

"Where's here?" Ceci asked, peering at the marks on the earth.

"According to Willy, deep in North Carolina, almost Virginia in fact. It's just a guess, mind you. Without a proper map and landmarks it's hard to say."

"I told you not to travel north for my sake," the girl said. "You should have had Willy guide us back to Charleston."

"Listen." Griffin sat back on his heels and looked at her. "I don't want to hear any more about it. We made this decision because Willy said it was the safest choice as long as they were out there." He jerked his head in the direction of the wilderness around them. Since they'd seen the renegades there had been an unspoken agreement not to mention the word *Iroquois*. Griffin didn't really know why those particular Indians elicited such terrified responses from both the half-breed and Ceci, but he was willing to accept it without probing. He turned back to the rough map. "My only question is why we haven't turned east before now. When do we start in that direction?"

"Not yet," Willy said. "Go north three more days, then take river to Jamestown."

"Very well." Antony scuffed the marks from the ground with the toe of his boot. "You're the guide. Let's go."

A few minutes later Ceci told him, "When we get to Jamestown I want to pay your passage back to South Carolina. It's only fair."

Griffin kept walking as he answered: "You are the damnedest, most infuriating woman I ever met. You have more pride than most men. Just save your breath, will you! And keep moving."

She did as she was told and he sneaked a look at her from the corner of his eye. It was remarkable how well the girl was bearing up. She hardly slowed the two men. In her own way she was as tough as any female he knew, including Hannah Ludlow. The thought of his aunt made him grimace. He'd told Ceci nothing of all that and didn't know if he would. He didn't know what he planned to do once they reached civilization either. He'd see she got passage to Canada, then make up his mind about his own future. As for his declaration of love back in the clearing, she'd obviously forgotten it. Well, he'd do the same. He'd gone begging to Mademoiselle Cecile LaPointe for the last time.

Will Randall had learned a few words of Cherokee during the months the Philadelphians spent in the Indian camp. He was the one who communicated with Achechi, leader of their guides. "Achechi says we reach the river tomorrow. We'll be on the James by afternoon if I understand him correctly."

The others looked with longing at the canoes the party carried. "I for one will be damned glad to be traveling on my backside and not my feet," Timothy said.

The rest of the men nodded agreement and settled themselves to sleep. By now their city clothes were so worn and threadbare that they didn't even bother to remove their jackets when they lay down. Still, they had worn them unfailingly since the day they'd set out on this adventure. Returning to Philadelphia in those same tattered and soiled garments had become a mark of honor.

Amory pulled his own frayed velvet coat closer and tried to make himself comfortable on the hard ground. Nights were longer and cooler now. Autumn would be here in earnest by the time they got home. He had a fleeting vision of the delight of a long, hot bath and a meal of steak and kidney pudding—with about a quart of claret, he promised himself. Then, chuckling softly at his mundane fancies in the midst of the wilderness while a Cherokee sentry stood nearby like some mythical being, he slept.

Dawn. A chorus of birdsong. One note seemed slightly more persistent and demanding than the rest. A few moments passed and again the strange note was repeated. This time it seemed a bit closer. The Cherokee guard stiffened and fingered his knife. Nothing. Only the sounds he knew to be right in this place at this time. Then, before he could open his mouth to scream, he was dead.

The Iroquois descended like Armageddon on the sleeping campsite. One Cherokee awoke in time to inflict a knife wound on the face of his enemy, but he too was dead seconds later. Few of the ten, Philadelphians or Real People, lived long enough to hear their assailants' war cries. Will Randall's brains spilled from his cracked skull the instant the ball-headed club descended. The blow intended to dispatch Joseph Deering was less perfectly delivered. He remained alive long enough to crawl some four inches from the spot on which he lay. One brave needed only two efficent passes of his knife to cut out the hearts of both Stuart Reed and Timothy Hanson. The Indian stood between their twitching bodies with the organs held high over his head and bellowed his triumph to the rising sun.

Not twenty seconds passed from the start of the awesome onslaught to the moment when Jacob Amory stared into the painted face of the executioner who had selected him as victim. There wasn't even time to be frightened. Amory's blue eyes opened wide and the hand holding the club began to descend. Then, for no apparent reason, it stopped. The brave didn't move from his kneeling position astride Amory, but he called softly to one of his companions.

"This one has the look of powerful *orenda*. He will be worthy."

"Long Feather said none were to be taken."

"But look. Look in his eyes."

The second brave moved closer. His chest was bespattered with the blood and smashed bone of those he had killed, and when he leaned over to peer into the captive's face some of the gore dripped onto the boy. Amory didn't speak or shout or cry. He couldn't. He merely stared in puzzlement that slowly became horror as realization dawned.

"Yes," the second brave confirmed. "Powerful *orenda*. Take him. I will tell Long Feather it is good."

Jacob was pulled to his feet and led away. Once he stumbled on ground made slippery by the spilled innards of the others. Only when he saw the head of Achechi lying some distance from his body did Amory fully comprehend the events of the past minute and a half. Shock and fear vied with each other. He was numb. Too numb to wonder why he had been spared or what the Indians had been saying. Of the meaning of the word *orenda* he knew nothing.

Willy Blood led Ceci and Antony eastward just when he said he would, three days after their discussion around the map drawn in the dirt. Within an hour of making that change in direction Griffin knew something was wrong. The Choctaw slowed their pace to a crawl and carried himself like a bird poised for flight.

"What's the matter, Willy?" Griffin asked. "Did we make a wrong turning?"

The guide shook his head but didn't speak. He pressed his fingers to his lips instead, and Antony turned and passed the message for silence to Ceci. They continued to creep forward—toward the river, Griffin fervently hoped, toward Jamestown and civilization. The tension was unbearable, just as it had been in those awful minutes when the Iroquois passed by. Finally Blood held up his hand and they stopped.

Willy pointed to a spot on their right and indicated that Ceci and Antony should hide themselves in the heavy undergrowth. He made signs to say that they were to wait there while he scouted ahead. He left them with a final gesture to remind them of the need for absolute silence. Antony nodded his head and took Ceci's hand. They remained like that for a long time.

When Blood returned he came so stealthily and with such suddenness that he startled them as badly as any hostile Indian could have done. Ceci gasped and Griffin's finger started to squeeze the trigger of his gun. Just in time he recognized the Choctaw.

"Come quick," Willy said.

Apparently it was safe to speak, for the moment at least. "What did you find?" Griffin asked.

"The Iroquois. Camp by the river. Many canoes. We go near. Wait. Soon, tomorrow maybe, they go. Then we follow river. Maybe they leave canoe."

"Why are we going near them?" Antony demanded. "That sounds crazy to me. Why don't we go in the other direction?"

"Better this way. They no look for enemies close to their camp. No care about us tonight or tomorrow."

It was useless to press for further explanations. Griffin would have to take the Choctaw's advice on faith. Besides, it would be dark soon. They couldn't go far in any direction until morning.

They heard the Iroquois before they saw their camp. Snatches of chants and laughter and whooping noises drifted toward them, growing louder as they moved on. For a moment Griffin was convinced that Blood had somehow lost his mind and was leading them straight into the lion's den. He was holding Ceci's hand and he could feel fear in the tight grip of her fingers. He was about to stop, refuse to go any farther, when Willy called a halt.

He'd led them to the top of a small, thickly wooded rise. They could smell the Iroquois campfire and see a curl of smoke in the dusk. Ceci could go no farther. She sank in exhaustion at the base of a large tree. Griffin left her there and crawled after Blood to the edge of the copse.

Below him spread a scene more terrifying than any nightmare he was capable of conjuring. The Iroquois camp was on the bank of the river. In the gathering dark the glow of their fire was reflected and enlarged in the water. The scalplocked warriors were all in motion—swaying, dancing, shouting. They looked drunk or drugged, but no less malevolent than they had in their silent passage through the forest.

"They make ceremony to their God," Blood whispered.

Griffin realized why it was safe to speak. No whisper of theirs could be heard above the noise of the camp. "What's got into them? What makes them act like that?"

Blood shuddered. "It is the Iroquois way," he said. "Their God makes them drunk."

"Oh no!" Ceci had crawled up beside them and her gasp made the two men realize her presence.

"Don't watch," Griffin said quickly. "Get back, Ceci."

She ignored his words. "Look, over there . . ."

A stake stood a short distance from the campfire. Antony hadn't noticed it until she pointed it out. There was a man tied to the stake—a white man. Griffin edged forward, stared, closed his eyes and stared again. "Sweet Jesus," he murmured at last. "Oh sweet Jesus, I don't believe it!"

For a few more seconds he simply looked, making himself believe that the seemingly impossible was true. Then he grabbed Blood's arm and pulled him back into the protection of the thicket of trees. Ceci followed them.

"That man down there," Griffin said through clenched teeth. "What are they going to do to him?"

The Choctaw didn't answer, merely dropped his eyes.

Antony turned to the girl. "Those damned Iroquois, you said you knew about them. What are they planning, Ceci? Tell me! I have to know!"

She swallowed hard. "I . . . I've heard . . ."

"Yes? For God's sake will you both stop looking like that and tell me!" Still neither answered. "Is it torture?" Griffin asked at last in a small, dead voice. "Do the Iroquois torture captives?"

Ceci nodded. "They say, in the long houses where they live, it's like seeing hell itself to see what they do. Once I knew an old Micmac who lived with them for a time. He said—" Her voice broke off. Then, as if the thought had just come, she went on: "But it's the women! They say the women do the torturing among the Iroquois."

"They renegades," Blood said dully. "Got no women."

"Yes. Well then . . ." She saw from the Choctaw's face that the hope was feeble.

"I've got to get him out," Antony said quietly.

Ceci and Blood stared at him incredulously. The girl spoke first. "There're so many of them, Antony. What can you do? You've just one gun."

"No way," Blood said firmly. "No way to rescue white man. He's dead, we're alive."

"He's not dead yet," Griffin said grimly.

"Same thing," Blood insisted. "Same as dead. Nothing we can do. If we try, we die too. You, me, Missy."

His words made Antony look at Ceci. Her green eyes were wet with tears. It was the first time in this whole long, difficult journey he'd seen her give way to any sign of weakness. She knew he'd seen and she rubbed her hand across her face in a defiant gesture. "I'm not crying for me, I'm crying for him. That poor man down there. If only we could do something."

"No way!" Blood was so angry he almost shouted. "You crazy, Mr. Antony. You want to die?"

"Take the girl, Willy," Griffin said quietly. "Take Ceci with you and lose yourselves in the forest. I'll give you an hour if I can. Then I'm going down there."

Blood stared at him. Ceci shook her head in protest.

"Listen to me." Antony sounded like a man speaking from a far distance. "You don't understand. That man, tied up down there—he's not a stranger, not just some poor devil I can feel sorry for and forget. He's my cousin, Jacob Amory. Don't ask me how he came to be here or how the Iroquois got him, I don't know. But that's Jacob and I can't stand by and watch him slaughtered. Now get going."

Four years he'd been an absolute master, a man to be unquestionably obeyed. It didn't occur to Griffin that Blood would defy him. The Choctaw's blow was so sudden Antony never saw it coming. One second he was telling them what he meant to do, and the next he was lying unconscious between the half-breed and the girl.

In silence Willy tied Griffin with the coil of rope he carried at his waist. Only after the knots were as secure as the Choctaw could make them did Ceci help to roll the inert body deeper into the protection of the trees.

At that moment a scream of terror and pain and anguish rose above the frenzied howls emanating from the Iroquois camp. It was a sound beyond human imagining, and it continued until it seemed that no man could have so much breath in his body.

Ceci closed her eyes and moved her lips in a prayer she hadn't uttered in years: "*Je vous salut Marie* . . ." It didn't help. The screams went on, growing more terrible. "Let him die. Oh Mother of God, let him die."

"He no die for a long time," Blood said simply. "Not the Iroquois way." He wasn't watching her while he spoke. His eyes were on Griffin, ready to strike again the minute the man stirred. Ceci looked from Antony's still form to the vigilant half-breed. The very forest quivered with the audible agony coming from the Iroquois camp.

"No! No! Lord Jesus Christ! No! Mama . . ."

The last, long, wailing cry eddied in the air around them. Ceci trembled, retched, could not vomit. Only Blood and Antony were motionless. Clasping her hands to her mouth to suppress her own screams, the girl turned and ran.

She struggled to the edge of the line of trees. He was dead, he must be dead. It was over. She could hear nothing but the whoops and exultations of the Iroquois. Ceci peered down at the campsite to find the confirmation of her hopes. She could rouse Antony, tell him the nightmare was ended.

One scalplocked figure danced around the staked-out body of the victim where he lay, spread-eagled and inert, on the ground. The brave was screaming in ecstasy. He was naked and his erect penis, limned by the firelight, bespoke the intensity of his excitement. The white man didn't move. He is dead, Ceci thought. Oh thank God, he's dead! The Indian laughed, raised something over his head. It was a bucket of water. He poured it over the face of the captive and the man sputtered into moaning consciousness.

Laughter and joy and delight filled the air as the Iroquois cheered the victim's awakening. "That's why they made camp by the river, they need water to keep reviving him." Ceci spoke the words aloud. They were the sounds of a child—fearful, unbelieving. Like a child she could not turn away. Part of her, some deep hidden part, continued to believe it was all fantasy. None of it was really happening; it was a bad dream. She would wake, and her mother would come.

The naked braves were closing in on the staked figure. They brandished knives and burning torches, and one held something that looked like a shell. The victim wasn't screaming now. He was watching them. The Indian with the shell knelt beside the man. Ceci saw them look at each other for a few seconds. A hush descended. The brave seized the white's genitals in his hand. There was one strangled moan followed by more silence.

Ceci pushed her fists into her mouth to stifle her terror. The Indian was scraping the soft skin from the victim's male organs with his shell. Still the white man made no sound. Then one terrible, shuddering scream pierced the night, went on and on, and Ceci could watch no more.

9

When Griffin regained consciousness it was beginning to be light and the only sound in the forest was the chirping of birds. He opened his eyes, looked around, and saw that he was alone. Then he realized that he was trussed up like a chicken and he remembered: Jacob, waiting to die some terrible death, Ceci, Blood . . . What had happened? Where were they?

When he tried to move, his head pounded. The Choctaw had knocked him out. Repeatedly, it seemed. He couldn't feel his arms or his shoulders—they'd gone numb in their bonds—but his legs were free. Griffin staggered to his feet and looked around once more. No one. Moving in a jerky, ill-coordinated fashion because the top half of his body was immobile, he made his way toward the edge of the copse. Ceci's green dress had become so dark and stained it blended perfectly with the undergrowth. The only reason he knew she was there was that he could see the gold of her hair where her head lay buried in her arms.

He dropped to his knees beside her and stared at the scene below. The campfire had become only a few smoldering embers. The ground around it looked battered. The dancing and jumping and running of the braves had torn the soft earth by the water, wounded it. There was no sign of the Iroquois. They'd moved on, just as the Choctaw had promised they would. The only thing remotely human down there was the mutilated carcass of Jacob Amory.

There were no eyes in the head; even from this distance Griffin could see they'd been gouged out. There were bloody stumps where Jacob's arms and legs should have been. The remainder of his torso was crisscrossed with cuts and burns of every possible description. Around Amory's body lay chunks of flesh and bone. He'd been hacked apart slowly, made to suffer as long as possible.

Griffin stared in silence. Ceci didn't look at him, didn't speak. "Untie me," he said at last. Then, after she'd managed to loosen the ropes, "Where is Blood?"

"Gone, back to Carolina I suppose. The Iroquois went west; they left a few hours ago. Willy left shortly after that. He said we didn't need him any longer."

Griffin didn't reply. He staggered down the hill to the deserted campsite, vaguely aware that Ceci was following him. Viewed close up, the remains of Jacob Amory spoke yet more eloquently of the diabolical rites that had transpired during the night. "I'm going to kill him," Antony said softly. "I'm going to find Willy Blood and kill him, but it won't be vengeance for this. Nothing could be."

"You'll never find him," Ceci said tonelessly. "You couldn't.

You know that. Besides, none of this is his fault. What he did saved his own life and yours and mine. It's nothing to do with him." She jerked her head toward the dismembered corpse.

"His name's Jacob. Jacob Amory. Don't say 'him' like that! Like he was some creature, something unknown!"

He had hold of her shoulders, was shaking her, shouting at her. Ceci allowed his explosion of fury to spend itself. Then, when he let her go, she said, "We must bury him. I'll help you."

They dug the grave with their bare hands, as there was nothing else to use. Then they gathered up the fragments of Jacob's mortal flesh and placed them in the shallow trench. Later, even after many years, Antony would never understand how they had done that. He couldn't believe how silent they were throughout, how neither of them even retched as they pursued their grotesque task. Toward the end, Ceci removed the leggings she'd made from the remnants of the green dress and used them to wrap the inanimate bits of flesh and bone that had been Jacob. Finally they scooped earth over the hole in the soft, marshy ground and piled stones atop the mound.

When it was done Griffin sat by the water and shivered. He couldn't stop his trembling. Ceci bathed his face and held him, pressing his head to her breast and crooning soft, meaningless words of comfort.

"I can't make myself believe it," he said finally. "I was right up there, a few yards away. All this happened and I did nothing. I didn't even shoot him. I could have done that. I could have killed him painlessly, swiftly."

"No, you couldn't." she said. "They would have found us if you had. It would have multiplied the horror, Antony, not ended it."

He didn't answer that. He knew it was true but he couldn't make himself say it. He'd traded Jacob's life for his own, Ceci's, and Blood's. The fact that the bargain had been struck not by him but by the Choctaw didn't make it any easier to live with. "Do they always do things like this?" he asked at last. "What kind of creatures are these Iroquois?"

"I don't know. The Micmac, the one I told you about, he said they only torture some captives, not all. They have a word, *orenda* I think it is." She slipped back into French, for the concept was too difficult for her to explain in English. "It means something of the spirit. Some communication between a person and God. At least that's what the Micmac told me. He said they choose victims because they believe them to have a powerful *orenda*. They believe the person tortured will have some high place in the spirit world afterwards."

All that soul-destroying night she had thought about it, remembering the words of the old Indian she'd known long ago in Acadia. It had been impossible to reconcile the Micmac's story with the awesome reality. Ceci didn't say that to Antony. He needed comfort, not riddles. She pulled him closer, kissed his forehead, his cheeks, his eyes. "Don't think about it anymore," she whispered. "It's done; nothing can change it."

When she realized that he wanted her, she froze. It seemed so base, so unbelievable. Now, in this place, after what had happened. But there was no mistaking the way his breathing had become hard and shallow, the urgency with which he responded to caresses she'd meant as gestures of sympathy. The moment of disbelief passed. Ceci felt Antony's pain, his shame. She had been able to do nothing for the other one, for Jacob. It was within her power to ease the anguish of the man yet alive.

She pulled away and stood up. Griffin looked at her, a question and a plea in his eyes. "Come . . ." She held out her hand and he stumbled to his feet and took it. "Here, in the trees, not by . . . by the river." She had almost said "by the grave."

When they reached the shelter of a stand of firs they stood facing each other. He didn't grab her. There was no mindlessness in this act, none of the spontaneous anger and need that had typified the night on the Ashley. Antony was asking for something human to wash away the repeated inhumanities that had occurred since their first meeting aboard the *Notre Dame*. He needed to deny the perversions that had culminated in the unspeakable events of the past twelve hours.

For some time they didn't speak or touch. Each knew what was being asked in this encounter in the forest, what it would mean. Finally Ceci raised her hands and began to remove her dress. Antony watched her. After she was naked he took off his own clothes. Then he drew her into his arms.

The kiss was a long one, gentle at first, tasting of the salt of both their tears. She could feel his hands on the bare flesh of her back, the pressure of his broad chest against her breasts. They parted for a moment and sank to the carpet of pine needles. She could smell the pungent scent of the trees mingling with the male smell of his skin and his breath.

Then, for one awful instant Ceci didn't see Griffin's face close above her own but Bonde's. The memory of the brutal captain of the *Notre Dame* superimposed itself on the scene. And that of the Iroquois, their erect penises witness to the sexual thrill of torture. Then Antony spoke her name and the vision evaporated. He was no one but himself; this had nothing to do with anything that had happened before.

"I love you," he said.

She didn't answer with words but she opened her legs for him, wrapped them around his hard, narrow hips. "I want to give myself to you," she whispered, surprised by the truth of the statement. Until this moment she had not known.

She could sense the swollen heaviness of him as he sought entry, feel the thin skin of his maleness hot against her thigh. In the instant when his member slid between the moist lips of her womanhood she perceived something tearing inside herself, giving way. A kind of spiritual virginity was being pierced. It was a much more important thing than the moment of her physical deflowering. Ceci gasped, knowing a sensation she'd never before experienced. Of their own accord her hips rose to make the contact deeper, more intimate. Her legs tightened around him.

They lay like that for two or three seconds, eyes locked as they'd been locked that night in the sloop on the Ashley, but saying different things. Griffin thrust slowly, tentatively, aware that a part of her previously inviolate had been opened to him. She moaned and he could not restrain himself any longer. His movements quickened, beyond any conscious control.

Deep within her Ceci could feel every powerful inch of him, every stroke of flesh on flesh. When he poured his seed into her she knew it, and the hot flow was a kind of balm that healed the wounds of twenty years of life. It was for her a gentle, quiet thing. She did not share his explosion of passion, the climax that carried him beyond any sensation she could understand. For this moment she didn't need to. She was a woman, no longer a girl. It was enough.

"They left this canoe," she told him, pointing to the small boat. "Willy looked at it before he left. It's not in the best condition—that's why they didn't take it—but he said it's good enough to get us to Jamestown."

"Yes," Griffin said, examining the thing, "it's good enough. We don't have far to go."

They settled themselves in the birchbark craft and started down the James. In a few hours it was apparent that they were leaving the forest and heading for the world they knew, the world of white men and women.

"Listen," Ceci said. "I have to tell you something." Suddenly it was important that she speak before they were wholly out of the wilderness. "On the *Notre Dame*, with that pig Bonde, I was a virgin. Then, in New Orleans, there wasn't anyone. Not even Emile. He didn't like women in that way. No one knew, no one would have believed it, but he didn't touch me. No one touched me."

Antony didn't stop the steady rhythm of his paddling. "I know. I don't know how, but back there I knew."

She nodded and for a while they said nothing more. Then she asked, "Where are we going after we get to Jamestown?"

"I have to go to Boston. My aunt and uncle—Jacob's parents—I have to tell them. I owe them at least that."

"Yes, I understand." Her voice dropped, became tentative. "Am I to go with you?"

"I hope so. But only if you want to."

"I want to."

It was settled. They looked at each other and exchanged shy smiles.

3

THE CHOICE

"I imagine a man must have a good deal of vanity who believes, and a good deal of boldness who affirms, that all the doctrines he holds are true, *and all he rejects are* false."

—Benjamin Franklin

1

In Jamestown they were accepted as a married couple who had escaped from hostile Indians. Such stories were common in the settlement and few questions were asked. They were given clothes, food, and shelter. When Antony tried to pay for the kindness his offer was refused, and that left him with enough cash to book passage as far north as Philadelphia.

"I can find a Griffin ship there, no doubt," he told Ceci. "When I tell them who I am we'll get royal treatment back to Boston." He grimaced when he spoke and she knew he didn't enjoy trading on his name, even in this time of necessity. She said little but made her own plans.

They arrived in Philadelphia the third week in November. Antony left her at a small inn and went back to the docks to inquire about a ship flying the purple and gold Griffin insignia. He'd seen none such at first glance, but someone could surely tell him how long it would be before one was expected.

"Is there a jeweler in this town?" Ceci asked the landlord's wife as soon as Antony had gone. "Someone who might be interested in buying a fine emerald?"

The woman was a Quaker. She had little interest in jewels, not even emeralds, but the girl touched her. "I can think of no one thee might ask . . . A ship's captain perhaps? Someone who can take thy stone to London and sell it there."

"I can't wait that long," Ceci said. "I need the money now."

"Yes, I understand." The landlady looked at Ceci. Her golden hair was tied back in a simple bun, her brown dress was of homespun and not particularly well-fitting, yet she had an emerald to sell. Still, the woman knew it wasn't stolen. "There is someone," she said hesitantly. "He's no need of thy jewel for himself but he trades in many business matters. He's an honest man, a fair one. Thee might find him of some help."

Thirty minutes later Ceci was walking along the High Street. When she came to the printer's shop she stopped before entering and examined the notice board outside, where a number of books and pamphlets were advertised. One called *Reflections on Courtship and Marriage* cited the printer himself as author. There was an announcement about a slave for sale if one "applied within," and another about some land. This Benjamin Franklin was indeed a man of many parts. Clutching the handkerchief-wrapped emerald pendant in her hand, Ceci stepped inside.

"So that's how Jacob came to be there." Antony leaned his head against the high back of the wooden settle and stretched out his boots to the fire. "Bloody unbelievable. But then, I suppose it isn't. The Amorys were always big on politics. At least Uncle Paul and Jacob were."

"Mr. Franklin said your cousin and the other young men were 'martyrs to the cause of English freedom.' She grimaced over the words. "Your uncle came last spring to try and stop Jacob from leading the expedition to the Cherokees."

"He was too late, I gather. Poor bastard. He won't thank me for the news I'm bringing."

"Mr. Franklin said your Uncle Paul was a fine man. He said he'd want to know."

Antony reached out and poured himself another tot of spiced ale. The cold winds of winter were beginning to blow in Philadelphia. "You and Mr. Franklin seem to have had a lot to say to each other."

There was just a hint of jealousy in his voice. Ceci tried not to smile. If Antony could see his "rival," he wouldn't be so foolish. "I explained," she said patiently. "I told you how it happened. When I asked him about buying the emerald Mr. Franklin said he might be able to oblige but first he needed to be convinced it was mine to sell. I had to tell him something and he's not a man one lies to. One thing just led to another. Then, when he heard we'd been in the woods, he asked after your cousin and the others, if we'd seen them or heard of them. That's how the whole story came out."

"Yes, well I'm glad to know about it anyway." He reached out and took her hand. "And I think you're quite marvelous. It would never have occurred to me to ask you to sell the thing, you know that."

"I know. But I'd rather have the money than the pendant now. Besides," she said with an impish grin, "it didn't go with this frock."

"That's something else," Antony said quickly. "You must take some of this and buy yourself some new clothes." He fished a coin from the little pouch she'd given him but she shook her head.

"No, not now. When we get to Boston perhaps." She was adamant and he gave in.

Her attitude was sound. Franklin had admitted he couldn't pay what the gem was worth, not if she wanted ready cash. Antony and Ceci didn't have much money, despite the splendor of the emerald. Some ship's captain would strike an excellent bargain when he purchased that bauble from Franklin and subsequently sold it in London. Well, never mind, Antony told himself, everyone made a profit along the line. That's what was wanted. All his growing years he'd heard what a good businessman was Benjamin Franklin, and today Ceci had proved it. Franklin was good at other things, too, from the news he'd heard at the docks. Which raised another point he must discuss with the girl, no matter how painful.

"Listen," he began tentatively. "The day after tomorrow when we go to the docks to meet the *Elizabeth G.*, you keep quiet. Let me do the talking."

Her green eyes widened in surprise. "Why should I have to talk? It's one of your family's ships, isn't it? Naturally I expect you to make the arrangements."

"I don't mean just that . . ." He stopped, realized he must continue, and plunged ahead. "It's your accent. Anyone hearing you will know you're French."

"I see." She turned away and the set of her stiff shoulders betrayed her reaction.

"No you don't, you don't see at all. It doesn't make any difference to me, Ceci. For God's sake, surely you know that! It's the people here, the Philadelphians. Some of them . . . Oh Jesus, you may as well know. This past summer there was trouble. Three different French privateers sailed in, looted and pillaged a number of places up the Delaware. All Pennsylvania was threatened. At least that's how they saw it. Your friend Franklin was the one who raised a company of volunteers to defend the colony. He even got the pacifist Quakers behind him."

She hadn't turned around and her back was still ramrod straight. Griffin rose and crossed to where she stood. When he lay his hand on her shoulder he knew just how rigid she was. "Ceci, listen to me, darling, it's nothing to do with you. Or with us for that matter. It's politics, that's all. Men's affairs. Forget about it. Please. I only told you so you could avoid any unpleasantness."

"Unpleasantness," she repeated softly. "Like the 'unpleasant' men in that place in Charleston. The ones who wanted to shave my head and send me back to New Orleans naked."

"Idiots and rabble-rousers," he said through clenched teeth. "You needn't fear them, Ceci. I can take care of you." He pulled her into his arms, buried his face in her hair. "Please trust me. I love you so."

"I know." She tipped back her head and smiled up at him. "And I do trust you. Let's stop talking about such terrible things. Mr. Franklin wants to meet you. I said perhaps you'd call at his shop tomorrow. He knows all your family so—"

"No." He shook his head. "I've enough family business on my mind at the moment. I think I'll give your Mr. Franklin a miss on this occasion if you don't mind."

Later, lying next to him in the big feather bed, Ceci thought about the family business he'd mentioned. He meant of course telling them about Jacob. But what, she wondered, was he going to tell them about her? How did Antony plan to introduce her into the select circle of the Griffins of Boston? She fell asleep with no satisfactory answer.

Antony Griffin expected one of Uncle John's girls to open the door of the Ark on this January morning of 1748. Or perhaps his mother or Aunt Martha. Maybe even one of the serving woman that came and went with such regularity in this establishment. Certainly not this vaguely familiar young woman. He peered at her in puzzlement for a few seconds before her eyes jogged his memory. One blue and one brown. "Sophia! I didn't recognize you. This is Cecile LaPointe. Ceci, this is Sophia, my cousin."

The girl didn't say anything but she did smile. "You don't recognize me either, do you?" Antony said quickly. "It's Antony. I mean I'm Antony . . . Oh hell! Is my father here? I'd best see him first."

Sophia still didn't speak but her smile broadened and she held out her hand to the strange blonde girl at the same time that she nodded her head in the direction of Charles Griffin's study.

"In there, is he? Well, I'll beard the lion in his den then. Take care of her, will you."

He watched Sophia lead Ceci toward the big sitting room. From the sound of it, nothing much had changed at the Ark. He could hear a babble of voices from every corner of the house. And he could smell the familiar cooking odors from the kitchen that never stopped producing food.

The captain of the *Elizabeth G* had told him none of the twins were married. Antony had warned Ceci about all of them and told her what to expect in this extraordinary household. She'd be all right. Sophia looked different though. Her hair, for one thing. There was so little of it—just a short fringe around her face, like a small boy's. And what was she doing here? Griffin shrugged and started down the hall to find his father.

"So, Antony." Charles leaned back in his chair and openly examined his son. "Home at last. I must admit, I've been sitting here wondering what I'd say to you."

"I don't understand, sir. You knew I was coming?"

The elder Griffin withdrew a pocket watch and examined it. "For the past twenty minutes I did. A runner arrived on the doorstep at ten past eleven from the *Elizabeth G*. The captain thought it best I have as much advance notice as he could provide. Don't look like that, lad. The man works for me. It's natural."

"I suppose it is. And now I know why he was so long about

finding us a carriage." Griffin gestured to a chair. "May I sit down?" Then, after his father had nodded and he'd taken the seat, he said, "Did the captain also inform you I paid our passage? The going rate. I didn't ask for credit. Not from you or any of the rest of the family."

"I'm glad to hear it," Charles said mildly. "Not that I begrudge you a passage, Antony. Just that it means you haven't come home a pauper. I think," he said, his voice softening appreciably, "it would be difficult for you to do that."

Antony swallowed hard and thanked God for Ceci and the sale of the emerald. "I'm not wealthy, sir," he said. "Not as one might expect, considering how well Blackwater's done these past few years. That's a long story. I'll save it for later if you don't mind. Actually, none of that's why I came home anyway."

"No, I didn't think so." Charles fished into the drawer of his desk and withdrew an envelope. "This arrived for you two weeks ago. From South Carolina. That's your Aunt Hannah's hand unless I miss my guess. It came with a Jameson's ship and I was instructed to hold it until you arrived, if you arrived. The Jameson's captain also made a point of telling me how Blackwater prospered under your stewardship. In truth, I knew that. I've heard about it repeatedly these past few years."

Antony didn't respond to the implied praise. He merely reached for the letter and stared at it for a few seconds. "I didn't walk out on her if that's what you're thinking," he said finally. "Nothing like that."

"My dear boy." Charles stood up and leaned forward. "Never in my wildest dreams did I imagine you'd walked out on your Aunt Hannah, or on the job you'd undertaken. I may not approve of some of what you did—running off like that without a word to me or your mother, no letters in all those four years—but as to what you've accomplished since . . . I'm proud of you. I thought you'd know that." He sat down again, passed his hand over his eyes. "We don't understand each other very well, do we? Never have apparently."

"It's all right, Papa, really. And the part about Blackwater is a very long story."

"Yes, I'm sure. I knew about your being there early on, of course. Your grandfather told me as soon as he got your letter."

"How is the old man?" Antony interrupted.

"Indestructible," Charles answered, smiling. "He's sixty-nine, so naturally he's failing a bit. But indestructible in all the ways that matter. He'll want to see you."

"I'm not so sure. Not considering what he wrote when he heard I was managing nigger slaves. And not after..." Antony's voice broke and he let the sentence trail away.

"After what?" Charles asked softly. "What's the real reason behind your return, lad? I think you'd best tell me."

"It's the Amorys, sir. Specifically Jacob. He's dead. I saw it happen and I couldn't prevent it. I felt the least I could do was tell Aunt Rachel and Uncle Paul."

"Rachel's dead," Charles said. He stared straight ahead without focusing on anything in particular. "A rotten business. There was a fire up at Sophia's house in Rowley. Rachel was visiting—"

Antony exhaled slowly through his teeth. It came out a low, ugly whistle. "Oh sweet Jesus! And now I bring news of Jacob—"

"Not just Rachel," Charles went on as if he hadn't heard his son's remark. "Sophia's husband too. And her three sons. Just babies. All of 'em burned to death. Sophia's never spoken since. Some injury she sustained, we suppose. Damned doctors can't tell us anything."

"So that's why she's here. I wondered about that."

"Aunt Martha brought her back from Rowley as soon as she could travel. She's been here since last June—six, no seven months." He rose and went to the window, stared at the frozen landscape. "Hard winter this. Very hard."

"I'll have to go to The Roses straight away," Antony said. "It's a miserable errand but it had best be done quickly. There's a girl with me, sir. A French girl from Acadia by way of New Orleans. Name's Cecile LaPointe. Can I assume she'll be welcome here? For a while at least. Until I've seen Uncle Paul."

"Of course she's welcome," Charles said gruffly. Only one who knew him as well as his son did could hear the tears in his voice. "Don't fight political battles in our home. Not any of us at the Ark. As for Paul, you won't find him at The Roses. He's in some damned shack up on Mount Whoredom. Come greet your mother and the rest of the family. Tomorrow's time enough to see Paul."

2

Mattie watched the young man tramp along the snow-covered track to the cabin. He must be coming here; there was no place else to go. Behind was only scrub growth and the ocean, beyond the copper works. If he'd been going there he'd have taken the road, not the path by the cabin. So what did he want? Not her, certainly; she'd never seen him before. Paul then. It was the only explanation.

The mulatto woman turned from the door to gaze at her lover. He was sleeping, a half-empty jug of rum by his side. These days he only slept when he'd consumed enough rum to make him unconscious, and even then he didn't sleep long. Mattie sighed. Somebody from town, something about his business maybe. She'd try and head him off so Paul could rest a little longer. She wrapped a heavy woolen shawl around her head and shoulders and ducked through the low doorway.

"You want somethin'?" she asked, intercepting the caller a few yards from the cabin. "What you doin' here?"

He knew who she was; his father had told him. Still Antony couldn't repress his instantaneous reaction. She was colored. A nigger. What right had she to address him in such a tone? "I'm going to speak with Mr. Amory," he said. "You just go about your business, girl. When Mr. Amory wants you he'll send for you."

"Send for me, will he?" Her voice was soft and musical and she was chuckling. "And did he send for you? I don't think Paul's sent for you, boy."

Griffin froze. "Keep a civil tongue in your head," he said. "And get out of my way."

She stood her ground. The wind whipped the shawl from her head. He could see the short ebony curls and the emerald eyes. There were small lines around those eyes—she wasn't as young as he'd first thought—but she was beautiful. No wonder she was Paul Amory's mistress. And no one knew better than Antony how compliant a black woman could be as a bedmate. Still, when he spoke next his tone softened. This was Boston, not South Carolina. "Mr. Amory's my uncle. I've a personal matter to discuss with him. It won't take long."

"I'm Mattie Sills," she said as if his change in manner warranted the introduction. "Your uncle's sleeping. He don' sleep good these days. He needs the rest. Go away and come back later."

"It's important," he remonstrated. Griffin felt like an ass standing here and arguing with a colored woman. Still, he couldn't bring himself to shove past her.

Just then Paul appeared in the doorway. He was hunched over, peering out into the glare of the snow beneath the sun, shading his eyes with his hand. "What is it, Mattie?" he called. "What's wrong?" Then, taking a step forward, he said, "Why it's Antony, isn't it? Antony Griffin. For heaven's sake. Bring the lad here, Mattie. He's my nephew."

She looked at him wryly. "You heard the man, boy. Get your ass over there." She chuckled again at the expression on Griffin's face when she spoke, and she was still laughing when she walked on in the direction of the Bucket o' Grease tavern. She'd leave them alone, but on her terms not the impudent stranger's.

Ignoring her, Antony hastened across the distance separating him from Paul. When he ducked inside the tiny shack he was surprised by its warmth and coziness. There was a fire and bright colors and cleanliness, not at all what he'd been led to expect. "He's taken up with some half-nigger woman on Mount Whoredom," his father had told him. "Gone native, the poor devil. Hard to blame him, but . . ."

"Have a drink," Amory said by way of greeting. He extended the jug of rum and waited while Antony took a swallow. "No fancy glasses down here, lad," he said. "We don't need 'em. What brings you? Last I heard you were in South Carolina making Blackwater the new Jerusalem. But then, I don't hear much these days."

Antony lowered the jug and got his first real look at his uncle. The sight shocked him. He remembered an enormous man, hearty but gentle, always ready with a smile or a kind word.The hulk facing him looked a total stranger. Paul's frame seemed permanently hunched, shrunken. Flesh hung from him in loose folds, without life. His cheeks were hollow, grizzled by a stubble of beard. The brown hair had turned gray in places and the glazed eyes wouldn't meet his.

"I heard about Aunt Rachel," Antony stammered. "I'm sorry."

"Yes," Paul said. "So am I."

Griffin groped for something to talk about, anything other than the terrible thing he'd come to say. "I told Sophia I was coming here. She's at the Ark, you know, with the family. I didn't expect to see her. She's looking well, though, considering." He fumbled in his jacket pocket and brought out a note. "She sent this."

"Thank you." The hand Amory extended to take the paper was as big as Griffin remembered, but it trembled and the nails were uncared for, broken. The two men said nothing more for a moment. Amory stepped closer to the fire to read Sophia's message. Outside the sun shone but there were no windows in the cabin. It was dim despite the hearth and the bright colors.

Antony stood and waited, shifting his weight from one foot to the other, trying to decide how he could begin. He'd thought about it often enough, God knows—particularly since he'd arrived at the Ark yesterday and learned of all the other tragedies that had beset the Armorys this year. Now, having delayed the meeting for twenty-four hours, he didn't think any of the speeches he'd rehearsed made sense. In this bizarre setting they all seemed inadequate to the point of cruelty.

Paul folded the note and looked up. "Sit down, lad, over there on that chair." It was one of two, the only such conveniences in the cabin, and Amory himself took the other one. "Before you tell me why you're here, perhaps you'd like to read this." His voice had lost some of its liquory vagueness and now sounded more familiar in Antony's ears. When he held out Sophia's letter his hand seemed a trifle steadier too.

"Dearest Papa," Griffin read. "Antony arrived at the Ark today and I think he comes to bring us—you—sad news. It will be hard for him. He too has suffered of late, I think. He's said nothing but I see it in his eyes and in those of the young woman with him. Be gentle. I know you will. Your loving Sophia."

"I didn't say anything to her," Antony said incredulously when he'd finished reading. "How did she know?"

"Sophia knows a great many things," Paul said. "She doesn't speak—she won't or can't. Not even I know which. But I think she understands more because of it." He sat very still, hands resting on his knees, a kind of dignity about him despite his ravaged appearance. "It's Jacob, isn't it?" he asked at last. Then, when Antony still didn't answer. "He's dead isn't he? I've expected it for months. But I hoped—"

"I buried him myself, sir,"Antony said softly. "A few miles from Jamestown. In the forest."

"Indians?"

"Yes. Not the Cherokees he'd gone to treaty with. Iroquois—a band of renegades. I don't know anything about his dealings with the Cherokees."

"I see. And you escaped?" Amory wasn't looking at him when he spoke; he was staring at the dirt floor.

Antony swallowed hard. "I escaped, yes. But it wasn't exactly as it sounds—" He broke off, willing the words to come but they would not. Never, he'd promised himself, never would he lie about what had happened. He couldn't live the rest of his life with such a lie. But it was no longer his feelings, what was left of his honor, that counted. His uncle was the picture of a beaten man; Griffen could not increase his burden.

Amory looked up, stared at his nephew, then nodded his head in some enigmatic communication with himself. "Yes," he repeated. "I see." He reached out and retrieved Sophia's note, fingering it as if he could absorb the meaning of her words through his flesh. Then, apropos of nothing it seemed, he asked, "Have you ever heard the story of the Kirkslee nun? The family legend?"

Antony was puzzled but grateful for the digression. "Only vague references, sir, from Grandma before she died."

"Lizzie saw her too, but she wasn't the first. Near as anybody knows Sophia was the first. Not my daughter, but Sophia Griffin. The first Sophia—she'd be your great, great aunt I think—saw the nun in the west wing of Harwood Hall in Yorkshire. Afterwards she became a Roman Catholic and a nun herself. You know all that, about the Griffins losing the Hall and getting it back. Then, in the next generation as it were, Lizzie saw her. Somehow the Kirkslee nun played a part in saving your grandparents' marriage; we'd never be sitting here otherwise. Because of something she told Lizzie, Rachel was born and after her came your father and his brothers. But Rachel was the child who 'healed the wound.' At least that's what Lizzie thought. Rachel too for that matter."

Amory didn't move as he spoke. The recitation bore some resemblance to an oral history chanted by some pagan storyteller in a distant land. Antony had read of such customs years before under his grandfather's tutelage. He'd never thought to participate in the ritual. He sat mesmerized by the tale.

"When I first met Rachel in England she didn't want to marry me. She ran away in fact, back to America, to her home. Then I saw the Kirkslee nun. She told me to follow Rachel, to come here to Boston, and that I'd never return to England. And she told me that we, Rachel and I, had a debt. That we must see it was paid. Everything that's happened since flows from that. It's not your doing, son. Don't torment yourself with it."

Griffin shook his head as if released from a spell. "I'm sorry, sir. I don't understand."

"No, I don't understand either. If I did I might be able to explain better. As it is . . ." Amory reached for the jug of rum and took another swallow. He offered it to Antony but didn't press when the younger man refused. "I don't blame you," he said. "Not much consolation really. An illusion, like so much else. Do you know about Valiant?"

The question startled Griffin. He'd not thought to ask about the youngest Amory boy in the time he'd been home. "No, I don't think so. I suppose he must be at The Roses."

Paul laughed but there was no humor in the sound. "The Roses. No, Val's not at The Roses. He isn't living in the tomb. He has a place somewhere in the North End, where he lives with a gentleman friend. He's . . . Valiant prefers men to women. I believe the popular term is a Molly, or perhaps a flute—in a word, a sodomist. Don't look so shocked, lad, it doesn't matter. He's happy in his own fashion."

Unable to sit still any longer, Antony rose and paced the room. It didn't allow much space for pacing. Ten steps in one direction, ten in the other. "You remind me of Rachel," Paul said. "She always paced when she was agitated. Must be a Griffin thing."

"I wish there was something I could say, sir. Some explanation—"

"There is no explanation except the one I've given you," Paul said. "Star-crossed, that's what Shakespeare would have called my children if he'd known them. Not only the children. Rachel, me—star-crossed. God help us all."

Griffin knew then he couldn't tell the rest of the story. He'd come here wanting to confess, to purge his guilt. Now he realized how selfish the notion was. Paul Amory had enough to live with. It wasn't necessary for him to learn of the agony Jacob had endured before dying. Or that Antony himself had been a short distance away and hadn't helped him. "Is there anything I can do, Uncle Paul?" he asked softly. "Anything at all?"

Paul pursed his lips and examined the young man. "How old are you?" he demanded.

"Twenty-three next month. Why?"

Amory ignored the question. "Yes, I should have remembered. A few months older than Jacob. Antony and Jacob, Tonyjay's namesakes." Then, as if it was an unrelated thought though it wasn't, he said, "I've heard a bit about you these past four years. Made a good job of managing the Ludlow plantation near Charleston, didn't you?"

"Yes, a damn good job if I may say. Blackwater's become profitable again."

"Good. You'll be going back there then? With this woman Sophia mentions?" He waved the note.

"No, I won't. Daniel Ludlow returned last September. He'd been gone eight years but the place is his now. Hannah will give it to him, if she hasn't already." Griffin had not yet read the letter from Hannah but there was no doubt in his words.

"So you're at loose ends. What are your plans?"

"I'm not sure. Canada maybe. Cecile LaPointe, the girl Sophia refers to, is from Acadia. There's land to be had up there. I'm not really a farmer but I am a manager. I expect I can make something of a piece of land."

"A manager," Paul said softly. "Like Rachel in more ways than one. Yes, I rather thought that. You've that Griffin look about you. All managers, the Griffins. Doers, survivors . . ." He'd been leaning back in his chair, balancing on the two rear legs. Now he slammed forward with a sound that seemed particularly loud in the small, low-ceilinged room. "Listen, Antony, I've a proposition for you. Take over my business. It's been floundering these past six months but I expect it's still worth having. There's not been enough time since Rachel died for it to go completely to hell."

"Your business? The Amory markets? You're offering me a job then?"

"Not a job. I want you to have them. I want to give you the damned markets."

"Give them . . . But that's absurd! They belong to you, to Sophia and Valiant."

"Sweet Jesus, lad, haven't you been listening to a word I've said? What do you think Val would do with them? He has less notion of how to run them than I have, and far less interest. As for Sophia, well you've seen her. Do you imagine she's likely to become a businesswoman?"

"No, but . . ." Griffin shook his head stubbornly. "It's crazy, sir. I couldn't accept."

"It's not crazy and there's no reason for you not to accept. Don't answer straight away. Think about it for a while. Here's my proposal. I'll make the markets over to you as a gift. We'll have it all drawn up legally. You don't want to be fooled twice by the same trick, do you?" He grinned to show he'd understood more of the Blackwater story than Antony's brief explanation had seemed to tell. "I'll stipulate an allowance to be paid to Valiant and Sophia, even a small one for me. Not out of profits, mind you, but off the top as it were. The rest is yours. Think of it, lad. It's a good offer—for both of us."

Paul Amory rose and it was as if the brief burst of energy that had made him seem more like the man Antony remembered had burnt itself out. He was again the gray ghost, more haunted than haunting. "It would please me to give you Jacob's legacy," he said softly. "Come back in a few days and let me know your answer."

Antony had to fight back the urge to run from the cabin. The thing was beyond irony. It was a malevolent trick by a diabolical God.

3

Given the numbers of people and the available space at the Ark, a room of one's own was a luxury. When her prodigal son appeared at School Street with a beautiful French companion, Mary Griffin evaluated the situation in one quick glance. This was no chance acquaintance. Antony had brought home someone about whom he cared deeply. Nonetheless, she told herself firmly, they'll not share a bedroom without benefit of clergy, not under my roof!

Antony she put in with his brothers, the younger of her sets of twins, Castor and Pollux. Cecile LaPointe presented a different problem. Sophia had the only single bedchamber in the house, a tiny cubbyhole in the attic. It had been assigned to her when she came to the Ark, in deference to her physical and emotional wounds. But as Mary stood by the kitchen fireplace lost in thought, attempting to decide where to sleep her French guest, Sophia tugged at her sleeve. She pointed to the ceiling, to herself, and to the sitting room from where the newcomer's voice could be heard.

"Share with you?" Mary said. "Your little room, you mean?"

Sophia nodded her head vigorously. "Yes, I suppose it's possible," the older woman continued. "But it's so small, Sophia—only one bed and no hope of getting another in."

The girl's smile widened. She ran her hands along her own tiny frame, then drew an equally small shape in the air while nodding her head to indicate she meant Cecile.

"Yes," Mary said, laughing. "You're neither of you bigger than a minute. Very well, you can have her in your room. Antony won't approve," she added with her lips pursed, "but he can like it or lump it. He fancies himself a grown man, but there'll be no immoral goings on in my house." Sophia turned away so her aunt wouldn't know she was giggling.

Antony certainly didn't like it but he said nothing that first day. Then, when he returned from Mattie Sills' cabin, Griffin looked as white as a new sheet and he was trembling. Ceci noticed the moment she opened the door. "Oh dear," she said softly. "Your uncle took it badly, didn't he? I suppose it's to be expected."

"No, not like that, not what you think. He—" The youngest set of twins, John's seventeen-year-olds, Martha and Mary, chose that moment to charge through the front hall. They were shrieking with laughter and were pursued by an assortment of other people, most of whom Antony didn't recognize. "Damn this place, it's a bloody jungle! Always has been. We can't talk here."

"They're playing a game," Ceci said lamely. "Something to do with hiding a button."

"And we haven't even a room of our own to talk in." He stood in consternation a moment but then his face lit up. "C'mon. I know where we can go. It must still be there."

He led her through the hall to the kitchen, which was also full of people. Antony spared only the briefest nod for his mother, his Aunt Martha, and the others who were preparing lunch at the big table. Ceci trotted after him obediently. Together they went out the back door, ignoring the knowing looks and giggles.

"In here," Griffin said, pushing open the door of a shed in the yard behind the house. "Wood store. I used to come here when I was a boy. It's the only place in this whole damn house where you can be alone."

"You're shivering, Antony," Ceci said. "It's cold out here."

"I'm all right. Are you?" He lay his fingers on her shoulders, then pulled the soft woolen shawl she wore closer around her breasts. "It's a big change in climate, after the south."

"I wasn't born in New Orleans if you remember," Ceci answered, smiling. "I'm used to the cold. Now, what about your uncle? You look terrible. Did he—" She broke off, unable to imagine what a man might do when confronted with news such as Antony had brought Paul Amory.

"My uncle offered to give me his business. The Amory markets. He said it would please him for me to have Jacob's legacy."

Ceci's eyes widened. There was nothing in Antony's voice to explain the extraordinary statement. He spoke the words in a flat monotone.

"Incredible, isn't it?" he said when she didn't reply. "And if you conclude that it's because he doesn't know the whole truth, you're right." Griffin ran his fingers through his hair, leaning against the wall of the wood shed as if he didn't trust his legs. "I tried, Ceci, as God is my judge I tried. But he's so beaten, been through so much. I couldn't tell him. Now he wants me to take Jacob's place. It's monstrous."

She pressed against him in an effort at comfort. "You were right not to tell him everything. I wanted to suggest that from the first, but I didn't think you'd listen. It wouldn't have been fair, Antony, to give him so much to live with on top of losing his son. You're young and strong; you can carry that burden for him. It's your atonement, if you will." Ceci was murmuring in French, as she always did if a subject or thought was too complex for her English, crooning her words into his chest, holding his head in her hands.

"I can't stay here and do as he asks," he whispered. "The idea's macabre." He dropped his face to the top of her head. Her hair smelled of fresh herbs and vanilla, and beneath his hands the curve of her hips could just be felt through the thick fabric of the homespun dress. "Ceci, Ceci, Ceci," he whispered. "I can't stand being separated from you like this. We've got to get out of here, go away, make our own life."

"We can go to Canada," she answered. "We've still got the ruby ring to sell. It will fetch a decent price, I think. We can do what we've talked about—buy a farm in Acadia. It's so beautiful there. You'll love it, Antony, I know you will."

The words spilled forth, the spinning of a dream. The very speaking of them was more of an aphrodisiac than his body pressing against hers in the silence and solitude of the wood shed. "Take me home, Antony," she said. "Take me home to Acadia." Ceci lifted her face for his kiss and at that moment his bulk sagged against her. He had fainted.

"Antony! What is it, what's wrong?" She tried to support him, realized she couldn't, and let him slide along the wall to the ground. There was no room to stretch out his long legs in this cramped space filled with sawn logs. She wasted only another moment trying to revive him, then ran toward the house to seek help.

"Sophia thinks it's an illness he picked up in Carolina, or while you were traveling. A kind of fever one gets in the swamps," Mary told the girl. She looked as worried as Ceci did—she was his mother after all—but she was obviously sincere when she said, "We're lucky. If anyone can cure him, it's Sophia. She has her grandmother's touch. There never was a better herbalist than Lizzie Griffin, and Sophia has the same gift."

"He's trembling so," Ceci said hoarsely, "and soaked with perspiration. I saw a man with such symptoms once, in New Orleans. He—" She'd been about to say that he died, but then she bit her lip and shook her head, moving to the cot on which Antony lay.

They had put the little bed in a small space behind the great kitchen chimney. The warmth should be strengthening. But Antony was still unconscious and his skin was a sick, gray color. Ceci stared at him, trying to stop her hands from twisting themselves in the skirt of her frock. There was barely room for her to stand beside the cot. She watched him for a few seconds, then turned back to his mother and cousin. "Yes," Mary was saying in response to her niece's gestures. "I understand, Sophia. I'll stay with him." She wrung out a cloth in a basin of cool water, moved to Antony's side, and bathed his forehead while she spoke. "You're going to Beacon Street? To the still-room? Yes, I thought so." Then, as an afterthought,

"Take Cecile with you, Sophia. She's very worried—it will do her good."

Ceci had not yet learned to decipher Sophia's signs as rapidly as the family at the Ark managed to do. There was little communication between the two women as they plodded through the snow up a steep hill. They reached the front door of a fine brick house topped by a white turret and a widow's walk. Without knocking, Sophia let herself in and drew Ceci after her.

Tonyjay was in his study but the door was open; he saw them as soon as they entered. "Sophia! And you've brought a friend, I see." He began on a cheerful, welcoming note but he read the distress in his granddaughter's eyes almost immediately.

"Something's wrong. What is it, Sophia?" He didn't wait for her to make signs but took a slate from a table near his desk and gave it to her with a sliver of chalk. "Antony," Sophia scratched quickly. "Home yesterday. Ill. Swamp sickness."

"I see," Tonyjay said. "You've come for herbs then. Go ahead, child, you know where everything is."

Just before she left, Sophia wrote the name "Cecile" on the slate and nodded toward the girl with her.

"That's your name, is it?" Tonyjay said, looking from the slate to the strange young woman. "And you've come with Antony?"

Ceci could do little but nod her head. She was too worried to make conversation. She had figured out who the man must be, though. When he said, "I'm Tonyjay Griffin, Antony's grandfather," it came as no surprise. She saw a man as tall and slim as Antony himself, although he was stooped a bit with age and his shoulders could never have been as broad as Antony's. He was still handsome, better-looking perhaps than his grandson. Silvery hair and black eyes, and lines in his face which added rather than detracted from his looks. They spoke of experience and good humor won from life's lessons. Tonyjay noted the girl's appraisal and smiled. "Am I what you expected?"

"I . . . I didn't mean to be rude," Ceci stammered, blushing.

"No, of course you didn't. Forgive me, my dear, I've embarrassed you and it wasn't my intention. You're very upset, aren't you? Worried about Antony, I expect. But Sophia is a genius with herbs, like my wife. She'll—"

Tonyjay had no further opportunity to say what Sophia would or could do. The girl herself returned just then, clutching a small box and indicating by her manner that she and Ceci must hurry back to School Street. "Go ahead, child," Tonyjay said, kissing Sophia's cheek lightly. "See they keep me informed of the lad's progress." They were almost out the door when he added, "Cecile, you tell that young rascal I expect to see him as soon as he's well enough to walk up here. We've a lot to discuss, he and I. I'm owed some explanations and I intend to have them."

Ceci was more comforted by the brusque but confident note on which the meeting with the senior Griffin ended than by any of the sympathetic noises made by the family at the Ark. They crowded into the kitchen and chattered advice, most of it conflicting and all of it useless. Sophia took one look at the melee and started pushing them out the door.

"She's right," Martha Griffin said at once. "We're all just going to get in her way. Out. Everybody!" Then she turned and said to her sister, "Mary, I'll be nearby if you need me." Martha started to lead Ceci from the room with the rest but Sophia stretched out her hand and indicated she wanted the French girl to remain. "All right, you and Mary and Cecile," Martha agreed. "The rest of us will wait."

Some of the numbness that had gripped Ceci the moment Antony fainted in the wood shed began to disappear. If Sophia had requested that she remain, that meant she could be of some use. Mary Griffin was still sitting by her son, sponging his fevered body; Sophia was busy moving a huge kettle of water over the flames of the fireplace; and Ceci began unpacking the box of things they had carried from Beacon Street.

Even if she'd been knowledgeable about simpling, which she wasn't, Ceci probably wouldn't have recognized the English names lettered on the close-wrapped vials and tins that she lined up on the table: HENBANE, NIGHT SHADE, ELCAMPINE, JIMSON WEED, RUE. None of it meant anything to her but obviously it did to Sophia.

Deftly the parcels were unwrapped and sorted. Each time, Sophia sniffed the dried powders and leaves with a testing manner, nodding her head when she found nothing amiss.

"Are they all right?" Mary Griffin asked. "Fresh enough? Lizzie's been dead almost five years and no one's been near her still-room in all that time. How can they be all right?"

Sophia smiled reassuringly. Her face looked particularly thin, even wan, beneath its scant fringe of brown-gold hair. Her odd two-color eyes seemed as huge as saucers as she concentrated on her task. But her confidence and the sure way she moved made the other two women relax. Within five minutes she had prepared a decoction and was spooning it between Antony's lips.

Ceci watched carefully, noting that Sophia used the hard seeds from the tiny bottle of rue to make the potion. They looked too shriveled and ancient to produce any reaction. When Antony suddenly lurched into consciousness and began to retch, Ceci was so startled she screamed. The sound erupted in the steamy silence of the kitchen. Then she saw Sophia's smile of satisfaction and the calm way she held Antony's head. This strange young woman knew what she was doing. In a way Ceci didn't understand, and for the briefest moment, Sophia made her think of her mother. After that the French girl was kept too busy to think of anything but the task at hand.

4

"Sophia's done well by you," Ceci said with a smile. "Three weeks and look at you, almost your old self."

"Yes," Antony agreed. "I'm damned lucky she was here.

Can't say I care much for her prediction though. She gave me a note yesterday saying that the swamp sickness is bound to return. I'm to expect bouts periodically for the rest of my life." He grimaced and took another sip of the broth Ceci was feeding him. "Must say it's a rotten prospect."

"Nonsense!" Ceci said brusquely. "Don't start feeling sorry for yourself. There's lots worse sickness. Look at Sophia."

"Mmm." He nodded and took the soup bowl from her hands. "Give me that. I'm well enough to feed myself." Then, when the broth was gone, he asked, "What do you think of her?"

"Sophia? I think she's marvelous. We're together a lot, even share the same bed—"

"Ha!" Antony interrupted. "Don't remind me of that. My mother and her fiendish prudery. How's a man to get well without his woman beside him?" He reached out and let his hand rest on her breast.

"Now you behave, Antony Griffin! You're sick. Besides, your mother is right. It's not . . . not seemly. Isn't that the English word?"

He chuckled. "Yes, it is. You're learning fast, my love. I've been meaning to ask you—does Sophia talk at all? When you and she are alone? I thought perhaps . . ."

Ceci shook her head sadly. "No, never. Not even in her sleep. It's not that she won't, Antony. I'm convinced of that. She can't. Something must have happened as a result of the fire." The girl shivered and moved away from the blazing hearth despite the cold and the snow falling outside the window. "Her arm and her shoulders are terribly scarred. And when I think of what she lost . . . That's what I meant about your not feeling sorry for yourself compared to her. And you mustn't worry. She gave me the herbs she used to cure you and showed me how to make the simples. I'll know what to do next time."

Antony hoisted himself in his bed and looked out at the blizzard. "I'll be well enough to travel in a week or two but this weather isn't going to help. God knows how long it'll be before we can take ship for Canada." He didn't say it but he was also worried about the political situation. He'd been talking to his father about that the night before. Charles Griffin wasn't pleased that Antony still wanted no part of Griffin's Importations, but he was resigned.

"Canada, is it?" he'd said. "Very well, if that's your choice. But you'd best be warned, lad. Things are getting worse here. They say England and France may make peace soon. Can't see it helping much in America. It's hard to find a peaceful ship allowed to travel from New England to Canada. Certainly none of ours would go there. Your Uncle Benjamin won't hear of it. He's a *patriot*." Charles spoke the word with distaste.

Antony was thinking of that now. "Do you suppose you could keep an eye on Long Wharf, until I'm well enough to do it?" he asked Ceci. "Watch for any French vessel there might be, one we could book passage on."

"Yes, but before that . . ." She let the sentence trail off. Her cheeks flushed slightly as they always did when she'd something to say she didn't relish saying.

"Go on. Before that, what?"

"You must visit your grandfather," she blurted out. "We can't go until you do."

"My grandfather! What do you know of him? And what possible difference can it make to you?"

"I go there," she admitted. "To his house. Often. With Sophia."

Griffin's eyes narrowed. "To Beacon Street? I don't think I understand." But he had a suspicion he did—a notion that the old man was filling Ceci's head full of rubbish about blacks being equal to whites, telling her of the quarrel between himself and his grandson.

Ceci didn't respond to the unspoken anger in his eyes, only to his question. "Sophia is fixing up your grandmother's old still-room and I've been helping her. We whitewashed it last week. In the spring she means to work on the garden. It's a sight now; no one's cared for it since your grandmother died."

"What's that to do with me and my grandfather? What's he been telling you, Ceci?"

Her green eyes narrowed. "Certainly nothing that should make you use that tone of voice! He's a marvelous old man, Antony. I love him," she added shyly. "I really do. And he's asked to see you. That's all."

"We were very close once," Antony admitted. "I guess that's why the argument between us is so bitter."

"On your part perhaps, but not on his," she said. "You can't leave without seeing him. It would be cruel and I won't permit it."

He couldn't be angry at her audacity. She looked adorable when she got that determined tilt to her chin. "We'll see," he said softly. "At any rate, the old boy's apparently lost none of his charm for women. You get dewy-eyed when you speak of him, and he'll be seventy his next birthday!"

"He is wonderfully handsome nonetheless," she said, giggling. "You know, darling"—Ceci leaned forward and put her two small hands on his stubble-covered cheeks—"I think you should grow a beard again. Like the one you had when you came to New Orleans. You look more like him with a beard. It covers up that funny square jaw and that crooked smile."

"Square jaw! Crooked smile! You'll pay for that, woman!" He grabbed her shoulders and pulled her down beside him. It might have gone a lot further had his mother not come into the kitchen just then.

"I see you're recovering, Antony," Mary said tartly. "Good. I'll tell Sophia we can discontinue your purges. After this one." She came toward them brandishing a bottle of brown, sulphrous syrup, and Antony groaned. Ceci was grinning when she disentangled herself from his arms and the bedclothes but she didn't dare let him notice.

"I don't need you holding my hand," Griffin muttered as they walked across the Common toward Beacon Street.

"I promised Sophia I'd finish washing the shelves in the still-room," Ceci answered mildly. "I'm not going for your sake."

He didn't reply, just kept walking the familiar route he'd once traveled so eagerly. One thing at least was the same: it was good to be out of the Ark, away from the hurly-burly and confusion of that noisy establishment.

Beneath their feet snow had become brown slush in a February thaw. Warm sun was melting the ice, causing the breeze to smell deceitfully of spring. If the weather hadn't turned so mild the women probably would have ganged up on him and refused to let him go out, even though he felt quite well again. As it was, they'd supervised the donning of a heavy knitted jerkin beneath his jacket and his mother had even resurrected his old muffler.

Griffin could feel the scarf as it rubbed against his incipient beard. Like the Common, it smelled and felt familiar. But in this case the familiarity wasn't pleasant; it fact he had a sense that he was losing something—some independence he'd won by the hard toil of the Blackwater years, a feeling of being his own man, and not just one of the crowd at the Ark.

"Please," Ceci said, interrupting his thoughts, "you're walking too fast. I can't keep up." She was breathless with the effort of trotting beside him.

"Sorry, love," he said quickly. "I was thinking." He shortened his long strides and took her hand again. "After today," he said, "after I see Tonyjay, we're going to the docks and try to book passage. I want to leave, Ceci. I've been in Boston long enough."

"Very well," she said. "But we haven't sold the ruby yet. Don't we need to do that first?"

"No," Antony said. "We don't. You can keep your ring. I have money enough." She looked at him inquisitively and he realized he owed her an explanation. "I didn't borrow it from my father, if that's what you're thinking."

"I didn't think that."

"It's my money. I earned it." Then, because he couldn't just leave it there, he added, "It came from my Aunt Hannah. There was a letter waiting here when we arrived. I got sick before I could tell you about it. She sent a bill of credit drawn on Jameson's, the Blackwater factors. My wages as it were."

Ceci knew better than to ask more. His voice wasn't exactly bitter, but it had a hard, brittle quality that foreclosed further talk on the subject. "Very well," she said. "I'll keep the ring for now. If we need to sell it later, we can. In Acadia."

Tonyjay watched the couple approach. He stood behind the curtains of his study and knew a peculiarly intense pleasure at the sight of the lad and the girl walking hand in hand up Beacon Street. Antony was little changed; the same tall but square form—Antony had never had the Griffin elegance—the unruly mop of dark hair. The French lass looked strangely out of place beside him; she was a true beauty. But the currents between them seemed right. Antony adored her—that was obvious just from the look on his face. Tonyjay was smiling when he went to the front door. Only at the last second did he remember that he had cause to be angry with the boy. He banished the smile.

"Come in. I'm glad to see you well, Antony."

"Thank you, sir. I might say the same." His grandfather certainly didn't look his years. A small knot of trepidation dissolved in Antony's gut. He had not resisted this meeting just because of the quarrel; he'd been afraid to see what time might have done to the man he'd so loved and admired.

"I've work in the still-room," Ceci murmured. "May I . . . ?" She hesitated to push past the two men standing in the front hall.

"Of course," Tonyjay said hastily. "You know the way, my dear. Make free—the house is yours." Then, turning to his grandson, he said, "Come in here, Antony. It's not as tidy as when your grandmother was alive but nothing else is different." He opened the door to the study and stood aside so the younger man could pass.

Antony surveyed the room with a sudden, altogether unexpected nostalgia. It was indeed the same. There was even his favorite leather chair drawn up beside the old man's desk, within arm's reach of the shelves of books. When he walked to that chair his knees were trembling and it had nothing to do with his recent bout of swamp sickness.

"You're growing a beard, I see," Tonyjay said by way of preamble. It struck him as an absurd opening to this particular meeting but he too was tongue-tied by the emotion of the moment.

"Yes. Ceci says she likes it."

"Mmm. I agree. Brandy?" He poured a tumbler without waiting for a reply. When Antony took it their fingers touched. Shyly Tonyjay put forth his hand. "Welcome home, lad. Despite everything . . . I mean regardless of . . . Oh hell, Antony, welcome home!"

They indulged in a swift but intense bear hug and then Tonyjay took his accustomed place behind the desk. "Now, get that book over there. The one I've left open for you. I want you to read what I've written about the evils of the slave system."

"Forgive me, sir," the younger Griffin said. "You don't know anything about the system or the blacks."

"Very well. Enlighten me then," Tonyjay said. "I'm always willing to listen to a man's arguments."

"First of all, there's no way on God's green earth you could run a plantation like Blackwater—or any other in the south—without the blacks. The extent of the work, its nature, the conditions of climate . . ." He threw up his hands in a gesture of frustration. "Damn it, sir, all you have to do is spend one day in the rice fields to know no white man could survive."

"The economics of it, yes, I know that," Tonyjay said mildly. "And the truth that Negroes are fitted for the task. I have no quarrel with either of those assumptions."

"Then I fail to see—"

"They're slaves, lad!" The older man banged his fist on the desk. "Bought and sold like chattel. Owned outright. Not just for a term like an indenture, but in perpetuity. Their very children are born into slavery. I've even read of breeding programs—as if the Negroes were livestock. It's disgusting."

"The precedents go back to the beginnings of civilization. Surely you know that."

"Oh Antony, to think you've fallen into that trap." Tonyjay sighed. "The psuedo-scholastic argument by which the fool tries to appear educated. It's rubbish I tell you! Those ancient civilizations you're citing . . . For one thing they made slaves of nations they'd conquered. They viewed slavery as the price of losing a battle as it were. They didn't convince themselves the enslaved were no different than their horses or donkeys or beasts of the fields. And I hasten to remind you those same cultures practiced crucifixion, and gladiatorial games to the death, and a lot of other unsavory bits of barbarism. Do you fancy your average southern gentleman, your slaveholder, would defend those other things simply because the ancient Romans did them?"

Antony was slightly bewildered by the onslaught. He'd forgotten the power of the old man's personality, the way he could always win an argument by relentless, and usually faultless, logic. "But you're forgetting something," he said in desperation. "The niggers are perfectly happy. They sing from sunup to sundown in the fields, while they're working."

"Oh Antony," Tonyjay said again with the same sadness in his voice. "I thought you had more sense, more sensitivity. And more powers of discernment."

The younger Griffin squared his shoulders and took a deep breath. He didn't intend to be defeated by rhetoric. "There's something you're not discerning, sir. An essential truth. The black Africans, the niggers, aren't the same species we are. I think myself they're some kind of intermediate creation. Something between men and ordinary animals. In time, given the civilizing influence of life on the plantations, they may grow to be more human. There are some who deny that possibility. They say all creatures are irrevocably fixed in their proper place. I had a bitter argument about that with a clergyman from Charlestown. But I think not. Some form of evolving may take place."

Tonyjay had listened to the long speech with a changing expression. "You have given it some thought then, not just accepted it trunk and branch as it were. That's good. It makes me feel better about things. Now, let's look at your theory. If indeed . . ."

5

They went round and round the subject of slavery for an hour but it ceased to be an acrimonious discussion. Once Antony raised a well-thought-out theory, the nature of the conversation changed.

"Very well," Tonyjay said at last, "you believe what you're saying. I see that. It's not sheer opportunism at least. That's what made me angry, Antony. The thought that you'd given in because it was easy, profitable. Do you understand?"

"Yes, sir. But it was never that. There's nothing easy about it."

"Are you going back there?"

"To Blackwater?" Antony was startled by the question. He'd assumed his grandfather knew. But then, why should he? "No. Daniel Ludlow returned just before I left. I'm not needed there any longer."

"Well," the old man said, nodding his head. "That's an interesting development. You don't sound bitter."

Antony shrugged. "I got over that after the first day. Waste of time. Hannah Ludlow's an extraordinary woman. It's in keeping with her character to do as she's done. I was a fool not to get something in writing." He had made that admission to no one else. It was a mark of the swift healing of the rift between himself and the old man.

"I'm glad," Tonyjay said honestly. "Glad you're not bitter and glad you're not going back. Your father implied as much. He said something about Canada, but I didn't understand at the time."

Antony allowed himself a small smile. "I'd forgotten how it is with this clan. Nothing can ever be a secret."

"You've managed, however. Unless I miss my guess Charles doesn't know a thing about Paul's offer."

"Sweet Jesus Christ!" Antony exploded. "You really do know everything."

"Not quite," Tonyjay said wryly. "I wasn't sure about Blackwater and I really didn't know about Daniel. I only have the other information because Paul came and told me. He thought I might influence you."

A dark look passed over Antony's face. "I'm afraid I don't want to discuss that," he said. "There's more to it than either you or Uncle Paul realize. Anyway, it's out of the question."

"Too bad," the older man said matter-of-factly. "I've been going over these books Paul left with me." He dragged a pile of ledgers to the middle of the desk. "There's a hope of saving the markets if someone takes them in hand now. It's not much of a hope—a business doesn't take long to go to ruin, not these days. But with the right management the Amorys could salvage something."

"According to what he told me, none of them wants it," Antony said glumly.

"Wanting's got nothing to do with it," Tonyjay said. "The

thing is that without it they'll all be paupers—Paul, Valiant, and Sophia. The family won't let them starve, of course, but it won't be pleasant. Not for those three wounded souls." He sighed and pushed the books away. "I'm afraid your Uncle Benjamin is in charge of matters like that. I made the lot over to him years ago. And he can be damned insensitive where men like Valiant or Paul are concerned, men who don't measure up to his ideas of the 'done' thing—not to mention Sophia."

"Stop trying to play on my sympathies!" Antony said angrily.

"Very well," Tonyjay said without shame. "Cheap trick on my part," he admitted. "I apologize." He poured them each another drink. "Let me speak plainly then, lad. And have the kindness to hear me out, for old time's sake at least. I fully understand that you don't want charity. But you should at least consider buying the markets from Paul. That's what his allowance scheme is meant to achieve. He sees those moneys as payment for the business, paid to him and his children over a number of years, the rest of their lives in fact. I've been doing the sums. The amounts involved will probably come to a good deal more than the markets are worth in their present state. He'll never get that deal from Benjamin. Ben will take over the lot and pay their fair value. After that, every penny the Amorys get will be charity—and they'll know it."

"I'm sorry for that. Really I am. Certainly Uncle Paul and Sophia deserve better. As for that poor, perverted bastard Valiant . . ." He shrugged. "I can't take the lot of them on, Grandpa. There are reasons why I just can't."

"Your little Cecile," Tonyjay said softly. "She told me—"

Antony's head shot up and his spine went rigid. "Told you what?"

"Nothing disloyal," the older man said quickly. "I should think you'd know her better than that. She only said your reasons for refusing to buy the markets were both deep and personal."

"You keep saying 'buy.' As if it were some straight business arrangement. That's not Uncle Paul's intention. He said he wanted me to have Jacob's legacy. It's monstrous."

"That's not the point, is it, lad?" Tonyjay pressed his fingertips together and stared at his grandson over the top of that small, familiar gesture. "Not for you and not for me. I want you to stay in Boston because I'm a selfish old man. You want to leave."

"It's not just Boston, though I admit the Ark gets me down. It's simply that I've no right to what belonged to Jacob. I'm the last man in the world with any right to that."

"Will your refusal bring Jacob back to life?"

"I wish to God it would," Antony half whispered, rising and beginning to pace.

Tonyjay watched him for a moment, swallowed hard, and then made himself speak the question born in the past fifteen minutes. "Did you kill him, Antony? Did you kill Jacob?"

The boy's back was to him when he answered. "Not the way you mean. He was tortured to death by a band of Iroquois renegades. Slowly. You can't imagine it; don't even try. I was some forty yards away. I didn't stop it. I didn't even grant him the mercy of a quick gunshot."

"Why not?"

"We were in the woods. Me, Ceci, and a half-breed guide from Charleston. We'd been trying to stay out of the clutches of the Iroquois for days. When we came on their camp and I saw Jacob I told the half-breed to take Ceci and hide in the forest while I tried to rescue Jacob. He knocked me out instead and kept me that way until it was over. I should have seen it coming but I didn't."

There was silence for a while. When Antony turned back to his grandfather the old man was gray with shock and pain. "Poor Jacob," he muttered. "My poor Jacob. Paul doesn't know the details, does he?"

"No. I intended to tell him but I couldn't. I just didn't think he could stand it. I'm sorry I told you, for that matter."

"I'm not," Tonyjay said quickly. The old man's effort to master his grief was visible. "It's about the first sensible thing you've done since you got home. Sit down, Antony, and listen to me."

"No, if you don't mind I won't. I respect you, sir, and admire you more than any man alive. But I just can't cope with another lecture right now. It's my problem and I've got to sort it out for myself."

"Very well, no lectures. Will you at least stop pacing? Good, that's better. What about Cecile?"

"Ceci? What about her?"

"Are you going to marry her?"

Griffin's gray eyes opened wide. "Of course I am! Eventually. When it's convenient—I mean after we're settled. What do you take me for?"

"A damned fool," Tonyjay said. "I've plenty of evidence. So you hide off to Acadia and the northern wilds and you marry that adorable child. Then what? You know there's going to be war here in the colonies, don't you? How do you imagine you'll fare then? An Englishman in a French country, a Griffin no less. Your family's ships will be at the king's service, you know. It's inevitable. Do you plan to change your name, deny your heritage?"

"I couldn't do that."

"I didn't think you could. So then what? After they conscript your land, and they will, what will happen to Cecile then? Not to mention any children you may have."

Antony stared glumly at the floor. "I don't know. I haven't thought about it."

"No. And you've not thought about the rest as well. I know, I know. I promised not to lecture. But I mean to speak my piece, damn it! At my age I'm entitled. This house is yours. At least it will be when I die. Don't start protesting. That's been my will since you were ten years old and I've no intention of changing it now. After you get thrown out of Canada, or escape if you're lucky, you can come back here. At least you'll have a place to live."

They were silent for a few minutes. Tonyjay blew his nose noisily and complained of something in his eye. Finally Antony stretched out a tentative hand to the ledgers still on his grandfather's desk. "You've looked at these you say?"

"Yes. Spent all last week with them. They're a mess. Until Rachel died it was another story but after that . . . Well, Paul was never a businessman. Not even before all the trouble."

"Trouble," Antony repeated. "There's been a lot of it lately, hasn't there?" He was remembering for the first time that Rachel had been his grandfather's daughter, Tonyjay's favorite child according to the family stories. The old man must have taken her death badly. Griffin's fingers were resting atop the stack of records. He stared at them, then pulled back his hand as if he'd been burned.

"Don't feel trapped, lad," his grandfather said softly. "The last thing I mean to do is make you feel trapped."

"It's not you," Antony answered. "It's me, myself. My blood, if you will. I was born a Griffin and nothing can change it."

"No. Nothing ever will."

"Tell me, sir, in your considered opinion—there's hope? For the markets I mean. They could show a profit again?"

"With careful farsighted management, undoubtedly."

Antony laughed without humor. "I'm an excellent manager, you know. You'd be surprised how good at it I am. I was myself."

"No, I don't think I'd be surprised," Tonyjay answered in an attempt to lighten the mood. "After all, I took a hand in your education."

Antony didn't respond to that banter but he did have another thought, a last straw to cling to. "What about The Roses? Can't Paul sell the house and get enough to make himself and Sophia and Valiant secure? On top of what Uncle Benjamin will pay him for this lot I mean."

"He could. And The Roses is for sale. But Paul won't touch that money, not for himself or his children. He's convinced it's blood money of a sort. Something like Judas and his thirty pieces of silver. The funds realized from the sale are to go to England, to Harwood Hall. I don't understand all of it myself, but I know nothing will make Paul do differently."

"That's something to do with the ghost, isn't it?" Antony pursed his lips in an effort to remember. "He said something about the Kirkslee nun first being seen in the west wing of Harwood."

It was Tonyjay's turn to rise. He'd given up pacing some years back. His legs weren't up to it anymore. Now he went and stood by the window. The winter sun glinted on his silvery hair and highlighted the wrinkles of age and experience. "Paul claims the nun appeared to him and said he had a debt. He means the money from The Roses to be held in trust to rebuild Kirkslee Priory on Harwood land. If and when it's ever possible."

"Sweet Jesus," Antony sighed. "It really is a hornets' nest."

The old man managed a smile. "It is, but you needn't be

stung. I said you weren't to feel trapped and I meant it. Forget the lot of them, lad. Take your Cecile and go to Acadia. I'll lend you whatever you need if that's a problem."

"You did say careful and farseeing management, didn't you?" Antony ignored the other man's last words and flipped through the top ledger in the pile. "Uncle Benjamin may be careful but he's about as farseeing as a toad. I can run rings around him, and my father and Uncle John if it comes to that."

"Glad to hear it," Tonyjay said, chuckling. "My sons have much to recommend them but if they'd not been handed a thriving business the three of 'em would be clerks."

"Well, not your grandson. Can I use a room here to work for the next few days? A man needs earplugs to think at the Ark."

6

Ceci saw the vessel three days after Antony's reunion with his grandfather. She hadn't asked him about that meeting; she'd had no need to do so. It was clear from the attitudes of both men that the rift between them was healed. That gave her great pleasure. She was wholly captivated by the senior Griffin and pleased that Antony had made peace with him. As for what Antony might be doing at the Beacon Street house, closeted in an unused bedroom with piles of papers and ledgers, she didn't really care. Some task for his grandfather undoubtedly, some business thing concerning only men. She would go on with her own jobs. Sewing a new wardrobe, for Antony as well as herself, and keeping an eye on the docks so they could find a ship to carry them north. On the Tuesday morning she spied the schooner *La Madalaine* at Clark's Wharf, Ceci was beside herself with excitement.

"Where is the captain?" she demanded of the deck hand, staring up at him and the handsome ship.

"Below, Mademoiselle," the man answered. "Have you business with him?"

He'd replied in French to her English question. Cecile felt slightly uncomfortable. *La Madalaine* was openly in port and everyone would know her as a French ship, but the memory of the night in Charleston was still fresh in the girl's mind. She hesitated to flaunt her own Canadian background. The crewman was waiting for an answer, however. And surely he'd be more cooperative if he recognized her as what she was. "*Oui*," she said after a quick glance to the right and the left. "*Maintenant, s'il vous plaît.*"

The sailor grinned at the blond young woman. He seemed to be delighted that a girl so lovely was a kinswoman. "Marvelous, Mademoiselle!" he answered, laughing. "I will fetch him *tout de suit*. Business with you will doubtless put him in a good humor the rest of the day."

The captain indeed seemed pleased to welcome her aboard his ship. "I never thought to find such a lovely lady in this place," he said, jerking his head in the direction of the town. "What is a beautiful Canadian girl doing in Boston, Mademoiselle? And how can I be of service to you?"

Ceci smiled flirtatiously. "How gallant you are, *mon capitaine*. And how fortunate I am that you've arrived. My fiancé and I wish to travel to Acadia. We've been waiting for a ship that can provide passage."

"Then it is a lucky day for us both," the captain said with a smile. "We sail in three days time for Grand Pŕe. Will that do?"

"Oh yes!" Ceci said enthusiastically. "That will do very well indeed." Then, because she knew no better time would arrive, she added, "I must tell you, however, that my fiancé is English." She looked him directly in the eye, offering no apology by way of tone or inference.

"*Eh bien,* Mademoiselle," the man said, chuckling. "Life and love are often removed from politics. For one as charming as yourself I will even have an Englishman aboard my ship."

"Antony!" Cecile called as soon as she opened the door to the Beacon Street house. "Antony, come quick. I've found it! The ship, I mean."

"Hey!" He collided with her as she rushed down the hall. "Slow down. What's all this about?" Then, without giving her a chance to reply, he said, "No, don't tell me yet. Give me a kiss first."

"Mmm, wait." She struggled against his embrace, then gave in and let her lips yield beneath his for a moment. He tasted of tobacco. Antony had taken to smoking a pipe during his hours of work in the spare bedroom. And there was something else unfamiliar, some sense of suppressed excitement that communicated itself to her in his caress. "You're pleased about something," she said when she could tilt her head back and look up at him. "What is it?"

"No. Your news first. I'll tell you mine later."

"Very well. Mine's better anyway. There's a schooner called *La Madalaine* at Clark's Wharf, just back from Guadeloupe with a cargo of cocoa. They're trading that for cloth and iron—that's why they're in Boston." She stopped and let her green eyes search his face.

She'd deliberately drawn out the narrative, telling him first the things of little relevance. It was a ploy born partly of her natural flair for the dramatic and partly of a desire to heighten his pleasure in her news, give him time to respond to it. But she saw no excitement in his face. If he'd guessed the end of her tale it showed in an expression of consternation, not of delight. "They leave for Grand Pré on Friday," she finished quietly. "The captain has agreed to accept us as passengers."

He let her go then, relaxed his grip on her slender form and taking hold of her hand instead. "Come into my room," he said. "We can talk there. I've a fire, and it's warm."

"What is there to talk about, Antony?" she asked. "I told you everything I know. You're to go to Clark's right away.

I told the captain to expect you. He knows you're English, and that's all right. I said you'd make the financial arrangements—"

He silenced her words by laying one finger across her lips. "Shh. Sit down. I've something to say. Are you warm enough? I can build up the fire."

She wasn't warm; she was cold. An icy coldness was seated in the pit of her stomach and spreading rapidly. But she shook her head. "The fire's fine. Tell me what you mean. I don't understand. I thought you'd be excited. Is it money, Antony? I still have the ruby. Don't forget that."

"I haven't forgotten. And it's not money. We have enough, as I told you. It's all this." He waved his hand at the pile of ledgers on the table that had become his desk.

"All what?" Ceci stared at the books, which meant nothing to her. "What is all that stuff?"

"The records of the Amory markets for the past half dozen or so years."

"The Amory markets? Your uncle's business . . . here in Massachusetts Bay . . . ? But you said—"

"I know. I know what I said."

"You said it was monstrous," she went on, ignoring his interruption. "You said you'd have nothing to do with Jacob's legacy. Why are you working with these things? What does it have to do with us? With our future?"

"Everything," he said. "I wasn't sure before, that's why I didn't tell you. But there is money to be made from those markets, Ceci. A great deal of money." His voice warmed. "It's a real challenge. The markets have a potential no one's fully realized, not even my Aunt Rachel while she was alive. They're too spread out now, too far-flung. But if some consolidations are effected, some tightening of control, and if a real effort is made to supply other shops and markets, why then Amory's could become the biggest—"

"Stop it," she said in a whisper that was more arresting than a scream. "Stop telling me all this. I don't want to know. Did he do it? Your grandfather? Did he prevail on you to take what isn't yours?"

"Not the way you mean." Antony moved closer to where she sat, dropped to his knees beside her. "I know what you're thinking, Ceci. And I know it seems outrageous for me to take over what belonged to Jacob. After . . . after what happened. But it's not really like that." She was staring at him, her eyes darkening with some emotion he was afraid to name.

"I think I owe it to him in a queer sort of way," Griffin continued, his voice almost pleading. "Without these markets Paul and Sophia and Valiant will have nothing. They'll be paupers, dependent on the family for charity. If I make the business pay, the Amorys will have lifetime incomes from it. Don't you see?"

"I see that you aren't going with me to Acadia," she answered in that same soft whisper. "That you're deserting me."

"For the love of God, Ceci! Do you imagine I don't mean for you to stay here with me? To be my wife? How can you think such a thing?"

"Stay here," she repeated. "Not go home. Not go to Acadia. Not bear my child in Acadia. I can't. I won't."

Her flat tone was like the sound of mourning, the sound of a gull keening in the wind. Antony heard only one phrase. "*Your child* . . . Ceci, are you telling me you're pregnant? That we're going to have a baby?"

"Yes." She nodded. "In August I think." Her voice was still without expression.

"But why didn't you tell me before this! It's wonderful news, darling. I'm overjoyed."

"I wanted to tell you when we got home. I wanted to tell you when we were in Acadia."

Griffin swallowed hard. He could not ignore the look of desolation on her face, the fear in her gaze. "My dearest Ceci. I love you so." He took her face in his hands and kissed her forehead before continuing. "Wherever we're together, that's home. I'll take care of you, protect you and the child. You'll have a wonderful life in Boston, you'll see."

"No!" She screamed the word, tore away from him, and stood like a trapped creature with her back to the wall. "I won't stay here. I won't! I'm going home, to Acadia."

She ran from the room. Antony stood where he was for long seconds. He looked at the pile of ledgers and the mountain of notes he'd made in his careful study of the books. He could feel the Beacon Street house around him, sense its claim on him, the Griffin heritage it represented. And he could hear Ceci's words echoing in the silence. She was expecting a child, his child. "Ceci," he yelled as he ran after her. "Ceci, wait!"

He caught up with her halfway down the hill. The ice was frozen solid again. The thaw had ended. The slippery road made walking a perilous thing and it had slowed her headlong flight.

"Don't," he said as he grabbed her arm in an almost punishing grip. "Don't you ever run away from me again. Not ever, do you hear?" She didn't answer but she didn't try to break free.

"I didn't realize you cared so much," he said more quietly. "About returning to Canada I mean. I thought it was just an alternative, something fairly sensible to do about our future."

"I care," she whispered. "I can't tell you how much I care."

"Very well. We'll go to Clark's Wharf now. I'll speak to the captain. We'll sail with him on Friday."

7

In the melee of the Ark privacy didn't exist. It seemed unimportant to the Griffins who lived there. They looked alike, thought alike, sounded alike, were unembarrassed by performing even intimate personal tasks in full view of each other. When one of them wanted a bath, a big copper hip tub was hauled in front of the cooking fire and filled with steaming water. The bather simply ignored the procession of people who came and went in the kitchen.

Ceci couldn't bring herself to adopt that attitude. On Thursday afternoon Sophia climbed to the tiny attic room the two girls shared and found Cecile immersed in the tub. She had dragged it, and the kettles of water required to fill it, up two flights of stairs. Sophia looked chagrined at thus interrupting the privacy Cecile had purchased so dearly. She started to withdraw.

"Don't go, Sophia. I don't mind you. I'm not a prude. It's just that there are so many of them."

Sophia smiled and nodded. The little room was full of steam but still icy cold. Frost was thick on the window, obliterating the outside. Sophia hugged herself and made exaggerated shivering motions.

"Yes," Ceci said. "I know it's cold up here. But it was worth it. I don't want to go aboard that ship without a bath."

Sophia's eyes clouded over and she turned away. She knew there was something wrong about this proposed journey. There was no excited planning, no apparent currents of joy between Cecile and Antony as they prepared for their new adventure. The rest of the family accepted their leave-taking as they'd accepted their arrival—philosophically, too preoccupied by their own concerns and lives to think of much else. But Sophia was different.

She reached for the big towel lying on the chair and held it out as the French girl emerged from the tub. "Thank you," Ceci said and accepted Sophia's brisk rubbing. They had established the physical intimacy of sisters in the weeks they'd lain together in the narrow bed; there was nothing unusual in the gesture.

Sophia worked from Cecile's arms and shoulders down her torso to her waist. Suddenly she stopped, ran her hands along the upper half of Ceci's body once more. Then she touched the girl's belly and looked at her questioningly.

"Yes," Ceci said. "A baby. In August. I just told Antony. How could you know? I didn't think I was showing yet."

Sophia reached up and cupped Ceci's breasts, indicated that they were beginning to swell, that her waist was thickening. "I see," Ceci said. "You would know, wouldn't you, what with having three of your own? Oh Sophia! Forgive me, that was cruel. To remind you like that. I'm just not thinking straight right now."

Sophia shook her head. Her hair was beginning to grow at last, making a golden-brown halo around her heart-shaped face. When she drew Ceci into her arms and sat with her on the bed, her small, thin frame seemed to radiate strength. Her gestures said that no apology was necessary, that she was happy for her friend. Ceci was emboldened by that bigness of spirit. "How do you stand it, Sophia?" she whispered. "Losing them as you did. I don't think I could go on living . . ."

Sophia shrugged as if to say there was no choice. "I lost a baby once," Ceci continued, the words pouring out of her in a sudden need to talk. "I've never told anyone. Not even Antony. When I went to New Orleans I was an indentured servant. I told you about that, how I met Antony on the ship. I didn't tell you about the captain." She shivered involuntarily and Sophia tightened her grip on the girl, drew the eiderdown quilt around them both.

"He was an animal, that Captain Bonde. He did things to me, terrible things. He made me pregant. Then, in New Orleans, an old woman cut the baby out of my body. I didn't know anyone could do such a thing. Oh it hurt so." She was crying, tears streaming down her cheeks. "Ever since then I've felt so empty. So hollow in here."

Sophia's hand still rested on the girl's belly. Ceci lay her own hand over it and pressed against the taut flesh. "But not now, not anymore. Ever since I found out, almost a month now, I've felt alive. And I'm not sick or anything. Not even in the mornings. When we get to Acadia, when Antony takes me home, it will be so wonderful. I'll have my baby in my own country . . ."

Her voice trailed off. Sophia wiped the tears from Ceci's cheeks with her free hand. Her eyes found the other girl's, signaling that she wanted to communicate something. "What?" Ceci asked. "What is it?"

Sophia moved away and took her slate from beside the bed. "Does Antony want to go?" she scratched on its surface.

"I can't say exactly," Ceci answered. "I guess he had some idea about staying. But that was just in the last few days. Before that he promised to take me home."

Sophia's eyes widened. She shook her head in almost frantic disagreement.

"You think I'm wrong to hold him to his word," Ceci said.

"I can see it in your face. But I want to go home, Sophia. I must go home. My baby—" She was weeping again, the sobs choking off her words.

"If thee loves, thee gives." Sophia held out the slate with its simple message.

"What about him? What does the man give?" Ceci demanded angrily. "All they do is take. Even Antony. They lie over you and pant and groan and do things, and when it's over they think only of themselves again."

Sophia shook her head, sadly this time. She wrapped the quilt tighter around Ceci's shaking shoulders, forcing her to lie back on the bed. "All wrong," she wrote.

"Why Sophia? Why is it wrong? Was it different for you, with your husband I mean?" Then, when the girl nodded vehemently, Ceci said, "I wish you could tell me about it. How you felt, how he made you feel. Why it was different. Is it because of your faith, Sophia? Your aunts told me you're a Quaker."

"No. Not a Quaker," the girl wrote on her slate. She underlined the words three times in bold, decisive strokes.

"But they said you were," Ceci insisted.

"My husband was a Friend," Sophia wrote. "I loved him."

"So you adopted his faith even," Ceci whispered. "But you didn't believe in it? You don't now?"

"There is Someone . . ." Sophia started to write. Then she rubbed the words out with a quick, vicious swipe of her hand. Again she shook her head, the tawny hair punctuating the gesture.

"Very well," Ceci said. "I won't ask you about that. I'm sorry." When she propped her head on her elbow the quilt fell away from her breasts and the cold air made her nipples swell. "But if only you could tell me about the rest," Ceci continued, ignoring her exposure. "I wish I could talk to someone about it. These last two days, watching Antony . . . I know he's unhappy about giving in. But I don't understand why his unhappiness makes me feel so guilty."

"Woman's instinct—natural," Sophia scratched on the slate.

"To give in you mean, to let the man have his way? Just like when you're in bed together?"

"Loving meant for joy of both," Sophia wrote.

Ceci smiled wanly and this time it was her turn to shake her head. "I'm afraid we have very different outlooks. I guess I could never feel as you do."

For some seconds Sophia sat still, with the chalk poised over her slate. Then she squared her shoulders and wrote, "Stay here. Don't move."

"Very well," Ceci agreed. "But why?"

For answer the other girl only pointed again to the message on the slate. Then she ran from the room.

Antony knocked but didn't wait for an answer before he opened the door. "Ceci, what's the matter? Sophia gave me a note. Said I was to come up here right away. That you needed me."

Ceci's eyes opened wide. "I don't know why she did that. We were talking—that is I was; Sophia was writing. Then she told me to stay here and ran away."

"She meant to give us some time alone, I guess," Antony said as he sat down beside her. "What were you two talking about?" His voice had a kind of reserve, an element of sadness present since the scene on Beacon Street, which Ceci pointedly ignored.

"Men and women," she said now. "You and me. Sophia and her husband. I think she loved him a lot."

"Yes," Antony said. "She must have. She ran off and married him without her mother's permission, you know. She had Uncle Paul's but that was never the same thing, not with the Amorys." He put his hands behind his head, stretching as if the weariness of a lifetime weighed on his shoulders. "It's really some queer kind of fate, I think, Sophia's husband and her children dying in the fire that killed Rachel. All very obscure."

Ceci was watching him, examining him as if for the first time: the way his nose ended in a slight upward tilt, the deep-set nature of his gray eyes—it all looked new to her, oddly unfamiliar. "Are you really very unhappy about going to Acadia?"

He waited for a bit before he answered. "No. I promised you. I never meant to go back on my word. I just didn't think it was so important. When I saw the possibility of remaining I was judging purely on business grounds."

"Just business?" she insisted.

"Other things too, I guess," he admitted. "My family, my name. It's complicated, Ceci. I don't think I want to talk about it. Anyway, it doesn't matter. We leave tomorrow. I saw the captain again this afternoon. Everything's arranged." He turned to her then and his crooked grin was touched with irony. "Do you know he's unloading his cocoa in the Amory market on Lyn Street? And buying his cloth and iron from my father. We'll never get away from the Griffins, Ceci. Their empire stretches everywhere."

"It's not that," she said. "I don't want to get away from them. At least not the way you mean. But I couldn't live in this house. Not permanently."

Griffin looked at her. There was some undertone to her words, some quality of unsureness he suspected more than heard. "We needn't live here," he said tentatively. "My grandfather is willing me the Beacon Street house, whether or not we go to Canada. If we stayed we could live there."

"Could Sophia live with us?" Ceci asked.

"If you wanted it and she agreed, of course she could." He lay one hand on her cheek, the first time he'd touched her since he came into the room. "Ceci, are you saying you'd reconsider?"

"Sophia wrote me a note," she said quietly. "It said 'If thee loves, thee gives.'"

"Do you love me?" he asked. "That much? You've never said it."

"I do." She took hold of his hand and moved it to her breast. It was his first intimation that she was naked beneath the thick quilt. "I think I do. I've never felt about anyone as I feel about you, Antony. Never really trusted anyone so much. Not even Emile. I think that means I love you."

"I hope so, oh God I hope so." He bent his head and kissed her gently. "I want you to love me, Ceci. I've wanted it so much for so long."

She raised her hands to his head and the quilt fell completely away. There had been so much emotion spent in the last hour, she was limp with it, exhausted by her own self-probing and admissions. Now, clasping his face in her hands, she closed her eyes and whispered, "I want to feel what you feel. Make that happen for me, Antony. Please."

He could barely hear her words, so softly were they uttered. When their import dawned he knew a moment of fear, even panic. He realized what she meant but he didn't have any idea of how to grant her request, if it were even possible. "It's different for men and women. At least I think it is."

"Sophia said loving was to give joy to both," she answered. "I want to feel joy."

He groaned and kissed her, knowing the effort she was making when her lips opened, her tongue sought his. She'd never done that before. For a fleeting second he thought about where they were, the way people bounced in and out of rooms here at the Ark. Then he remembered Sophia. She knew they were up here; she'd stand guard.

Almost every time he'd made love to Ceci there had been an element of haste, even of urgency. Maybe that's why she never seemed to enter wholly into the act. This time he moved slowly. He kissed her eyes, her cheeks, her hair, let his lips travel along her neck to her breasts and rest there. He was startled when she guided his hand below her belly to the moist, secret places between her thighs.

"Sometimes," she whispered, "I think about you touching me there. I want you to. I want to feel you touch me there."

He did as she asked, remembering a Boston barmaid, the first woman to whom he'd ever made love, who had enjoyed just such fondling. Ceci wasn't like the barmaid. Antony rejected any comparison between them. She was the golden goddess, the soon-to-be mother of his child. He eased his hand away from between her legs and freed the buttons of his britches.

When he stretched out full length beside her he sensed a change. Each time since the morning in the woods, the morning they had buried the remains of Jacob, Ceci had given herself to him in a conscious act of permission. She seemed to be allowing him the freedom of her body, making a gift of herself. In large measure that was part of his pleasure in the act. She who had denied him so long, denied him no longer.

This time was not like the others. Somehow Ceci had withdrawn into herself, was concentrating on herself and not on him. It was as if the long, slow buildup, the tender caresses, had wakened some childlike self-absorption. Antony didn't understand that to be a necessary prelude to the kind of explosion of feeling that Ceci craved, the kind he took for granted. He only knew that somehow the difference made him angry. For a moment he almost felt as he had that night on the Ashley, the night he raped her.

Griffin made a low throaty sound, not a question but a demand. Swiftly he rolled on top of Ceci's soft, rounded body. When he pushed his thick tool inside her he hesitated, feeling a moment's uncertainty. Ceci gasped and the sound was different too, unlike any sound she had made before. "Yes," she murmured urgently, "like that. Slowly."

He tried to comply. Despite his confused and conflicting reactions he wanted to give her what she desired. For a few seconds he moved with slow, deliberate motions. She was moaning and there was a slight tremor in her body beneath his. That hadn't happened before either. But he couldn't sustain it. The powerful drive that marked every encounter with a woman Griffin had even known took over. Gritting his teeth he plunged deeper, repeated the thrust twice, three times, finishing in a burst of glorious sensation that spread from the top of his head to his toes and left him gasping for breath and soaked in perspiration.

Ceci felt the weight of his body as it settled over her, limp and flaccid, the taut rigidity of his muscles now totally relaxed. Inside her she could still feel his turgid member, could feel, too, the twitching of her flesh. It was as if the secret, woman-spaces in her body were trying to speak, to call out their desires. Slowly the feeling ebbed. It was more than she'd ever felt before. Perhaps it was all there was. It must be.

They were married a week later in Tonyjay's study, in the house where they would live. Sophia stood beside Cecile, smiling at her and at them all. Later, in private, she would weep, mourn her losses as she always mourned them. Alone, with none to see or feel pity.

The senior Griffin beamed on the newlyweds. He was delighted with the turn of events and didn't care who knew it. No one had been happier than Tonyjay when *La Madalaine* sailed without Antony and Cecile. He had many grandchildren but Antony was the firstborn. He was special to the old man, as he'd been from the day of his birth.

"I'm glad it's all worked out this way, lad," Charles Griffin told his son in a private moment after the ceremony. "It will be good to have you nearby."

"I'm glad, too, sir," Antony answered, smiling. "I'm sorry Uncle Paul didn't come though. I sent a note specially to invite him."

"Well," said Charles with a shrug, "you know how he is these days. He couldn't very well have brought his woman and I don't think he goes anywhere without her."

"Doesn't matter," Antony said. "I just would have liked to have him here."

"I take it you and he have fixed up your business arrangements," Charles said.

"Yes, signed and sealed in the lawyer's office yesterday."

"Fine." Charles nodded with satisfaction. "I'm sure you and your bride will be happy. You've done the right thing, son."

"Yes, I'm sure of it." Antony glanced over to where Ceci stood talking to his mother, smiling and looking incredibly beautiful. Women, he thought. They aren't so difficult once you get them to face up to reality. "I'm sure we'll both be happy," he repeated.

4

THE PHOENIX

". . . All you who have been baptized in Christ's name have put on the person of Christ; no more Jew or Gentile, no more slave and freeman, no more male and female; you are all one person in Jesus Christ. And if you belong to Christ, you are indeed Abraham's children; the promised inheritance is yours."

—*Galatians 3: 27,28,29*

1

On a bleak February day in 1754, her twenty-eighth birthday as it happened, Sophia walked along Lyn Street purposefully averting her eyes. Eleven years ago this very day she had first seen Jonathan, just here at the central Amory market. Sophia did not wallow in that memory. She was on Lyn Street of necessity, not choice. She made her way through the crowds quickly, not looking up, not stopping.

When she drew abreast of the market she didn't falter. From the outside it was the same two-story brick building Rachel had built thirty years past. The additions were in the back, not visible from Lyn Street. That was true of most of the improvements Antony had made in his six years as owner and manager of the Amory markets. The changes provided more profit and more security, but were not externally dramatic. If Sophia had raised her eyes she would have seen the same big green double doors through which Jonathan had chased after her with the unwanted hinges. "Thee forgot thy hinges," he'd said. She could hear his voice as plainly now as she had then, could see his earnest, beloved face beneath the crop of red hair. Stop it! she told herself. Don't think about it; thee knows better. Squaring her shoulders, Sophia walked on.

"Morning, Mrs. Crandall," a man said, bowing and lifting his tri-cornered hat. She smiled at him and walked on. Every step was a penance but no one watching her would know that. They would see what they frequently saw: the mute Sophia

Crandall wearing gray bonnet and cloak, carrying her satchel of woven straw and hurrying to some house where there was sickness or disease. Today she was expected at Henchman's Lane where her simples were slowly curing a child of a dreadful skin ailment. Had the child been less pitiable, the lane more accessible, she'd not be on Lyn Street. Certainly not on this of all mornings.

The family admitted her to their comfortable house with little fanfare. Her patient was a young boy with a leprous, oozing patch on his forearm. He held the diseased member out to her and managed a smile. "It's getting better, I think, ma'am," he said eagerly. "Don't you agree it's getting better?"

Sophia smiled and nodded. The child's pleading tone could elicit no other response, but she was being truthful. His skin was improved. The pustules had ceased to spread and the stench from them wasn't so terrible. Working with the economy of motion that was her hallmark, Sophia bathed the sores with warm water and then applied a poultice of flaxseed, mallow, smallage, and fumitory. Finally she bandaged the arm afresh and stepped to the pump at the back door.

She always carried a lump of strong brown soap on these sorties and invariably she washed her hands after finishing her work. Many of the women of Boston laughed at her for that odd practice. "Like Pilate she is," one of them had said. "Thinks to cleanse evil with water." That remark was simple jealousy, brought on by the girl's success in cases where so many older women had failed. It never stopped Sophia. Her grandmother had advised the practice, based on a theory Lizzie had about the transmission of sickness. Sophia agreed. When she was clean to her satisfaction, she turned to the lad and held up two fingers.

"You'll be back in two days," he said. "You promise, ma'am?" Then, when she nodded and ruffled his hair, he said, "I wager my arm'll be all cured by then."

The mistress of the house was waiting to show Sophia out. "Thank ye, Mrs. Crandall," she said. "Thank ye and God bless." She pressed a coin into the girl's hand. Sophia bowed her head gravely, accepted the payment, and secreted the coin in the folds of her muff. From the poor she took nothing; from people of adequate means such as this family she accepted payment as her due. This coin, like so many others, would go into the jug in her bedroom on Beacon Street.

In the beginning, when she first took up residence with Antony and Ceci, Sophia insisted on paying for her room and board. "For heaven's sake, Sophia," Antony had remonstrated, "you're not a charity case. It's all arranged between your father and me. I've bought the markets and the payment is spread out as income for you and Valiant and him. I'll just deduct it from your account."

She wouldn't have that though, not at first. But in August of '48 the Griffins' son, Antony Jacob, was born and shortly thereafter the senior Tonyjay grew very ill. The work in the small household multiplied by leaps and bounds and Ceci couldn't have managed without Sophia. Only then, knowing herself to be necessary, did Sophia become less sensitive.

Life moved on: Tonyjay died and was mourned; three more children, daughters, were born to Antony and Ceci; the garden prospered under Sophia's care, and the old still-room was filled to overflowing with the results of her labors. Money ceased to be important. Against what end she was hoarding the jug full of coins Sophia could not say. But it was there, and it grew, and when she needed cash as well as herbs to help some of her poorest patients she was glad of it.

Sophia was thinking of all this as she made her way home. The quality of light had changed; the gray of the sky was deeper and more mournful; the air smelled of snow. Beneath her neat black boots the packed ice of the roadway, vestige of three harsh blizzards in as many weeks, made a dull squeaking sound. That and the low hum of her own breathing were the only disturbances in the quiet street. It was the dinner hour and few were about. Sophia thought of the big dining room on Beacon Street, of the Griffins and their four small children. The little boy they called Tonyjay after his namesake would be six next summer; the three girls, Mary, Sarah, and Louise, were four, three, and two. The youngsters were all blondes like their mother. They made a charming picture sitting between their parents at table.

Sometimes Sophia would look at them and feel intense, overwhelming pain. It wasn't just that she remembered her own scrubbed pine table in the kitchen at Rowley. Memories like that she could bear—they were a source of bittersweet joy. But when instead she saw her son Stephen's round baby face as she'd last seen it, pressed against the glass of his bedroom window, the bedroom into which she'd locked him, with leaping flames encircling the vision and the child's mouth shaped into a silent scream of terror, then she prayed to die.

Antony appeared to have forgotten about her past and all she had lost. Ceci had not, but if she saw Sophia's pain in the rare unguarded moments when it showed, she only looked away. Ceci understood the charity of pretending one didn't know another was suffering. It occurred to Sophia that the other woman's understanding was the product of her own secret griefs. No one would imagine Cecile LaPointe Griffin to have any cause for unhappiness. Her husband was successful and devoted, her children healthy and beautiful. What woman could ask more? She does though, Sophia sometimes thought as she lay abed in the long silent nights that shaped her existence; she does grieve. Like everything else it was an unalterable fact of life. Neither woman referred to it.

Today Ceci would not expect Sophia to join them for the midday meal. "You'll be late at Henchman's Lane, I expect," she'd said earlier. "I'll put your dinner at the back of the fire." When Sophia opened the door to the house she could hear laughter and chatter from the dining room and she was glad she need not join them. The fact of her birthday—the Griffins didn't know the precise date and each year it passed unmarked—and the forced walk along Lyn Street had combined to make her despondent. It wasn't an indulgence she permitted often, but this afternoon Sophia would just as soon be alone.

She went into the kitchen and found the covered plate waiting on the ledge beside the hearth where the kettle usually stood. Sophia took off her bonnet and cloak and went to stand by the fire. Its glow was warming. Outside, the first few snowflakes started to fall. Big and distinct and very wet, they clung to the sill like separate jewels. She reached for the plate, removed the cover, and walked to the window, staring out at the gathering storm, smelling the savory steam generated by roast mutton, potatoes, and carrots.

"Sophia."

The voice didn't startle her, though it might have. She knew instantly it wasn't familiar, but neither was it threatening. When she turned and saw the woman she didn't tremble or feel fear. The black-garbed figure with the starched white wimple framing a face obscured by shadow was inexplicably ordinary-looking.

"You know who I am, I expect," the woman said.

Her speech was more unusual than her clothing. The accent was slightly familiar, but unlike any Sophia could remember hearing in Massachussetts Bay. She shook her head slowly. She did not know who the creature was or what she was doing in the kitchen of the house on Beacon Street.

"No? Well, it doesn't matter. I've a message for you, child. It's been waiting a long time. In the other room, the one with all the books, you'll find a volume lying on the desk. It is open. Read what is written there."

The strange figure didn't dissolve into a vapor or walk from the room. She simply ceased to be present. Sophia stood staring at the spot where the woman had stood. It was empty. She was alone in the kitchen.

From the dining room the sound of the family at dinner could still be plainly heard. Outside the snow continued to fall. Sophia looked at the plate in her hands. Steam yet rose from it. Carefully she replaced the cover and put the saved dinner back beside the fire. Then, walking as if in a dream or a trance, afraid her legs would betray her if she were not very cautious, she started for the hall. The room with all the books could only be her grandfather's study, which Antony now used. She had not been in it in years.

The door was ajar, as if Antony had forgotten to close it when he went to dinner. Sophia pushed it farther open and stepped inside. Nothing there was extraordinary or mysterious. It was dark, however. A fire was laid but the grate was cold. Perhaps Antony hadn't been in here this morning. No light came through the window and the curtains were drawn against the chill. Besides, it had grown as black as night outside. Sophia fumbled with a candle and finally managed to get it lit.

Lying on one corner of the desk was a slim volume bound in faded black leather. It was open and face down, as if it had been in a reader's hands a moment before—as if it had been left thus for the duration of some brief errand by one who intended to return and continue.

She was shaking now. The reaction had been slow in coming but delay had intensified it. She stretched out her hand to take the book but couldn't do it. Twice she pulled back before she succeeded in grasping the thing and turning it over. Slowly Sophia dropped her eyes to the page. There had been no marking on the cover. What book it might be she had no idea. Then across the top margin she saw the heading, "The Psalms of David the Israelite King." Thirteen words leapt up to meet her gaze: "O Lord open Thou my mouth and my lips shall declare Thy praise . . ."

"Dear God," Sophia whispered aloud. "Dear God what does it all mean?" Then she gasped and dropped the book as if it had turned to fire. Pressing her hands to her mouth, she stood staring at nothing. Her teeth were biting into her knuckles and she could taste the salt of her own blood.

She wanted to try again but she was afraid. Slowly she dropped her hands and spread her fingers on the desk, leaning on them as if she might otherwise fall. Sophia shut her eyes, concentrating every particle of her being on repeating the miracle. "Jonathan," she said in a strained, high-pitched little voice. "Stephen, Paul, Hiram . . ." The spoken names of her martyred husband and children tinkled like broken glass in the silent room.

2

Cecile's world was bordered by her husband, her children, and her home; there was nothing else. In the early days of her marriage she had thought it might be different. Antony, scion of one of the most prominent Boston families, swiftly became a noted businessman in his own right. Social opportunities should have been plentiful for the wife of such a man, even in staid and stolid Boston. But shortly after little Antony Jacob was born she learned the price of such pleasures.

It had been a fine late September evening in 1748 and the air smelled crisp and fresh with autumn. Her figure had returned to its normal proportions. Riding in a handsome carriage to a party at the home of Benjamin Griffin and his wife Eve, Ceci had been full of anticipation. She knew her blue velvet gown looked lovely. In Antony's eyes she read pride and satisfaction with her appearance. "You'll be the most beautiful woman there," he'd said, smiling. "I can't wait to see the looks on their faces."

It was Ceci's first such evening since her marriage, as her pregnancy had foreclosed any earlier parties. When they arrived at Marlborough Street she was impressed with the elegance of the house, the poise and polish of the assembled company. It didn't take her long to realize that most of the guests were from England, not true American colonials for all they spoke the same language.

Her fluency had progressed to the point where she could

hear the subtle difference in accents. Besides, these ladies and gentlemen in satins and brocades, with their polished manner and their silky wigs were a different breed from the locals, she could see that. Here and there were the brilliantly colored uniforms of his Majesty's various regiments. Even the governor of the colony was present, resplendent in medals and ribbons and braids. The newest Mrs. Griffin was overwhelmed. In all her twenty-one years she had seen nothing like this.

Ceci was young and gay and beautiful and she enjoyed herself. "I say." A red-coated officer appeared at her elbow. "I've been trying to meet you all evening. Permit me to introduce myself: Captain Roger Pratt of his Majesty's Royal Americans."

"I'm Cecile Griffin," she answered, smiling. "Mrs. Antony Griffin."

"Yes, I know." His grin was rueful. "Worse luck."

"I beg your pardon." Her green eyes opened wide.

Captain Pratt chuckled. "That you're Mrs. anybody I mean. Bad luck for me."

She had laughed with him, taking enormous pleasure in the casual flirtation.

Antony arrived beside them a few minutes later and Ceci smiled at the look on his face. It wasn't serious, any of it. A touch of jealousy wouldn't hurt him. And it flattered her. She turned back to the gallant Englishman. He was speaking. "May I ask where in France you're from? Originally, I mean," he hastened to add. "I know you Huguenots take great pride in being true English settlers now—"

"But I'm not," Ceci began at once.

"What my wife means," Antony interposed smoothly, "is that she's not any longer interested in theology or politics. Isn't that so, my dear?" He gave her no opportunity to answer before he whisked her off to meet someone else.

Ceci said nothing until they were alone in their bedroom. The blue gown looked ugly to her when she took it off and hung it away. She thought herself ugly too. How could she not be with that pinched look around her mouth. "Why did you say that?" she asked finally. "Why did that man think I was a Huguenot?"

"It's better that way," Antony said, pretending not to notice how upset she was. "I just let it be circulated around town. There's a long tradition of Huguenots in Boston. Old families like the Faneuils. They're much admired."

"But Canadians, let alone Acadians who happen to be Catholic rather than Protestant dissenters, are not. Isn't that what you're saying, Antony?"

"Forget it, Ceci," he said grimly. "It's nothing to do with you. Not really. I'm just protecting you as is my duty. Besides, it's nothing but politics and obscure theological arguments, just as I said."

After that she went only to those parties that he insisted she attend and she took no pleasure in them. Her contacts with the ladies of Boston were equally limited. Mostly she spoke only to the other Griffin women. There were enough of them God knows, and at least they accepted her for what she was. She even refused to have a servant despite Antony's protests. "No," she said. "Sophia and I can manage. It's a waste of money."

And it was Sophia who provided her only real companionship. Because of her and because Ceci was blessed with four delightful children, life was tolerable. She couldn't even be really angry with Antony. He meant his subterfuge only for her protection and well-being, she knew that. Antony wasn't ashamed of her; he was merely a practical man, a manager who made all the bits and pieces fall together and work to his ends. She couldn't resent his ruse.

Ceci told herself those things many times and went doggedly about the business of living. She would not permit herself to dwell on moral dilemmas, nor on the increasing hostility and bitterness between the Canadians and the Americans. In October of 1748, England and France had made peace at Aix-la-Chapelle. The treaty was complex and Ceci understood few of its terms. But she took a particular secret delight when Louisbourg was returned to France. The New Englanders who had captured the Acadian town in 1745 were incensed; now it would be impossible to admit she was a French Canadian and not a Huguenot. Ceci told herself she must count her blessings and ignore everything else.

She couldn't ignore Sophia, however; they were too much a part of each other's lives. During the long harsh winter of 1754, Ceci grew increasingly aware that Sophia had changed.

Something had happened to change her but Ceci didn't know what. She watched the other woman closely and made one or two overtures designed to invite confidence. Nothing came of either ploy.

Sophia could not quite accept the reality of her restored speech. It seemed to her a fragile, illusory thing. She examined the gift repeatedly, with small, tentative sounds—but only when she was sure she was alone. Sentences, even phrases, seemed beyond her; she could think but not speak them. She would slip a single word between her lips, play with it, taste it, then shake her head and deny the reality of her own ears. It had happened too suddenly, too inexplicably. Sophia could not make herself believe that any of it was real. The strange woman in her extraordinary garb, the open book, the mysterious message of the psalm . . . It was all too bizarre to be real, certainly too bizarre for her to share.

Always the words she used to test the miracle were the same she'd uttered that February afternoon in the study. "Jonathan," she would say, "Stephen, Paul, Hiram . . ." Over and over like a litany. It inevitably made her cry and she grew thin and tense with the puzzle and the sadness of it all. One April day when she was alone in the garden and knew no one was within earshot, she said without thinking, "God." The word hung in the cool, early spring air. She repeated it. "God." Then, "Jesus Christ, Son of God, Saviour." It was the longest string of sounds she'd attempted since the day in the study. Her tongue felt thick and unwieldy. The emotive phrase brought no comfort, no sense of peace. Only more questions.

Sophia stood up and wiped the mud from her trowel. She carried it and the basket of weeds to the little potting shed and neatly disposed of everything—the weeds to the compost heap to rot into fresh soil, the trowel to its customary place on the shelf. Smoothing her skirt of gray homespun, she walked to the house. In the kitchen she donned a starched white apron and started to assemble the ingredients for the bread she'd intended to make this day. Then, as if she'd planned it all along but hadn't wanted to admit as much to herself, she turned and headed for the study.

The books on the shelves were as they'd always been when

her grandfather was alive. They were Tonyjay's most perfect and fitting memorial and none of the household would have dreamed of altering them. Sophia knew their arrangement, had grown up knowing, as all the old man's grandchildren had. She knew too that no subject was missing. It didn't matter whether Tonyjay had agreed or disagreed with an idea; if it moved men he was interested in it. Thus, despite his lack of religious belief, there were many books on sacred topics.

She let her eye scan the titles. There were works by both Mathers, father and son, Milton, Donne, Butler, and many earlier writers, as well as Saint Augustine's *City of God*, Thomas a Kempis's *Imitation of Christ*, and dozens more she'd never heard of, many inaccessible to her because they were in Latin or Greek. Finally she reached up and removed one volume: *The Gospel of our Lord Jesus Christ*. Sophia moved a chair to the light of the window.

In the four years she'd worshipped with the Quakers, Sophia had grown to love them. She loved their simplicity, their silence, their uncompromising insistence on truth and justice. How could any creed that produced someone as fine as Jonathan Crandall be wrong? She had never thought it was, but neither had she deluded herself into thinking she shared their vision. The Friends' spontaneous outbursts of praise or revelation, restrained though they always were, meant little to her. She'd had no message of her own to share.

Of the theology behind their practice, she knew nothing and cared less. She'd had too much joy and peace in those years to become exercised about doctrine and dogma. But now, when joy had turned to cinders and even hard-won peace had been stripped away, it was different. She had to understand this thing that had happened to her. Otherwise she courted insanity. Sophia opened the Gospel to the first page and read, "The book of the generation of Jesus Christ, the Son of David, the Son of Abraham . . ." She continued thus for almost half an hour. Then, realizing that Ceci would come looking for her, she closed the book, carried it up to her bedroom, and returned to the kitchen to finish her work.

Time was in Puritan Boston when Quakers were whipped and stoned and dragged from the colony by a team of horses;

when the attempt to build a temple for worship in the Church of England fashion caused a riot in the streets. But those times were no more. The grip of the Puritans had first relaxed and then all but disappeared. Puritanism still colored the life of the town, remained the dominant faith, but one could live easily in Boston these days without espousing its beliefs—unless one were a Catholic, that is. Rome was anathema, seat of the anti-Christ, the Whore of Babylon. Sophia had grown up knowing that.

She was shocked when she first realized that Roman Catholicism was the professed faith of many of the desperately poor whom she nursed. They didn't advertise the fact of course. Even the ignorant Irish of the hovels and shacks in the outlying districts of the town knew better. Sophia learned their secret by observation. The fact that she was mute led many people to mistakenly think her deaf as well. They would shout when they spoke to her, make unguarded comments in a normal voice.

She had seen one old woman make the sign of the cross when her leg was cured of a suppurating wound, another furtively clutch a string of wooden beads and move her lips while Sophia treated her husband for a flow of blood. At first these expressions of idolatry disturbed the girl. They were so crude, so superstitious, so contrary to the simplicity and purity she'd known among the Quakers. Eventually she learned to tolerate and in some small measure to understand them.

They've so little else, she would muse. No one has attempted to teach them right thinking. It's wrong that they should be persecuted for their beliefs, foolish though they may be. It would never have occurred to her to betray them and the Catholics came to know that. Few in number, with no opportunity to practice their faith, they simply lived with their stubborn insistence on the old religion.

The day in June when Sophia knocked on the door of Tessie Riley's home she wasn't expected. It was unusually warm for the time of year, but all the windows were closed tight and the shabby curtains drawn. For some seconds she imagined no one to be home. But that was unlikely. Her patient, Tessie's husband Padraig, was ill with consumption. He couldn't have gone anywhere and Tessie was unlikely to leave him alone. Sophia shifted the heavy burden of her basket and knocked again.

"Oh, it's yourself is it." Tessie opened the door a crack and peeked out. "I weren't expectin' ye."

Sophia nodded her head to indicate she knew that, and pointed to her basket. There were three fresh eggs on top, a pail of new milk, and some salad herbs. These things would be good for her patient.

"Give 'em to me then," the woman said surlily. "I'll cook 'em up fer himself. Though Lord knows if he'll be able to eat 'em. Right poorly he is."

Sophia made urgent signs that she should be admitted.

"No," Tessie said stubbornly. "Ye ain't 'spected today."

Sophia shook her head and pushed the old woman aside. These Irish peasants could be so difficult, so peculiar.

"Don't!" the woman shouted. "What ye come botherin' us fer today?"

Sophia ignored the protests and entered. Then she stood very still in the middle of the tiny room. Her patient lay in a bed by the hearth, obviously dying. That didn't startle Sophia; consumption often took just this sudden and irreversible turn. What caused her to stare in shocked surprise was the man kneeling beside Padraig Riley. He wore a long black gown and a narrow purple scarf around his neck. The surface of the scarf was embroidered with arcane symbols and he held a glass phial containing Sophia knew not what. The scene sent shudders of horror along her spine. The stranger was making marks on the dying man's hands and feet and forehead.

"What is thee doing to him?" she whispered hoarsely. "Can thee not let the poor soul die in peace!"

"Holy Mother of God," Tessie muttered. "Sweet Holy Virgin. Ye is talkin' Mrs. Crandall. I never thought—"

Sophia gasped, pressed her hands to her mouth, and gasped again. She'd spoken. Not tentatively, not alone—but normally, without first thinking about the words. Here in this place, with a dying man and a devil present, and Tessie Riley and her superstitious incantations as background.

The black-gowned man turned to face the two women. His hand still hovered over Padraig's motionless form. "In a moment, Madame," he said softly, "I will be finished. Then, if you wish, I will explain what I am doing."

He went on with his murmured Latin phrases and his anointings. Tessie and Sophia stood where they were, neither moving nor saying anything. Finally the stranger was finished and he drew the quilt around the thin shoulders of the old man.

"He is sleeping now. He may not wake but he is peaceful." Carefully he removed the purple scarf from his neck and folded it, pressing it to his lips before putting it away. "You are not a Catholic, I take it," he said to Sophia.

She shook her head. He looked to her rather like her childhood imaginings of Satan—tall and very thin, with jet-black hair that came to a point in the middle of his forehead and eyes to match. His long black robe accentuated the effect.

"She don' talk, Father," Tessie whined. "Least she never has. Been dumb since I knowed, since anyone knowed. But just now she said somethin' to you. I heared her meself."

"Yes," the priest said calmly. "So did I. When did you regain your speech, my child? Or did you have it all along?"

Sophia stared at him, at the old man and the old woman. She opened her mouth but no sound came. Concentrating, she tried again. It seemed to her at this moment that nothing in heaven or on earth was more important than knowing. "What . . . was . . . thee . . . doing?" she managed to say.

"Praised be all the saints," Tessie murmured. "Tis a miracle. Must be."

The priest ignored Tessie. "I was giving a dying man the last rites of Holy Church," he told Sophia. "That is his right as a Christian and my duty as a priest of the Society of Jesus. Do you find it all so strange?"

He had an accent. It was rather like Cecile's had been when she first came to Boston. "It's an . . . offense . . . here," Sophia stammered. Then, spurred by the concern she felt for this ignorant old couple, she added, "It's dangerous. Thee could be hung, and them as well."

The priest shrugged. "We all know that, child. We are willing to take the risk. We're not the first and we won't be the last. Do you intend to report us to the authorities?"

Sophia shook her head. Tessie had crept over to kneel beside her husband. The interchange between the Jesuit and the girl was beyond her ability to assimilate, the miracle of Sophia Crandall's speech too obscure for her to comprehend.

"You say 'thee,'" the priest continued. "Are you a Quaker?"

Again Sophia shook her head. "My husband was a Friend," she whispered. "Jonathan was such a good man. So full of love . . ." The words were tumbling out in a singsong monotone mixed with tears.

"He was her husband," Tessie volunteered. "So I heared tell. Died in a fire with her three babies. Long time ago."

"I see." The Jesuit reached out his hand and touched Sophia's tear-stained cheek. "Is it since then that you haven't spoken, child? Since the fire?"

"Yes. I couldn't. But Jonathan was so good. And the children were so pure, so innocent."

"Yes. It's a terrible mystery. All suffering is. We can never hope to understand it."

"Then why . . . ?" She looked up at him with eyes blurred by her tears. "Why do we believe anything at all?"

The man put his hand into the pocket of his black gown and withdrew a wooden crucifix. The figure of Christ was intricately carved. Suffering and anguish showed in the lines of the face; the hands and feet pierced by nails were horribly graphic. "Because He suffered this," the Jesuit said. "What other reason can there be?"

3

"The Canadians are capable of such behavior." Benjamin Griffin pursed his lips in distaste. "They have no moral fiber whatever."

"But spying, really Ben!" Charles looked questioningly at

his brother. He didn't allow himself to look at Antony.

"Yes," Benjamin said. "Spying. How else do you imagine this aberration took place at Great Meadow?" He tapped an angry finger on the gazette lying atop the desk between the three men.

"I daresay, Uncle Benjamin," Antony commented dryly, "it's not necessarily an aberration to lose a battle."

"Nonsense, lad! This chap—what's his name?—Washington, Colonel George Washington. Fine soldier, excellent commander. Heard it from Governor Shirley himself and he had it from Dinwiddie of Virginia. Only way the French could have beaten Washington at Fort Necessity was to know his tactics beforehand. Spying. Just as I said."

The younger Griffin rose and pointed to a map on the office wall. "Look, the whole problem is greed. If we'd stay out of here"—he drew a blunt finger along the Ohio valley—"we'd have peace."

"Stay out! Why the hell should we stay out!" Charles didn't share his brother Benjamin's hawkish views. Still, the suggestion angered him.

"Because the French now have forts along the entire stretch. And they've made allies of all the Indians in the territory."

"Young man." His uncle drew himself up to his full height and thrust out his chest. It made him look rather like a pigeon. "Those lands belong rightly to his gracious Majesty, George the Second. We have the duty to colonize them."

"Yes, and when we try, England will have to send troops to aid us. America is too vital a part of the British economy for them to do otherwise." There was a weary undertone to Antony's voice.

"Nothing wrong with that," Benjamin said. "And now that we're wise to their spying tricks, we'll make short work of them."

"For God's sake, Papa, don't you see it either?" Antony turned to his father in desperation. "We're playing right into the hands of the French."

"I'm afraid I don't see that," Charles said.

"All they're really after is a chance to tie up English forces here and relieve pressure on their maritime commerce and their West Indies colonies. We're pawns, the lot of us," he ended morosely.

"Defeatist rubbish! Just this week I told Shirley our young men were going soft. Now my own nephew proves it." Benjamin sat down as if the last word had been spoken on the subject.

"Very well, Uncle," Antony answered. "We'll agree to disagree. I came here to ask about that shipment of bananas you're expecting. Am I to have them or are they going on to London?"

Charles said nothing. He and John were responsible for the ships and the crews, while Benjamin took charge of the cargoes. The senior partner was squinting at his nephew now, weighing the possible weaknesses available for exploitation. "You could do with them, lad," he said. "You've not had bananas to sell for months. I'm told there may be some available soon through Faneuil's. Doesn't do to let them get ahead of you like that."

"Yes. Well, that's why I'm here. Four hundred," he said evenly. "For the entire shipment just as it comes out of the hold."

"Four hundred's not near enough, Antony." Ben shook his head. "I can double that at Wapping Dock."

"Yes, on a per-bunch basis. But you'll get nothing for those that have rotted in the extra time the journey to England takes. I'm offering to buy the lot. For a flat price."

Charles allowed himself a small chuckle. His brother looked at him angrily, then broke into a wide grin. "Takes a Griffin to do business with one, doesn't it? Very well, Antony, they're yours for five hundred."

"Four fifty."

"Done." Benjamin stretched out his hand.

"Done." Antony shook it and turned to go.

"One more thing, lad." His uncle's voice stopped him from leaving. "This business about spies. It's a real threat, you know. I'm not imagining it. I told the governor I'd keep my eyes and ears open. I'd appreciate it if you'd do likewise. You do have contacts . . ."

Antony froze. His back was to the pair of older men. They could see the way it stiffened. When he slowly turned to face them his expression was neutral but his gray eyes were icy. "There are no spies in the Amory markets," he said softly. "And none at Beacon Street."

"Beacon Street . . . Good God, lad. I'm not referring to your wife. I never meant to imply that Cecile—"

"Thank you," Antony said. "I prefer to have that understood between us."

After he was gone Charles shook his head ruefully. "That was tactless, Ben. You should know better."

"So should he, damn it! We're talking of men's business. Nothing to do with women. Besides," he added apropos of nothing, "four fifty's a damn good price."

"Better than you thought to get, and you know it," Charles said mildly.

Two or three times a year Paul Amory went to Beacon Street to visit his daughter. Sophia had never been to the cabin on Mount Whoredom. So when Mattie entered the room with her arms full of washing and said, "Your daughter's on her way here," he looked at her incredulously.

"Sophia? But that's not possible."

"Possible or not, that's her comin' down the path. I seen her when I was takin' this stuff off the grass."

The girl appeared in the doorway just then. The door was open to the warm July sun, so she could not knock.

"Sophia! What's wrong? What are you doing here?" Paul went to her quickly and placed his big hands on her shoulders. He expected no spoken answer, but he searched her face for an explanation.

Sophia swallowed hard, opened her mouth, then closed it. She could not do it. Not here in front of Mattie. She was fond of the mulatto woman but she did not count her an intimate.

"I's goin' up to the tavern to see how they's gettin' on," Mattie said easily. "You don' mind my goin', chile, do you? Them fellers is so lazy I gots to keep after 'em every minute. Place would never get cleaned if I didn't." She flashed a broad smile at the girl. "You an' your papa have a nice visit here. Maybe I'll see you afore you goes home."

"Come, Sophia," Paul said when they were alone. "We can sit out here in the sun. What is it, child? Why have you come? Did you bring your slate?" He gestured to the big bag she carried. "You can write it out for me. Or if not, I can find a bit of paper."

"I don't need the slate, Papa." Her voice dropped like pebbles into the pool of early summer heat. Nearby a bumblebee droned.

Paul stared at his daughter. "Did you . . . ? Can you speak, Sophia, or did I dream it?"

"I can."

She said no more. Neither did he for long seconds. "When?" he muttered at last. "How?"

"In February," she answered. "It simply happened. My voice returned."

"February. But that's months ago. I've seen you since then. I don't understand."

"I was afraid. I told no one. Thee can't know how I felt."

"I should like to try, Sophia. Have you told the others now?"

She shook her head, the habit of silence ingrained by time.

"Why not, my dear? They would be pleased to know. Ceci particularly, I should imagine." When she still said nothing, he asked, "Are you afraid they'll think you were shamming all the years when you didn't talk?"

Sophia shrugged.

"No, you're right. That doesn't matter." His response to her wordless replies was as habitual as the replies themselves. "Tell me what you mean by 'It simply happened.' I'd like to understand."

Her eyes searched his face. It looked very old in the strong light of the sun. "I saw a woman," she said slowly and with effort. "A woman dressed all in black with a white thing around her face."

Paul took both her hands in his and raised them to his lips. "It must have been the Kirkslee nun," he said finally. "And she brought you a miracle."

"She said I should know who she was. I didn't. Her accent was strange but familiar."

Paul chuckled. "A ghost with a Yorkshire accent. Who would imagine such a thing. Sounded a bit like your grandfather, didn't she?" Sophia nodded. "As to why you didn't know who she was, we never talked about it. Not me or your grandmother or your mother. Particularly not your mother."

"Who is she?"

He told her the story much as he'd told it to Antony seven years earlier, but with a few more details because Sophia knew even less of the legend that Antony had known.

"What did it mean?" Sophia asked when he was through. "The part about Mama healing the 'wound of Kirkslee'?"

"I don't know. Rachel always said it was something to do with her mother and father, with Lizzie and Tonyjay. But I don't know." He thought about telling her of the money he'd sent to Harwood Hall with instructions the Kirsklee priory be rebuilt if possible. He decided against it.

"The first Sophia, the one who became a nun," his daughter said, speech coming a bit easier now. "Why did she do that?"

"I've no idea," Paul said. "I'm sorry, child. I've few answers for your questions." Then, realizing that there was something she wanted to say but hadn't yet, he asked, "Why did you come here like this, Sophia? You've kept your secret all these months. Why did you come and share it today?"

Slowly she reached into the bag she carried and withdrew a book. It was the leather-bound volume of psalms that had been the instrument of the miracle. "The one thee calls the Kirkslee nun told me to go to Grandfather's study and read the book I would find on the desk. This is that book." She handed it to him opened at psalm fifty. "This is what I read." Her finger directed his eyes to the words.

"O Lord, open Thou my lips and my mouth shall declare Thy praise." He read the line aloud, then turned to stare at her. "It's beautiful, Sophia. Why are you crying?"

"Because I cannot. I cannot declare His praise. They're dead—Jonathan, my babies . . . How can I praise God?"

"My poor little girl," Paul whispered hoarsely. "How can anyone give you an answer to such a question."

"He says there's an answer. In here." She withdrew another book, thicker and more imposingly bound. "In these Gospels."

"For some there is, Sophia." Paul took both books from her and lay them on the grass. "Who do you mean? Have you been speaking with the vicar at King's Chapel?" She shook her head. "Who then?"

"A Jesuit. Father Parelle."

"A Catholic priest! But where did you meet him?"

Sophia shrugged again. "That doesn't matter. Some of the poor, the old Irish people, are Catholics. He's come to minister to them. From Canada."

"Your Jesuit is taking a great risk," Paul said quietly. "I expect he knows that."

"He says he would glory in martyrdom for his faith."

A faint smile played around Paul's mouth. "Yes, one always thinks such things. Before they happen."

Sophia turned to her father with a frightening intensity in her two-color gaze. "Papa," she said, "I couldn't think who else to ask. Thee has always been wise."

For a moment Paul was conscious of his unshaven face, of the way his ill-fitting clothes hung from his gaunt, outsized frame. He looked at the hovel where he lived and the desolation of the surroundings. Then he reached again for the hand of his daughter. "You are kind to say it, dearest. I've not been very wise. Neither about myself nor my children."

Sophia shook her head. Her hair was as long as it had been before the fire, but now she wore it in a severe bun. "It's not thy fault," she said. "Nothing that's happened is thy fault."

"You use the Friends' speech still," he said. "Why have you not gone to the Quakers for religious comfort?"

"I cannot desert Jonathan's tongue," she said simply. "It's nothing to do with belief."

"Yes, I see. You don't believe but you feel you must. Because of the nun and the miracle that restored your voice."

"Not just that," she whispered. "There are other things. In here." She reached across him and retrieved the Gospel. It flipped open to the page she sought, "Look. Tell me what this means."

She had given him John, Chapter 6, and he could see where she'd faintly underlined a few words. "Whoso eateth my flesh and drinketh my blood hath eternal life and I will raise him up at the last day."

"What does it mean?" she repeated and there was anguish in her words.

"I don't know, Sophia. I cannot help you. I wish to God I could."

"The Jesuit," she whispered as if she hadn't heard him, "Father Parelle. He told me what he thinks it means, what Catholics say. But if he's right, then Jonathan, the children . . . Are they not to be raised up? They took not of this Eucharist he tells me about."

"And this Jesuit says that means they're damned!" Paul exclaimed. "It's monstrous, Sophia. You must believe no such thing."

"He has not said it," the girl protested in a small, weak voice. "I have not asked him, for I cannot bear to hear his answer."

"It doesn't matter anyway," Paul said, searching for a way to comfort her. "Priests are notorious for twisting words and ideas—Jesuits worst of all. Ignore him, Sophia. He's nothing to do with you."

She shook her head, stood up, and gathered together her bag and her books. "It's not Father Parelle," she said. "He's only a man. Tis no man that frightens me, Papa."

Paul watched her white-knuckled grip on the Gospel and the volume of psalms. He swallowed hard, trying to think of something else to say. Sophia smiled at him—a gentle, tender smile. "I thank thee, Papa," she said as she kissed him.

"For what?" he demanded bitterly. "What have I ever done for you, Sophia?"

"Thee has been willing to risk my pain." She did not explain the comment, only walked off toward town with her back very straight and her bag swinging at her side.

4

He wanted to make love to her. Ceci had known it all evening. Antony's concern with business seldom extended to the hours they spent in bed. He shed them sometimes earlier than that, often over the dinner table. He would catch her eye across the top of his wineglass and she would know what he was thinking.

Tonight had been one of those times. Her husband had flirted with her outrageously. She should be flattered. After Sophia went to her room, early as she'd been doing recently, Antony had treated Ceci like a girl he was wooing—kissing her hand, stroking her cheek, paying her pretty compliments. Most women would envy her such attentions after nearly seven years of marriage. Now, lying beside him, Ceci felt his hand on her hip, felt it slide upwards along her midriff and cup her breast.

"Take your nightdress off," he whispered. "I want to touch your skin."

It was a pretty garment, white and long sleeved and high necked and trimmed with lace and pink satin robbons. Ceci undid the tie at her throat, then realized she couldn't manage lying down. She rose and stood by the side of the bed and pulled the gown over her head. One little pearl button tangled itself in her mass of blonde hair and she paused a moment to free it with her arms extended over her head and the nightdress bunched up in her hands.

"You look beautiful like that," Antony whispered. He was propped on one elbow, surveying her in the moonlight that shone through the open window on this hot August night. "I love the way your breasts look when you stretch your arms."

Embarrassed by this unashamed discussion of her anatomy, she felt her cheeks redden but knew it was too dark for him to notice. The recalcitrant button gave way and Ceci dropped the garment and slid back into bed. He reached for her eagerly and kissed her neck, her shoulders, her breasts. Ceci moved closer to him, rubbed her pelvis against his hard-muscled thigh. His fingers played over her buttocks, kneading, even scratching. Her breath came in shorter more shallow gasps and a thin film of perspiration dewed her skin.

Antony, judging her ready, lifted himself over her. When her legs were spread to receive him, he lowered himself into position. Their bodies merged in one fluid motion.

Ceci ran her hands along his back. His skin was almost as silky as hers where the base of his spine curved to meet his waist. She delighted in the feel of it, in the weight of him atop her. Raising her hips, she tried to bring his heavy member in closer contact with those soft, moist secret places that longed to be touched. For a moment she succeeded and she moaned with the intense pleasure of it. Then she felt him stiffen, explode. It was over.

Later, with the beautiful nightdress replaced and the special intimacy of skin on skin ended, she said, "Something funny happened."

"Just now?" he asked with concern. "Did I hurt you? I didn't mean to."

"No, of course not. I'm not talking about that." She never talked about it afterwards, never admitted her disappointment. "I mean this afternoon. I went to the miller's to buy flour. There was a woman there. I don't know her name. Not very well dressed—a poor woman, I think."

"What's funny about that?" he asked sleepily. "There are lots of poor women."

"No, not that. The way she looked at me. And I heard her saying something. Whispering to the miller. They both looked at me oddly."

"You're too sensitive by half, Ceci. You always have been."

"It's not that. They really did look at me as if they thought I was . . . diseased. And when the miller weighed out my flour he didn't say a thing. Usually he chatters and makes jokes. Today he didn't."

"He had an off day," Antony insisted. "Nothing to do with you." He drew her closer and stroked her hair until she fell asleep, and he said nothing of the anger making an icy knot in his gut.

Sophia did not hear the rumors about French spies, the increasing talk of war. She did, however, continue her rounds of the homes of Boston. She could have heard the stories, would have, were she not so preoccupied.

The things she read in the Gospel and discussed with the priest filled her thoughts, causing her such anguish that sometimes she wanted to stop whatever she was doing and scream—just stand where she was and scream and scream until she had no breath left. Her mind was a mass of confused and conflicting questions and needs. It took every ounce of determination she could muster to keep her hands from trembling, her palms from breaking out in a sweat.

When she went about her tasks at Beacon Street or with her patients she gritted her teeth until her jaws were sore with the effort of control. Ceci looked at her strangely. Once or twice she asked, "What is it, Sophia? Can't you tell me what's wrong?"

The mute who was mute no longer merely shook her head. Except for the one time a few weeks before when she'd gone to her father, she had spoken to no one but the Jesuit. He alone shared her secret. Tessie, the old Irishwoman, was convinced she'd witnessed a miracle the single time she heard the girl talk. She reported it to all her friends and neighbors but they dismissed the notion as a product of her imagination. Tessie was known to be fond of her gin, and they had concerns of their own. Father Parelle would be with them only a short while. His presence was a singular blessing but it was also dangerous. The small, clandestine Catholic community held its breath even while participating in the sacraments the priest made possible.

The Jesuit moved among his little flock like a black wraith, never in one house for more than a day or two, sometimes disappearing for as long as a week. "Where does thee go?" Sophia asked him one day when they were alone. "I visit all the houses where thee can stay. I have patients in all of them. Sometimes I don't see thee in any."

He looked away. "I have business to attend to. It's not wise for me to stay in any one place for long."

"It's not wise for thee to be here at all," she said.

"Here, you mean, in this field?"

"No." She shook her head and threw out her hands to indicate the overgrown field in which they sat. "This place is as safe as any in Boston. I told thee that."

"Yes, so you did. It's a pretty meadow. Why is it so deserted?"

Sophia shrugged. "I don't know. Summer Street has always been like this. The Roses is the only house for nearly a quarter of a mile."

He looked across at the outline of the white brick mansion that could barely be seen through the sumac and blueberries and wild grasses. "It's a beautiful house. Who lives there?"

"I don't know. My father sold it five years ago. I grew up there, though."

"Really." His surprise showed in his voice. "I didn't know that."

"No, why should thee?" The enigmatic answer was typical of much of their conversation.

"Sophia," the Jesuit said at last, "why do you meet me like

this? What do you want of me?"

"To know the things thee can tell me. The things thee believes about God."

"But I have told you everything I know. Everything you've asked me. Yet you ask the same questions again and again. I cannot make you believe, Sophia," he said softly. "Faith is a gift from God Himself. It's not mine to give. I wish it were."

"There's something else," she began hesitantly. She'd made up her mind to ask him today. "About this thing thee calls the Eucharist. About what it says in the Gospel."

"Except thee eat of the flesh of the Son of man and drink His blood . . ." the man quoted quietly.

"Thee has no life in thee," Sophia finished. "Yes, about that."

"But I've told you," he insisted. "It's a miracle. The Eucharist, the Mass, the way He gives us His flesh to eat . . . It's beyond human understanding. It's a miracle."

She shook her head. "It's not that I mean. Not exactly."

"What then?"

She opened her mouth but no words came.

"Speech comes hard to you," he said at last. "Even now. You've not told anyone else about your own miracle, have you, Sophia? I wonder why you feel you must go on being mute."

"I told my father."

"Good. It must have given him joy."

"Perhaps," she said.

Sophia twisted a stem of grass in her fingers. The priest stared at the unaccustomed sight of his legs encased in buff breeches like those of a laborer. It was unthinkable to walk the streets of Boston in a soutane; still, he marveled at the picture of himself as a layman. Marveled at much of what shaped his days in this time and this place where he had no right to be and where many had thought him a fool to come.

"I must go," he said at last. "I'm to baptize three babies today."

"Yes."

They rose and impusively he took her hand. It felt hot and sweaty, and when he turned it over and stared at her palm he could see little white semicircles where she'd dug her nails into the soft flesh. She must have been doing it all the while they sat in the peaceful meadow. "Sophia," he said urgently. "Whatever is making you so unhappy, worrying you so . . . You've only to give your cares to the Lord Jesus. He will carry them for you."

She felt a flush of anger at the simplicity of his words and their pathetic inadequacy. "I wish I could," she answered through clenched teeth.

"Listen. Tomorrow afternoon, at the cobbler's house, I shall be offering Holy Mass. The last time before I leave this colony." She looked at him in surprise. She hadn't known he was going so soon. He ignored her reaction and said, "Come and celebrate the Mass with us. The people won't mind. They trust you. I'll tell them it's all right."

"No." She shook her head and pulled her hand away. "I cannot do that." She turned and ran from the field.

Sophia knew something was wrong the moment she opened the door. She could sense the presence of fear in the house. Her first thought was of the children but she could hear them laughing and playing in the garden. The door to the study was closed. She turned to the other side of the entry hall and walked into the drawing room, whose door was ajar. Ceci was standing alone. Blood ran down the side of her face.

Sophia rushed to her and began at once to tend the wound. It was a nasty cut but not deep. "I'm all right," Ceci murmured. "It's nothing."

Sophia did not ask her questions aloud but spoke them with her eyes. The practice of silence was deeply ingrained even in moments of stress. Now she followed Ceci's glance to the shattered glass of the window and the rock lying on the carpet.

"A few minutes ago," Ceci said. "I don't know who threw it. This was attached." She held out a piece of rough paper.

Sophia took the note. A barely literate hand had scrawled, "Take this as warning. We know how to deal with French spies."

Antony's reaction was rage. He ranted and raved, then left the house to circulate among the taverns and taprooms in search of the perpetrators. Ceci knew such efforts to be fruitless. "He won't find them," she told Sophia. "How could he? Anyway,

I knew it was coming. I should have expected it."

Sophia changed the poultice on the wound with deft fingers. Once she opened her mouth, close to revealing her secret in her desire to comfort and reassure her friend. Ceci's green eyes were dull with pain, her mouth pinched with anguish. Sophia wanted to speak but she couldn't. It wasn't as if the gift were gone. She simply could not overcome the imperative that had concealed the miracle until now.

"It's all right, Sophia." Ceci reached up and touched her friend's cheek. "It's some political trouble, the same threat of war we've known about for so long." When she added, "It doesn't matter," she looked away and Sophia knew it mattered very much.

Later she saw Cecile watching her children anxiously. Sophia felt a terrible fear. She understood Ceci's concern for her babies. These youngsters were half Acadian. Any animosity directed at their mother would also be directed at them. Suddenly Sophia thought of the Jesuit. Business, he'd said. When he was gone someplace none of them knew, he was on business. She pressed her hands to her cheeks and turned away.

She had to confront him with her suspicions. Sunday quiet shrouded the streets of Boston and mingled with the August heat. It was oppressive, choking. Sophia walked on and ignored the rivulets of perspiration running down her back. The cotton dress she wore was limp and dusty by the time she reached the little cottage in Whistling Alley. The cobbler's house, he'd said. This was it.

Sophia lifted her hand to knock, thought better of it, and walked in. A few heads turned swiftly. Here and there she heard a gasp.

"Tis all right," someone said. "Tis just Mrs. Crandall."

Near her one woman stared with open hostility. "What you comin' here for like this?" she asked. "This is our religion. Got nothin' to do with you."

Another silenced her. "Hush, Becky. He said she might come. Father Parelle told us."

Sophia ignored them all, searching the gloom for the priest. He entered a minute later, wearing his black soutane and the purple scarf he'd told her was called a stole. Its odd embroideries filled Sophia with distaste, as they had the first time she saw them. Idolatry and superstition, all of it. What was she doing here? Jonathan would be ashamed.

The Jesuit looked at her, found her eyes across the head of the cluster of people, and smiled. Then he looked away and took his place behind a makeshift altar. There was a crucifix, the wooden one he'd shown her many times, and a shabby white cloth. The only other furnishings were splendid and wholly out of place: a silver goblet and an ornate silver plate. Sophia wondered where such things had come from, how they could be in this house. Then she realized he must carry them with him, like the stole and the representation of the impaled Lord.

She had written a note before leaving Beacon Street. "I must speak with thee. Please meet me in the usual place at dusk today." She'd intended to pass the message to him and leave but no opportunity presented itself. She and Father Parelle were separated by a dozen people, all intent on the Jesuit and the ceremony. She could not interrupt. She could only wait.

He bent over, touched his lips to the cloth, knelt, and spread his arms. The fingers of each hand were held in precise formality, thumb and forefinger pressed together, the rest splayed.

"*Introibo ad altare Dei*," he said. From somewhere a muffled voice made a response.

It was all beyond Sophia. She remembered none of the Latin the tutors had tried to teach her in the house on Summer Street. She watched only the priest, every movement and gesture. It was as if they were alone in the room and he was communicating with her by signs. In a queer way it was as if he were making love to her.

The image flitted through Sophia's mind. She pushed it away in shame. What truth there was in the analogy she did not recognize. But she did feel love. Directed at her, enveloping her. The sensation increased as the strange rite went on.

The mood of the assembly became hushed, centered on the actions of the Jesuit. Each man and woman strained toward the altar. They thrust themselves into her consciousness by the intensity of their reactions. Then her awareness of them faded. It was just the priest and herself once more. She'd not budged from her position by the door. Now she leaned against it for support, not joining the small congregation when they knelt.

"Hoc est enim corpus meum." The words floated over the bowed heads, mingled with the smell of dirt and sweat. The Jesuit was bent on one knee. When he rose he held something aloft. She knew it was the Eucharist he'd told her about. That which he claimed to be the body of Jesus Christ.

"Sophia." She heard Jonathan's voice even while she stared at the sacred thing, the thing she wanted to despise but could not. She knew it was her husband; no power in heaven or on earth could make her doubt it. Not then, not ever. "Sophia. It is the truth, dear heart. The blessed truth."

"I heard Jonathan's voice," she told Parelle later when they were alone in the meadow. "My husband's voice. It was not the sound of a damned soul."

"Damned! But why should you think—"

"Because," she interrupted, "he never knew. Never ate of the bread."

"But that's not the teaching of Holy Church," the priest exclaimed. "I never said such a thing. All men who follow their conscience, men of good will..." He launched into a lengthy theological explanation. Sophia didn't listen.

"It's all right," she said simply. "I know."

She never asked him if he was a French spy. His last act before leaving the colony was to receive her into the Roman Catholic Church.

5

Antony Griffin had begun to be afraid. "Can you not do something with her, Sophia? The way she stays up there in the attic room or out on the widow's walk..." He shuddered, looking out the kitchen window at the leafless trees blowing in the cold March wind. "All this winter, in every weather. It's insane."

Sophia lay her hand over his and nodded in sympathy. Her gesture left a small trail of flour on the table. Antony drew his finger across the pale, gritty meal. It made a beautiful contrast to the golden oak of the table. "Before I went to Blackwater . . ." he said softly. "Do you remember the stories about Aunt Hannah? The way they said she was mad?"

Sophia shook her head swiftly, indicating first yes and then no. She didn't pause in her kneading.

"You mean yes you remember, and no Ceci's not mad. I know she isn't. Neither was Hannah, at least not the way people said. But it is a kind of madness, Sophia. This single-minded preoccupation with one idea. It will ruin Ceci's life if she doesn't get over it. All this hostility to the French Canadians has nothing to do with her. It's politics hatched in Europe with us as the pawns. I keep telling her. Why can't she see it?"

Sophia shrugged, removed the dough to the table, and began portioning it into loaves.

"Anyway," Griffin said with a sigh. "Braddock's come from England with two regiments. Over a thousand regular British soldiers. Think of it, Sophia. They'll make short work of the French and leave us to bury the dead and heal the wounds. Isn't it glorious?" His bitterness was palpable. "Damn fools, all of us." He rose to go. "I'm expected at Lyn Street. Back for dinner. Just do what you can, will you, Sophia?" She nodded and he left.

Numerous times she had looked her wordless appeals at the other woman, written her messages on the slate. None of it had any effect. Ceci was allowing herself to give way to depression, and Sophia knew as well as Antony that that was the road to madness. Had she not stood on the brink of the same abyss? Half a dozen times Sophia had opened her mouth to speak to Cecile, considered the possibility that the shock of learning her friend was no longer mute would snap Ceci's morbid introspection. Always something stronger than herself held Sophia back. Now she set the pans of bread to rise by the fire. She would try again.

She removed her apron, folded it neatly, and patted her hair into place. Lord Jesus, she prayed silently, give me leave to speak. There can never be a better time. We're alone, the children are at the Ark. Thee knows how important it is, Lord. Please help me.

Her soft shoes made no sound on the stairs as she climbed to the attic. The door leading to the tiny space was well oiled; its hinges did not creak when Sophia pushed it open. A shaft of light illuminated the place. It came from the high, narrow widow's walk that skirted the turret of the house. Sophia looked up and saw Cecile. She was leaning on the rope railing, her back to the attic, the wind whipping her hair and her shawl.

Sophia opened her mouth. No sound came. I must, she thought. I must. Nothing. She reached into the pocket of her dress and found the familiar talisman. It was a bit of string she'd tied into a series of knots. Five units of ten knots each. The closest thing to a rosary she possessed. Blessed Mother of God, help me to help her. It was as if a hand on her shoulder forced her to kneel. Sophia obeyed, fingering the bit of string.

"Hail Mary full of grace, the Lord is with thee . . ." She did not realize she'd spoken the words aloud until she saw Cecile whirl around.

"Sophia!" Ceci said nothing more. She stared in shock but she did not doubt. The other woman was continuing her prayer, ignoring the presence of her friend.

Slowly Ceci descended the stairs. The murmured invocation went on: ". . . now and at the hour of our death, amen."

Ceci reached out and took the makeshift rosary from Sophia's fingers. What it bespoke was as extraordinary as the girl's speech. "Where . . . ? how . . . ?" she began tentatively.

"I regained my voice through the mercy of God a year ago February," Sophia said. "He led me to his Holy Church last August."

"I don't understand. You said nothing, in all this time, not even to me . . ."

"I'm telling thee now," Sophia said, smiling. "Come, we will go downstairs and talk."

"If thee continues thus thee will lose thy sanity. Hatred poisons the soul, rots it."

"How can I not hate?" Ceci asked as she'd asked half a dozen times in the past hour. "This town, these small, bitter people. They will destroy me and my children and think nothing of it."

"Thee exaggerates. They whisper and gossip. They will do no physical harm to thee or thy babies. They would not dare."

"No, because I'm Antony Griffin's wife. The children are Griffins." Ceci made a fist and punched the soft fabric of the quilt on the bed where she sat. "Am I to take solace from that, Sophia? Would you? For myself, my blood, I'm rejected. For the sake of the name of Griffin we are protected from physical danger. It's monstrous."

Sophia bit her lip, staring at her hands folded in her lap. "Thy people," she said, "they were Catholics, were they not? Why has thee given up thy belief, Ceci, the practice of thy faith? It would sustain thee through all this."

Ceci laughed without humor. "Sustain me. Oh yes, panacea for all the ills of this life, count on glory in the next one. I can't believe that, Sophia, not after what I've seen, what I've been through." The other girl's head shot up and her look spoke volumes. "Oh, Sophia, forgive me! I didn't mean it like that. I know what you've suffered, how brave you been. I don't mean to imply—"

"It's all right. I understand. And I'll not preach to thee about religion. But for Antony's sake, for thy children's, thee must try not to brood as thee has."

Ceci rose from the bed and walked to her dressing table. "I will try, Sophia, I promise. I'd already made up my mind to that. Meanwhile, there's something here I want you to have." She fumbled in a drawer and drew a string of wooden beads from its depths.

"Tis a rosary, a real one." Sophia fingered the thing with love.

"Yes. I've had it since I was a child. It's funny, all through the years, long after I ceased to believe in anything, I kept it. I never let anyone see. It was sewn into the hem of the green dress I was wearing the night Antony and I met in Charleston. Just a coincidence, really. I could have worn another dress."

She looked at Sophia. The girl was staring at the beads, couting them as if to assure herself of their orthodoxy. "That dress," Ceci whispered. "We used part of it as a shroud to bury your brother Jacob. I took the rosary out beforehand. I don't think Antony ever saw."

"I've never thanked thee for that." Sophia's cheeks were wet but she didn't acknowledge her tears. "Thank thee for burying Jacob. He was a sweet and fine boy. I pray he's happy in heaven."

Ceci turned away lest Sophia read in her face the memory of Jacob's terrible dying, the echo of his tortured screams. "If anyone is, he must be," she said. "Keep the rosary. It's yours. Better than that bit of string you made."

"Very well," Sophia said. "But thee must take the string. As a reminder."

They exchanged tokens. Sophia placed the wooden beads in her pocket and Ceci dropped the knotted string into her jewel case. Sophia broke the silence. "Come downstairs with me. There's something I want to show thee in the study."

"I can never get over all these books," Ceci said. "Every time I come in here to dust I marvel at them. To think your grandfather read them all. Antony says he did."

"Yes. He was a wise and learned man. I do not know if he ever read this, though. I found it a few months ago. It was my grandmother's. At least I think it must have been. It's written in her hand."

She withdrew a thin, square book. It looked like the kind of thing women copied receipts into, not at all like the other books of the library.

"Where did you find that?" Ceci asked. "I've never seen it in here before."

"Neither did I," Sophia agreed. "But it was here among the books of history. Something just made me open it. Here," she said, holding out the volume. "Look."

The cover was unadorned and untitled. Ceci began leafing through the pages. "It's a history of the family. At least that's what it seems. I can't read all the writing."

"Yes, tis a history. I think Lizzie wrote it all for us, just as she wrote my herbal, as a kind of legacy for her grandchildren. I think no one found it until now." She took it from Ceci's hands and located the page she wanted. It was almost at the very beginning. "Can thee read this part?"

Ceci drew her finger along the lines of crooked lettering. "What a spidery hand your grandmother had. Yes, I can read it: 'After Sophia Griffin saw the Kirkslee nun she went to France to be a nun herself. The abbey she entered was called

Saint Saviour's and twas near Paris. Twas of the same order—as such things are styled by Romans—as that priory of Kirkslee which had once stood on Harwood land.' But how extraordinary! How did Lizzie know all this?"

"When they were first married Tonyjay took her on a visit to England. She often used to tell me of what she'd learned there."

"Sophia . . ." Ceci hesitated, then closed the book. "Why are you showing me this?"

"So thee will understand. It's the meaning of my miracle, the reason the Kirkslee nun appeared to me and restored my speech. I know it now. The book explained everything. I am to go to France and be a nun. Just like the first Sophia, my namesake."

Ceci promised to keep the secret. She didn't want to, but Sophia insisted. "Can't I tell Antony at least?" Ceci pleaded. "I know he'd be pleased. And anyway, I don't think I can pretend you're still mute."

"Please, Ceci. Please. I don't know why, only that it's important. I'd not have told thee except that I was so worried about thy brooding. Antony was so worried . . ."

"Very well. For the present at least. But I cannot agree to help you in this other thing. It's mad, Sophia. Why should you go to France and be locked up in a nunnery? Surely God doesn't demand such a sacrifice when you've already made so many."

"He does not demand," Sophia agreed. "Tis I who dare to think I've a right to the privilege."

"It's daft," Ceci insisted. "The whole idea."

"But thee will keep my secret? Thee swears it?" She held out the string of wooden beads and made Cecile clasp them in her hand. "Promise me, Ceci. For all our years of friendship. Promise me."

"Very well, I promise." She withdrew her hand from the rosary as if it burned. Then she looked again at the other girl. "I don't see how you're going to do it anyway. With all this talk of war, how are you going to find a ship to carry you to France?"

"God will send a way," Sophia said calmly. Then she threw up her hands. "My bread! I left it to rise before I went to seek thee on the widow's walk. Twill be ruined!"

Ceci watched her as she sped toward the kitchen. The thing was so mysterious, so unbelievable. With Sophia out of the room Ceci could almost convince herself she'd dreamed the whole business, that Sophia was as dumb as she'd been in the eight years they'd known each other. "Lord open Thou my lips and my mouth shall declare Thy praise," Ceci quoted softly to herself. And after that Sophia said nothing for fourteen months, she mused. Nothing anyone else could hear at any rate. Extraordinary.

It was time to collect her children at the Ark. Most days this winter Ceci had refused to perform any such errand: if it meant walking the streets of Boston she left it to Sophia or to Antony. Now the Frenchwoman went to the front hall and put on her cloak and bonnet. She moved to the door of the kitchen. "I'm going to get the children," she said. "Can you start dinner while I'm gone?"

Sophia nodded and smiled.

Ceci waited a moment, but the other girl said nothing. Silence had become a way of life again. The brief time of revelation was over. "I won't be long," Ceci said and started for the door. She knew Sophia was pleased by this gesture. Ceci was pleased herself. It fitted in with a decision she had made earlier this day—before she knew Sophia could talk, before the other girl had pleaded with her to stop being a recluse. "I'll not let these villains drive me to insanity," she muttered as she headed down Beacon Street. "They won't win. I will. I and my children." She was not aware that her whispered words were spoken in French.

6

The summer of 1755 spread itself benignly over Massachusetts Bay. The days were easy—warm but not hot, soft with blossom and scent and sea breezes. It was a stark contrast to the mood of the colony.

In the shops and the taverns and the docks the talk was of battles and the preparation for battles. The men muttered and swore and pounded their fists with urgency.

"They say every injun tribe tween here and the Alleghenies is sidin' with the damned French."

"Bloody savages. What would you expect?"

"Tain't just that. Tis natural, considerin' how Braddock and his troops got their asses whipped at the Monongahela."

"Nacheral mebbe, but not smart. Damned French ain't seen the last o' us. Not by a long musket. Next time them stupid English generals will listen to us Americans. We knows how to fight a war in these parts."

"Aye. Like Winslow an' his lads did in Acadia."

This remark always brought nods of satisfied agreement. In June, a month before Braddock's defeat, Fort Beausejour had fallen to two thousand New England colonial forces. Aided by a small fleet of British warships, the Americans now controlled everything from Baie Verte to the Bay of Fundy.

"Rather what I expected," John Griffin was heard to tell his brother. "Your friend Franklin's wrong this time, Ben. Talking the Pennsylvania farmers into sending their horses and wagons to join Braddock is foolish. This business needs to be settled by ourselves. By Americans."

The women of Boston were less interested in military tactics but they cared as deeply about the battles their husbands and sons were fighting. "I heared," one goodwife said, "bout a letter what was sent by a spy in Virginia. A Jesuit priest told them French devils all bout the plans to capture them 'Cadian forts. Only the mercy of the All Mighty brought our lads the vict'ry they deserved."

"No! Where'd you hear that?"

"From me own son. Twas me Tommy what told me. And warn't he there with Winslow and all? He'd not lie to his own mother. Not 'bout somethin' like that."

So the need for vigilance was impressed upon the ladies as they made their way from the markets of Hanover Street to the shops of Treamount. It was a lesson well learned.

Cecile knew it too. She went out at least once a day during those sunlit summer months, often with her children in tow. Cecile had exchanged a policy of hiding for one of open defiance. "Can you send this material round to my home on Beacon Street?" she asked the draper on one noteworthy occasion. "You know me of course—Mrs. Antony Griffin. Cecile LaPointe Griffin from Acadia."

The man flushed and busied himself writing a receipt. The three other women in the shop pressed hands to mouths to stifle gasps of shock. The cheek of it! Ceci nodded graciously to them as she ushered her children out the door.

"For the love of Christ, Ceci," Antony exclaimed that night. "Do you have to rub their noses in it like that! You're only heaping coals on the fire."

"Would you prefer I hide again?" Ceci said. "Would that please you better?"

"Of course not. But—"

"But nothing. Eat your dinner." She passed him a bowl of new peas. "I have decided not to be afraid of those miserable hags. Don't expect me to let them forget it."

Sophia looked from husband to wife, then dropped her eyes.

Most communication between Ceci and Sophia was conducted as it always had been, with signs and gestures replacing words on the part of the American woman. "I hear there's a Jesuit spy abroad in the land," Ceci said laconically one August afternoon. "It must be your Father Parelle."

"No!" Sophia exclaimed. "He could not do such a thing."

Ceci looked at her. The notion must be distasteful in the extreme to make Sophia speak. "Why not?" she asked. "He is a patriot perhaps. A Canadian who loves his country."

Sophia shook her head with negative vehemence.

They were working together in the garden. Ceci dug her trowel into the soft black earth and sat back on her heels. "Listen to me," she said. "Are you still thinking of this crazy idea of yours? About going to France and becoming a nun?"

Sophia nodded.

"Well, how do you think you're going to feel? Being on the other side of this war? Won't you consider yourself a traitor? Won't you be miserable?"

The barrage of questions summoned a verbal reply from Sophia. "It is of a different order. Does thee not see that? The truth of Jesus Christ is above any matter of patriotism, any boundaries between nations. Besides, I should not be a spy. Whatever others might think, I would know that."

"You're sure, Sophia, really sure?" Ceci asked the question with as much gravity as she could command. The other woman nodded. Slowly, surely, with utmost conviction. "*Eh bien*," Ceci muttered. "That's settled then."

Sophia wondered what she meant but Cecile offered no explanation.

A few months earlier Antony had feared his wife was losing her mind. Now he knew fear of a different sort. When they were alone together Ceci was withdrawn, introspective. It seemed she only came out of her shell to fight. "Won't you let me help?" he asked as they lay together in the big familiar bed. "You keep pushing me away. Not physically but mentally. I love you so, darling. And this whole business will pass. I know it will. You mustn't worry so."

"Will the New England troops pass out of Acadia?" she said. "Will they go home and leave my people in peace?"

"Of course they will. Eventually, once this thing is over. It's always that way. Besides," he said, drawing his finger along her cheek, "I'm not the enemy. I didn't storm Fort Beausejour."

"Your brothers did."

"Cosmos and Damien. Yes. But they're young, Ceci. War seems like a great adventure. Anyway, they're not me."

"No." She turned to him and pressed his hand to her lips. "I know that. I don't blame you; it's not your fault."

"Do you mean that?" He rose up on one arm and gazed into her green eyes. They were unreadable in the light of the candle flickering on the bedside table. "Sometimes I think you do blame me. If I hadn't wanted to buy the Amory markets and stay in Boston we'd be in Acadia now. I haven't forgotten that, Ceci. I don't expect you have."

For answer she did what she had been doing more and more frequently of late, pulled his head down to hers and opened her mouth to admit his tongue. Antony groaned and held her close. She'd taken to sleeping nude on these warm summer nights. At first the practice had shocked him, seemed wanton. She'd laughed at his objections, saying it was common practice in her childhood.

Antony was wise enough to understand the gesture and the explanation. It was one more avowal of her origins, one more way of showing her disdain for the people of Boston and their attitudes. That didn't prevent him from being aroused by it. Ceci wouldn't share her thoughts but she gave her body with new generosity. Their nights had become a wordless feast of lovemaking, even more frequent and intense than it had been during their first days together.

Something else was different too. Ceci's responses to him were abandoned, urgent. It was as if some dam had burst within his wife. She did things he would never have asked her to do, things he never expected. Now she slid down in the bed and began tonguing his organ. "Oh God," he murmured, tangling his fingers in her hair.

"*Non*," she hissed, raising her head. "I told you before: speak to me in French, only in French when we're like this."

"More," he whispered in the language of her choice. "More, please." He would refuse her nothing if it resulted in such ecstasy. She was driving him wild with pleasure. He pulled her up beside him and started to roll over her.

"Not like that," she said. "I want to be on top." She matched the deed to the words, climbed on top of him, and struggled to take his member inside herself in the unfamiliar position. He had to use his hands to help her.

Ceci felt the stiff cock slide into her body and groaned with satisfaction. Everything was concentrated in that one spot between her legs where she could feel his hard, hairy flesh rubbing against her. All the sadness and regret of the desperate decision she'd made, the plan she'd confided to no one, least of all Antony, was present in the frenzied speed with which she twisted and squirmed.

"In New Orleans," she whispered in his ear, "the whores used to talk. I heard them. They said it was best like this. Deeper, harder. It is."

He groaned and dug his hands into her buttocks.

Suddenly she stiffened. A long gasping moan escaped her lips. "Oh! Oh!" Her shuddering climax mingled with his.

"I've never seen you like that," he said afterwards in English. "I . . . it frightens me, Ceci. I like it but it frightens me."

"Hush," she answered. "Go to sleep." She did not want him to know that she was crying.

7

Ceci let herself out the door of the Ark. Behind her the voices of her children mingled with the babble that was endless in the house on School Street. They loved to visit their grandmother and Mary delighted in having them come. No explanation was required of Cecile.

She hurried along the road, looking neither right nor left. Her black frock and veiled bonnet were somber for this bright August day but they suited her mood and her errand. When she left the Bowling Green behind, the temper of the city suited it too. Boston was different on the fringe of Mount Whoredom. Her intentions seemed less extraordinary here.

The man was waiting for her in the doorway of a nondescript hovel. "Did you bring it?" he asked.

"Yes. Have you the money?"

"Right in me hand, ma'am. But I ain't meanin' t' give it till I seen the ring."

Ceci looked around. The few other people on the dusty street were lost in their own misery. "Very well."

She held out her hand and the man grasped it. His touch made Ceci's flesh crawl but she didn't pull back. He studied the stone from a number of different angles. "Tis a fine ruby," he admitted. "Ye weren't lyin'." Still he did not release her. His toothless grin bespoke his pleasure in her submission. "Can't say I think it's worth nine hundred though."

She snatched her hand away. "Then you won't buy it. I don't mean to bargain."

"Hold on, lass," he said, chuckling. "I didn't say I wouldn't pay." He withdrew a sack of coins. "Got it all right here, just like I promised." Ceci reached out to take the money. "Not until I got the ruby," he said.

She stripped the ring from her finger with a sense of relief. This morning was the first time she'd put it on since leaving Charleston. "Take it. Give me the money."

There was a moment when she thought he would cheat her—take the jewel and refuse to pay. What could she do if that happened, a woman alone in such a place? Her fears were groundless, however. He could not, after all, know how unlikely she was to set the bailiffs on him. He might guess—why else would she be doing business with him rather than a reputable jeweler?—but he could not know for sure. He pressed the pouch into her palm, prolonging the contact as long as he dared, and chuckled again as she sped away.

Ceci went some fifty yards before she realized he could still have tricked her. How did she know how much was in the little bag? Her eyes darted up and down the road. The buyer had disappeared. An old crone was sitting on a doorstep, another leaned out the window of her hovel. Two men, more disreputable-looking than the one with whom she'd dealt, stood watching her. No, she could not count the money until she got home. It was too dangerous.

When she reached the empty Beacon Street house she finally began to feel safe. Sophia was not yet back from her nursing rounds and Antony was at Lyn Street. Ceci ran up the stairs to her bedroom and turned the key in the lock before dumping the coins on the table. Miraculously the count was fair. He had paid what they'd agreed. She sighed and placed the money between layers of silky lingerie.

Later she found an opportunity to speak to Sophia. They were alone in the kitchen, cleaning up the remains of the evening meal, their steady rhythm born of long practice. "Can you be ready to go to France in a month to six weeks?" Ceci asked.

Sophia looked at her and nodded, her eyes grave, her lips parted in surprise.

"It may be short notice. A day or two, perhaps no more."

Sophia nodded again.

"Good. I will let you know as soon as I can."

The plan had been born in March, soon after Sophia had confided her secrets, after Ceci realized that if she continued as she was she would go mad. It had required weeks of incubation to ripen. First she had to overcome her distaste for the unfairness of the scheme. Antony loved her, loved his children. He was a good man and he deserved better.

"You always push me away, always reject me," he'd said years before. Another time, once only, he'd asked if she loved him. It was on School Street, in the attic room she shared with Sophia, the room where she and Antony had made love and she'd agreed to remain in Boston. "I think I do," she had answered then. The years had taught her that she did. It had been hard reconciling that knowledge with her choice. Recent weeks had made it even harder.

In the eight years that she lay beside him, gave herself to him, Ceci had known frustration, a sense of some greater satisfaction always beyond her. Then guilt and anguish had driven her to a frenzied abandon that broke her wall of self-imposed reserve. Because she despised herself for what she was going to do to him she was wanton and thus climbed those heights she had always been unable to reach. That irony was but one more cause for bitterness.

The most difficult aspect of the scheme lay ahead. Cecile prepared herself for it by walking the streets of Boston and observing the hatred and distrust in the eyes of all she met. A week later, on the first day of September, she made the contact she sought.

She had to take the ferry to Charlestown to find the man. "They tell me you know of ships looking for passengers," she said by way of introduction.

"Sometimes I do." The man looked her up and down. She was not his usual sort of customer. This woman wasn't fleeing an indenture. A jealous husband perhaps. Yes, that must be it. Running off with a lover, more than likely.

"I have a difficult request." Ceci ignored his speculative examination. "I wish to reach France."

"France. That isn't easy. Not these days."

"I know. Can you do it?"

"Maybe. Maybe not. Cost a fair bit if I can."

"How much?"

"For you, fifty at least. Maybe more. And that's not including my commission." His eyes narrowed. "You planning to travel alone?"

"No. We will be five. Two women and three children."

He whistled through his teeth. "Harder still. There's vessels advertising passage every day. You can find them up and down Ship Street. Why'd you come to me?"

Ceci smiled. "My name is Cecile Griffin. It does not suit my plans to seek passage on Ship Street."

He nodded. "I see. Leastwise I think I do."

"You know as much as you need to know. Give me a fair price for the five of us and keep your mouth shut. I'll double your regular commission."

"I'll see what I can do. Where do I reach you?"

"I will reach you. Here, the day after tomorrow."

"Too soon. Need a week at least to find what you're after."

"Very well. A week from today then. Same time."

Watching her go, he wondered what the powerful Griffin

family might pay for advance information about a runaway wife or daughter. In the end he shrugged and decided to do the Griffins no favors. He would make an excellent profit either way. Might as well have the satisfaction of seeing the high and mighty take a small tumble.

Cecile was desperately tense for the next few days. If Antony learned anything the explosion would come soon. It had been a calculated risk telling the broker her name. She had decided on it after much thought. It would not be long before she knew whether the gamble was won or lost.

Her worry was intensified by Antony's behavior. He was watching her every move. Sometimes she caught him staring at her with indescribable sadness in his gray eyes. The look tore at her heart but she did not falter.

Three days after her trip to Charlestown her husband lay his hand on her shoulder as she sat by the dressing table brushing her hair. "Ceci, listen darling, I have to talk to you."

She did not break the rhythm of her strokes. "Yes. What is it?"

"The things we've been talking about, the things bothering you . . ." He hesitated, could not continue.

"What about them?" she asked. Better to know now.

"I had word today—"

Ceci put down the hairbrush and turned to face him. "Yes, word of what?"

"The Acadians." He sighed. "Some of the governors, Lawrence and Shirley to be exact, they think—"

"What? What do they think?" She felt relief because he did not know, fear because he was bringing her some new problem.

"They think the Acadians in Nova Scotia may prove a dangerous liability."

"In what way?"

"Spies, saboteurs. People who would be sympathetic to the enemy if they tried to regain the territory."

"The enemy. You mean France, I take it."

"Yes." He ran his fingers through his hair and turned away from her steady gaze. "Damn it, Ceci, there's some logic to their position. You have to see that."

"What is their position? What are they going to do?"

"Transport the lot of them, according to what I heard today. My brothers, Cosmos and Damien, are just back from Beausejour. The news came with them. It's not public yet."

She was staring at him open-mouthed. "What do you mean 'transport the lot'? There must be hundreds of them."

"More," he said tonelessly. "Many more. Thousands. According to Cosmos, they're including the Indians of the area as well. They're supposed to be shipped to Georgia and points south."

"Georgia," she repeated incredulously. "What will they do in Georgia?"

"Officially, be assimilated into the native population. In point of fact, most will be sold as indentures."

Ceci said nothing. She stared straight ahead and only her clenched fists betrayed her feelings.

"I had to tell you," Antony said. "I couldn't just let you hear by accident."

"Yes." Her voice was toneless. "Many will be anxious to tell me. Antony, are you going to oppose this thing?"

"I don't see how I can. I've no political influence."

"You're a Griffin. Your family has as much power as any in New England."

"Economic power. That's not really the point. Besides, if I made the wrong enemies it could be very bad for business." He saw the look that statement elicited. "I don't mean that as it sounds," he added. "You should know better. If there was a chance of stopping it I'd go ahead and damn the consequences. As it is, I'd be doing us irreparable harm and gaining nothing. There's no chance, Ceci. None at all."

"No," she repeated softly. "No chance."

8

The news of the proclamation reached Boston on the very day Cecile made the final arrangements for passage. She was returning from Charlestown, her receipt for half the fare, two hundred and fifty dollars, tucked in her bosom, when she saw the broadsheet being hawked on the corner of Dock Square and Cornhill. She handed over a coin and stood reading the document.

> ". . . your Lands and Tenements, Cattle of all kinds and Live Stock of all sorts are forfeited to the Crown with all your other Effects saving your money and household goods and you your Selves to be removed from . . . this Province."
>
> The Acadians are now under military guard. Every loyal citizen should rejoice that thus will be firmly dealt with these People who will swear no TRUE allegiance to his gracious Majesty George II and who continue to cling to their infamous and superstitious Catholic beliefs.

Ceci read the words a second time and looked up to see a man watching her. He was smiling. The woman next to him tittered behind her hand. Carefully Ceci folded the paper and, head high, walked up the hill to Beacon Street.

Sophia was in the garden. The children were playing nearby. Ceci surveyed the tranquil domestic scene, pressing her hand over her bosom and the receipt for passage. "Sophia," she said, going forward to where the other woman worked among the gray fronds of lad's love. "It's all arranged."

Sophia stood up. "When?" she asked softly. She spoke so seldom that speech remained an alien thing. It was a mark of her excitement that she asked the question aloud.

"The day after tomorrow. By a small brig from Charlestown to Barbados. Thence by schooner to Gaudeloupe and on to France."

"I have the money," Sophia said. "I never thought to tell thee before. In a jug in my room. I can pay for the passage."

"We'll settle all that later. I've paid for the time being. Sophia," Ceci said, taking a deep breath and folding her hands tightly. "There's something else. Something I haven't wanted to tell you until now. We're going with you. The children and I."

Sophia searched Ceci's face. "I do not understand. Why does thee go to France? Surely Antony will not agree to such a trip at this time—"

"Antony doesn't know. He mustn't know until after we've gone."

Understanding widened Sophia's eyes. "Thee is leaving thy husband," she whispered. "Leaving Antony."

"I know how awful it sounds," Ceci said. "I didn't make the decision lightly. I've no choice, Sophia. You must see that. There's no future here for me or my children. I cannot remain. Don't you know what they will do to us?" She turned to watch young Tonyjay as he hoisted little Louise to his shoulders so she could reach an apple. It hung red and ripe above her blond head.

Sophia looked at the scene with her. "It is wrong, what thee plans to do," she said. "Thee is tearing these babies from their father, their home. How can thee do such a thing, Ceci?"

"I will not allow them to grow up with hate," Ceci insisted. "You don't know what that's like, Sophia. I do." She saw the stubborn disbelief in her friend's eyes. "Here." She thrust the broadsheet toward the other woman. "Read this. Then tell me we should stay in Boston."

Sophia took the document and read it twice. "This is a wicked thing. An evil thing." Her voice was choked with tears.

"Yes. That is why we cannot stay here."

"But if thee told Antony what thee felt, surely he would—"

"I've told him. Over and over. He keeps saying it will pass. He means well, Sophia. He's a wonderful man and I love him. He doesn't understand because he cannot. No one born to the security of being a Griffin can understand." She turned to go, then paused. "He knew about that four days ago." She pointed to the announcement of the expulsion of the Acadians which Sophia yet held. "He told me about it so I'd be prepared. He says there's nothing he can do because it would be bad for business."

Both women were silent for some seconds after that. "I'm going to start packing," Ceci said finally. "You must say nothing to Antony. It would hurt him worse to see us leave, and in the end he could not prevent it. My mind's made up."

Sophia watched Ceci walk away, shoulders bent, steps heavy with fatigue. Turning, she looked again at the children. For the space of one silent prayer she stood still. Then she let herself out the garden gate and sped down the hill.

Antony saw the official announcement on the docks. He was looking for a captain with whom he hoped to conclude arrangements for bringing in hemp when a casual acquaintance hailed him.

"Hey Griffin, heard all the family ships are going into the indenture business as of today. You're always first in line when there's a profit to be made, aren't you?"

Griffin smiled slightly. "This is one Griffin not in the shipping business, you know that. What are you on about anyway?"

"Them lot o' traitors and fools they's gonna bring down from the north. Need ships to load 'em on, won't they? I heard half a dozen Griffin schooners would be leavin' tomorrow. Frankly, I figured that might mean you and me could do a little business. If they Griffin ships are up in Acadia they won't be bringin' in cargoes for you, will they? Now I know about a load of coffee you might be able to buy cheap."

"What lot of traitors?" Antony demanded. "I still don't know what you're talking about."

"Here." The man fished a copy of the announcement from the front of his shirt. "Here's the whole story. Thought you knew. Rum lot the Acadians, serves 'em right—" He broke off. "Sorry, I just remembered bout your wife. Course I didn't mean her."

Antony ignored his informant. He read the broadsheet, then dropped it on the dock and ran toward Ship Street.

"Come in, Antony. You've given up knocking, I see." Benjamin didn't really look at his nephew, he merely acknowledged his presence and turned back to the men sitting with him in the office.

There were five Griffins present: Benjamin, Charles, John, Antony's brother Cosmos, and John's eldest son William. All were intent on the senior partner. "I agree," Benjamin was saying, "that this is an opportunity not to be missed, but we must remember it's a one-time operation. A single venture as it were. We can't spare more than four or five vessels without endangering our commitments for other, more regular cargoes. It's out of the question."

"Still," John said, "we can carry a goodly number on five ships. Something near a thousand indentures as I see it. That's an excellent return. How much do you calculate, William? Before expenses."

"Well, if we—"

"Shut up." Antony's command dropped into their conversation. Every head turned toward him. "Shut your mouths, you bloody fools. If you stop talking now, maybe we can all forget this conversation ever happened."

"You try my patience, lad," Benjamin said. "You always have. Charles, will you kindly find out what your son is talking about."

"What indeed, Antony?" his father asked. "I think we're owed an explanation. I suspect an apology as well."

"Apology . . . Sweet Jesus! I wouldn't believe it if I weren't hearing it with my own ears." He turned to Benjamin. "Where are the rest of them?" he asked. "Your sons are missing and I only see one of my brothers. Isn't the whole clan in agreement on this little, what did you call it, venture?"

"This is a large firm, lad." Benjamin's voice remained mild and even. "We're seldom all here at one time. Now if you don't mind . . ."

"But I do, Uncle, I mind very much. So much I'd like to punch that smug smile off your face."

"Antony!" His father's shocked voice wasn't the only one raised in protest. "If you can't keep a civil tongue in your head you can get out of here. And I'd like to see you later. We can discuss the nature of your apology to your uncle."

Antony ran his fingers through his hair, took a deep breath, and fought to suppress his rage. "I'll apologize now. I'm sorry, Uncle Benjamin. I'm very angry but I don't mean to insult you or go at things this way." The senior Griffin grunted and sat back. Antony tried to muster his thoughts, bring his temper under control. He wanted to achieve his end, not give himself the satisfaction of a punch-up.

"Look," he began as calmly as he could. "You can't do this. The Griffin ships cannot be involved in transporting the Acadians."

"I see," John murmured. Then, a bit louder, he said, "We understand your feelings, Antony, now that we know what's behind this outburst. And you know we're all very fond of Cecile. But surely you realize that's nothing to do with anything. It's business, lad. Plain and simple."

"It's not just because of Ceci," Antony said. "I care about that, of course I do. But it's a larger issue. You must see it. This thing they're doing—it's outrageous, barbaric."

"I say, old man." William's voice was friendly but his eyes weren't. The cousins were only two years apart and rivalry had marked their relationship throughout their growing-up years. "Isn't that rather an odd position for you of all people to take? I mean, considering you spent four years managing black slaves."

Sophia still knew her way around the Lyn Street market. She went straight to the office in the back and looked through the window. No one was there.

"Afternoon, Miss Sophia." The old man who spoke had known her since she was a child. "Lookin' fer Mr. Antony? He's not here. Gone down to Long Wharf, I think. I'll tell him ye called, shall I?" He smiled benignly at her when she left.

Most of the men on Long Wharf knew her too. Those who hadn't been part of her childhood had been recipients of her simpling skills. "Who ye seekin', Mrs. Crandall?" one lad asked. "Here." He held out a stick and pointed to the sand. "Scratch the name."

She wrote "A. Griffin," in the dirt and looked at him questioningly.

"Was here a while back," her informant said. "Think I saw him headin' in the direction of Ship Street. Why don't ye try the office?"

She nodded her thanks and sped away.

The distance between Long Wharf and the headquarters of Griffin's Importations was slight. Sophia covered it in less than five minutes. The outer office was empty but she could hear voices from the rear. Sophia went to the door and raised her hand to knock. Then she heard the shouting and stopped.

"That," Antony Griffin told his cousin William, "is a poor excuse for an argument. Black slaves have nothing to do with transporting the Acadians. If you want to debate the plantation system I'll discuss it any time you like. Right now we're talking about wholesale dislocation of thousands of white people. Stealing from them what is rightly theirs."

Benjamin cleared his throat loudly before any of the others had a chance to speak. "We're wasting time, gentlemen," he said. "Antony, it's my unpleasant duty to remind you that you chose not to come into this business. You have no vote. Now if you'll excuse us, we've things to settle. Charles, how soon can the ships be ready to sail north?"

None of them heard the door open. They were all looking at Antony, waiting to see what he'd do. When Sophia came into the room they didn't notice her. Then she raised her voice.

"Thee must not do this," she said.

Six pairs of eyes fastened on her in shock.

"Sophia!"

"In God's name child, when—"

"But how can you—"

"What are you doing here?"

She ignored their questions and their amazement. Slowly, clearly, the words were repeated by she whom they had believed mute. "Thee . . . must . . . not . . . do . . . this."

Silence. Even Antony was speechless.

John regained some measure of his composure before the

others did. He remembered the charred wraith he'd seen in Rowley right after the fire, the terrible funeral at which they'd buried Sophia's mother, her husband, and her three sons. "Sophia," he said softly. "Your ability to speak is a great shock, but a happy one. Naturally we all want to know how it happened. But this is not the time child. Perhaps we can all meet at the Ark tonight. Yes." He warmed to his idea and smiled at the group. "We'll have a party, a kind of celebration. I'm sure Martha and Mary—"

"I thank thee, Uncle John," Sophia interrupted, "for all thy kindness to me. But it is not time to speak of that now, as thee has said. It is time to put aside this terrible deed thee are contemplating. The Griffins must take no part in the transport of the Acadians."

"Well," Benjamin said drily, "we've another nonvoting partner. Antony's been telling us the same thing. His words were not quite so unexpected, on many counts, but I tell you the same thing I told him, my dear. This is not your affair."

Sophia turned to stare at him. Her look was intense, unfathomable. Slowly her gaze traveled around the room, examining each of her relatives in turn. "Thee are the heirs to the kingdom," she said at last. "And thee are a generation of vipers."

Benjamin jumped to his feet as swiftly as his paunch allowed. "Look here! I've had quite enough of this—"

"Be quiet!" She issued her command and didn't wait to see that it was obeyed. "Thee has forgotten much. It is time someone reminded thee of what brought thee to this position of might and power." She wore neither cloak nor bonnet. Her departure from Beacon Street had been too swift. They could see her breasts rising and falling beneath her simple gray frock. Nothing obscured the passion in her face.

"Does thee not know that the Acadians have commited only one crime? This terrible punishment is payment for the fact that they have remained true to the old faith. Their sin is that they're Catholics."

"Well, Sophia," Charles said placatingly, "you must admit that casts some doubt on their loyalty as British subjects. We can hardly be blamed for wanting to protect our future."

"Loyalty," she repeated. "Thee should be shamed to speak

the word. What was it that sent Mark and Clare Griffin to martyrdom on Tyburn Tree, Uncle? Was it not their Catholic faith? And did the charge not claim that they had plotted against the life of the king? Did not all the Griffins know that to be a lie? Did they not stand together at the execution? After it? Was that not true loyalty?"

She moved around the room and stared at each of them in turn. "Do thee not all know that this very business, this thing which clothes thee, shelters thee, puts food into thy mouths and the mouths of thy wives and children, was built by a man who despised cheats and frauds? Did Roger Griffin not take his stand on the questions of right and justice? And what of his son? What of my grandfather? Does thee think if Tonyjay were alive he would sanction what thee is doing here? What thee is planning?"

She had touched a nerve at last. The memory of the old man seemed suddenly alive in the room. Even Benjamin dropped his eyes. He could well imagine his father's reaction to this affair.

"I will tell thee more," Sophia continued. "If thee does this thing the very heavens will howl with rage. Thee will bring blood and desolation on this family and generations unborn will not be free of it. Do any of thee not know of the Kirkslee nun? Has thee forgotten the first Sophia, my namesake?" She closed her eyes and turned her face to the window. A shaft of sunlight lit her tawny hair and the men could only stare. Suddenly she was not the girl they all knew so well. This was a voice reaching out of the past and into the future.

"It is through her that I regained my tongue," she said. Through my namesake and the Kirkslee nun. Through them has God revealed Himself to me." She faced her relatives once more. "I too am a Catholic. In two days' time I leave for France to become a nun of the Abbey of Saint Saviour. God willing, I will one day see the priory of Kirkslee restored on English soil. Now, does thee wish to sell me into indenture too? I'm only a woman. Surely thee would not find it difficult."

She paused. No one said anything. "In Grandfather's library," she continued, "thee can find a book written by Lizzie. It tells the story of the Griffins in England and in America. Thee should read that book. Thee should grave its words on thy hearts. And thee should learn to measure thy deeds against the standards of the Griffins who have gone before us."

Her head dropped to her breast. She was quivering with exhaustion. "Take me home, Antony," she whispered. "I do not think I can walk the distance alone."

9

"Sophia," he said before they reached Beacon Street, "I don't know when you started speaking, or how. But what you did today was magnificent. Your courage . . . Well, I just wanted you to know what I think."

She paused in mid-step, coming out of the trance that had gripped her as they left Ship Street. "Antony, there's something else. I nearly forgot." She paused and bit her lip. "Tell me first," she said. "Will they do it? Despite everything thee said, everything I said . . ."

He looked at her in mild surprise. "I didn't know you'd heard my arguments. They were pretty small beer compared to yours. But no, they won't do it. I could see it on their faces when you finished with them—particularly when you mentioned Tonyjay. You saved them from their greed, this time at least."

She nodded and put her hand on his arm. "Antony, does thee remember the day at the Ark? Before thee and Ceci were wed?"

"The day you came and told me she wanted me," he said. "Yes, I remember. That's when she said she would stay in

Boston. I guess I never thanked you for that."

"Thee has no cause to thank me," she whispered. "She is leaving thee. Taking the children. Ceci will hate me for telling thee but I could not keep silent when it's all my fault. I was looking for thee just now. That's how I came to Ship Street."

"Leaving . . . But I don't understand."

"Today she told me she plans to go with me to France. We are to sail from Charlestown in two days time. All the arrangements are made. I must be on that ship, Antony. Ceci must not. It is a terrible mistake." She saw the expression on his face, knew his pain and his need to confront his wife. "Go ahead home," she said. "I can walk the rest of the way by myself."

Antony needed no further encouragement. For the second time that day he broke into a run.

"Why did she tell you?" Ceci whispered, staring at her clenched hands. "I told her it would only make it harder."

"Why . . . ? For the love of God, Ceci! You're my wife. How could she not tell me? Oh Ceci, Ceci . . . What can I say? How can I make you understand?"

"I understand everything," the girl said. The green eyes she lifted to him were wet with tears. "We are powerless to change it, Antony. I am French and you are English. They will never let us forget that."

"No." He took her shoulders in his hands and they felt like unyielding wood. She was stiff with anguish and control. "It's not true. You're simply playing into the hands of every bigot and petty autocrat. We can't change the big things, Ceci, the system. But we can be responsible for our own actions. And teach our children to be responsible for theirs."

She shook her head and moved away. "If it were only that simple," she whispered.

"It is if you allow it to be."

They were standing in the kitchen. That's where he'd found her and they had not moved. Outside, the children were still playing in the garden. The kettle sang merrily on the hearth, the smell of venison stew rose from one bubbling pot.

Without thinking, Ceci stirred the meat. The habits of years were not erased even in the terrible emotion of the moment.

"Ceci," Antony said, clasping his hand over hers, ignoring the hot steam that rose around their joined flesh. "Ceci, do you love me?"

"Yes."

"You're sure? Once before I asked you and you said you thought you did. I've never forgotten that. I'm asking again. Perhaps for the last time. Do you love me?"

"I love you."

"Then in God's name, in the name of all you hold holy, don't do this to me, to us."

They stood together in silence. The clock ticked. A fly buzzed through the air and escaped through the open window.

"I love you," she repeated softly, "but I can no longer trust you."

He tried to assimilate the magnitude of that remark. Before he could find some answer to it Sophia came into the kitchen. She looked at both of them, raised her hands in supplication, then dropped them in a gesture of hopelessness. Ceci opened her mouth to accuse Sophia of betrayal but remained silent.

"I have meddled in thy lives more than I've had any right to do," Sophia said finally. "I beg thy forgiveness. Especially yours, dearest Ceci." Then, when the other girl turned to her, Sophia held up her hand. Wait. Do not say anything. Thy concerns must not be with me at this moment. There is one last thing I must tell thee, however. After thee said thee was leaving I went looking for Antony. I found him at Griffin's Importations on Ship Street. He was beseeching them not to participate in the transport of the Acadians."

Ceci looked quickly from Sophia to Antony. "Do not think he did that only for thee," Sophia continued. "I heard him, Ceci. He was pleading for the right of the Acadians to be free. If thee does not believe that is a man good enough for thee to stand beside, then I pity thee, my dearest friend. For thee will never find a better one."

Antony let go his grip on his wife. He turned away from both women to face the wall and find some measure of control.

"I am taking thy children to the Ark," Sophia told Ceci. "We will spend this night there. Tomorrow I will bring them home. Then I must go to visit my father and say good-bye."

"Sophia," Antony called after her. "If they make it difficult at the Ark, if they abuse you, don't stay." Despite his own terrible anguish he could not abandon her to the wolves. Not after what she'd done.

She laughed now, although she was spent with emotion. "Don't worry. I shall simply remain silent. They won't believe I ever spoke at all. They'll think they dreamed it."

"She spoke to them?" Ceci asked when Sophia was gone. "To your family? All these months, over a year, she refused to admit that her voice had returned. I don't understand."

"She came to Ship Street looking for me, just as she said. When she heard they were planning to send Griffin ships north to transport the Acadians, she spoke." He closed his eyes with weariness and pain, then opened them again. "She was like an Old Testament prophet. None of them will ever forget the things she said. Neither will I. And no ships of ours will be part of this thing. I suppose you consider that cold comfort."

"No," Ceci said slowly. "No, I don't think I do. What you were saying before, Antony, tell me again. About individual actions."

"I've nothing to add," he said quietly. "We can't always change the way things are. We can only stand by our own beliefs."

"And our commitments," she whispered. "We can stand by our commitments. Like Sophia is doing."

"It's not good enough, Ceci," he said in a voice that sounded as if it came from a far distance. "I don't want you to stay with me because you promised to. If you honestly believe you can't trust me, we've no future."

She did not answer right away. When she did, her words came slowly and painfully. "I think I mistrust myself. I said first I had to go because the people of Boston hated me. Then I said it was because you wouldn't stand up for the Acadians. After the other night I mean."

"I told you I wouldn't protest formally to the governor. At least that's what I meant. I can't make Shirley change his mind. I hoped I might have a chance at changing my family's minds. That's the difference."

"Yes, I see that. But it's not really the point." She couldn't look at him. "It's myself I've mistrusted all along," she repeated. "Every time. On the *Notre Dame*, in New Orleans, even at Blackwater. Every time I run it's because I don't trust myself to stay and fight."

"I'll fight for you," he said. "Always, if you'll let me."

"Yes. That's good. It's wonderful. But I mustn't be afraid to fight for myself." She lifted her face to his. "Will you help me, Antony? Will you help me learn to fight for myself? Help me teach the children to be that strong?"

For answer he kissed her.

Later, as they lay in each other's arms, spent with passion and love, she said the wisest thing any of them had said that day. "Antony, I've been thinking about the children. Tonyjay goes to school soon. The war may be real when he does. The other children will taunt him about me, about his Acadian blood."

"I think I'd best start teaching him the manly art of self-defense," Antony said.

Ceci chuckled. "That's probably a good idea. But I know a better one." She sat up and looked at her husband in the moonlight. His dark hair was disarrayed by their lovemaking and she smoothed it back with a tender gesture. "The important thing is to teach him the proper reply to such taunts. We must make sure Tonyjay always knows what to answer. He will say, 'I'm not French and I'm not English. I am Antony Jacob Griffin. I'm an American.'"

ABOUT THE AUTHOR

Beverly Byrne is an American, originally from the Boston area. She divides her time between the Isle of Wight and the Canary Islands. Her previous Fawcett books are JEMMA, THE OUTCAST, and THE ADVENTURER.